Cary J. Lenehan is a former trades assistant, soldier, public servant, cab driver, truck driver, game designer, fishmonger, horticulturalist and university tutor— among other things. His hobbies include collecting and reading books (the non-fiction are Dewey decimalised), Tasmanian native plants (particularly the edible ones), medieval re-creation and gaming. Over the years he has taught people how to use everything from shortswords to rocket launchers.

He met his wife at an SF Convention while cosplaying and they have not looked back. He was born in Sydney before marrying and moving to the Snowy Mountains where they started their family. They moved to Tasmania for the warmer winters and are not likely to ever leave it. Looking out of the window beside Cary's computer is a sweeping view of Mount Wellington/Kunanyi and its range.

T0118834

Warriors of Vhast Series
published by
IFWG Publishing Australia

Intimations of Evil (Book 1)
Engaging Evil (Book 2)
Clearing the Web (Book 3)
Scouring the Land (Book 4)
Gathering the Strands (Book 5)
Following the Braid (Book 6)

Warriors of Vhast Book 6

Following the Braid

by
Cary J Lenehan

Following the Braid

Book 6, Warriors of Vhast

All Rights Reserved

ISBN-13: 978-1-922556-82-0

Copyright ©2022 Cary J Lenehan

IFWG Publishing International
Gold Coast

www.ifwgpublishing.com

Foreword

I know that in my books I talk about the disruption caused by The Burning, but I really didn't expect to have to deal with the effects of a plague in my real life. Despite this, you now hold the sixth book of the Warriors of Vhast series in your hands (or on your screens). Thank you for continuing to read the stories.

With my Patreon page, the stories now extend for many thousands of years of the history of the planet and I have more in mind as novellas that may take it back even further in time as well as forward. I hope that you all get the chance to look at the various maps, eat the food from my recipes and, now, even play a character behind the scenes in Ashvaria.

Whether you have bought the books, borrowed them, or read them through the library, I hope you enjoy this latest offering, and that you share my world with friends. Please also feel free to leave a review anywhere you can (even a few words). For writers working through small press publishers, these are vital.

Feel free to talk to me and ask questions on my Facebook writer's page or through my website. I am more than happy to answer them.

Cary J. Lenehan
Hobart

A cast list and glossary of terms used in this novel can be found from page 281. I advise using them when you start in Vhast.

My wife, Marjorie, is my rock and my support. Without her I would not be doing this. She is very patient for a start.

Once again I thank Pip Woodfield for the beta reading she has done for me, checking my continuity errors and knowing many of my characters better than I do myself.

I respect and acknowledge the Muwinina people, who are the traditional owners of the Nipaluna land where I reside and write my stories. I give thanks to the Tasmanian Aboriginal people and to elders past, present and future. I acknowledge that they never ceded the land where I reside.

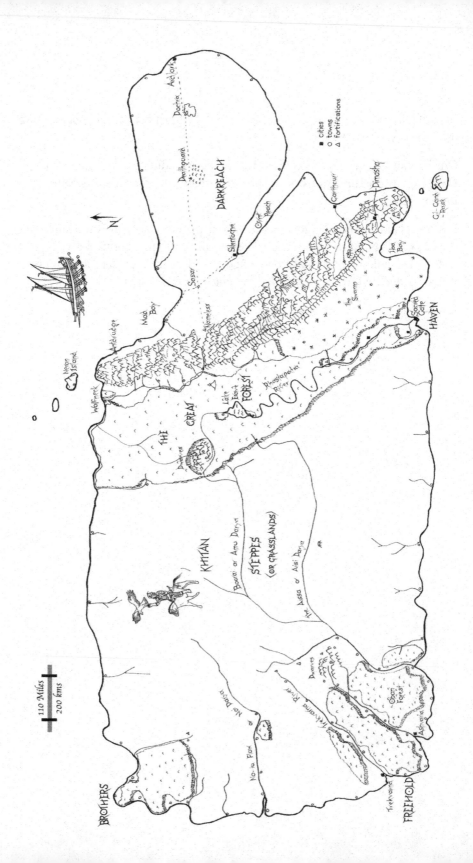

Seven Clans met at the One Tree Hill
Meet with the Mountains and the Coast
Long forgotten oath-taking needs to fulfil
But destroying the hate-filled[1] was foremost
No more to dread the emergence of their host
Treaty is made and compact agreed anew
Common cause and justice form the glue.
A Conclave of the North held in Greensin
Spring a new beginning for scattered folk
Agreed and signed on fresh-scraped skin
War plans put aside as leaders they spoke
Unity thus gained but not allowed to provoke
Or unwind what was accepted on battle hill
Lessons so learnt and part all with goodwill
Torn asunder by evil-incited older conflict
The time had come for past to be mended.
In a lost valley once haunted and derelict,
From all over the land Prelates wended
A new addition to their ranks commended.
Now again unified in purpose and in belief
Opening the way to end long-endured grief.
Three groups meeting in a spirit of amity
All different in tone, but hope for peace
Finding their way from dire calamity
Bring forth change as hopes increase.
Princess Theodora do Hrothnog
A ballade written in reflection

---

1 The Khitan name for the Brotherhood of All-Believers is the 'üzen yaddag düürsen', literally 'the hate-filled'.

The Village of Mousehole

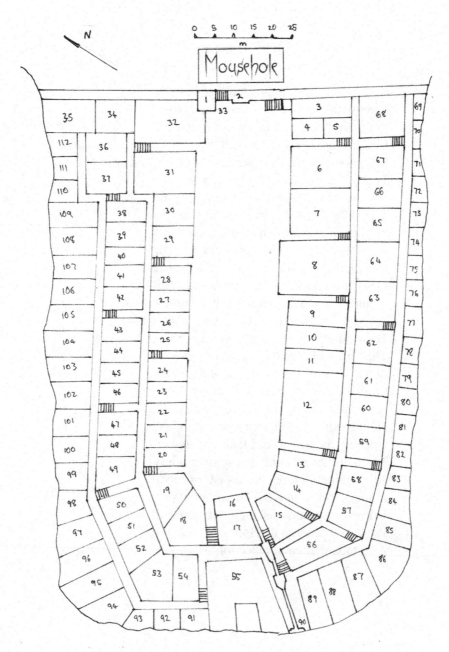

Mousehole's details can be found at page 306

Chapter I

Harnermês
17th Unique, the Feast of Anastasi, the Year of the Water Horse

I have the best eyes on the ship and the honour of the lookout in this attack. Anything could happen and I am the one to watch for it. So far, the sea and the sky have been empty, except for birds and a fish or lizard breaking the surface, but I will stay alert and keen scanning in the dark.

Even with his keen eyes, Harnermês could not see the barely visible rope that stretched in the dark between the two women that was all that lay away from the influence of their rings. They took those rings off just outside the small circle that the other saddles made around the *River Dragon* and then quickly moved to land their saddles on the ship.

"The saddles return," he called down to the deck. "The Cat is wounded. Call a priest and clear some space."

From it being a quiet and uneventful night, with people just sitting around, it is now all busy. Denizkartal is trying to clear space for them. All are looking out now and they can see that Astrid must have been badly wounded; her mail hangs off her in tatters. Furthermore, there are many things hanging off them and off their saddles.

On seeing the two women appear, Basil and Hulagu are bringing their saddles in to the ship as well, and the Princesses are soon pushing through the crowd. Enough. I need to stop watching what is happening below. They have been hurt and now something could come and attack us. I need to watch the horizon and the sky instead.

3

Ayesha bint Hāritha

L and and get off the saddle. Good, the Christian priest is already here. "Father...she is healed for most of the wounds that she took, but she still has broken ribs that pain her...can you...?" Christopher moved forward and led Astrid towards the hatch cover prepared for the priests to use.

Astrid the Cat

W hy is Basil fussing? "Basil, I am fine. You should see him...the one I killed. He is not well at all, I killed him, and he was so much bigger than me."

There is Bianca handing things to her husband. She needs to know that I have made my choice. "I have a patron saint now. I have chosen Saint Kessog... good Saint for fighting...I owe him an icon already." She coughed. It left flecks of blood on her lips and an expression of pain appeared on her face. Christopher hushed her and got her into the circle.

Ayesha

A yesha looked around. Where are the Princesses? Astrid is being taken care of. It is time for me tell them what we found. "It was good we did that. They had magic—and lots of it." As she spoke, she was taking items from pouches and laying them out in front of her.

"Astrid has more of it than I do," she continued, "and they had something that we do not think was a real magic. It was a machine like the weapons of light of the Brotherhood. It could see this ship and the saddles as little green sparks and when we killed it, it spat lightning at us. They had a talker—well, we think it is a talker—and something that sensed when you pass the barrier that Astrid mentioned. Astrid has those." *They listen intently.* She continued.

"We returned over Skrice and there is no sign that they know what we have done on the mountain. We kept low once we left there, so we could not see the boats from Wolfneck. They must be well behind you since the detection wand that the sentries used didn't find them. If we can find the fugitives, we should be able to all attack at once if the Wolfneck people do not get impatient."

"We have been lucky," she concluded. "If we had not taken the sentries on that mountain top, then we would have sailed straight into an ambush. Now they will be confused, and until they see the saddles, they won't be sure what is happening. They must have thought that the green glowing box would see us as we flew." With that she kissed her husband and went looking for a place to sleep.

Olympias Akritina

*N*o-one *has said anything to the contrary, despite the activity around my sister, so I will assume that the two were successful in their task. It is time to put the rest of the plan into action.* "Raise all sail and call up the wind." *Good.. my crew are quick to start unfurling the sails and the wind is catching them straight away.* The ship responds immediately. *We no longer need hold back.*

She looked around her at the sea and the clouds. *From what I know, we should be already south of Herjolfsness, the most southerly point on Neron Island. Even if it were full daylight, and we had a full suite of sails set, we very soon would not be able to be seen by a watcher on the shore at Skrice.* She looked to the rear.

The other craft are almost invisible behind us in the distance, and I know where they are and where to look. It will be a long time before they are in sight of anyone who may be a threat to them, and they are slow. They have not had to slow down at all. They can just travel as fast as they are able and yet still stay together.

Astrid

*A*yesha *can just go to sleep. For me it is harder. Now that Christopher has healed my bones, I first must wash the drying blood, both Murgrątt's and mine, from my clothes and then I get to sew the rents together. I should have grabbed more clothes in Wolfneck. I am sure that my old ones are still in the house somewhere. No-one will have tidied it since I left.*

Luckily, one of the Dwarves can do some repairs on my mail while I do that. It will only be butted together rather than the precise and tiny riveting of the rest of the mail I wear...but it will be better than nothing. When she went to sleep in her damp clothes and wrapped in sleeping furs a few hours before dawn she was uncharacteristically exhausted.

Chapter II

Olympias
17ᵗʰ Quinque, the Feast of Anastasi

With the natural wind coming from the west and the enchanted wind that belonged to the *River Dragon* both blowing about as hard as each other Olympias found that the cast log was giving a far higher reading than she had expected it to.

Previously I have just run with a natural breeze when it was strong enough and not used the enchanted wind. Now I find that the two winds together seem to act as if they are a far stronger breeze coming from fine off the port quarter, and since at this point I have all of the sails set, it is obvious that we will soon be out of the line of sight of the land near Skrice.

I wonder how that can be. I must ask the teacher woman that my sister thinks so much of about why this is when we are next in the village. We will see if she knows why it is happening. I suppose the most important thing is what the effect of it will be. We will be around the southern point of Neron and close to making the landfall that we want well before the pale autumn dawn even begins to first lighten the sky in the east.

Rani

As they sailed and got ready for the next step, Rani thought over what was about to happen. *I have had so many people tell me about Neron Island that I think that I can find my way over it without ever setting foot on its shore. For a start, it has two very different sides. On the far smaller, and much more* sheltered eastern side, huddled as it is behind the mountainous spine of the island, the land plunges straight into the sea down steep cliffs and over sharp rocks.

On the lower slopes of the Zarah Mountains and the small flat areas of the east, the trees grow as thick and tall as they do around Wolfneck. According to many, here they grow even thicker. They say that it is certainly harder to move through the area and the trees grow too thick to ski between them. There is deep soil and a quiet that is only broken by the sound of birds.

This is a distinct contrast with the wider, flatter western side of the island, and in its north. There the constant gales and winds sweep the vegetation into either low grass, which the sheep graze, or else into small hardy shrubs that spring up from the rocky soil. There are no trees over most of it. It is windswept and the plants are bent and twisted by the gales. They cling on hard to what shelter they can find for themselves.

Unfortunately for the locals there is no suitable harbour, or anywhere to land a small boat safely, among the cliffs of the eastern side of the island. On the inhospitable western side there is a very good harbour which, although small, has no bar across its mouth and which provides good shelter from waves in almost all weathers if a ship is drawn up on the shore or is firmly anchored.

The trade-off for them is that, with no shelter from the wind, which bends their stunted trees over double, the islanders must raise stone walls—walls that are higher on north and west—to shelter their small fields of short-stemmed oats enough to allow them to grow. The people apparently spend a lot of time huddled in their stone houses burning peat from bogs near the base of the mountain to keep them warm against the nearly constant wind from the west.

I am firmly of the opinion that, even though it is thickly wooded terrain in the east, seeing that there will be mages looking for the fugitives, the refugees must have both magical help in addition to some support from the other people of the island. It cannot be that they are surviving just with a reliance on luck and their skill at living in the wild.

Of course, once winter comes on them, they will be easily found. They will almost certainly have to light fires, or at least use strong enchantments, to stay alive and either of these will make them easily findable.

We have brought the enchanted loud talker from the Brotherhood general with us, and Presbytera Bianca is preparing to take a saddle and fly Father Simon over the east of the island. I think that it is likely that the fugitives will see us arrive in the River Dragon. They will not be able to avoid hearing the priest. Hopefully, they will listen to what he is saying. He knows some of the people who are likely to be there and, more importantly, several of them know him.

It is supposedly completely useless for us to try to find a place to anchor off that hard shore and so, with the ballistae manned, Olympias can run the

River Dragon up and down the coast, staying well outside any possible bow range, while Bianca and Father Simon do what they can. I rarely pray, but may Asvayujau smile upon us, and give us the good fortune of a quick result.

Rani (an hour later)

*T*he sun not even fully clear of the horizon…and Harnermêŝ, standing on the maintop, reports that Bianca has landed. I want to climb up and see if I can see what is happening. What does Astrid want so urgently? "My talker, the one we took from the dead mage up on the mountain, is asking Snæbjorn why he hasn't reported. They are speaking Darkspeech, and it is with a Neronese accent."

She has the talker up to her ear, holding her hand over it so that everything is muffled. She speaks in a whisper; I suppose so that it will not likely carry back to the other end.

"Whoever is talking is very upset. He thinks that they have all fallen asleep… it seems that they have done it before…he is telling Murgratt…I know that was the name of the Insak-div that I killed…to pick up the talker even if he doesn't like it…the voice seems to be getting quite upset…they are supposed to be watching for us."

"Little priest-woman…Bianca…is coming back," called Harnermêŝ in his halting Darkspeech, "she has woman on her saddle with her…not priest."

Astrid

*I*n the excitement, only Astrid noticed Theodora go to the other side of the River Dragon and throw up. *Well, that wasn't from seasickness on this flat sea. I guess that I was right about her behaviour, and I know the feeling she is having now. How did that happen? I wonder if Ayesha knows how. I'm willing to bet anything that Rani doesn't.*

So, it is not just me who has been watching her. Father Christopher went over to Theodora and had a few words before giving her something. Theodora nodded at the priest, looked at where Rani is, and put the something in her mouth. She began sucking on it. *I hope she likes mint.* Astrid gave a quiet smile of knowing.

Bianca

I brought Ingrid Holmsdottir out. She is the wife of the senior refugee mage, Thrain Vigfisson. I think that she trusts me, but she is coming out from the island to see if the River Dragon is a trap for them all. I have had to leave Father Simon behind as surety. It seems silly, but I suppose that being cautious has kept them all alive so far.

At least we were able to quickly satisfy her. We will be returning to their hidden camp and taking the carpet as well as more saddles to bring their entire party on board.

Astrid

B ianca and most of the other saddles are off to pick up the refugees and the River Dragon is picking up speed for the west of the island. It isn't necessary to keep the ship still and waiting. The saddles can catch up with her just as easily whether she is still or moving. Once they left, we straight away turned and sailed towards the rendezvous. The saddles are so fast that we didn't need to delay the far slower ship while waiting for people, even people laden with their belongings, to join the rest on board.

Now that they are all on the ship, and I am more composed, and far better rested, it is time for Basil and me to leave the River Dragon behind. It is the time to shepherd the Wolfneck ships in. Behind us, on the River Dragon, we can leave them all with introductions being made.

Ayesha

T he Neronese all defer to their Father Gildas as their acknowledged leader. They allow him to tell what has happened. However, just as the Mice (even I ...and always Astrid) often do, when Rani is relating what has happened, the bards in the group: Signy Skáld, Koll Hjortson, and their son Ketill Söngvari keep correcting him when they feel that the priest grows irrelevant or boring...and he does that often, just as Rani does.

Theodora

It seems that the mages Thrain Vigfisson and his son and apprentice Arnor *know this story too well. They have dragged me away from hearing it. It seems that the father and son are both air mages. They are the ones who have been instrumental in hiding these people from those who are seeking them. Now they are more interested in the River Dragon itself and how it sails against the wind.*

As they came down to round Herjolfsness, the natural wind blew strongly from the forward starboard quarter, and combined with the ships own wind, this made the River Dragon act as if it had a breeze from square off its starboard beam as she heeled over.

While they are interested in the way the wind behaves, the two mages have revealed that they have spent most of their exile making wands in anticipation of a desperate last defence. They have plenty of them in store, ready for the battle ahead. That interests me more than explaining the way that the winds act on our ship, something that even I do not understand.

Another pair from Neron Island that have boarded the River Dragon are the island's teachers, Kadlin Vitur and Æirik Lærði. They are also a married couple. They are both older than the rest, and it seems, are lucky in that their children all have holdings well out of the town, and have mostly been able to keep clear of the turmoil and the new religion. It is mainly their family who have brought supplies and news to the fugitives.

Bianca

I guess it is time for me to act as the Bishop's wife again. Bianca gathered Danelis, and they took Vigdis, Father Gildas' wife, in hand and were making a chance for her to talk to the other two Presbyteras on board, and to freshen up and eat some of Gundardasc's excellent hot food. *It is our job to comfort her. A nice soup always helps.*

Our husbands, the priests, will be occupied for some time with the telling of the tale and with other matters. From what I have heard so far, I think that there is no need for Vigdis to suffer again during the re-telling that is being done by her husband.

Ayesha

A *strid left me with this talker from the island. It fell silent some time ago,*
but Astrid thinks we should keep listening, and I suppose that she is
right. The last call indicated that the person calling still thinks that those up
on East Zarah are still asleep. He is threatening to inform a Master. Even
if the Master thinks the same as his minion, it is unlikely for this state to
continue long. I just hope that they say something about us openly, so that we
know when we are seen.

With the strengthening of the morning light in the east, as the River Dragon
comes around this headland that they are calling Herjolfsness, our sails will
soon be clearly visible to the south from Skrice, as will the craft from Wolf-
neck, coming up from the south-west.

We might all be hidden from a magical gaze, but I am sure that we will be
clearly seen against the horizon if anyone happens to look out to sea with their
eyes. It is still early but, just as mountaineers look up at the peaks and farmers
look out at their fields, I am sure that sailors tend to look at the waves as soon
as they get up, regardless of whether they are going to sea that day or not.

Already Olympias has struck the topsails to reduce the visibility of the
River Dragon until she can join with the other four. They are apparently
coming in from our left. I cannot see them from the deck, but Harnermês has
called down that he can already see them from his high vantage point.

Rani

A *s the story comes out, it seems that the advent of the Masters and their*
gaining control of Skrice had been quite a shock...a fatal shock for
many of the village. The attack had come about mainly from the ruler backed
by those who lived outside the village and who had been able to avoid the
scrutiny of the priests, and although there had been some odd rumours about
the return of the Old Gods, they were no more than some that had been heard
in Wolfneck before the arrival of Svein's drakkar.

It seems that the whole thing probably would not have succeeded at all if
it had not been for the Insak-div, the Kharl and the presence of three of the
Masters. They had seemingly foolishly sailed the dromond into the harbour
before disembarking, so people had been prepared to flee in case it was an
attack from Darkreach, and others had gathered to fight them.

The people of Skrice traded sometimes to Cold Keep, but never saw any large craft from there. From what they knew of the fishermen from there, they sailed very different craft both to this and to the sort of vessels the locals in Skrice use.

The priest says that the intruder was obviously a craft meant for war and it came insolently close to shore, suddenly opening its previously hidden ports and eliminated many of those waiting to object with one blast of its fire weapons. So, we do face the possibility of blasts of fire from it. We dare not get close to it then.

Father Gildas lost most of his family as they helped him escape, and as for Thrain and Ingrid, they now only have their eldest and their youngest children left...their young daughter Groa stands huddled against her mother. Six of their other children died in the fighting to allow their parents to break free. Some of their older children lost their families also, although some of them may still be alive.

At least my reasoning was sound about how they were surviving. The fugitives did indeed have help from some of those who stayed behind. They were pretending to go along with the priests of the Old Gods and went searching for their friends without ever reporting that they had been found and were having food delivered to them.

However, those left behind in the village are finding it harder and harder to keep going. The demands of the new religion are getting more and more onerous. Also, there were more and more people from outside the island arriving whenever the dromond returns. Seemingly they were supposed to all be in Wolfneck by now. As it is, there are perhaps only a third of the original inhabitants left, and at least half of them are firm believers in the new gods.

Moreover, there has not been much chance for the unbelieving locals to flee the island. Only the most trusted are allowed to put to sea, and escaping to the rest of the island is impractical and would only have delayed their death. It was expected that the entire village would be made to come and hunt the refugees soon after the first serious snows made their location more obvious.

The fugitives had refused to allow any of the others to join them as it would have only ensured that they too would die...and their families as well. Father Gildas is, however, sure that if they are given the chance there will be a number of people who will either choose not to fight or else will fight against the Masters and the Old Gods. I need to take that into account.

This made Rani revise her thoughts on how to make the attack and she went into consultation with the teachers about the layout of the village. She had the sketch that Astrid had made for her from the air, but it was rough and did not tell her what the buildings were.

Bianca

*I*t is as terrible a tale as I am going to hear, near as bad in the re-telling as the destruction of my caravan was in real life. Father Gildas says that he is very grateful that help arrived when it did. "You will have to confess me afterwards, but I will be very glad to help exterminate these so-called priests in any way that I can. We have been told that our oldest daughter was one of their first sacrifices and others died too. We have not heard about the families of our other children."

From the change in the expression on her face, Vigdis also overheard her husband's words. She addressed her own private prayer to Saint Ursula and drew the older woman's head onto her shoulder as they sat on the rear cargo hatch. She gathered her into her arms as the woman began to weep...*Danelis is just hovering anxiously...She hasn't needed to become involved in this part of being a Presbytera before and is not sure what to do. She is going to need to learn.*

Christopher

*B*ianca is consoling the grieving woman. She weeps for her children and for what her husband could become. We can stop the last at least. "You will take no part in the combat," he said, "unless they call up the bodies or bones of the departed. Our job is to keep our people alive, and you will, like the rest of us among the priesthood, be busy healing bodies and souls."

My wife may not like me going in to battle at all, but now she is smiling at me in an approving fashion from where she sits with the other woman's head clasped to her shoulder.

Mind you, even if I stay out of combat it will not necessarily stop her from going where she probably should not be. I am not sure if I approve of her devotion to Saint Ursula...mind you, I am even less sure about Astrid's new-found attachment to Saint Kessog. Why couldn't they have chosen safer patrons such as Our Lady or Saint Catherine?

Still, today is at least an auspicious day for our assault on Skrice. It was the Feast of Anastasi...the Resurrection...the main day of Easter...and I had better get to and preach the Orthros service before I run out of time. It is an easy theme for me to warm to with the rebirth of the Faith on Neron Island at stake and the Redemption of many souls.

As they sailed on slowly...waiting for the craft from Wolfneck to catch up...the crew and some others of the huge number of people on board sat high in the air on the yards...they sat in the tops and everyone else was now out of the holds and sitting on the closed covers.

I believe that nearly half of our force is concentrated on this one, very overloaded, ship. Even with four priests on board it seems as if Mass will take forever to be finished. Then it will be Confessions and the Eucharist all around, and only the Dwarves are staying clear.

Astrid

I cannot believe it. Astrid shook her head in wonder. *The priests of Wolfneck have indeed grown reticent in expressing their belief. I have had to prompt Father Fergus, in the rechristened drakkar Vindur-skrefi, Wind-strider, along with Captain Siglunda, to hold an Easter service. The priest said diffidently that he wasn't sure that it was appropriate to talk to God in such a fashion before they were about to kill so many people.*

Astrid disagreed. She did so strongly. "We are about to go into battle and some of these men will never see another service...of any sort...and they are fighting for the Faith. Are you going to deny them the Eucharist and the consolation of the story of Redemption? I will bet you anything you like that Bishop..." and she emphasised the title, even if he was not yet installed, "Christopher is holding Orthros now."

She even made Siglunda draw the four ships closer together so that all could hear what was said on this one. Although Fathers Maurice and Bjarni were on other ships to deliver the Blessing there, she had to get Basil to take Fergus across to the last ship. *He won't fit on to fly with me. I am too large, and Fergus has, so to speak, grown along with his job.*

We are drawing ever closer to the River Dragon. It is only a mile away now by the time they are all finished here with their service. From the people clearly visible sitting in the rigging and everywhere else, it is plain that Christopher is still in full flight in his preaching. Astrid drew Father Fergus' attention to this.

If you listen hard, you can even hear Christopher. Astrid smiled...*where has the shy priest that I met in the forest gone to...*She conveniently ignored her own changes.

With that thought she leant over the side of the ship and threw up. *Oh no...I wouldn't be seasick. I never have been before. I guess that it is not just the Princess who is pregnant. It looks like there are more children on the way for us too.*

Astrid looked around her...*Basil isn't on this craft now, so he hasn't seen me do that. I think it is best if I tell him after the battle. Yes, that is best. I don't want him to have to worry. At least I know that Christopher has some of those things to sweeten the breath for me to suck on. I am getting used to mint.*

Rani

*T*he Easter services are over. Olympias can unleash the River Dragon and Wind-strider towards the land. I may not know much about boats, but even I can see that, even without having its own wind, and just with its oars out to aid its sail, the drakkar is surging ahead of the slower knorr.

We will make landfall just south of Skrice at a beach there and behind a slight ridge. There we will secure the beach with these two ships and then wait for the other three to arrive before anyone goes far forward.

Rani (a short time later)

*F*rom the masthead Harnermês is reporting that some of the people in the village seem to have seen the approaching flotilla, but they are taking the opportunity to quickly flee the village with their families rather than to prepare to try and resist. It seems that this exodus is continuing with people running from house to house to tell others. As people move, they are apparently looking to the north.

As our ships draw near the beach, he tells us of a large group that can be seen coming back towards the village from the direction of the stone circle to the north that Astrid told us about. He reports that there are some there who could be the Masters... "one...two...three...maybe four of them..." and there were three "who are bigger than anyone on the ship...and make Ariadne look as pretty as Jahnifer." He said that with a grin.

Ariadne, sitting on her rock thrower eating breakfast, lost a part of it as she threw a hard bread roll up at him where he was perched high in the mast...and hit her target. He grabbed at the roll and caught it and started to eat the missile. Even Jennifer joined in the cheering and applause for her throw. *As we grow ready to disembark it breaks the palpable tension.*

Chapter III

Rani
17th Quinque, the Feast of Anastasi

Three or four Masters...there were supposed to be only a hand of them left around after Dwarvenholme. We killed one at Wolfneck. Olympias possibly killed one on the drakkar on her way north. If there are only three on Neron, then the last will be with the dromond...somewhere. If there are four on the island, then there should be no more.

Of course, there could have been far more than a hand of them left. I must be honest with myself. We cannot assume anything. Even after we finish here, we have not finished. Rani sighed. We will have to be sure that we have eliminated all of them. Leaving even one alive is not an option for us. It is like the dromond. Where is that now? I am sure that there must be at least one Master with it.

I need to pay attention to the battle that is about to start. Already the two boats from the River Dragon, along with the saddles and the carpet have begun ferrying the people from that ship on to the land. As they land, they head up to where it has been decided that we will set up our lines. It is time to be a Battle Mage again.

It will not be long before Wind-strider beaches and its passengers start to disembark onto the shore. Those from the Wind-strider will soon be running up the slope to join the others and take a position. I must be there first.

Ariadne

I *have made sure that my ballista and crew are among the first to be taken off by the saddles. In Wolfneck, I thought about what we are now facing. I have arranged for special backpacks to be made. These come out on the next flight. If we must move, the Hobs and I will carry as many enhanced balls as we can in them.*

The three Hobs, Aziz, Haytor and Krukurb — and I still need to sort out how I feel about him — are carrying the ballista to an advantageous spot forward of the landing on a small ridge between the beach and the settlement and closer to the village and…despite their strength…all are almost staggering under the weight they carry. They cannot do this for long.

Ahead of us, I can see our opponents starting to form up. The mage Atli and the Rangers of Wolfneck are already heading off at a jog towards the interior of the island, trying to circle around the village. It seems that their job will be to try and get behind the Masters and rally anyone that they can find to join them in attacking.

They will attack only once the mêlée has been joined, or to prevent any armed foe from escaping before or during the battle. The ridge that I am using to set up on is just tall enough to stop them from being seen from the village as they leave. All is going as it should.

Ariadne (a short while later)

*N**ot here! Siglunda has Leif unrolling an already drawn-out pattern near the ballista.* Ariadne chased the mage further away from her. "I don't want them aiming at you…missing you and getting me…or even the other way around. They will not like me soon and I have magic that will hopefully make them miss. It may then catch you, so you want to be clear of me."

She looked down the low ridge. *Ahead of me, and slightly to the right, is a cluster of buildings. I am at about the same level as the very top of its highest chimney. Despite the ducks and chickens, it doesn't seem to be a full-sized farm…there are not enough animals there…someone wealthy then…a ship-owner perhaps. It is close to a hand of filled hands away, so it will not provide cover for archers.*

Another few hundred paces to the right of that is a similar set of buildings and then…further around…some mills. Two are on the same ridge that I am on as it curves around the village — they use the wind — and another is on a stream that comes down through the village. In the distance, I can just see the tops of the stone circle over another ridge, or rather the same ridge as it keeps bending around.

Realisation hit her. *That is why they didn't see us approaching then. They cannot see the water to the south and south-west from there. They may not even be able to see anything beyond it.*

Below me is the little sheltered bay with two ships, rounder ones like the three craft that have not yet joined us, and several smaller boats drawn up on the strand around it. The River Dragon will be coming through its narrow mouth and anchoring there once it has dropped its people. Between my weapon and the smaller ones on the front of the ship we will make it a hot time for the defenders. Our ship will also prevent any escape by sea.

She could see just behind the last buildings of the village a battle array starting to be drawn up. *Unlike what both Stefan and the Brotherhood General did, this is something more like the barbarians that I heard about at home. Even though not all of them seem to be islanders—some are even Kharl—they are assembled as one single mob with archers just mixed in with the others. At the front of everything is a shield wall armed with axes, swords, and spears.*

Around her, she could hear Stefan and Eleanor yelling at the Wolfneck people to get them sorted out from exactly the same sort of clump. *I can see some looks of annoyance...but the two already have experience at chivvying the villagers of the North around to get ready for a battle and Stefan is not taking any shit from them.*

People are starting to do as they are told, even if they are casting dirty looks at the two and muttering under their breath. At least I have a lovely long slope that I can command with my fire. Anyone advancing to my position will have to walk uphill into the face of whatever I can throw. A saddle rider arrived and put down some more packs. *Good...more balls.*

Astrid

*R*ani *has set up further along the ridge from Ariadne and now the other mages are doing the same. Eleanor has bunches of archers near each mage. Stefan is still trying to get order out of the Wolfneck people who have axes and spears and swords. Oh dear. He has even hit a couple on the backside with the flat of his sword to gain their attention.*

It may be the sword that killed a dragon, and they will put up with him swearing at them, but that is a risky move with my home villagers, and I can see some annoyed looks even as they do what he tells them. Astrid sighed.

She landed and got Anahita to take her saddle. *Maybe they will have more respect for me.* She looked around and used her voice and waved her new weapon around. "Look ahead of us…you see those giants…they are Insak-div…I have killed a Master in single combat…well, this morning I killed one of these…Insak-div are a lot harder."

I have their attention, now to drive home my message like a nail into timber. She continued. "There are almost as many of them in that shield wall as there are of us…if you do not listen to me…and to Stefan and Eleanor, I will have to tell your wives and sisters that you refused to listen to us when I explain to them why you did not come back."

She looked around. *That really got their attention.* She formed them up as she wanted, or rather as Stefan was clearly trying to get them to. She kept looking at him and he nodded back. *I must be getting it right. I saw what the kataphractoi did in their charge against the chariots. There is no reason that…if we come off our ridge and time it right…our wedges should not do the same thing to the shield wall that is forming ahead of us.*

I have some changes though. I need to occupy the shield wall while I take on the Insak-div one by one. She looked around the men and women of Wolfneck who were there. *I was such a little thing when I left home…now I feel that there are none among the people of my old home with the experience to take on one of the giants. That will be my job.*

With that in mind she went to where Eleanor was getting the archers all in their places. *After the priests and mages, I want them to concentrate on the Insak-div. It is natural for the archers to want to take on the opposing archers first, but this time it is more important to… I have shadows.* She looked back.

Following behind her were her four remaining brothers. *They hang together in a little clump.* She grunted. *As long as they don't get in the way, and they do what I tell them to do…* After a quick word with Stefan, she picked out a few who she wanted to add to her family and gave them all their instructions.

Thord

*W*e *Dwarves are all very glad to make it onto the land. We were not happy out on the sea, and I am sure that Dwarves will never be so.* Thord formed them up well to the left of the ballista on the very shore itself. *Even the Baron is readily obeying me. Until we have a king once again, it is good to be the Crown-Finder.*

Apart from a few skirmishes with the wild tribes of the mountains, Dwarves have not been into a real battle for a long time, and although we might argue about most things, one thing that we are practical about is listening to someone who has experience in something important...like mining, engineering, and war.

If the battle shapes up the way it is likely to, there is going to be an attempt to outflank us along the beach, or at least an attempt to escape to the beach. Our task is to stop either of those. Unless we are on our sheep, Dwarves are much better at being charged than in charging. Crossbows were readied and shields put onto backs for when they reloaded. *The first part of the battle will be an exchange of missiles, and not everyone has the amulet that I do.*

He moved his people forward, past where the ridge met the water. *Due to the shape of the bay, we must take up a position ahead of everyone else...but well to the side.* He looked ahead. *The enemy line is almost at right angles to us Dwarves.*

Once we are in place hunkered down out of sight behind a stone wall, it is time for our druid to say a few words. On board a ship is not the right place to say words to the Gods of Earth and Stone. Having everyone sitting on the ground and holding on to the stones of an ancient wall that is well anchored in the bones of the earth is.

Ariadne

I hear a shout and a series of cries coming from behind us. She turned and looked. *On the beach, the last three boats are now grounding. Their crew and passengers are already surging up the ridge. My people are yelling instructions to them as they come up the slope and they chivvy them into the places where they are needed.*

She looked out to sea. *In the meantime, the River Dragon is already moving up the short stretch of coast to its position in the bay. I can see the Princess Theodora standing in her pattern on the hatch. Our opponents are starting to move slowly forward, and although we want the enemy to charge us, the allies do not seem to be ready quite yet...I have no orders, but I think that it is perhaps time to confuse them a little.*

Ariadne called for her Yamyam to pay attention as she carefully laid in her aim. *That is a priest or a mage or a leader of some sort giving orders, and those are probably Masters who are watching him with priests all around them. It would be a crime not to take advantage of our element of surprise.* She fired and immediately called for a reload...her team sprang quickly into action. *We are well practiced now.*

Rani

*A*svayujau, please grant us some good luck. Everyone is not even off the ships; we are not ready for the battle yet and they are coming on to us too soon. Should I release the saddles to delay them?* She turned to give an order and there was a roar of an explosion behind her. She turned back. *There is one less Master on its feet and Ariadne's crew are reloading their weapon. She must have seen the same as me and acted quickly. She has hit it directly.*

I *know what must be done next.* Rani turned and gave her orders to the saddle riders, who leapt into the sky. *Kāhina has my saddle, and it looks like Bryony is flying instead of her husband. I can see Astrid on the ground chasing axemen into little clumps…what is she up to now? Ariadne is firing again.*

This time not at the Masters. She has gone for the one giving orders…he looked like he was trying to make the islanders defend, instead of charging uphill. That would have changed everything and let him wrest the advantage back. I guess that is the Jarl, Egil Thorgrimmson. He was one of the ones who brought the Masters in. I hope that he enjoys his reward.

Yama take him. He is…unbelievably…still alive after being hit! He must have protection. Someone is giving him a healing draught…too late…Ariadne has noticed that also, and sent a second ball down to him. Two explosions centred on him, and he is not going to be getting back on his feet, nor are those who were clustered around him.

That gives some defenders pause, and yet makes others angry, and starts the reluctant ones moving forward. Ariadne has done what we need. I can see confusion as our opponents work out what they should do. At least it gives Stefan and Eleanor a longer time to loudly direct people to places as they arrive up the ridge. Gradually, our line is filling out at the top of the slope.

Astrid

*I*t took a while, but I have my groups in some sort of order. If only they can remember what I told them to do when things start to kick off. Now, what is happening around us?* She looked around the battlefield. *The move forward has ground to a halt for a while as our enemy mills around without leadership. Ariadne showed that she was good at those tactics at One Tree Hill.*

Finally. it looks like one of the Masters is calling out and waving around and has restored some order and our opponents have started off up the slope towards us again. Unfortunately for them, we are all in place and ready now.

Our foe is moving towards us at a slow jog. Their archers must move and fire, and so do their mages. That is stupid of them. We are the ones who must take the ground, not them. They should make us come to them. I guess that it would not be manly enough to do that. I can hear Eleanor calling orders and more explosions from the work of Ariadne and her boys. The River Dragon is now coming through the channel and Denizkartal has his smaller, bow-mounted, ballista working and so does Olympias.

They each have a crew...who is steering? Harnermês. He is bringing her in slowly under a staysail alone. I can see people in the back, and they are now letting go the stern anchors. No-one can escape by boat now. Both ballistae are in their bow mounts. They are firing their smaller balls along the line advancing to us. From the lack of explosions, they are just using plain balls, but balls that are designed to go through stout wooden hulls and sink a ship do wicked work along the length of a shield wall among soft humanoids. Each of them is firing at about half the speed of a bow and twice as fast as Ariadne.

Each shot brings down at least a hand of people dead or maimed. The screams can be heard from where I am each time a ball rakes along the line. She could see that Theodora was using a wand at the few she could reach. *Arrows are starting to come in and, far more, go out.* "Stay fast. We must wait." *It is dangerous and hard to just stand and take it, but it is only a small ridge that we are on, and if we come down off it too early, we lose our small advantage of height and there are not that many arrows coming up at us anyway. Most head towards our archers and our mages.*

Rani

I am glad that I am wearing my helmet that deflects missiles. It must be obvious that I am a leader. Arrows keep hitting all around me...some explosively. As the range closes, I can see that magical bolts are starting to be fired from wands on both sides. Our attackers will have difficulty casting on the run unless they use a wand. I was hoping that we could provoke them into losing their defensive advantage by taking up a position on the ridge.

Kartikeya has been kind. The Masters are good at planning ahead, but it really seems that they do not think on their feet very well. I wonder... They give people instructions...do they, in turn, have someone else telling them what to do? Is there someone, someone still hidden, who does the real thinking for them? And it is only when they are on their own that they behave so unthinkingly? The thought appalled her, and she put it aside until later.

I am only going to have time to use one good blast before going on to my wands...so it has to count. She grinned. *Watch this spell, provincial mages! Watch a Havenite Battle Mage in action and fear the power of Mousehole.*

She recited the words, and the blast that she had used against the Brotherhood chariot came out of her hand. This time she threw her spare pot as its flame kept going, and grew and grew. One of the Masters completely vanished and the other staggered, obviously hurt badly, its robe on fire. A circle of dead and dying priests lay around the target. *Now there is only one Master left and he is somewhat distracted.*

Astrid has started her people charging down the hill now. Rani waved in the air. The Mice on the saddles obeyed their instructions, and acting from on high, each of them threw some of the supply of molotails. Sections of the shield wall and one of the Insak-div were enveloped in fire. Instantly, the huge Kharl became like a giant flaming statue of ear-splitting pain.

The rest kept going, dodging around the screaming pools of fire, and trying to avoid the victims who run around blindly covered in flame, or who writhe on the ground trying to put themselves out. *They keep on coming towards us. The bulk of them must know that the losers of this battle are going to be dead soon. From what we heard in the questioning at Wolfneck, from their beliefs they want to die in a battle anyway. That way lies their Nirvana.*

What is that movement at the flank? From up the creek, a group could be seen moving down towards and into the village. *Hopefully, that will be Atli and the Rangers. They seem to have some others with them...Astrid will hit soon. Thord has his Dwarves running as fast as they can towards the wall of a second field just short of the end of the line...*

Eleanor

I have my archers in hand. I have the advantage of numbers for a start. The Kharl have few archers, and the Neronese have far less people with bows or slings than me. They make up for it by having a lot more troops armed with sword or axe or a spear.

The archers of Wolfneck have the same outsized weapons that Astrid uses and even on the flat they can outrange the short bows that most of our rivals use. Throw in the horse bows that nearly all the Mice use now, and the mages and archers of our opponents are well outclassed and are starting to go down even if many of the mages have some form of protection.

In addition, we have the ballista...and Ariadne is picking her targets well. Her balls do a lot of damage as they bounce through the shield wall, and those from the ship slay several each time that they fire.

Stefan

From where he stood with the line of spears, Stefan looked up at Bryony on a saddle as she climbed into the sky. *Adara is at least with the other archers behind me. It is bad enough worrying about one woman in a battle, let alone two of them.*

Stefan was using his experience from dealing with the northern alliance to hold the spears and swords in check and his voice was getting sore. *They want to charge recklessly downhill. I cannot allow that. They are the shield for the archers for a start and the longer we delay our charge, the less of my people will die and the more of our opponents.*

He looked left and right. *On each side are little blocks of people, mainly men with two-handed axes. At least my people are all in one solid wall. Astrid must run from one side to another as she tries to chase her people into the positions that she wants, and then hold them in place like a sheepdog in an open field without a fence to help it. I, at least, can see what she is trying to do. I am sure that most of this lot have never been in a real battle in their lives.*

By Saint Sebastian, I must either be standing out as a leader or else there is a sign above me that says, 'aim here'. He kept his shield high. *That is the third arrow to lodge in it. Add that to the one that glanced off my helm and those lodged in the ground around me….Now the foe are starting to charge up the slight incline.* Astrid nodded to Stefan, and he nodded back.

She is shouting her people forward and into action. I must hold mine in place a little longer yet. "Hold fast…hold fast…hold fast!" he cried out.

Astrid

Time for us to go…Stefan agrees. "Axes…start moving…walk slowly… don't charge yet until I say!" She looked up as she heard Stefan calling at the spears to stay still. *I hope that they do. The saddles are coming in for another run and ahead fire erupts from various parts of the charging wall.* Screams rise through the air as the smell of burnt flesh quickly came up on the breeze. *I hate that smell already…now we go…* "Run…now charge!" Her voice called as loud as it could, as first her group and then the ones on the other side started to run.

I can hear Stefan calling the spears and the swords to start walking forward now. Astrid aimed herself towards the two remaining Insak-div. *Why hasn't the fire taken them? On their own they are more dangerous than all the mages who are left and any others who have wands. My amulet must be working. People beside me are hit and I charge on.* She was moving aside from the rest of the axes as she ran on. "Saint Kessog, I call for aid. Saint Kessog."

Theodora

*H**e is definitely a mage. Astrid told me to look for anyone running with a wand and nearly being tripped up by their sword. She was right.* She fired a bolt at him.

Damn him, he must have protection to have deflected it. Now he has noticed me. He must be their Earth mage, judging from the flying clods from his wand. He is not as powerful as I am, but he is probably their senior mage. Now it is mage against mage. I need to put up with his clods and hope that I have more protection than he does...that one made me stagger.

She worked through her spell. *I stand firm in a pattern, and he doesn't; and he knows it. He has stopped and is now starting to begin a full chanting. It is too late for that.* She smiled as she unleashed on a single person the spell that had cracked open the roof of Peace Tower.

The fist of air forced the mage, and several people around him, suddenly to become missiles against their own people. They moved backwards as fast as an arrow to lie limp, and some rendered into pieces, after impact. *Now, what is left for my wands?*

Astrid

*I**t was soon too hot a task for Astrid to think about others. *The wedges are cutting through the surviving shield wall, but I have an Insak-div to contend with...some of those with axes have moved with me and...*She fenced with one while the other killed a man with a two-handed axe fighting alongside her... slicing him near in half...*getting too close to them means dying.*

Someone on the hill is showing off their archery as an explosion rocks that one. I must focus on my own. This time I do not have the advantage of surprise attack. And strong though I am with my magic, this one is far stronger. And big though I am, I am small next to him. But at least I am faster... She turned in the fight so that both of the Insak-div were in line.

My four brothers stand all around the second one...at least they have the sense to pack-hunt like wolves as one dives in from behind and hits and moves out and the others defend and dance back...it seems that everyone expects me to take this one on my own...damn, he just took another splinter from my spear shaft. She thrust...he parried and then swung around his blade in a two-handed stroke and she had no choice but to block square on. Her spear splintered into two pieces... *I no longer have a spear...I have a stick. My spear's head lies on the ground.* Astrid dived, rolled, and picked up the head, holding its short shaft in both hands as she danced around.

Saint Kessog help me... The Insak-div was roaring and drawing back for another blow as...without thinking...she sprang forward and dived into a roll between his splayed legs...thrusting up from the ground as she did so.

An almighty scream filled the air as her spear point struck deep in the groin of the giant with all her enhanced strength put behind the blow. She was showered in hot blood as she passed rolling between his legs and then pulled the blade out of where it had deeply lodged, at least a spread hand inside the giant.

It is stuck in something inside him and resists my pull... The blade of her wide-bladed hunting spear had not only pierced his groin but had cut at least one of the arteries to his legs and was nearly trapped inside him. Suddenly, it came free as she scrambled to get clear. He fell writhing face first to the ground with his screams ringing in her ears and around the battlefield.

Quickly, she took her spearhead and its short shaft in both hands and dived onto him. "Saint Kessog... Die, monster." She added her weight to the attack. Her target turned, and as he turned over, the blade went through an eye, opening the skull, and pinning his head to the ground. Suddenly, he went limp.

Astrid stood and looked around wiping her eyes clear. *My brothers have finished their Insak-div off and have the hide to be standing there watching me with grins on their faces.* She looked further... *Stefan's spearmen have completed the destruction with their charge. As short as it has been, the battle seems to be over.*

Although some are trying to get away, they are being cut down or rounded up. They cannot hope to escape the archers on saddles, who are now herding the routed up like sheep dogs would, and now there are Dwarves at one end of the field and the Rangers at the other. It looks like they are thoroughly screwed.

She looked up and around. *The rest of the archers are still standing on the low ridge with the mages and the ballista crew. The priests are starting to hurry down and the carpet has already landed among the wounded.* She stopped and spat some blood from out of her mouth.

The Insak-div blood I am drenched in from head to foot might still be warm, but it tastes bitter and foul, and I already stink as if I were a very charnel house. As she moved, blood squelched in her boots. She looked at her blood-soaked braids and down at her tunic under her mail. *I will never get the stains out of that. I guess that I need to keep this one for battles.*

Chapter IV

Rani
17th Quinque, the Feast of Anastasi

I thank Kartikeya. The destruction of our opponents has been nearly complete, and our losses seem to be light. Some of our foe tried to flee back to the village, or towards the boats and the beaches. The second group were stopped by Thord and the Dwarves and the first have run into Atli, the Rangers, and others that they have gathered.

The rest of them have either died...or are still dying in ones or twos surrounded by our people...or have surrendered already. It is likely that most of those will have to be executed for what they have done under the rule of the Masters, but for the moment they are just captives. They are being bound and they will be questioned.

Basil

*W*e *need to make sure that the prisoners are all secure.* Basil walked among the captives, binding them, and checking other people's knots. *We cannot execute them today on Easter Dithlau or tomorrow on Krondag. That is Kyriaki tou Pascha when we should be giving the red eggs to symbolise the blood of the risen Christ. It would be wrong for an execution to be held then.*

One man is causing a problem and rejects lying still with the other prisoners. He refuses to stay on the ground, even though he is tied. People are knocking him down and he still gets up. Basil came to quiet him down, but the man rebuffed any attempt to quiet him.

With his hands bound he is still struggling to his feet. He bears bloody open wounds on his head, and he was probably unconscious when he was captured. He is very unsteady on his feet now. He insists on speaking. Basil came up and stood in front of him. The man looked him up and down as if evaluating if he was a leader.

"My name is Skap," he finally said, "and you are going to kill me. If we had won, I would probably have killed you. I chose the wrong side and before I die, I want to confess to a priest. I will confess to anyone who will listen. I am not objecting to dying. I want you to kill me as it would be a sin for me to kill myself. I realise now that I have committed far too many sins to live, and I do not want to live with what I have done."

He stopped and looked around at the other prisoners with disgust then shook his head and spat on the ground in their direction. "I thought that I was doing what the Gods wanted...I was wrong...I really thought that they were Gods who ruled us and talked to us...they showed us things and wrought what we thought were miracles." The man paused and drew breath.

"I want to tell you everything about them. If they were indeed Gods, mortals would not have been able to defeat them. They are either demons, or they are just mere mortals like me who have lied and made us do...shameful things while they...watched. Either way I hate them, and I want to bring them down and make sure they do not survive me by long." He stopped.

Basil stood there silent and looked at Skap. Skap stood swaying slightly but with determination on his face as he returned the stare. "Well," he said "ask me whatever you want. I will answer you and I will tell you the truth."

Where do I start? We need the Princesses here to listen for a start. He beckoned others of the Mice over. "The Masters said that they were servants of the Old Gods, did they?"

"They didn't have to," was the bitter reply. "Those things...those Masters," he spat again onto the ground, "may have been people once, and they said they wanted to be people again, but they would have been servants when they were people the first time around...and would have been servants again if they were re-born.

"Do not get me wrong, they were powerful mages and very intimidating, but sometimes they behaved just like servants who were terrified of their masters, just as we were mostly scared of them." He coughed the cough of a person with wounds inside him.

"Every now and then, particularly if they were near the main Pattern, one of them would stop and sort of tilt his head a bit to the side as if he were listening to something in the air and then he would come out with orders. Sometimes they were orders that were even completely different to what they had just told us to do, and once one of them had the new orders, all the others did as well."

Skap stopped again, coughed, and spat. He looked at where he had just spat. This time there was blood in it. He looked sourly at the spit.

"When we were killing a girl...we always had to rape her first...as many of us as could do so before she was likely to die...they made it so that before we did anything one of the Masters, or the priests would say a prayer over her, and then they would make a tiny cut somewhere on her body with one of those stone knives."

"The girls always started screaming as if they were in torment as soon as that was done and before anything else happened. Most had to be gagged. The screaming was too distracting, and you couldn't do what the Old Gods...the god-cursed demons...whatever they were, wanted you to do if they were like that."

The man has a haunted expression on his face as he speaks. I have never seen its like before in a confession. There is no doubt that he is genuine. He is seeing and hearing things in his head that he does not want to either see or hear. Looking around me, I can now see his expression is echoed in the faces of some other of the other captives. He is making them think about what they have done.

He continued. "I don't think that there was one, except the first...Runa, Father Gildas' daughter, who hadn't lost her mind before she was killed." Skap stopped and shook his head.

"Runa...she was brave, and she was strong. She thanked the so-called priest for ending her suffering even as he was cutting out her heart with his knife. She had a look...I don't know what it was...on her face as she fought in her head with what was happening to her body and her soul. How she acted should have told me that I had chosen the wrong side."

He looked across at Father Gildas, who had joined them, his face a blank mask, "I am sorry, Father. Do not feel bad about hating me. I freely give you my leave to do that. I hate myself at present. Please do not ever forgive me. I do not deserve it from you, but I am desperately hoping that God will do so in time."

He shuddered and continued. "They used some girls from here and many more that they brought from elsewhere...I think the Brotherhood. As the girls were being raped and killed you felt a...sort of cold presence around you... if the rape was done in the Pattern, you sometimes saw six figures standing around the victim. They always seemed to loom over you as if they were drawing on what was happening and feeding on the pain and suffering."

"I asked one of the priests about this when he was drunk one night after a...sacrifice. He said that I was right, that I had been blessed to actually see a vision of the Old Gods themselves as they fed, and perhaps I should think about becoming a priest myself, but I am a simple warrior. Perhaps too simple, and it always seemed to me to be wrong for a deity to feed on suffering and pain...but who was I to judge a God?"

He stopped again and looked around. *I may not be a priest, but his face has a look of what can only be described as spiritual agony. Unlike most people, his hell has come to visit him while he is still alive.* Skap coughed and spat again. "What else do you want to know? There is another Master somewhere. He is away from here with the fire ship and most of those from Darkreach… he is not just at Arnflorst.

"I heard some of the priests talking with the Jarl. The Jarl was worried. He knew that you were going to attack, but he didn't know when. He expected something weeks ago when your ship killed the drakkar, the Blood-Letter, during the storm. He had wanted the fire-ship to be here the whole time, but the priests said that there were other places that it had to be…that the Gods had servants all over the world…that the Gods would look after us without it.

"They had set up the watch on top of the mountain," he jerked his head towards East Zarah, "and told us that nothing could sneak up on us now, that we would surprise you. We had to take turns up there, a week at a time. Your ship coming up was the first time the green box showed anything except at the edges and not coming here."

I don't need to prompt him. He is saying all that he knows as if it were a Confession, and I suppose that it is in a way. "I don't know what the box is. We just stared at it hour after hour and we looked for dots after each sweep that stayed there. We hated it. We fell asleep all the time we were doing it until they started putting a Kharl and a Big One up there with us.

We were told that the Greenskins could kill us if they wanted to if we fell asleep. They killed one man and ate his liver and heart." He stopped. *There are tears running freely down his face through the drying blood.* "That is all that there is unless you want me to say who did what to who, but that is not important as most of them are dead anyway and the rest soon will be. I need a priest…a real one…but not Father Gildas. He has suffered enough already without me adding any more for him."

He fell silent and held out his hands as he looked around to see if there were any other questions. *He deserves something. Having spoken up and shown his resolve perhaps he deserves to be relieved of some of his pain before he achieves the execution that he is waiting on.* Basil undid his bonds. Skap stood quietly rubbing his wrists as Father Simeon came over and took him aside to sit him down and to start to hear his confession.

Rani

*W*e may not be able to destroy the Patterns until our priests have regained their mana. However, we still need to look for where the Patterns are. She started to gather up some of the Mice to come with her when she saw Astrid coming closer with one of the weapons she had taken from the Insak-div on the mountain. *Where is her spear?* Rani looked behind Astrid.

Who are the four men who follow her several paces behind like puppies? Huge blonde puppies with long braided hair and beards. The smallest of the four is more than a hand taller than Astrid and the largest at least two hands and they are all far wider. They sort of look like her brother the priest...she has more than one brother, doesn't she? Why is Astrid dripping wet? She is coming from the creek...has she dived into it fully clothed? Why?

"It is time to see what we can find," said Astrid. In the hand that did not have the strange weapon in it she waved the magic-detecting wand that they had found on the mountain. "Do we start with the Patterns or look for magic?" *She is looking at my face and must divine my puzzlement.* Astrid waved her hand behind her.

"These are my brothers, and they think that I will forgive them for years of cooking and washing and being looked down upon by them just because the four of them were able to bring down one Insak-div between them. It may be a start, but they have a long way to go yet. I think that you will have to put up with them following me until I can get them home."

"We should look for the Patterns first." *While her tone is harsh, Astrid does look more than a trifle pleased with their endeavour. The brothers have obviously fought hard and three of them bear wounds, either bandaged or recently healed from the gaps in their chain shirts and trews.*

Theodora now joined them, and Astrid waved towards Stefan and his wives, beckoning a couple of archers closer. "We need to see if they need to have anything done to them...that is...if we can do anything to them."

I guess that I start walking towards the ridge to the north of the village and everyone comes with me then. It seems right to look near the circle first.

We need not bother to look any further for the first pattern. The entire new-built circle is filled with an arrangement of masonry that has been dug into the earth. In the centre is an altar covered with the dark stains of a sacrifice. The stones, and the soil around the stones, have another dark stain to them. Ants swarm over the entire pattern. There is a rank smell, even in the chill air.

Astrid went down on one knee and smelt the stain. "Blood," she said grimly and stood. "Some of it is fresh from this morning, but I cannot see the body. It is probably why they didn't see us...they were distracted." They all looked around the circle. *The Pattern in it is over a filled hand of paces across.* Astrid's voice grew angry: "how many died to make this Pattern?"

The design seems to have a similar appearance to the others we have seen...but not quite the same. It was only when Father Christopher was brought along with his book of sketches that they found out that it was the same as the one on Gil-Gand-Rask. It bore the names of the six that could not be spoken carved on slabs of stone that were then set into the pattern.

Astrid looked around. "Where is the other one?" she asked.

What is she asking? "What other one?" asked Rani.

"We know that the Masters were still communicating from somewhere. This is a pattern of something else, the things that Skap saw. Somewhere there will be another one. This one is new. The other one here on Neron will be the same. Neither of them was mentioned on our list from Dwarvenholme. That means that there is, even after here, yet another pattern.

"Furthermore, there is the larger circle that the Masters received their instruction from when they were in Dwarvenholme. Where is it? It won't be here unless these other beings that Skap talked of are here on this island and, if they were here in their body, then why weren't they more openly here when people died in this Pattern for them?"

How many other Patterns are there? I can feel the horror growing in me. I had thought, or at least hoped, that this attack on Skrice might be the end of it all. Now it looks like the hardest parts of what we must do still lie before us. Until now we have attacked targets that are visible and easy to find. Our targets, once we knew where to look, lay almost in the open and the advantage of surprise lay with us, the attackers. Now we will be going after beings that had the Masters afraid of them.

We neither know anything about this enemy nor do we have any real information on where they might be. Skap mentioned Arnflorst, but I cannot ask for more from him in case they are listening. From what he said there are more servants of the Masters and the so-called Old Gods all around the world and not just in The Land.

We have one small ship, and we don't even know how big the world really is. We do, at least, have a lot more books to look in and it is at least possible that prophesy will be clearer now. Rani paused in her thought for a moment. *We desperately need to get back to Mousehole for a while to read, to think and to plan where we cannot be overheard.*

The Mice began to spread out and started searching the entire village. Magic was collected and the smaller Pattern that was used for the Masters here to communicate with their minions in the Land was found in a building. *We have not found any others. I am not sure now if that is good or if it is bad. May Ganesh grant me the wisdom to decide that.*

One thing, at least we have found the partner to the opal and iron talker. When we leave the island one can stay here and the other can go to Wolfneck. If the devices have the range for it, then never again will the two settlements, with so much in common, be so totally isolated from each other that one can be over-run by enemies and the people at the other settlement not even know.

Chapter V

Siglunda
17th Quinque, the Feast of Anastasi

Tonight, my people of Wolfneck celebrate that they are alive. None of the locals that are left can deny us that, although the surviving Neronese have lost too much to be joyous, and to celebrate. Even if I did not know all my people, the Neronese could be distinguished by the haunted looks on their faces. In two days...after these Mice have destroyed these Patterns...all my people will board their ships and return home.

There are less of them to go home than what arrived. I need to admit to myself that my leadership of Wolfneck has been a disaster. We have lost near as many people as we would have from a bout of The Burning. I now have to go back and face their families.

Even with better tactics, and with far more powerful magic, and with all of our priests hard at work...using just bandages and potions and unguents and berries when they had no more mana to give...there are far too many who have died in this victory. Many of the people that I delivered as babies died today.

We still have the prisoners to deal with. We have largely left them tied up and all locked into one of the large houses of the former ship owners. I used to deal with him. At least it makes it easier to keep an eye on them. None of us knows if others will try to free them, but perhaps half of the surviving men of the island are inside that one building. At least all those from other places are already dead.

Astrid

We Mice have taken over the dead Jarl's hall while we are here. Those that are not on the River Dragon or on watch over the prisoners are all quietly inside in front of a warm fire. It was nice of him to leave us a whole pile of really nice furs to snuggle into.

Tonight, I get to show Basil the joy of having a pile of furs in a sleeping closet. I have claimed one for us and my new weapon leans against it to show whose it is. I may have new aches and pains, but I want the release of our coupling.

Astrid sat by the fire pit with a warm spiced drink in her hand leaning back onto her husband. *The bard Signy Skáld is coming over to us with a thoughtful expression on her face. She has been sitting down with the Princesses and she has talked a lot but has said nothing. She has something to say, but she does not know how.*

That is not like her at all. She is normally a good storyteller. I have heard her several times before and she has a way with tales. Now has dropped her voice and she speaks low as if not wanting to be overheard. Does she not realise that, if anyone but us is listening to us, they use magic and talking low will not help.

"What Skap said made me think," she said. "There is an old, old, story, and only a part of one at that, I do not know if it is important or not. It talks not of the Old Gods but of the Adversaries, but it says that there are seven of them, not six, and it calls the seventh the Renegade. It talks of the struggle for the soul of the world and for its fruits that we are all a part of." She stopped and looked around as if afraid of being heard.

"It is a story that is always passed on from master to student," she continued, "even though no-one understands it. I have always thought that it was an allegory but now, after these events here, after what has been said, I am not so sure." *No-one notices that I am listening hard to this story. How much more do we have to do? Do we have worse to face?*

Signy left and Astrid turned around to face the Princesses. "So, we have gotten rid of almost all of the Masters. Do we now have to get rid of these Adversaries? What is next after them? Are they the last? Do we have a life stretched out ahead of us that becomes one of us chasing one enemy after the other until one of them kills us? Will our children still be doing this long after we are dead? Is there an end? Is this the prophesy that you have brought to us?"

Astrid

Now Signy has left it is the turn of Ingrid, the wife of the mage, Thrain, to come up to the Princesses. It seems that even tonight it will be all business until I can get to bed, and we both have a watch soon before we can do that. She has her daughter with her, holding her hand. The girl stands there silent, her eyes downcast.

"I have been talking with your people about your valley and what you are building there," Ingrid said. She indicated the girl standing beside her with her eyes downcast. "This is my daughter Groa. She is the only child among us Neronese who was not under the control of these evil ones and yet she has lost most of her family."

She looked at the Princesses as if she was still working through her own thoughts. "Those young who are left here on Neron are mostly related to those who killed her brothers and sisters, well, we all are related to each other to some degree, but she is still young. When you leave here, I want her to go with you to this school that you are building."

"It seems that there are others there in your school. Some have suffered and others have not...She is bright, and I want her to be educated and...with all respect to Kadlin and Æirik...I want her to get a wider education than she can get here on our isolated isle." *Maybe the Princesses expected this. I suppose that we are lucky not to have a flood from here and elsewhere.*

"If she becomes a mage...and she is likely to...she will be a water mage of the sign of the fish and my husband will not be able to give her the teaching that she will need. Besides, I have looked into the future as best I can, and I cannot see her marrying into this village. It is something that we do far too much of anyway and it is starting to show."

Oops, now she is looking across the fire to where I am sprawled, with Basil's arms around me, in the warmth of my new white bear's fur that I found and am taking home with us. She is looking straight at me. I guess that I am now included in her remarks.

"Even one of the Wolfneck men or another part-Kharl like yours will be far better than a local boy...we are all too much cousins here on the island and I think that this may have helped in what has happened here. I am claiming some of the Jarl's treasure to go with you so that Groa...and any others that we send you," *I knew that there would end up being a flood of children coming to us,* "...will be taught as they need to be. Any boy who wants her can pay a good bride price...so she will not need a dowry. We will keep that much of our practice at least."

She is looking even more directly at me now. What have I done? "I am making you responsible for her in that regard and all others where a parent's decision is needed quickly. She will be part of the school, along with the other children we send, but I tell you that you are now her foster-mother and will make decisions for her in my stead."

Damn. Don't I have enough things to worry about? "And if I don't want that responsibility?"

"From what I have heard of you after asking around among your people," and Ingrid smiled, "that would be very unlike you." Several soft chuckles came from various places around the fire and Astrid herself had to smile ruefully. *I guess that she has me there.* She sat up and beckoned the young girl over. After patting the fur beside her the girl sat down and Astrid began to talk to her.

Christopher

Over the next two days, we need to disenchant the Patterns. We also need to dismantle as much of the larger one as we can. For the good of everyone, I think that its blood-stained rocks need to be broken up and cast into the ocean.

I said so loudly, and on hearing that this was going to be happening, some of the men already condemned to be executed, led predictably by Skap, have asked a final boon. They want to take part in the destruction of the circle and the Pattern before they die. He may have confessed, but his soul is still tortured, and this may help heal him before he dies.

This will also help with how their families are viewed by the other islanders. True contrition is hard to show, but I have interceded on their behalf and their wish has been granted. God already knows what is in their minds, but that it will show the rest, including their families and the rest of the village, that their repentance is genuine. It is a part of the needed healing for the others.

Siglunda (19th Quinque)

At last, the Patterns are gone. Those of the prisoners who want final confession have received it and now they will be executed by having their heads cut off on a wooden block. This is to be done north of the village, by the shore.

At least the long bearded two-handed axes of the Neronese and my village are ideal for this task and the end will be swift. Some of the condemned men weep and plead for their lives and have to be held down on the block. Some of these take several blows to dispatch as they try to dodge clear of the blade.

Some others, led by Skap, go unbound and thank their executioners before the blow. These men draw their hair and beard out of the way on the block before they lay their neck out. Some waited quietly and some weep as they did so. Unlike Wolfneck, there are none whose sins are small enough to just warrant exile. I guess that I can be glad that the blood toll of our cleansing was less in many ways.

I am surprised that, after all that has happened and been said, there are still many who call on their false Gods to help them. At any rate, they try to call. Any attempt to do so leads to them being gagged with strips cut from their own clothes. Those who are unrepentant have their bodies thrown deep into the sea. The others have their bodies handed over to anyone who wants to bury them.

The toll of the whole affair has been very heavy on the Neronese and poor Father Gildas ends up taking on the responsibility for many of the bodies. It looks like Father Bjarni will be leaving Wolfneck and staying with him to help. Father Gildas has insisted that any who fully confessed their sins, and been granted absolution, deserved a proper burial even if they have no-one to do it for them.

With the executions, the battle, and what had happened before, it will be very many generations before the population of the island returns to even a semblance of what it once had been. The whole affair has affected the people of the island even worse than The Burning did and far worse than us. I need to think hard and long and stop feeling sorry for myself. We are far better off in Wolfneck.

Rani

I guess that, now it is all over, Theodora and I are safe up here on East Zarah looking at the remains of this green glowing box that Astrid and Ayesha destroyed. I can make nothing of it. It spits no more little bolts of lightning around, but now is just a shattered thing of metal, glass, timber and some other materials that I don't know.

Just looking at it tells me nothing about it. I can try to look wise and stare at it and poke it as much as I want to, pretending that I know what I am doing. It matters not. It shows us no obvious correspondences that have been used in making it. The lightning could even have been a trap that failed but, from what we were told, it didn't act that way.

It is a mystery as to its magic. We have gathered up all of the shards and are bringing both boxes down to the River Dragon to come back to Mousehole. There Eleanor can try to work out if there are any jewels concealed inside while Harald looks at the other metals. "Perhaps we could even try a spell or two on it once we are safe back home. Who knows, we might even be able to put it back together."

I should have known better by now and not have made that joke. As soon as I did my wife's mouth has opened as if to say something in reply and then, almost immediately, her eyes have glazed over, and she has taken on her far-away look and the words that she was framing to say never come out of her mouth.

Rani sighed. *It is a far-away look I am coming to regret and resent, even if my Theo-dear has done some marvellous things because of it.* She groaned inside herself. *I had been hoping that we would have a joyous time of celebration together after the end of Easter and that ridiculous fast. It seems that this will not happen now until she has worked out her thought.*

Rani

*O*nce the executions and the business of the Patterns is over, then the *weather-gazers have looked into the skies and forecast a good sea in two days and accordingly that is set for our departure. The intervening time can be spent trying to get the village back into a semblance of order.*

The teacher Kadlin Vitur has been elected as their new village leader. She takes over the duties very reluctantly, but it seems as if, for the moment at least, none of the few surviving relatives of the Jarl want to claim the vacant title. I don't blame them. They would have a hard field to hoe if they did.

Rani listened and looked at the discussion about this. *I am staying out of the whole thing unless someone asks me a direct question. It seems to me that, as far as the islanders are concerned, being too eager to step into his shoes will be seen as an endorsement of what he unleashed upon them. It is the ones who took refuge who want to keep the title…and the traditions and the survivors from the rest of the village who want to abandon it and follow Wolfneck's example.*

It is not often that they interfere in the affairs of men, but interestingly Baron Cnut and his Dwarves have many words to say on this subject. I didn't know that the Dwarven titles are not necessarily hereditary.

The next holder of the title has to be elected, and although most often it is handed down, although not necessarily to the oldest child, if the family are seen as having failed, or as not having been successful enough. It seems that the Dwarves are harsh on this point, but then the title can pass to another family, and it can even be stripped away while the holder lives.

Cnut is very actively urging this practice upon the Neronese and many of them seem inclined to listen to him. I suppose that they could do worse.

Chapter VI

Olympias (22nd Quinque)

*T*he day of our departure dawns fine and clear with a nice breeze from
the northeast promising a quick return to Wolfneck. One by one, we get
the ships loaded and set off. The three knorr go first, one by one using their
sweeps to help them clear the small bay. They are still deep laden, but less so
than they were before. I will admit my sister was right. They are manoeuvrable
and weather worthy.

The drakkar, Vindur-skrefi, is pushed clear and backed out under its oars
before smartly going forward on one side and swinging around. Now is it our
turn. I refuse to bring the sweeps out. We should be able to do this by just
drawing in one of the stern anchors fully and making the other taut before
allowing the jib to swing us around to face the sea.

She then pulled the second anchor aboard as the other sails were set. *See, it
was simple.* The River Dragon immediately leapt ahead and picked up speed.
*It is not long before the other four craft are left behind in our wake and we are
well on our way to Wolfneck with the saddles hovering and playing around us
in the air like gnats over a mud-flat. The saddles may be fast, but they cannot
take the place of a good ship to carry things.*

Olympias (after lunch)

*W*ith her own wind blowing from behind her and all sails set the River
Dragon made it into the Methul quickly. *Most of the village of Wolfneck
are happy to see us, but they would have been happier if it were their own
boats that had come in first. The Vindur-skrefi will not be too long behind...*

it should be in before dark...but the knorr will not have a chance of being in until tomorrow morning at least.

The Dwarves are not waiting. Having finished what they came for, and now being on land again, they are headed back to North Hole as soon as they can and even without more sleep than they managed on the return ocean voyage. As far as they are concerned, their part in this is over until the last surviving Master re-emerges and they want to return to being under the land where they are comfortable instead of on the sea.

While most of the Mice will have to wait in Wolfneck to travel back home in shifts on the saddles and the carpet, I will be taking the River Dragon out for the return trip sometime tomorrow. It is a long way, and we will not have the winds with us on this voyage.

In the meantime, the ship is filthy from all those people being on board, and Shilpa already has goods she bought here in Wolfneck, ones that she purchased and put into a store while we were waiting for the attack. Now, after the holds are cleaned, she can begin loading them on board and the others can get on to cleaning decks and restocking food supplies.

It seems Shilpa has a fortune in furs to put in the hold. She says that she has never seen as fine a selection as she has been able to obtain here and is looking forward to selling them in Darkreach, and eventually, at Evilhalt.

She even has some superb heavy woven cloth of a weave neither of us has seen much of before. My sister has some. The locals use it for making anything where normal cloth would tear too much. It is apparently resistant to that and to being snagged. All the Rangers and most of the hunters wear clothes made of it in the wild.

While the village resented not being able to go out to sea before the attack, they will now have to head to sea to fish, despite the lateness of the season. Some small craft are already heading down river. The River Dragon has on board almost all the local stock of whalebone, oil and ambergris, as well as barrels of salted and pickled fish.

The Princess Rani has insisted that, although she wants the ship back home before winter is fully in place, we do not have to hurry as much this time. I am, admittedly under pressure from Shilpa, going to call in on more Darkreach ports to see what can be brought around to Haven. Shilpa wants to start selling there in addition to buying.

We will skip Cold Keep as we go. I don't like its shores anyway. My brother thinks that there is little there for us to buy that we have not picked up here, but we will call in to some of the other ports from Antdrudge on down the coast.

Chapter VII

Basil

I wish that she had told me before the battle, but as soon as it was over Astrid confessed that she was most likely pregnant. I admit that I would have tried to stop her doing so, and most likely failed, but fighting not one, but two Insakdiv and risking, not just herself, but our unborn child or children is excessive even for her.

She sat very quietly through my rebuke, and meekly consented to be one of the first to return to the valley and so not come back to Mousehole on the River Dragon as she had wanted to do. She must be feeling the strain to do that. Somehow, I feel that the next time such a question comes up, she will conveniently forget my words again. He sighed. *I need to get used to that, I suppose.*

Thorstein (10th Quinque)

It turns out that I arrive at Mousehole later on the same day that the last person left to go to the north. From what I have seen, I am a very different priest to both Bishop Christopher and Father Theodule. I was a hunter before I entered the priesthood. I am also alone and have no magic on me, so my natural caution made me keep quiet and unseen as I approached Mousehole.

I watched people fly back and forth above me as I travelled. It provided a good guide to show that I was on the right path without me exposing myself. Because of the lack of magic, and his caution, Thorstein was the first arrival not to have been seen by the watch until he finally appeared around the talus slope heading to the stream late in the day.

It seems that Father Theodule is very glad of the arrival of an extra priest, even if I am still inexperienced in that role. I guess that, like someone falling overboard from a ship, I will learn to swim by necessity.

He has given me special charge of the Brotherhood girls as my full-time duty. This lets Theodule keep up his normal duties, which now include even more teaching, mostly of me. I can concentrate on getting the girls to learn the languages that they need to function in this odd village of my sister's that is now my home as well.

I already speak the three main tongues of the village, even if my Hindi is poor. As I teach the girls, I must work on learning Sowonja in return. In this at least I have plenty of help when they can be spared from their other tasks. I have the girls called Verily and Make, and the captured priest's widow from Peace Tower.

As a girl who had been promised to a priest from an early age, it seems that she has received a lot more education than most of the other free women there were given. She speaks a smattering of Latin, Hindi, and Khitan, as well as having other skills that are considered suitable for a priest's wife to learn.

The poor girl has several major problems that she must face. The first of these is her age. Having just turned fifteen, she is nearly the youngest of those brought back and only stopped being regarded as a child once her marriage took place.

The second is her name. In Flaming Fire Take Vengeance on Them That Know Not God is not a name that is calculated to either show modesty or to hide what she once was. Even the contraction to Fire is not an inconspicuous name, even if it is the one that everyone uses. It is only just better than the alternative contraction of Vengeance.

The third is that, while all of the other girls from the Brotherhood were born as slaves and would have died that way, she was born free. The fact that almost all the former slaves were slated to die soon is also an impediment.

The fourth, and indeed most important problem is that she is the widow of a priest. This means that, although she had as yet received no training and knows nothing of the dark secrets of her religion, she was going to be a priest herself. Having scarce survived the attentions of the Brotherhood priests, the other rescued girls do not like having anything to do with her.

Being only newlywed and only married after they had been closed up inside of Peace Tower, she had not yet started her education as a priest, but that does not matter to the others. Thorstein found that he had to keep her close to him all the time or she would end up in quiet tears when she thought that she was not being watched.

She never complains about it, nor does she blame anyone, but it seems that she is constantly having 'accidents' that leave her bruised or hurt. They are only minor injuries, but they are constantly happening when she is near the others from the Brotherhood.

I have tried talking to the other girls, but everyone just looks innocent, and no-one will admit to anything. Around everyone else the rest of the girls are happy and co-operative but, while they will allow Fire to translate for them, they will not talk to her otherwise. Make wouldn't talk to her readily either, but I believe that is because Make has difficulty talking with any priest or their wife. This leaves Verily and I as the only ones, among those she is forced to work with, who will talk to her.

Eventually he asked Theodule what to do. "She seems to be a good girl," Theodule replied, "and from what they found out before they brought her back, she seems to have known nothing about the real nature of her religion." He thought for a while before continuing,

"If we are forced to act to reprimand or censure the others, then it will cause resentment among them, and they might never forgive her for being who she is. I think that it would be best if it worked itself out. As they see her true nature, we will see if it all settles down and disappears over the next few weeks. I want you to keep her close to you and watch out for her."

Thus, Fire quickly started to always be beside Thorstein and even to help look after Basil and Astrid's growing pair of children that Thorstein was trying to care for instead of leaving them with the other children who had been left behind. *She is, at least, good at running a house and cooking. She is, in fact, much better at it than I am, although I have to admit that is not hard.*

Now she was no longer destined to a marriage, she had wanted to practice the craft that she had first been brought up in—but lacked both the tools and the material. As a child she had started to learn how to make linen.

Lakshmi has promised to get her seed or young plants to plant further up the valley or in some of the small valleys up or down the outside road, but until then there is nothing that she can do. Making linen is a skill that no-one else in the valley has. Lakshmi is sure that it is one that the Princesses will want to encourage, as apparently, we have a big shortage of cloth.

Astrid (23rd Quinque)

Thorstein was busy working with his charges in the hall when Astrid arrived home, and so she was not even aware of his presence in the valley. After putting her saddle away, Astrid headed straight home to clean up. *I will see my children once I am clean and have clothes without quickly mended rents, ones that do not stink.* She took her two new weapons, two of the insak-div spear-axes, with her.

She discovered that Fire was in her house only by coming to the open door and hearing inside a soft, pleasant voice singing something quietly in a language that she did not understand. *It may well be the sort of song you would sing to put a child to sleep, but I do not recognise the voice as one from this valley.* Her senses prickled. *Who is in my house with my children?*

Quietly she put down her pack, and one of the spear-axes, and crept inside. She had forgotten that her appearance, with her exposed teeth, a weapon in her hand, torn mail and field-repaired clothes, might be a bit of an unwelcome surprise to someone left on her own to care for babies and was rewarded with a shriek as the young girl noticed her and quickly stood with her back to the babies.

It is only the priest's wife that we captured at Peace Tower. She has a look of fear on her face and has as much chance as a baby fawn of stopping me, but she still stands between a possible threat and the babies she has been left with. She scrabbles at her belt for the eating knife that she bears there. I approve of that.

The babies, of course, woke up again as a result, and there were assorted cries and much confusion, and it was not long before Astrid and Fire ended up walking slowly around with a child each in their arms trying to calm them down.

Chapter VIII

Rani (23rd Quinque)

*A*s soon as she came back to the village, my Theo-dear has just absent-mindedly kissed in the direction of Fear and very nearly missed her entirely with her lips. She has disappeared straight into her study without even changing from her travel clothes that went through a battle. It seems that I get to look after our child on my own again.

"Mummy Theodora is doing a new spell again...isn't she?" Fear asked Rani, getting a heartfelt sigh and a nod in return. *At least she already understands what it is like.* Rani wrapped her in a hug and sat her down on her lap to hear what Fear had been doing while they were away. *She is getting so big.*

Rani (sometime later)

*T*heodora emerged from her study much later that afternoon to go to where Rani sat in her own study, reading. "This one is going to be easy... I will only need some stored mana to do it," she said to her wife. "I was worried that it would be an earth spell, but I can do it as a water-based enchantment. There is nothing really risky...and that is just as well."

She looks smug and she is unconsciously caressing her stomach again. She has been doing that a lot lately. Rani looked hard at her wife. *She has apparently finished her work, and now I have time to pursue what is happening with that gesture.*

"That is good, dear. Now, are you going to tell me why it is just as well... and any other secrets that you happen to be holding from me?" She looked at where Theodora's hand rested on her stomach. *It is no longer as flat as it had once been.* Rani put down the book and stood up. *Something is changing with her, and I think that it is more than eating too many sweet things.*

My Princess looks guilty. She has that little girl caught out look she gets. Theodora went over and cuddled up to her taller partner. Tucking herself under her right arm, she took Rani's left hand and put it on her stomach as she whispered into her ear. "My love…we are going to be parents," she said. "Fear is going to have a sister…or a brother. I don't know which they are. You might like to look ahead to find out …" *Now she is even using her little girl voice.*

What do I do? What do I say? My wife…the woman I love…is holding me tight and making me feel her stomach as she nuzzles into my neck. Beneath my hand, it is very easy to feel the bump that presages a new life. At least I know now why we have not made love for some time. It would not have taken me long to realise that something is changing with Theo-dear's body.

Now my feelings and questions come in a rush. How do I feel? Only a few weeks ago I was very, very glad that I didn't have a baby to care for. Now I will have to care for one. Can I even cope? I can feel panic starting to set in. How did it happen? Who is the father? Will I have to share my Princess with a man now? I have no desire at all for a man in my life, even as a co-parent.

Theodora

I *need to say something, and I need to do so quickly.* "There is no man suddenly appeared in our life. I am still yours and only yours. I am pregnant to your younger brother, but he does not know, nor does he count. He just gave me the seed. It happened while I was 'lost' in your family's garden when we visited them."

"Now," she continued, "just as Goditha is for Parminder and Melissa, you are going to be the father of our baby…but you don't need to cut your hair all short like Goditha has to mark it. I don't think that I would like that."

She paused and looked up. *I am worried. My beauty is tense in her stance and body. Have I done the wrong thing by not consulting her? No. I know that my love would never have agreed beforehand, and my body was aching to have a child of my flesh from my husband.* "Please, tell me that you want our baby and that you will still love me when I grow fat and am no longer pretty."

Rani

*S*he used her adult voice, but now she has gone back to using her little girl *voice again.* Rani turned so that Theodora was in front of her and then held her with her arms resting around Theodora's waist and looked down. *Holding her like this I can now feel the bulge that I now know is a baby pressing against me. It is exciting in its own way, quite exciting.*

Rani leant forward and kissed the slightly shorter woman on the tip of the nose. "I will be honest. If you had asked me, I would have said no, but if you want to have a baby this much…well, I will always love you and I will love her just as much. It is just a shock to me."

She bent her head and kissed her wife in a way that showed that she was still very much loved as one hand slid down to hold and gently squeeze a buttock and the other strayed up to cup one of her breasts. *Is it already a little larger? I can feel Theodora's nipple quickly harden under the silk. She wants me just as much as I want her. I am looking forward to tonight.*

There was a sudden commotion, as an excited Fear appeared followed by a flustered, very pregnant and much slower Valeria. "I am sorry, she got away from me. I am getting slow and clumsy…come on Fear…leave the Princesses alone, they are…having a private moment." She reached for Fear's hand, but Fear didn't want to give it and was dodging and trying to say something.

"No…that is alright." Rani quickly removed an incriminating hand from a breast. "You can both stay, and you can both be the first to know. Theodora is pregnant. Fear, you are going to have a sister, or it may be a brother."

Valeria's jaw dropped as she looked from one to the other of the mages in astonishment. *From the expression on her face, it is obvious that she thinks that we have somehow managed to achieve a pregnancy between us and you can see her opinion of our ability soaring higher. I am not going to disabuse her of the idea. Who the actual father is is no-one's business but ours.*

Fear ran over and tried to throw her arms around her parents. Theodora grabbed one hand as she tried to do that and put it between her and Rani so that Fear could feel the faint swelling of her stomach.

"See?" Theodora said, "it is only a small bulge now, but soon I will be big like the cows are when they are going to calve. Are you excited?" *At least she has gone back to her older voice, there is a time for the other and that is not now. However, that is a silly question. Even I can see that Fear is almost bursting.*

She nods and pushes me aside. It seems that I am forgotten already. She is putting her ear to Theodora's stomach. "I can't hear anything…not like I hear Valeria's girls when she holds me." *Fear has an intense but abstracted look on her face. It is almost a mirror of Theo-dear's when her mind was elsewhere… wait…what did she say?* Fear didn't see the very different looks that the three women gave to her.

"Girls? Two of them?" squeaked Valeria, grabbing her stomach with both hands, a despairing look on her face.

"Hear them?" *My wife echoed me on that.*

"Yes," said Fear abstractly as she kept listening. "I can hear them in my head. It is like Parminder hears the animals, but I think it is different. If I am very, very, quiet I can sort of hear babies when I listen on someone's tummy. I forgot to tell you that. I can't hear my sister yet." *She knows that our child is a girl? Is she just guessing?* "She must be too young. I will listen every day until I can though and then I will tell her what is happening all of the time," she said seriously.

It took some time to sort it all out and then Valeria was sent hurrying off to see Christopher to see if he could confirm what she had just been told.

Valeria

The priest slowly and carefully feels all over my stomach. I need to hold still. He knew I was pregnant before I did. Now he is using the same senses, the feeling a priest develops for sensing life, to see if Fear is correct in what she has said.

"Yes, she is right. There are two," he said. "She said they were girls, did she? I cannot tell that sort of thing, but I can tell you that their life signs feel healthy. Now you only need to go back to Fear and see if she can tell you their names and you won't need to actually give birth."

Christopher grinned. "I can see that we need to start looking at Fear as an apprentice midwife at least during her work time from school. We will see what else we can get her to do. I wonder …"

The Bishop's face quickly takes on the lost look of a person in thought that I am used to from Princess Theodora. He absently lets me out before hurrying off. I will bet he is off to consult with Lakshmi and the other healers. I had better make sure that Fear is fed. I have a feeling that, once they have talked, she is going to be busy soon.

Rani

In all of that, someone else had to come and let the Princesses know that another trader was arriving in Mousehole. *That is what Fear was trying to say in the first place and did not get around to. This time it is the Hobgoblin Guk. He has only one of his horses with him in addition to his youngest son. He is still a big lad by Human standards for his age.*

The Princesses emerged from their house with Fear hanging on to a hand from each and saw him in conversation with Sajāh. They both turned at the approach.

"I greet you Princesses, and bring you best wishes and letter from Nacibdamịr for you. Letters cost a Dwarven Tólf-penningr to deliver, although I will accept the same in any coin, and the person who it is delivered to must pay. I have given new Bishop his letter from chief priest, Father Michael. He good priest. We like him. He writing Bible in Hob now. Not finished much yet."

He shook his head. "He says very slow work and he needs more to write in. We never have real book of own before." *He sounds proud of the first Hob book being written.*

He paused and recollected his thoughts. "I go from here to Bear people. I find them and see if want trade. I then go back to Dwarves, then home. More money than just go between Dhargev and Dwarvenholme. Will make own secret path up hills from Bear people now. That way not waste time going back way I came."

He waved at his son who was re-emerging from the stables. "Bring strong son to work. Not much else to do for winter. Wives can look after all that. This time have little on horse but food and tools to make path. Next time, when we know what people want, we trade more. What you want here? Me need lots of money. This woman," he waved at Sajāh "wants much money to stay. Better be good food."

Hobs are, at least, direct in the way that they approach things. "In that case Guk, we will give you several letters before you leave. That should not slow you down much. If you want to wait for another couple of days, I think that Aziz, Krukurb and Haytor will be back here in the valley. Krukurb and Haytor may want to go on with you, I do not know. Also, Aziz may want to send a letter to his mother."

Guk looked sideways at Sajāh as he spoke. "Cannot stay long. Me not wealthy man like she thinks." *The jewellery that he is wearing displayed around his arms and neck openly gives the lie to that statement.*

It is obvious that his decision to take the risk of trading is already paying off. I want to see it pay off even more. Not only is he the first trader to the Dwarves here, but he is the first person I know of, possibly the first since The Burning, to try and set up a regular trade run on the flank of the Southern Mountains.

I have already decided that like Skrice and Wolfneck, for us to be secure against any outside intruders that may come against us, the settlements of the mountain flanks have to actually pay more attention to each other instead of just hiding away and trying to survive on their own. If we can bring the Bear-folk in on that too, well, even better.

Chapter IX

Christopher (24ᵗʰ Quinque)

On her first night back in Mousehole, Ayesha came to see Christopher. "I am now married, and I have time to admit what I suspect. I may be pregnant. Although I should not let you touch me as a man in a time like this, you have laid hands on me to heal me and return me to life, so I think that what applies to any other man may not apply to you, Inshallah."

She continued. "Can you lay your hands on me and tell me if I am right? I have all of the signs, and I would tell my husband of this before he gets too wrapped up in the fact that his köle are going to give him even more children before they marry, or before he starts to think about getting my sister-wives pregnant."

I'm surprised. "You have not seen Anahita and Kāhina for some time. They should not have fought in a battle as they were, and they will both be showing much more than I am when they get back. Do not say anything. I will tell you that it is not considered polite to mention it until they do. I have told Astrid this, and you should tell others."

Once Ayesha had left him, having confirmed what she had thought, Christopher started thinking. *Sajāh will be delivered in less than a month, with Valeria not too long after that. I already knew about Parminder. With the Princess and Ayesha and the köle, it is obvious that the winter and spring round of pregnancies is again under way for the village.*

I wonder who else is a part of this round. For us to plan ahead, I have to assume that every female with a partner is likely to be. At least this time it seems that the children will be more spread out over a few months, but it is time to see Lakshmi and to make sure that we are prepared with all of the herbal help that we can have ready.

Now, we need to ask to see all of the women, but this time it will be with

Fear present. We will see what we can find out between us all.

Theodora
25th Quinque, the Feast Day of Saint Aldhelm

*W*e have a few days (of frustration for me and of peace and quiet for most of the village) ahead of us. Our people are starting to trickle back into Mousehole from the north, and yet nothing significant is taking place in the village.

The returnees settle back into their village roles as the changes to what Astrid tells me are called the Fagus trees soon turn the hillsides red, and the weather of an autumn in the mountain foothills blows chill around us. We need to make sure that we have prepared for the winter that lies ahead with all of these extra people with us this year.

Theodora
30th Quinque, the Feast Day of Saint Walstan

*D*uring the night, tales are told and scars and mementoes shown, but there is no grand celebration of victory. The feast for the patron of agricultural workers at least is welcome to us. It sees our most excitement for days with an enthusiastic sermon praising farmers, from our Bishop, that the farmers (even the Islamic ones) are glad to have attended.

During that day, the Devartetilcu Yamyam arrived with their ballista. Ariadne, leaving the men to arrange for its placement up on the roof of the hall beside the mage's pattern, hurried off to find the Princesses in their house. *Nervously, she stands in front of us, in what is starting to be called our reception room. It is obvious from the way that she circles around in meaningless talk that she is having more than a little difficulty in coming to the point.*

"Come on girl," said Theodora. "You have something important to say, or it would have waited until later when everything was tidied away. Let us know what it is, so that we can all get back to what we have to do." *I have a suspicion that the question will involve men, and can see no reason for it to be such a matter of umming and ahhing.*

Ariadne still looks nervous. "Let us all sit down," said Rani as she did so herself. *She has rung the little bell that Nikephorus puts between our chairs on a table. We have never had a use for it before.* In reply, Nikephorus quickly appeared from the rear of the house. "Are there some refreshments that we can have please?" she asked. Nikephorus nodded and ducked back out.

While they waited, Rani continued to chatter inconsequentially about the campaign, and how Wolfneck was coping after it. *She is trying to put Ariadne at ease. It is not working. In a remarkably short time, Nikephorus is back with both kaf and shortbread biscuits and sweets.* Valeria came in and arranged small tables and he put the tray down on one and handed out cups and small plates. The two household servants then tactfully withdrew from the room.

After a little while, Ariadne opened up, and Theodora's suspicions were partly confirmed, but the rest was a surprise. "During the campaign, I have grown fond of Krukurb," she blushed. "More than fond...I want to keep him here and marry him, but I don't know where we stand. I know that we, the women that is, were sent here because we wanted something different from life, and most didn't have many choices...for one reason or another.

"We were told that we would be looked after...and we have been...but what is our future? Here in the village, no-one pays us any money, but no-one asks for any either. When we were away, all our food was bought, and we had a bag of coin for expenses...but is it ours to keep or do we give it back? If I am going to set up here and have children to raise, I need to know these things."

She is very nervous about what she is going to say next. "I need to know if they will be slaves or if they will be free. Will they have money of their own, or will they just live on what they are given? No-one has ever said anything about these things, and it is important to me.

"I understand that the ones who freed the village have a share of the wealth, and the ones who were slaves here have another share, but what of the rest of us? Do we have wages, or indeed, do we have any money at all? Will we be just like the barbarian tribes of the mountains are; living on what they grow for themselves and on the gifts that they are given by their rulers?"

"You know that I am from Darkreach," Ariadne continued. "I am used to being paid for my work." *She has gotten it all out now, and to regain composure, she is sipping at the hot sweet kaf. She is still so nervous that she nearly scalded her mouth as she did so.*

Rani looks at me, and I look at her, and we both open our mouths and yet no words come out of us. I have never gotten used to the idea of regular money in the first place...or even the idea of being paid and so it is not a question that has occurred to me. I just spent what I needed to when I was in Darkreach; drawing on what I got from the Palace. Then, after I met Basil, he handled everything, even the money I earned entertaining.

There just always seems to be money there when I need it. One of the reasons I did not think of this question is that I have always been used to things just appearing when you want them. I suppose to me the situation in Mousehole is normal. Although I have servants here, and I suppose they do their job because they want to, I don't connect that with what happens with other people.

My husband also comes from a privileged background. Certainly not as privileged as mine was, but it is one where she is also not used to thinking very hard about money. Ariadne had said what she wanted to say, and was just keeping quiet and looking from one to the other as she nervously waited for an answer. *We are still just looking at each other; neither of us knows what to say in reply.*

Nikephorus moved back into the room. "Please forgive me for listening to what was being spoken," he said. "But I would also like to know the answer to that. I am here for my Valeria, and I understand that she doesn't want to leave and so I am happy to stay here. Besides, I prefer to work rather than to sit doing nothing as long as I really do not have to work too hard. I find that it is boring doing nothing.

"My Valeria is supposed to be a wealthy woman with lots of money, but we see none. She has her beautiful jewels…and they are valuable…but that is all. How does she get this wealth, and more importantly, how does our child? Will I be paid for my work here, or am I really a slave who does not know it?"

Theodora was the first to recover. *I feel so embarrassed, and my husband still looks stunned. She is better at planning a battle than running a village. This is a part of my role, and I am not doing very well with it.* "I don't really know the answer to anything that you have asked." Theodora looked from one to the other as she spoke.

"I am sorry. I feel that we have failed you as your Princesses by giving you that answer. It is something that we should have thought of. We now need to deliberate about this, and we will ask Ruth, who knows about many things, and we will ask Bishop Christopher, who will know what is fair, and we will come up with an answer for you. If it turns out that you are getting paid by the village or by us, then we know when you arrived, and will make sure that you get what is due."

We really have something unique here, don't we? "I hope that we can come up with a way for you to have money without it being like outside. I know that we will look after you somehow, and you will never be slaves, but I like the idea of everyone just working for each other, although I often feel that my husband and I do not do enough.

"I do know that I want to keep our little village of Mousehole the same as it is now if I can but…I am sorry…I just don't know. We will let people know some ideas when we can. Is that good enough for the moment?" *There may be more than just a note of anxiety in my voice. All of a sudden, I can feel my*

happy world starting to fray a little bit at the edges because of something that
I had not even contemplated.

"It is honest," said Nikephorus, "and I suppose that is all we can ask from
you at this time. Be assured, I do see why you want to keep the village like it
is. Even though you might think that it was a perfect place to be, the Palace
you were brought up in does not work nearly as well as this Mousehole of
yours does."

He went on. "This is a far happier place. Here people do not need to push
each other down to gain prestige or promotion. Here regard comes to you from
what you do and who you are, not how good you are at flattery and politics.

"I don't know how you can do what you want to happen, but I sincerely
wish you luck in it. Now that Ariadne has raised the question and you are
thinking on the matter, I am sure you will come up with the answers. I can
wait. I am not going anywhere." He turned to leave and then turned back with
another thought.

"If you will pardon me saying it, I also would not worry too much about
your not working hard enough. From what I have heard and seen you have put
your life and your mind at risk several times already for the village, and I am
very sure that you will keep doing that when you need to. It would take quite a
lot of my washing dishes or cleaning up the house to make up for that."

*It seems that Ariadne agrees with him, and reassured at least a little, she
is now leaving to confront Krukurb with her feelings. It seems that they have
already been intimate, now she confesses to wanting more from him.*

Theodora (5th Sixtus)

*I*t has been agreed that the marriage of the Insakharl and the Hob would
take place the next time that Guk comes through the village. Although they
might be able to catch a carpet ride up to Dhargev before it ever got there, Guk
is to leave a letter for Krukurb's family to let them know what was happening.

*I have told Ariadne to pay for it from her expenses purse. Krukurb's family
will not have that much money to spare when Guk delivers it. It will be a long
time before any among the Hobs do. They have only ever had the coin that
they have looted before now.*

*Haytor has already decided that he wants something else from life. During
the campaign, he saw too much of the world outside the valley of the Cenubarkincilari to go back to looking after a few poor sheep in the hills around Dhargev for
his whole life. In the end, Haytor has decided that he will be going on with Guk
for the rest of this circuit and possibly staying with and working for him. They can*

work that part out as they go. It is a long way back home the way they are going.

Theodora
later that day

I am surprised that it took as long as it has for word to get passed around the village about the question we are thinking about. Now that it has, it provides much for people to discuss, even if it is a question that leaves the girls from the former Brotherhood bewildered.

Apparently, getting paid is not something that had occurred to any of them. They were slaves. To them, freedom means choosing what work you want to do and learning things…and not being raped by any who want to take them… whether they wanted it or not. They have no more expectations than that.

Many people came up to the Princesses or to Ruth with ideas, and indeed, more questions, all of which were noted. *While people are thinking, the next question to arise is obvious. What will the village do next? It is obvious to all there are several pregnancies, and given the number of women in the village who cannot fight for some time, indeed there are many who are having difficulty just practicing with weapons, it will be a while before we can go out into the world to take up the fight again, even if we do find out where to go.*

Over the last few weeks Hagar, Adara, Umm, Aine, Bryony, Dulcie, Eleanor, Bianca, Fortunata, Parminder, and Ruth have all admitted that they are expecting a child after they were seen by the healers. Yet others have announced that they have plans to get married and Mousehole is starting to settle into what seems to be becoming its normal pattern for an autumn and a winter.

In the meantime, work proceeds with the mill and on other buildings, even on the basilica when there is time, with the unskilled workers pitching in to help when they could. It seems that we will have plenty of time to work out the matter of money. Still, I need to say something so that we are not overrun with rumours.

Theodora gathered everyone and addressed the villagers in the Hall. "We need to know that we are doing what is right. In coming back here for winter after a battle, we are just slipping into what is becoming this familiar and safe pattern. We know that there is at least one more Master out there, and we know that these so-called Old Gods are somewhere. I will bet that they are not just sitting still and waiting for us to come to them."

"Father …" *Several heads raised then.* "…I mean Bishop Christopher…

can you do what you do so well, and I will get my husband to do what she does and then we can be sure." Christopher agreed that it was appropriate for them to do this, and the next night was set aside for the endeavour.

Once all of our work is done for the day, and we have eaten, everyone will gather together in the large feast hall, where there is more room, and first my love can read her cards and then Christopher can do his stichomancy after he has conducted the Apodeipnon service.

Hulagu
6th Sixtus, the Feast Day of Saint Domenic

*T*he *next night there is a buzz of excitement in the room. I have not told the Princesses yet, but we Khitan have decided that Dobun will later be entering a trance to see what he can determine. He has never done this on his own before on an important matter and so he is unsure in himself about it, but the rest of us are eager for him to try.*

"If you are going to be a shaman of power, you will need to be able to do what the Princess and the chief priest of the Christians do with ease. I have seen them work with their predictions and they are both very powerful seers. I have seen my grandfather make potent predictions as well. It is now up to you to learn how to do the same."

"If we are to be a strong clan, then you need to help me make it so, as the chief shaman of a clan should." *The other tent-born women are nodding at that already and even my sister realises the truth of it and joins in.*

Theodora

*I*n *the hall, people sit on benches and on the floor, while others stand behind them. They are all where they can see what will happen. The children have been brought along, and everyone is there except those on watch. No-one wants to be left out.* Rani waited until they were all in and then nodded to Astrid. *I can smell the heavy incense of myrrh, her aroma, burnt to help her thoughts. How considerate of someone to think of that.*

"All of you be quiet now," she said, "we need to get this underway, so we can find out if we have to go out again. For those who have not been here before… this is what will happen. The Princess will ask someone to shuffle the cards. That person needs to think about what we should be doing next…not about what they want to do themselves…but what we all should be doing. As they are doing it, we should all be doing the same. Princess …"

Rani looked around. *She told me that she has given a lot of thought about who to ask this time. The wrong person shuffling could give the wrong result. It has to be someone who knows what the long-term goal is, and who feels it keenly, far above their own personal needs.* "I have asked the Presbytera Bianca to do this task before and tonight I have decided that I will ask her to do it again."

Rani handed the cards over to Bianca, who was seated with her husband at the front. Each of them had a small child on their lap trying to play. *Bianca hands Rosa to her husband, and as he juggles the two squirming children, starts her practiced shuffle and cut.*

I may play cards better than she does, but she handles the cards better. I can see our three kataphractoi from Darkreach, all of whom fancy a game or two of chance I believe, are looking at her dexterity with the parchment rectangles with some admiration. I will bet that they are making a vow not to engage the priest's wife in a serious contest of cards.

She continued shuffling and cutting for a while, with a grave expression on her face, as she deliberately did not look at what her hands did. Eventually she was happy with what she had done, and she handed the cards back to Rani before regaining her seat and taking a child back on her lap.

My husband begins to lay the cards out on a small table, covered in a soft cloth, which has been placed before her. The first card laid out shows a woman. She is dressed in robes, and seated on a stone chair. At her feet are piles of sacks and mounds of produce. Some of the sacks have coins spilling from them. Behind her is a scene of a marketplace, and in the top corners are two figures of robed women offering sheaves of corn. Those who have seen Rani at work before will remember this card. We have seen, or at least heard of her before.

The second card…the one on the left…is a new card. It is upside down and it shows an armoured man lying on the ground, shielding his face with his arm, as a bolt of lightning strikes a tower behind him that resembles a taller and narrower version of the great structures of Gil-Gand-Rask. In one top corner, a man with melting wings is falling from the sky, while in the other a man is falling from a flying chariot, which has winged horses pulling it.

The third card, on the right, shows a Hindi woman on a throne. In one hand she holds a fan, and in the other there is a round-headed mace like those used in Haven. A woman stands to one side behind the throne holding a ceremonial umbrella over it, and the woman seated in it. Behind her, but on the other side, stands another woman wearing a crown that is like mine. She has one hand on the throne and the other is holding a red fruit of some sort.

It could almost be us. On the other side of the throne, behind the umbrella-holder, is a male peacock with its tail raised.

The last card is placed below, and it shows a naked woman with blonde hair and pale skin standing in the shape of a Latin capital 'Y' and holding on to a large circular garland of flowers that extends from her knees to over her head where she grasps it in her spread hands. She stands in a field and behind her, in the distance, is a city built on a series of islands.

In the background, a ladder runs from the top to the bottom of the card, from the ground to the sky and disappearing into a cloud. In each corner, there are the glyphs used to show one of the four elements on a magical pattern. The symbol for Fire was in the top left, and then sunwise Air, Water, and finally Earth.

Rani put the other cards aside, and looked at the cards before her, pausing with her hands held flat over the cards with her palms down and her eyes closed. *Silence extends over the room for a short while, even the children stay muted, and then she begins to speak. Her brow is a trifle creased, and as has been the case before, when she reads the cards, her voice takes on a slightly distant quality. It is a tone I have never heard in her voice at any other time.*

"The first card is in the position of the Enquirer, and is the Queen of Talents," she said. "Her card speaks of security and richness and a rich place for new growth. She is also, with the connotations of harvest, the ruler of the season of autumn. She represents us here secure and rich in our valley at this season. There is no doubt about this as we saw her before as a part of our limits and destiny.

"The second card that we see is far more interesting. It represents the history of us and our question and where we are coming from. Here we see the seventeenth numbered card of the major Arcana, the Tower, and it is reversed. If it were upright, it would be a dire card to see as it speaks of the sin that Bishop Christopher tells us is called the hubris of deserved downfall and unexpected events. Reversed it is a very different card and that is what we see here.

"We see a card before us a that speaks, nay it shouts loudly, of avoided disaster and of dramatic rescue. It seems to show our past, and to show that what we have done so far is very, very, important. According to this card, what we have done to this point has allowed us…or perhaps a lot more than just us…to steer clear of a major catastrophe."

Rani stopped. *Her eyes close for what is probably nearly a minute, but it feels like it is much longer to me, and I suppose the rest of the audience. Finally, she opens them, at least a little, although they stay lidded, and she continues with her exposition of what she feels.*

"The first two cards just let us know that we have the right question, and so that we know that what is to come is what we are looking for. This third card tells us exactly what we should do next. It is the fourth numbered card of the major Arcana, that of The Empress. It is an unusual card to see in a story of warfare and strife, because it represents the maternal and the fecund. It speaks of feminine fertility, and power or domestic tradition, and of family and childrearing.

"Much as happened with us in the valley during the last winter, I believe that this shows that again we should just tend to our children, and rest here away from war until we see the need to go forth again. I do not know if this will be next summer or even further away. Perhaps it is even something that will become readily apparent without us worrying about it, just as happened last summer.

"The last card shows us the result that should come, and I admit that this card puzzles me even more than the one before it, as I cannot see how we can reach this result given the course of action. It is the last and twenty-first numbered card of the major Arcana…actually it is the twenty-second card, as the first is not numbered. It shows the card called The World.

"It represents the whole vast design of nature; what Bishop Christopher tells us is called the Great Chain of Being. It signifies completion and perfection, fulfilment and success, and the final coming together of plans. I may not understand how we will reach this point, but it is the very best card to find in this position of resolution, so I know that we can sit in our valley in confidence. For us, it means that all will be well with the world, if we just continue as we are meant to."

Rani stopped speaking, opened her eyes fully and gave a shake of her head. *She looks around at us all watching her for a little while before continuing. When she speaks, it is in her normal tone of voice.*

"I am pleased with this reading. I certainly do not fully understand it, and it is hard to explain how or why, but am I left with a feeling of contentment inside me. That is good to have after doing any reading." She paused and concluded contentedly: "I look forward to seeing what our priest finds from his divination."

Everyone without a child on the lap joins in rearranging the seats into a suitable layout for the Divine service, and people move their seating around so that the Orthodox can get the front seats. The Brotherhood girls still do not know where to sit, but it seems that Father Thorstein won't let them go to the back. He seems as firm as his sister in many ways.

I have to admit that I can understand scarcely a word he is saying, but I will warrant he is insisting that they are studying to accept Christianity, and so should be close to the front. I note that, as he normally does now, he keeps Fire near to him, but on the opposite side to the other girls. She is a pretty thing and so shy.

Dobun is looking on with an expression of curiosity on his face. He has not attended one of Christopher's formal services before, although he has seen plenty done in the field. He is about to find out that Christopher conducts himself the same regardless of where he is. To him, a service is a service, and unless it really is unavoidable, should not be either scrimped on or shortened.

Today is the feast day of Saint Domenic, the patron of teachers, and Christopher does not let the anticipation over the waiting stichomancy distract him from thanking God for the teachers in the valley, in terms that have Ruth blushing and asking the Saint for his intercession on their behalf. He might not like the Order that operated in his name, and what they did in terms of questioning those they regarded as dangerous to the faith, but he obviously has no problems with the Saint himself.

When the service was finished, Bianca quietly came up to Christopher and handed him her Testament. Christopher took it, and holding it in his hands, directed a short prayer towards Heaven. He thanked God for the advice that had been given so far, and asked Him for further intervention to guide them as to what course they should follow next.

He then closed his eyes, and lowering its spine to rest on the table in front of him, allowed the book to just fall open. For a short while, his finger hovered in the air, as if it were in doubt, before coming down. He opened his eyes and looked down at where it lay before looking up again at the audience.

"My finger manages to cover two verses." He smiled at his audience. "It is not hard. I have large fingers and the writing is very small. In front of me, I have the book of Lamentations, chapter three and verses twenty-five and six. This is what they say." He cleared his throat before looking down again and beginning to read:

"The Lord is good unto them that wait for him, to the soul that seeketh him. It is good that a man should both hope and quietly wait for the salvation of the Lord." Christopher looked up again. *He sounds a little bewildered as if not actually expecting to be told to almost relax.*

"I think that, once again we have a concordance of opinion. God looks in favour upon our course of action. We should wait, pray, and look after our souls, and we will find the time to act again. In the meantime, we can still do things. We need to work on our basilica, and in particular, our village. I have been told that we are to pay host to at least three and possibly up to six Metropolitans and the people that they bring with them soon.

"I am not sure where we will sleep them all, and we should at least show that we are trying to properly start our basilica. Besides, it will need a name. I am open to suggestions about who our church here in Mousehole should be dedicated to. This is an important decision for us. Seeing that I see many people from other faiths at services, I will accept suggestions from them just as much as I will from the Christians.

"It may be a Christian church that we are building, but I hope that you will always feel welcome in it, whatever your creed. If you have been listening since you first met me, you will have heard of most of the Saints by now, but feel free to ask one of us priests if there is a particular patronage that you are interested in." With that, he closed the book and pronounced a Benediction on everyone before they all began to drift off in different directions.

Chapter X

Hulagu (6th Sixtus)

I may have gone to see Lakshmi with what I thought was a discrete enquiry, but it seems that she has been expecting this request. She already has a special storage box set aside. It has the herbs that can be used as hallucinogens in smaller containers secure inside it.

She says that prominent among her purchases in Chulün Arlüd was Sünsjims. It was hard for her to obtain, as it is a plant of the plains, but without us telling her she found out that it is the best and most potent drug available for the purpose of entering a trance such as our böö use. She is right and we all know it is what they prefer.

Once she had been able to make Hulagu confess what he wanted it for, she went and fetched it. "I got this in case you needed it for this purpose. I know that the shamen of your people often use such plants, so I wanted to have them in case they were needed. Next time, however, you can tell Dobun to come to me himself. Before I give him any more, I want to be sure that he is not addicted and that he is healthy."

She handed some berries over in a small jar. "I have not used these before, but I talked to Rani about dosages after I bought them, and this should be the right amount for what is needed for a night. Please bring me the jar back."

Hulagu went back to where the other Khitan waited, and after passing on the message from Lakshmi, they gathered horses, and all went out to near the small patch of woods and began to garner fallen timber. When they were ready, he looked around them all. "It is not a secret in the village what we are doing, but it is still up to us whether we tell anyone the results of what is found. We will decide this when we are finished."

This time Ayesha is with us. She has not been tested yet, nor will she while she carries a child, but as my wife she has the right to be here. This is her first time among the tribe on such an occasion and I can see that she is a little nervous, but the other women seem to accept her presence, occasionally giving her a hint, with a glance or a nudge, at anything that she should do.

While the divination would be done by the shaman of their totem, the Khitan did not insist on any particular religion among their people and so firstly Bianca, and now Ayesha, was just as welcome to take part in what was to come as any of the others.

Eventually, they had enough timber for the night, should it take that long, and a small fire was lit, and smoke began to rise. Everyone seated themselves around the fire and food and drink began to come out of the saddlebags that they had ensured were full, even for this very short trip. Dobun ate the three berries and settled down comfortably on a hide with his legs crossed staring into the flame.

Around him, the others sat companionably in the growing chill, talking in the manner of the tribes of their days and what was happening to them, the hand of women discussing pregnancy and marriages. Food and drink were companionably passed around among those waiting. Babies were nestled into rugs and Bianca's three horses hovered behind her.

As the only other adult male, I am largely excluded from the talk of the women. I will just remain seated here beside Dobun. I will stay silent for most of the night roodling, I will stare into the coals of the fire as the mind drifts along thinking both empty and vast thoughts, letting things wash over and around me. He sipped on some drink and nibbled on the food, but spoke little, only answering if he was asked a question.

It was morning before Dobun stirred, as if to acknowledge the growing light around him. As soon as he started moving, Anahita handed him a mug of strong kaf that they had ready and Kāhina gave him some sweet things that she had been given by Lādi especially for this purpose. *We will wait for him to slowly return to us, watching him as we do so.* Gradually, his eyes re-focussed as he ate the food and sipped at the fragrant kaf. The women had arranged a rug over him.

He looked at Hulagu. "Your grandfather sends you greetings and is glad that we have finally decided to start to enter the real world. He showed me things...I cannot say what...but I believe that we are doing the right thing. The veil has been lifted a little, not fully but just enough to see more of the way ahead. There is still someone or something trying to prevent this. They are beings with great power but little control. This tells us that there is a lot more yet to do.

"I believe that we have a year ahead of us, and possibly even more, before we must act fully. Others may yet join us, and we must all learn how to use the saddles as easily as we use our moriid and to train the others. The irony is that, in the future, the Mori will rarely ever ride our Üstei akh düü except in ceremony." He looked back over his shoulder at the herd gathered there as if including them in his words.

"Our children will use our brothers and sisters to learn how to ride, as is right, but they will almost always ride the sky. The moriid we gather will be mainly of use for our valley in the sky and for play." He stood up and stretched. "I believe that we should tell this to the Princesses and to the head priest. They shared their divination with us, and we should share ours with them. Your grandfather has agreed with me."

Hulagu nodded, and once morning prayers were done the others went back to their homes while the two men went to see Christopher and then the Princesses.

Chapter XI

Theodora (7th Sixtus)

Although she thought that she had worked out how to repair the detector from Neron, the remains were still on board the River Dragon.

This left Theodora with little to do except to make more wands and some other things for the village, and she grew jaded with doing the same thing over and over—even when it was needed. It did not take her long to grow bored, think about what Dobun and Hulagu had told them, and then to go and see Stefan and Dulcie the carpenter.

Theodora
18th Sixtus, the Feast of Pentecost

Once again, there was a closed workshop and covered items were being carted around the village while mages were forbidden to cast at certain times. After another few weeks, through the feasts of the Saints Columba, Bridget, Bartholomew and Phocus, the feast of the Pentecost arrived. After the service, the three proudly unveiled the result of their work...six new flying saddles.

"And we are going to keep making them," Theodora proclaimed. "We should have the materials for not just six, but twenty more. From what we were told by Danelis and Shilpa, Fatima and Valeria are due to deliver roughly on the same day. If some want to go to this wedding of Theodora Lígo, and the guard that is soon after the birth, then we can do as we did last year and visit Darkreach to see the baby, go to the wedding, and be back before winter sets in fully."

"But where are the pots?" asked Astrid. "You didn't ask us to...ahhh...

contribute anything to help you make them."

"I have grown in the interval," *I may sound smug. I certainly feel it.* "I only had to do it last time because I was not as strong as I am now and the spell itself was a new one that I was not familiar with. Although I changed it a trifle, this is now almost a familiar spell for me and so the risk is so much less. I can still only make one every three days, but it is a lot safer for me to do it."

I had better explain. "They will still only work for the people of Mousehole though…but I suppose that is good in many ways, and I think that I will always keep the casting set that way and not make one for anyone else, nor will I teach another from outside the valley how to make them. I think it is best that way."

Rani

T *he new people in the village can now begin to be introduced to the joys…
and the perils…of flight. Due to the way they have been made they still
cannot use the old saddles, only the new ones. I have Astrid starting to work
out the tactics that should be used with this many saddles, while Hulagu and
a visibly pregnant Eleanor start drilling riders in how to use a bow from the
saddle as it flies.*

*I had already decided that, seeing that the saddles hold the key to our
military success, the short horse bow should be the first weapon that the
new people learn. Whilst the Mice will still train to fight on foot, for that is
something that we will always need when we go out on raids, it is probable
that only the very heaviest of our cavalry, the kataphractoi, will still be useful
in most open battles and probably then only to lead others from outside the
valley.*

*The rest, the kynigoi, will now be mounted in the air if there are enough
saddles for them. Seeing that most of the new riders can neither fly nor use a
bow properly, Robin is kept as the busiest person in the village making arrows
and more bows as they damage and break things.*

*Not only that, but Stefan must make many bracers for arms, and breast
shields for the larger girls. Meanwhile, Eleanor takes time from something
else that she is keeping secret in her workshop to carve bone and horn thumb
rings. At least she can do a lot of work on those while she is sitting and relaxing
after the evening meal just as others sit and knit.*

Rani (23ʳᵈ Sixtus)

*N*ow we can let Thord take advantage of the increasing number of saddles to more regularly visit Dwarvenholme and his parents. At the same time, Aziz and Verily can take the soon-to-be wed couple up to Dhargev. As it happened, they did not beat Guk there. He had managed to come in two days before them and was now, with more horses and trade goods, already preparing to come back to Mousehole and his circuit.

Marking the passing of time, the feasts start to pass. The Havenite feast of Onam, little remarked in Mousehole up to now, was celebrated. It was mainly being done by the students as Ruth taught them about what a harvest festival meant. *It came as a surprise to me to accidentally find the whole school going through the ceremonies, with Ruth, Lakshmi and the two new Havenite girls showing them what it was all about. I had forgotten it.*

After that, Holy Trinity was followed by Saint Pandonia. *I agree with Astrid on the area we should claim influence over. To show that is the case, and as part of their training, Astrid can start to lead groups of saddles in sweeps around the area. It helps show our power to the other villages.*

Some can go down to Lake Erave to check to see if the River Dragon is back from the north yet. There has been no sign of the ship thus far. I am told that the winds will be more against them this time, and they are supposed to be taking their time to come back around, and this time they will mainly be sailing into the wind, but Olympias took less than a month to reach the north and Saint Pandonia's feast marked the thirty-seventh day, one day more than a month, since the River Dragon left Wolfneck.

Weddings began to be celebrated as Bilqis married Tariq, and Ata and Asad both took their second wives Zafirah and Rabi'ah. The three marriages were held on three consecutive days. Bilqis' wedding was by far the most memorable of the three. Norbert and Sajāh's daughter, Huma, was born towards the end of the night.

Sajāh had organised the wedding feast and had then succeeded in going into labour during it. She was rushed to the chapel to deliver still giving instructions as she left and had insisted on being carried out to supervise the next two marriage feasts, even if she did consent to sit in a soft chair on a cushion while she ran things.

Of course, a person being delivered of a healthy child during a wedding is regarded by all as the most fortunate of omens for the bride and groom in almost every culture. I am getting used to the idea of having a child of our own, but I am just glad it is not me that has to go through with it.

Ayesha
29th Sixtus, the Feast of Saint John the Baptist

*B*y the Will of Allah, a Christian Feast marks the second anniversary of the freeing of our village from the bandits. Both our Christian priests and I give thanks over this and then we all have a feast of celebration that we share.

Here we tell again the stories of our village, and what happened to us, and what we have done about it. This way the new people hear all of them, and those growing up will grow up with them in their ears and being reinforced each year, and those of the Faith will praise the mercy and justice of Allah in sending us.

The Princess Theodora and I tell the story of the liberation, and Verily speaks of her life before she was freed and of the brothers who brought her there. After they finished, Astrid told of how Thorkil had come to join the bandits, and she told of Svein so that the people understood more about the ones that they were fighting. She is getting better in her storytelling.

Lastly, Princess Theodora tells of how we found Dwarvenholme and cleansed it of the Masters, and then completes this by telling the new additions of what happened at One Tree Hill and then at Neron Island. The whole tale of our adventures is rapidly becoming a full cycle of stories, and likewise some songs.

Ayesha (30th Sixtus)

*W*e finally have a full Khitan wedding held outside around a fire and indeed between them, as my husband takes both Aigiarn and Alaine as his second and third wives in the same ceremony. Again, the swords fly although perhaps a trifle slower than is usual as several of the dancers are well on the way to showing their pregnancies.

It is good to show his importance as the clan leader now that he has three wives, and Inshallah, I can perhaps work on the faith of all of them, or at least that of the children.

Ayesha (34th Sixtus)

*W*e should have no more marriages for a while, Inshallah, but last night was the first among the Christians for some time. The farmer Arthur married the newly baptised Brotherhood girl, Make. The silly girl made a truly blushing virgin bride. Elsewhere that would be normal, but here in Mousehole it is a thing to note.

Her blushes are even more evident this morning when the couple first appear in public. Astrid asked those around her, asking loudly and indelicately, if anyone had heard someone who was loudly praying several times in the middle of the night. It took a little while before her victim realised what had been meant. I must admit though; even I thought it funny, although I had to explain it to my husband.

Lakshmi

*I*t is interesting to be the midwife in this village. Christopher and I have Fear pressing her head to the stomach of every one of the mothers to be. We have her listening to see what she can hear in her head as we take notes on our slates and tablets.

No-one amongst us has ever heard of anyone doing what she seems to be able to do before and we still don't know its limits, or even if it is real. For all we know it is just her imagination, although I doubt it. I think that it is one of these new gifts that are starting to be heard about over the last few cycles.

In the world outside this valley, far too many women die while giving birth, even when there are priests ready and present. Anything that we can do to try to stop this happening in Mousehole is worthwhile. We need to have Fear do these listenings more than once. We need to make sure that she checks each woman once a week. We need to take down anything that she says and then write down exactly what she tells us in the journal we keep with the pregnancies in it.

Fear was listening to Verily, who was only just beginning to show as being pregnant, and was having her first check after Christopher had detected the signs of real life. *We all gather around and watch and listen and write.*

Eventually, Fear spoke up in a worried voice. "One of your little girls is sick," she said. "She is very sick. I am not sure that she will live for very much longer, and her sister feels very worried about her." She stood up and looked around at the adults watching her. "What does that mean? How can a baby be sick? How can she die before she is born if someone is not trying to kill her?"

Christopher looks at me and I look at him. Their gazes locked for some time as eyebrows were raised and the two tried to talk to each other with their faces without saying anything out loud. *Eventually, he wins and I get to explain to Verily, and also to Fear. We have discussed whether something like this was going to happen.*

"There are many births outside where the baby is born sick," Lakshmi said. "Seeing that Fear always seems to say that babies are healthy, we have wondered, sorry Fear, if she was just saying that or if she would pick up when something is wrong with a baby. Given the problems you had with your last birth, we have been particularly worried about you."

Lakshmi took a deep breath. *Now, the explanation gets harder. I must tell her without alarming her. A mother who is too afraid can have other problems brought on just by the fear. I need to keep going and sound calm.*

"Hobs and Humans are built quite differently in very many respects, even if it seems they can have children together. This is especially true when they are just born, as Hobs have a larger skull, and from what we can tell, Hob women have a different shape to the bones making up the hips to that of Humans, and you are small in that area anyway."

Lakshmi looked to see how Verily was taking the news. *For once it is not hard to tell.* "Like many of the cross-race pairings, we think that the mating of a Human and a Hobgoblin is fraught with extra risk for both the mother and the child. You will notice that Christopher is already getting ready. He has been working on a new prayer. It is one that no-one has ever heard of before and he is still unsure if it will work as he wants it to."

He told me that he regrets not having asked about such things last time he was in Ardlark. It must have occurred to someone there that it would be a useful aid although perhaps a Hob is more different to a Human than an Alat-kharl is, for instance. But I am not telling Verily that. She looks worried enough already.

"However, he saw the need and he has prayed over it, and worked on what is needed and written it down and prayed some more over what he has done. Now it is time to put the new prayer into practice and to see if it works." *Already Thorstein has been sent off to fetch Aziz. He has the right to be here too.* She signed to Christopher to take over.

"You are having two daughters," the priest said. "But I have to tell you that Fear thinks that something is very wrong with one of them," he said to a very distressed girl while that was done. "I thought that it was possible that this could happen, and I want to try and cure her…your daughter that is… before she dies.

"Thorstein has gone for Aziz, and he will be with you when I do it. I have thought and prayed about this, and have developed a new entreaty to God for his Mercy and I think that it should work…but no-one that I know of has ever done this sort of thing before so I cannot be sure. Do you mind? May I go ahead?"

A very worried Verily is quick to consent. People have seen Christopher bring Ayesha back to life. Acts like that tend to imbue patients with confidence in their healer. Surely that means that she can trust him with the life of her unborn baby. Fear laid her head down and again checked which baby was ailing.

While Christopher prays, Fear will stay listening to the unborn, trying to see if anything changes in what she feels. I will make the more normal check of the mother, and keep feeling Verily's pulse and watching her breathing to make sure that she is healthy. I have potions for her at least if we need them.

By the time Aziz was there, the priests were getting ready to perform the service for the Third Hour. It was a little early, but they were sure God would understand. Everyone was in their place. *The healing chapel is all set up, and Christopher has the icon of the healer saints Cosmas and Damien, who the Chapel is dedicated to, on the wall above us all.*

The table, of course, stood in place in the centre of the room, surrounded by the most elaborate pattern painted on the floor with sacred words placed in the appropriate places. *The room smells of incense, blessings have been done and all that is needed is at hand. I have a supply of herbs and potions ready if needed.*

Christopher started into the service. Verily was half-lying and half sitting on the table supported by cushions, Aziz stood on one side holding one hand in both of his and with a very worried expression on his face. *Her little hand disappears inside his grasp.*

Fear stands on the other side; her head is still pressed to Verily's stomach. They concluded the short service and then, straight away, Christopher launched into the new prayer. Thorstein stood beside him holding his written text, while Theodule held a copy of the Bible in one hand while keeping up a constant low chant of Kyrie Eleison in the background and swinging a censer in the other.

Christopher finished. *I can see a movement visible from within Verily. It is the sort of movement that should not be seen for many months, the sort of motion that a baby makes when it stirs and turns around inside its mother. Christopher looks down at Fear's face. We all await her report. We know that something just happened.* A smile lit it up as she looked from where she still had her faced pressed.

"She is well now. She and her sister feel so happy." She ran around the table and hugged Christopher while Aziz and Verily hugged each other and said a few words. "Thank you, Father," said Aziz, looking up. "And you too, Fear." He looked at his wife, who nodded. "Now, it is up to you to keep track of which of our daughters was just healed…because her name is now to be Fear."

The young girl is nearly beside herself and runs out of the room to find a mother. Aziz turned to Christopher. "I think that it time me spoke to you about having vocation." He squeezed his wife's hand. "Time me become priest." Verily squeezed his hand back and started nodding in agreement.

Rani

*F*ear *didn't have far to go when she ran out. I watched the whole thing from just outside the room and she nearly collided with me in her enthusiasm. Our daughter has developed a great talent it seems. Such a miracle is the first that I have ever heard of, as well.*

It is not uncommon for such babies from two so different races to die in the womb, or emerge as monsters that die soon after birth. When this happens, they usually take their mother with them into death. It will not take long for the rumours of Christopher's latest wonder to sweep around the village either. Whether or not our daughter can ever become a mage, she has a powerful talent of her own.

Chapter XII

Astrid
35th Sixtus, the Feast Day of Saint Magnus

Twenty-one saddles were in the air. Astrid looked around. *Half of the riders are experienced, and the other half are trainee riders taking out the new saddles that Theodora and the others are making as fast as they can. It is back to our first attempts to use them. God help us if they have to fly individually and dodge anything. Keeping them in a formation is hard enough.*

On these rides, she usually went northwest towards Forest Watch and often took the riders in to visit the soldiers there. *This one is a far longer ride. They must get used to being in the saddle for hours.*

They left soon after breakfast and were swooping west from Mousehole out of the mountains with the sun rising behind them. As they went, they were slowly practicing their formations, wheeling and shifting their positions as they flew. Lake Erave was in sight ahead.

Astrid was calling out to stragglers using the loud-talker from the Brotherhood general. *It does make it easier that I do not have to try and shout.* Now that they were away from the mountains, she was flying her saddle backwards, and was keeping the speed low, and making them change formation often, circling around and criticising if people flew too high or too low, too fast or too slow.

Although our magic is expensive and hard to make, despite what Theodora says, it surely will not be too long before other places have their own saddles once they figure out how to cast the spells. If we Mice want to keep our advantage, we will have to always be far better at using the saddles than any others are.

Astrid was about to bring them down low over the lake when she looked ahead of them towards Erave Town. She cried out…which became a very loud and deafening sound as she forgot that she had the loud-talker…and she turned and accelerated. Looking ahead, most of the riders could just make out a tiny white blob in the distance. *It looks like my sister is back. The River Dragon is arriving home.*

Christopher

*T**he** news of the arrival of the River Dragon is somewhat muted by the arrival of Angelina and Eugenia Cheilas. I have everyone ready in case of problems with Fear, present at her first birth, listening and saying when the babies are ready, talking to the babies and reassuring them about the changes that they can feel around them.*

Maybe it was because of that, or it could be for another reason, but Valeria had a quick and easy delivery, and the twins are both born healthy. Fear was devastated when, as the girls were born, the voices of the children that she had heard in her head gradually faded away.

I am very relieved now the twins are delivered. I have been hoping that Fear has not been imagining hearing the twin girls. If she had, it would cast doubt on everything else that we are counting on and that we have done. At least this time, both Theodule and I were able to confirm before the birth that they are twins, even if no priest can tell what sex they are.

His first birth, and young Thorstein is embarrassed by being present. He will get used to it in time. He is so unlike his sister in many ways. The other priests went on to tell him gleefully of their first experiences.

Although, as midwife, Lakshmi does almost all the work, it is a good idea for the priests to be on hand in case of any problems, and as far as I am concerned, it is essential that he learns to become a physician to his flock, just in case there is no experienced midwife available. Lakshmi heartily agrees with me. She wants to have easy and safe deliveries herself and she cannot perform her role on herself then.

The delivery reminded them that today Fātima could also be giving birth. During the day's service Christopher addressed their prayers, not just for the health and safety of Valeria and her children but also for the Empress-Ambassador and hers. Ayesha had already done the same when she was leading the prayers of the Muslims earlier.

Danelis (36th Sixtus)

One item that came up from the River Dragon was a present for the valley from Metropolitan Taraisios. He had realised that, even with plans, it was unlikely that the work needed would be able to be done by the craftsmen of Mousehole so, while the ship had been in the north, he had ordered that an organ be made for their basilica.

I have to admit that I am nearly beside myself with excitement. It has come up to us packed away in boxes, with instructions on how to put it all together. The first organ outside of Darkreach will be ready for when our building is ready to house it. That is unfortunately still some time off, but when it is ready, we can hopefully make music...once I learn to play it properly, that is.

It apparently even has a magical device attached to it that provides the wind. The plans that I got on the way up north called for a person to be pumping away with a bellows the whole time to keep it working. This will be far better.

Basil (2nd September)

Stefan asked the Princesses if he could take the first turn at guarding the ship now that it has returned.

He will be taking his wives down with him to Evilhalt for a week, and Astrid has decided that she will also go down with them for a while. I suppose that this means that I should go with her to make sure she does not offend too many people.

My wife may claim that it is because she wants to use the bath at the inn, but I know her far too well. She just wants to see what the reaction is from Stefan's parents, especially seeing that both of his women are now quite visibly pregnant, and yet they still hang off each other, and off their husband. She thinks that his parents are both very stick-in-the-mud and Stefan did well to leave them.

However, at least it does allow my sister and her crew from the River Dragon to all come up to the village, a place where none of them has spent much time, and where some have never been at all. There are so many reasons that this is good. For a start, it will allow them to hear the stories of the valley. My wife started this, but Rani agrees that it is most important. It also lets the priests check all of the women on board, with both Fear and Lakshmi helping.

Christopher

*N*o one is surprised that Shilpa, Danelis, and Jennifer, all of whom are showing signs, are confirmed as pregnant by Fear. She is also saying that Shilpa has a boy, Jennifer, who is hardly showing much at all, is having a girl, and Danelis, whose tiny frame is already showing the strain, has both a boy and a girl inside her.

"Olympias," said Simeon, "I think that it is time that you got married and stopped pretending to not be with your man." *I am sure that I would have put it more delicately than that, or even waited for her to make up her own mind.*

Olympias may try denying that anything has happened...that she could not be pregnant...but the grins on the faces around her show her that her protestations are not believed by any of us. It is early, but Simeon had suspected it and now Theodule and I can confirm it. She is pregnant, too. It seems that it is far too early in the pregnancy for Fear to hear anything from the baby.

I have decided that she can only hear something once the baby gains what makes it unique, perhaps its soul, perhaps something else. I do not know. I do suspect, however, that we priests will argue about this for a long time and probably never agree.

The other three women were not confirmed as pregnant, although Anastasia was asked to come back in a few weeks as they were not sure in her case. *We think that it is likely she is with child, but that is all.*

Theodora

*O*ur latest count of the village said that we have a population of nearly one hundred and fifty people, including the students. Our hall can still take a lot more people in it, but it is a very different sight, with three times the people and noisy and happy children underfoot, to the first time that we assembled after the village was freed.

"Now that we have everyone home, except for the watch here and on the River Dragon it is time to settle a few things," Theodora looked around the room.

There are still many more women than men. It seems to be the fate of Mousehole that, although we are adding men to its numbers, we seem to be able to add women even faster. "We need to resolve a few issues that have been raised. The major one is how people pay for things or, indeed, if they pay for things and how they get money." She stopped and looked down at what was etched on the wax tablet that was before her.

Ruth has given me notes, and I must understand them and pass them on. My husband may be the better teacher, but I am the better speaker and thus much more likely to keep this many people interested. I have to put that skill to use. Besides, neither of us understands what I am about to say, so being able to speak lines is more important.

"As you are aware, I am not much used to the idea of money myself, so please bear with me if I make mistakes." She looked around briefly, trying to look at nearly everyone as she did so, before continuing. "Because of that, when I am finished, Ruth will be here to answer your questions and she will fix up all the wrong ideas that I give you."

She smiled at everyone. "We have decided to put these ideas to you as your Princesses. If people can see flaws in what I say…please let us know… but we think that this is the fairest way and the way that will keep things in the village as much like they are now as we can while answering people's concerns.

"For the people who were the original residents of Mousehole…that is the former slaves…they have a share of the profit of the village, and I will deal with how we get that later. That share is already laid out, and they pass that share on to their children for all time. My husband and I and those who came with us, and our descendants are likewise covered by what was agreed then.

"The question that is important is how all the new people in our village get treated. We don't know how much you will get paid yet…none of us know enough about that issue, but we are going to ask people for lists of wages and prices when we go back to Darkreach in a few weeks. We have decided that we will pay everyone more than what we are told is usual. People will get paid for their normal job and we will keep track of what people do."

"That task will fall to young Fire there." She pointed at the Brotherhood widow who shrank back in her seat. *Several women, and indeed all the former Brotherhood girls, are glaring at her as an almost automatic reaction as soon as they see her, or her name is mentioned. Astrid was right. We must stop that.*

"Because of what she *was going* to be," she stressed the words 'was' and 'going' when she spoke, "but was not yet, she had some training in accounts. Bishop Christopher has had a long talk with her, and you all know him to be a holy man. He says that she is a good girl, and cannot be blamed for agreeing to an arranged marriage, and I trust his word. She will note if you do one job or if you do two, and you will get paid accordingly."

Theodora looked at her notes. "We have decided that we will deduct from your wages for keep. We have yet to work out how much, but anything that you eat or drink, or that you draw from the common store to cook in your home is already accounted for. Any normal cloth of wool or hemp that is used from the common store, or any everyday clothing that is made, is also counted. One day we may add linen and other cloth to that list, but it will not be until we can grow our own.

"In addition, we will regard anything normal that Norbert or Stefan or any of the other craftspeople of the village make for you, or any of the building work that Goditha and Dulcie and the others do for you, will also be covered. Only special things like jewellery or special clothes will be charged for." She paused and looked around. *This is important for them to understand.*

"All children born in the village get free schooling…as much as they need. Their teachers, and them alone, will decide when they can leave school. That is not going to be a decision for either the parents or even for the child. It will be a decision of the teachers and if you disagree with that decision, then you must convince us, your Princesses."

She looked at her notes again. "No-one will be paid in coins unless they ask for it to be so. We will set it up as, I am told, is what is called a 'bank'. Fire will keep count of how much you have in it, and you can ask for it in coin or you can leave it there. That is her job, and you must pity her, as she has to now work out how much we have and count every coin we have in store, and we have a lot of them. She then has to keep track of how many there are as it changes.

"That also means, with the help of Eleanor and Lakshmi, knowing the value of everything that someone does not already own, or is not in general use, all of the magic and even the gems that we have in store, to see how much wealth everyone has now.

"We will be using some of the money that we have…and you will need to ask Ruth about how this works as I do not pretend to understand it at all…we will use it to lend money to money lenders outside of the valley, and perhaps even to rulers or whole villages, and she says that they will give us more money back later than we give them now." Theodora shrugged.

I may look doubtful at this, but at least Ruth is nodding, as are Fire and the women who have experience as traders. It seems to make sense to them and if it does, then they can help explain it to the others.

"Anything normal that people make…I mean food, or any of the other ordinary things we do all the time…for me that means magic items, for others it might be sewing a dress…will belong to the village. If you make something that is not a part of your customary job, then that is yours and you can sell it however you want. I suppose that would mean if I actually sewed a dress and someone was silly enough to give me money for it instead of making me pay them to take it.

"We expect people to be proud of what they do, and what they make, and we hope that many of our rewards will come, not from the money we get, but from the way the people that we live among and care about think about us. We haven't worked out what we will do if people are lazy, and we hope that we never have to. We hope everyone will want to work hard for their own sake. At the same time, we expect people to be wealthy according to the rest of the Land.

"If you are going outside the village, you can take your money from the bank to spend it as you will, and if you have any left over when you return then you can put it back." She looked at Ruth again seeking an answer to show that she was right on this and received a nod in return.

She started counting things off, trying to make sure that she covered everything that she had been told to say. "Lending money is one of the ways the village will make money...I mentioned that. We will have the school, and we expect it to grow, but we do not expect or count on it ever making much money. We will have the inn, and that will bring in a little money to the village from travellers.

"Another way we will make a lot of coin is through selling things to merchants. That will mean any profit we make from Carausius and Guk as they pass by, along with the gems, or antimony, or herbs and potions, or horses, or anything else we want to sell. It includes anything Shilpa makes when the River Dragon sails to Sacred Gate, or to Ardlark or anywhere else; and she did very well from that on the last trip.

"We also get plunder, even if we cannot count on that. We took wealth when we took the village and a lot more at Dwarvenholme. We got treasure in Haven, we got even more from the dragon, and we got it in Rising Mud. We even gained some in Freehold, in the Brotherhood, and on Skrice. Anyone who, in addition to their normal work, comes out to fight will also get paid for that. We have even less of an idea how much to pay for that than we do for normal work.

"Jennifer and Vishal and some of our sailors may have recent experience with how much they were paid, and we have talked with them, but otherwise all that we know is that kataphractoi get more than kynigoi and that artillery receives more than infantry do. We also know that you get more if it is likely to be a dangerous mission than if it is just guarding something. Tithes come out of what the village earns, and there will be no other taxes. We don't need to take back any of what you are given. That would be silly."

She stopped and looked around. *I know of no village or town or nation that runs like this, although it is similar in some ways to what happens with moneylenders in Freehold, and in other ways it is similar to Darkreach, and in still others to the Brotherhood.*

"We know this is different to what you are used to, and we realise that perhaps the only reason it will work is that Mousehole is rich...very, very rich. The village will be giving everyone so much...I nearly forgot...unless you want something really special or unusual, weddings and funerals and other celebrations are part of the deal and possibly dowries or bride-prices if children marry outside the village.

"We ask you to bear with us as we work it all out...ohhh...another thing I nearly forgot...students will get paid when they are doing their work in the fields or with a trade after studying. It will not be much, as it is part of their learning, but this will get put aside and they can draw it out and spend it, with permission of a teacher or parent, if a trader has anything they want or when they visit another town. What is left will be given to them when they leave the school and return home."

The older children in the school look pleased at that. Theodora looked down at Ruth. "I think that is all that is important..." Ruth nodded "...so I will finish, and Ruth will take questions while we have something to drink...and the drink is also covered." She sat down.

There are surprisingly few questions to Ruth. It looks like everyone in the village is happy to wait and see how it works. From the look on some of the faces of those from Darkreach, they are more than happy with what they will be getting. I think the only person to lose on this is Fire. I have a feeling she will be so busy, she will not have a chance to feel slighted.

Chapter XIII

Astrid (3rd September)

Stefan and his wives are almost ready to leave the *River Dragon*. "Do you want me to come with you?" *See, despite what Basil says, I can sound casual. Who could tell that this is the whole reason I am here on this trip?*

Basil has both of our babies happily crawling around on the deck with tethers around them and I am just standing here playing with one of my new weapons, which according to what I have been able to find out from the books may be called a bardiche. I have nothing important to do at all...except listen in to the conversation that will happen later.

"No, thanks," said Adara. *For the moment, she is the one with Aneurin on her hip...I think.*

"Yes, please," said Bryony at the same time. *She has met Stefan's mother before.*

Stefan just looks back with a stunned expression. He has worn the same expression on his face from the moment that Bryony convinced him they cannot avoid this moment much longer. Astrid grinned. "Then I will come along for a bit before I go and have a bath. Are you going to tell them everything about the three of you, or just that you are married to two women?"

I made a good hit there. Stefan is looking even sicker, if that were possible. The two girls even briefly look at each other. Adara looks a trifle concerned with that after she notices Bryony wears an expression that is more than a little worried. She is looking as if her stomach is a little unwell. She looks sick and nervous, and as if she is ready to go straight back to the valley and never ever come out again.

"At least every man in town will be jealous of Stefan...have you got that letter from the Bishop with you?" *Stefan has started checking his pouches and there is a relieved look on all three faces as he pulls it out.*

"Just go and stop teasing them, Puss," said Basil. "I remember someone, someone who is not too far away from me now, that was very, very, nervous about meeting her mother-in-law for the first time and who has never, ever, admitted it."

Astrid stuck her tongue out at her husband and began to lead the others off the ship, and down the ladder to the ground from where the *River Dragon* stood in a cradle in the yard where she had been built. *The River Dragon has been pulled high and dry and is out of the water for the first time since she was launched.*

She is waiting to have her hull cleaned of barnacles and seaweed after which the two coppersmiths from Erave Town will be crossing the water. Her maker will re-caulk her hull and the two smiths will clad her entirely in copper. One of her holds has many sheets of the metal and boxes of copper nails in it that have been bought in Ardlark for just this purpose. Once work starts on the ship tomorrow we will be moving into the inn. For the moment, we are staying on board.

Astrid looked around. "Oh, look," she said in a lively tone. "It is too late for any of you to change your mind now. Stefan's brother Amos is already outside the village, and he is coming towards us. I hope you are all ready."

Astrida (few minutes later)

"I have been sent to see if you are actually coming to see our parents now that we have heard you are here," Amos said to his brother. "Hello, Bryony," he said to Adara, who still held the baby. "Hello, Cat," he added to Astrid. *Then he turns to Bryony with a puzzled look, and then back to Adara with even more curiosity, and then returns his gaze back to Bryony.*

The two women are, as they often do, playing on their appearance and only a person who knows them well can tell them apart. I do it by looking at the pattern of their freckles. "I am sorry, we haven't met," he said to the wrong one. *The two women smother smiles badly.*

"And you won't until we get to your parent's place," said Astrid. *Why spoil the surprise?* "Lead the way and be quick. I am going to blame you for us being late." She slapped his backside with the butt of her weapon. Amos moved smartly ahead as Astrid grinned. *He might always be a far better leatherworker than his older brother is, but he is also a full three years younger than Stefan, and sometimes it seems that the gap in their ages is even larger than that.*

Astrid

U nder the circumstances, the visit went fairly well, even if the letter from Bishop-elect Christopher had to be produced and read, and Father Anastasias had to be brought from the church to confirm what was in it. The priest was surprised by what he read, but he did confirm that the verses quoted existed, and if two Metropolitans and a Bishop agreed with it...who was he, as a simple village priest, to argue.

The fact that both women are beautiful, and both are pregnant with more grandchildren does not hurt either. As the food was brought out, Astrid launched into tales of Stefan's role in the Army of the North as one of its Great Captains and how he had done the same on Neron. Astrid looked at the table as she spoke. *It is a wonder that Stefan does not weigh twice as much as he does.*

I can see Stefan's father expanding, as neighbours are brought in to be introduced and have the explanations and stories run through time and again. Amos may be inheriting the house and the business, but never let it be doubted that the prodigal is now the favoured son. Astrid never did get to go to the inn to bathe that day and food had to be sent out to the ship for Basil.

Chapter XIV

Theodora (4th September)

The broken remnants of the devices from Neron had been brought up from the *River Dragon*, and now lay in front of Theodora on her desk, and on the floor around her in a display of mangled wood and metal and other substances.

I have tried to sense if there is any magic at all coming from them, and Verily has checked them over with her sense, which usually is able to pick up traces even of departed magic from something that has been dispelled. She confirms that there is not the faintest smell of magic about any of it. So, what is it?

Both my husband and Ruth have looked at the bits and pieces with what they know about how machines work, and both say that these items are far beyond their ken. Ariadne only glanced at it and laughed. She said she understood ballistae and she doubted that what we have would even make a good projectile.

Harald, Lakshmi, and Eleanor have all looked over the fragments. There is wood and they can identify different metals. There is some gold, some silver, some copper and even quite a lot of mithril. There is also glass... lots of broken glass. There is a strange soft material too, often wrapped around the copper. She sighed.

Did Astrid and Ayesha have to be so thorough in making sure that it no longer worked? She found something black and with a dot that flicked one way and another. *It does nothing now, but when the device was working perhaps it was like a trigger that set the machine to work. There is a lot of smooth material. Some is flat and green, and seems to have lines of silver or copper metal on it and some is white or other colours.*

No-one has any idea what the smooth material is, although little pieces of it bubble and dissolve when Lakshmi puts them in an alkahest and they burn with a very bad smell and drip like wax if you put them near a flame. Additionally, there is a little sealed metal box, all of one piece, but too light to be solid inside, that I don't want to open.

The little box has some broken or cut wires coming out from it, and some are still connected to other bits of the machine. The big cord like a heavy metal rope is made up of more wires. Once they are inside their boxes the wires in the cord split up and run to different parts. The cut ends of the big cord show that some of the wires are made up of the smooth white material and some are copper and have more smooth stuff around them of different colours.

Also in the ruins there are green squares...sort of like the rest of the smooth material, but different and waxy and with metal lines and little hard things on them. Most of the inside of the round box on legs is made up of an almost flat thing that looks like it wants to spin around. That is the only thing that has Ariadne excited. She wants to take it apart even further to see why it spins so smoothly as far as it can before jamming in its dented and broken cage.

I will not let her do that, but Ariadne got a small piece of glass with some silver on the back of it that she could use as a mirror and thrust it inside after gluing it to a stick with wax. She started muttering words about little balls in a track as she moved it backwards and forwards. I have not seen her since then. I think that she may be trying to make her own.

Just sitting and looking at the broken boxes can only go so far. Eventually, Theodora had the apprentices gather the remains, while she took her notebooks and her mana storage and everything else that she would need for the casting and they all went off to the roof of the Mouse Hall. She looked at the pattern there to check it. *Its lines have just been renewed by the apprentices under my husband's direction and all is ready to proceed.*

I need everything in my favour for this cast. I am going to be well and truly overdrawn again, and my husband and the apprentices have all augmented the roof pattern with a reinforcement of mana to bolster my chances. I am going to chance my luck as well. After reading the words again and preparing them carefully she started casting. It was a very powerful spell that she was using, and it took a goodly time while she recited the phrases that she had determined should do what she wanted done.

Inside my head, I can feel the spell teeter on the verge of success and failure, but my decision to appeal to chance has worked in my favour this time. I can feel the fabric of reality shudder in my mind and even in my bones. In front of her, in the middle of the diagram where she stood, the two boxes were standing joined by a long coil of cable. *There is a collective gasp from my audience.*

That was close. At least the next time I do the spell it will be far easier. It always is the second time you cast, and by the tenth time around with using a particular spell, tearing these particular gaps in what some call the normal world becomes routine and easy. Our so-called reality is really so malleable and uncertain. It just needs the right nudging to fall in line.

Eagerly, she leant forward to pick up a box; only to nearly fall over. *That really had been close.* Quickly, her husband was at her side, and led her over to where there was a chair and some refreshments waiting. The apprentices brought one box and placed it in front of her on a small table and set the other up on its legs some way away.

Ceremoniously, she opened the box as the others clustered around. *Where is that trigger thing? There it is…black on black…the white dot is on the end that is in the air. In the centre, on a slope of the smooth material, also black, is a circle of glass. That is all of it: a slope, a circle, and a trigger thing in a box with a lid, and something to hold it open, and screens that fold down the sides and would make it all darker.* She looked around. *Everyone is looking back at me.*

The watchers must have turned it on without any problem. She passed her hands all over it. *I can still feel no magic when it is whole.* Slightly nervously, Theodora pushed the trigger thing on the white dot and the device slowly seemed to come to life. Gradually the glass began to glow with a series of green rings that were equally far apart.

I can faintly see a green line on the glass…it is getting brighter and brighter. Now it starts to sweep around it. It takes about a slow count of five to complete a circle. On the screen are a nearly straight line and a series of jagged ones that are bright when the line sweeps over them and gradually fade to be gone, just before the line reaches them again. All of them are inside the smallest of the circles on the screen and the nearly straight one is right in the centre of the screen. Likewise, near the last circle, are some other short green lines.

Theodora looked at the screen. *The lines seem to be sort of familiar.* She looked up the valley in thought, and after a little while, back at the screen in shock. She looked up and down again a few times as the line swept around, and then she turned the box around. *Now I have it right…the lines are sort of an eerie green glowing picture of what I can see ahead of me of the shape of the valley.*

"Someone get a saddle and take it for a flight. Get a couple of them… fly one around the valley, and make the other go up and far away to the top meadow. Go in and out of sight." She waited as Hulagu and Goditha ran downstairs. They soon appeared and took off. With astonishment everyone watched two dots appear on the screen and over the image of the valley mimic what they could see the saddles doing.

They could see them, but they could not see how high they were. *Hulagu is taking a saddle up the valley towards the falls. I can see him sometimes… both as a dot and with my eyes.* Eventually, he went past the cliffs and started soaring beyond where the line was on the screen. *He is a green dot and still in the smallest circle but only Fortunata can just make him out as a dot in the far distance in the sky.*

"Can someone please find Ayesha? Make sure that she has her ring and get her to fly around the valley a bit. She needn't go far, but get her to take her ring off a couple of times and put it on again." Again, there was a wait. But not a long one, as Ayesha was downstairs wondering where her husband had disappeared to in such a hurry. Soon they followed her with their eyes and on the screen. She must have put her ring on as she disappeared both from sight and on the screen at the same time. After a while she appeared again in both places.

"Hulagu is coming back" said Parminder, pointing at the screen as Ayesha disappeared again. Soon everyone was assembled again, and after passing word around and letting anyone who wanted to, have a look, it was turned off. *It is obviously a machine of some sort that lets you see what is out there as if it were a set of eyes…only it sees a lot further.*

Theodora (that night)

*W*ell, *it seems that it does not need light to see. It shows the same in the day or the night. It is almost as if it were a new way to see the world.* "Does anyone have any ideas about this?" she asked those who were standing around looking at the night test.

Olympias nodded and spoke, almost to herself. "That would be useful on the ship at night if there was heavy cloud or during a storm." Theodora looked at her. Then she spoke louder and more confidently. "You could tell where the land was and not run into it. From what Astrid indicated to me, when they saw it working, it might see out as far as a hundred miles if everything was right."

She continued. "I wonder if that is why it was on East Zarah. Like us, it wants to have no break in its view, and the higher it is, the better the view it will have. You can see more from a masthead than you can from the deck, and I suppose that you would see a whole lot more from the top of a mountain.

"They could have seen where the drakkar was that night. In fact, if they had a far-talker, the ones on the mountain could have told the drakkar where we were from their watch point and gotten them to steer straight for us. I was wondering how they managed to find us in that storm. I thought it would have been magic that they used."

"Do you think that you could put it on the River Dragon where it would be able to see?" asked Rani. "Would the masts get in the way?" Olympias went over to where the circular box was and pointed at it, looking back.

"This is the part that sees?" *Everyone nodded.* "And the other box is what you look into?" *Again, there are nods.* She laid out the cable between the two and began pacing. "There is enough cable that we could put the box under the spanker mast where the helmsman could see it and run the cable up the mast to the spanker topmast." She looked at the tripod for a while and turned. "Can you turn it off please?"

Theodora leaned forward: "Done."

Olympias looked at the circular box and fiddled with where it joined the legs. She turned back holding the legs under her arm and the box in her hands. "The legs were added to it. They are not part of the device. We can do the same sort of thing to that," she pointed at the top of the tripod, "and fix it to the side of the mast on a beam. We might have a little bit of the view blocked by the mast, but it is worth a try."

"I will fly down to the ship with Galla tomorrow and we will see what we can do. We will keep it under cover until we are on board so that, unless they actually see it mounted on the ship with their eyes, our opponents will not know it is there.

"I wanted to check on the progress with cladding the *River Dragon* anyway. You lot might be happy sitting down on dry land high in the mountains. Apart from it being a nice break to have a large bed and no-one to disturb me with problems, I am not. I like to have a wooden deck under my feet, not mud and dirt."

Chapter XV

Rani
6th September, the Feast Day of Saint Ursula

*T*he girls from the Brotherhood are starting to be seen as a normal part of our village life. With the kataphractoi Neon, Menas and Asticus beginning to pay court to Maria, Loukia, Verina and Zoë…even if no-one was sure which one of the three is courting which of the four girls at any one time, then except for Lādi, who still does not have a suitor, and Rakhi and Zeenat (the pair of young girls rescued in Haven) they are almost the only unmarried women in the village.

However, the fact that there are twenty-nine of them, as well as Fire, makes for a large, unmarried, and very visible block of girls. Except for Fire, who has shown no potential for magic, I have still not been able to test any of them as an apprentice. It is something that they all feel is wrong for them to do. I have the feeling that I only need to get one of them to agree, and then the rest will fall in. But just getting the first one to agree is the hard thing.

I find it hard to wait to get Astrid back from lying in a bath. She must be wrinkled like a prune by now. Whether she likes it or not, the girls are about to become Astrid's project. They seem to be more scared of her, perhaps because she is a warrior woman or perhaps it is her teeth, than of the consequences of anything else.

At least Goditha is near to completing our own bathhouse, just outside the wall near the practice area. It has two hot water tubs and two cold ones each in separate rooms. There is a larger set for the women and a smaller one for the men. After all, there are a lot more women in the valley than there are men. Having that will tempt Astrid back.

There has been a special timber bit added under her instruction at the edge of the building that you can get to from either the men's or the women's *side. It will hold about three hands of people seated or lying on two rows of wooden benches, one higher than the other against the wall.*

I have, although I am puzzled as to why it is wanted, made something in the way of a spell for it that will heat some rocks until they are very, very, hot when you command them to do so. They are in a sort of cage so that you cannot touch them. The annoying girl has just smiled at what has been made and told me to wait.

Astrid has refused to say why she wants it but she, as well as Thorstein, Ayesha, and the plains-born are all very excited about it. The hard bit in making the bathhouse is, apparently, connecting everything into the village drains and water supplies so that we do not have to do anything by hand except pull some handles or turn some small wheels.

At least, we have the advantage that, being built above the ground, we don't need a spell to empty it all as they do below the tavern in Evilhalt. It will all empty of its own accord…if you turn the right handle.

Olympias (8ᵗʰ September)

Olympias and Galla returned and immediately went to see Rani.

"We have fitted the green-light box to the *River Dragon*," said Olympias. "From where she sits out of the water near the village, we can sort of make out the mountains and the shape of part of the lake and even see the church spire in Evilhalt as a very close green light of its own.

"It takes practice to understand what we are seeing, and we will need to get experience reading what it says to us if we are going to use it to find our way. It is not as clear and easy to work as the expensive spells of clairvoyance, but it works well in its own way and is always available to anyone without needing a mage."

Next Olympias went to see Father Christopher. "You are right. It is time that I was married. Denizkartal has wanted to do so for a long time, and it is only my stubbornness that has prevented us doing so. You are sure that I am pregnant?" Christopher nodded. "Then I will go and ask him. Will you be offended if we ask Father Simeon to do the ceremony? He is our ship's priest and our friend after all, and it only seems right that we get him to act for us."

"You can have Thorstein marry you if you wish," replied Christopher. "I am just happy to see marriages taking place." *He has a joyful smile.*

Christopher
9ᵗʰ September, the Feast Day of Saint Maurice

*W*e *have seen the birth of Elizabeth's daughter Virginia. Fear predicted a daughter and again the birth is worry free, although Elizabeth needed some healing of her body afterwards. It was then the turn of Saint Ursula to have her day, to the delight of my wife, who managed to say more than a few words in the service on her behalf, reading from a copy of her Life that she picked up in Greensin.*

Next, Anahita has given birth to her son, Baul. It was an easy birth, and most noted by having two nervous men waiting outside: Hulagu, the father, and Dobun, the husband to be. It may not be normal in a Christian village, but I suppose that I need to get used to the other cultures we are surrounding ourselves with.

Today is the feast day of Saint Maurice, and the scene outside the chapel is duplicated as Kāhina gave birth to her first son, Yesugai. Fear said that both Khitan births would be sons, and I am getting more confident in the truth of what she says.

Both women had births that were quicker and easier than their first, and although that is normal for most women, I am beginning to suspect that having someone coaching the baby through what is happening might also be making things faster and smoother for the mother. It is well that we did not need the men; neither is very sober this time.

He joked to his wife that they had better not let Fear's ability become known to the world outside the village. "If it becomes known what she can do, she will soon be kidnapped by anxious mothers-to-be from all over Vhast, and wars would be fought over her services."

Rani (12ᵗʰ September)

I am again reminded just how far I am drifting from the way I was brought up.* She had come across Ruth and the school students, with Zeenat and Rakhi. They were doing a celebration for Vasant Navratri, the quarterly celebration for women that lasts for nine days. Again, she pondered her faith. *Now that I look into the hall, I can see that even my wife is sitting there with Fear on her lap.*

To the dismay of my parents, I have never had a high level of belief in the Gods of my people. I guess that I have studied the practicalities of magic far too much. I believe in Father Christopher and what he does personally, I have constant proof of that, but as for his religion, or indeed my own, I have little feeling one way or another.

I am not sure if that affects how God or the Gods feel about me, but I suppose that, until my feeling changes I will still cling to going through the motions with what I have been brought up with but, and she added a caveat to herself, *I will also still listen to the one man that I have met who I am truly sure is holy and go to his services.*

Ruth (19ᵗʰ September)

The day that winter started was the day that Dobun married both Anahita and Kāhina. *The Khitan have an unusual culture, and it is apparently only today that the women cease to be köle and become free again. They gain their freedom over two years after the rest of us in the village became free.*

Ayesha, who is too pregnant to dance the dance that she has been learning, is to be left holding the babies...all of them except the smallest, like a nest of puppies, in a large fur rug mounded at the edges over cushions.

Bianca, Aigiarn, Alaine, and Verily perform the marriage dance without her. At last, I now know that the choice to be married on this day is a deliberate one, as the changes of seasons and the equinoxes are regarded as the most propitious and sacred days for the Khitan. Having one of these at just the right time is thought to be too good a chance for them to pass up. Again, the celebration itself is held in the chill night air that marks the beginning of winter.

Our bathhouse was also completed today, and although they don't have a sweat tent, the use of the wooden room on the side of it is explained. Astrid calls it a sauna *and admits reluctantly that women who are pregnant past the time when they should no longer be too active should not use it as it is a danger to their unborn child. She says that it is the best way to cure colds and such diseases and for sore muscles and is even good, with more alcohol and lots of water, for hangovers.*

The Khitan are glad to have it for quite another reason. It seems that, for a proper marriage ceremony, as a part of the normal purifying ceremonies, the participants cleanse their sins from their bodies with steam and heat.

I have...at long last...found out some details of one of the Khitan ceremonies and what it means and now I have an explanation for the fires that were lit on the afternoon of Hulagu's wedding. The sweat tent, or in our case the sauna, is considered to be a better alternative than fires for something like a wedding.

Rani

*O*ur village is beginning to look less and less like a temporary camp. The bathhouse is not the only new building. For a start, the mill is now finished and working. It is small, but it will be all that we need for quite a long time.

Although far less than a quarter of the buildings of the village are being used, several people have decided to gradually move to where they might best live and work. We have discovered what some of the abandoned houses have attached to them, sometimes only through clearing away collapsed cellar walls inside the buildings.

Thus, both Jordan and Giles have new places refurbished for them as the tunnels that were dug into the rock behind some of the houses were discovered. Jordan now has a place to hang smallgoods, instead of having to dodge things that were hanging up in his house and workshop.

Giles now has many shelves to replace in another tunnel so that he can store all the cheeses that he is now making as fast as he can. The shelves will apparently give everything the right temperature so that they can mature properly. Aine has, long ago, already found the tunnel for her wine and is using it.

Even more importantly, before she had even started on making more saddles, my wife has made some devices for the builders. Now, when they are working on walls or roofs Goditha and Ariadne no longer have to worry about climbing up scaffolding and then falling off it. They, and some of those helping them, can slowly walk on the air, rising and falling as they need.

Moreover, she has made a set of small straps that can be fitted around a block or stone. Once this is done, the block will become almost weightless. It is still slow to move and very hard to stop once it is moving, but it does mean that one unskilled person can, with attention, shift a huge block of stone that will normally need a whole crew of people and a crane. Even some of the smaller women can now move stones direct from the quarry to where it is needed, if they are cautious.

To help even more, working alongside Norbert, our blacksmith, Christopher and the other priests have several times combined their mana to make some actual stone-working tools. The best looks like a normal toothed stone-chisel, but instead of taking several days to cut a block of stone and shape it, it merely requires the correct guiding.

Just as a skilled person can make statues out of ice while an unskilled person just breaks it up, it is hard to guide the chisel properly and requires a hand experienced with working stone to use it as it should be used, but it means that a whole block can be cut out and shaped in less than half an hour. They have made several of these and have now started making more than they need and are *putting them away as gifts, or to sell to Carausius, or to the Dwarves.*

With what they make from them they might be able to pay for some of the work on the basilica themselves rather than ask the village to do it. Finishing it will need someone from outside with skills that do not exist in the village. They have also made another tool that smoothes cut stone once it is passed over it. It cuts and scrapes away the stone as if it were a warm butter knife with a rough block of butter. It allows a block to be trimmed just right or a cornice to be carved once it is in place. Having been working with them, Goditha is now beside herself with excitement about both.

Ariadne has left behind her role in sieges and has been busy making both tiles and bricks. Mostly she makes the former, as we need more of them at present, and between her work, and the tools of air and earth, building goes a lot faster here than anyone has heard of or seen before, even when there have been many more people on the site as people all generally work on one building. Now they are more spread out on different projects.

The first building of the school, set up as part of one side of what would one day be a grass quadrangle with a cloister around it, an idea that is modelled on what our priests say is the inside of the abbey, is finished. At present its windows are just made of stretched oilskin or sheep's guts, but they hope to do something better than that when they can. Its walls are of white-painted plaster, and it has a smooth stone floor.

I have made lights for it, and a small device that will keep it warm in winter. The rest of the school is just pegging, string, and ideas and it has stretched Ruth's and my combined ability to design a building to get this far. We need to get more books to help Ruth finish the designs when we are next in Darkreach.

We have built a much larger room than we really need for teaching at present, but I plan for the school to grow and that will mean larger classes. For the moment we must do everything in just this one room and so it is full of items from many subjects stacked around the walls, and on and under rough tables.

In a like fashion, the bases of the walls of the basilica are under way, but we lack the knowledge of how to properly build the series of arches and the great domed roof over the half-circles at the sides. Once we have those complete, we will still need someone else to come in and make the mosaic floors and paint the icons.

However, the shape of the building, its doorways, its entries, and its stairs can now be made out. There is even a small part of rough-hewn floor of stone ready to have mortar and mosaics applied to it once the rest of the building is finished. Our priests are just hoping that we will learn how to finish their building before they need it.

Chapter XVI

Ariadne (20th September)

The scouting saddles reported a large band of Hobs coming down the road from the north. They had weapons, and were painted, but they waved happily at the saddle as it flew over. It was reported that there was at least one human among them. Aziz and Ariadne flew out to see who it was.

It seems that my wedding is about to happen. Also in the party are Guk, and his son, and his new worker Haytor, along with horses carrying trade goods for his new run. Guk is not going to let something minor, like the approach of the snows of winter, deter him from trading. They have with them Krukurb's relations, Aziz's mother, and other Hobs coming down for my wedding. My wedding...it sounds very good.

I have so much to learn. Aziz tells me that the paint on the Hobs is of an appropriate pattern for this purpose. The Humans, for there are two, are Father Michael and his wife. They are also painted more or less as their parishioners are, but are wearing more clothes. The priest is coming down to talk with his Bishop-elect, and his wife is coming to talk to the other wives.

Ariadne sped back to Mousehole. *In the new deal, I was promised a wedding. The cooks and others have a bit over a day to prepare for it. Now Christopher must work out a ceremony that is Hob in nature, but that also caters for my tastes, and in addition, is still a valid Christian rite. Since we posed him the question, I hope that he has given it more thought than I have.*

Bianca (21st September)

I will have to get used to this sort of meeting I suppose. The Presbytera were sitting together in the Hall of Mice sharing kaf, tea, and biscuits and talking together. *Seeing that her husband has now started to be trained as a priest, for the first time I have told Verily to join us. It seems that Sofronia is even more worried about adapting to local custom than her husband is.*

"Except for Michael," she said to the other four women, "no man has seen me unclothed since I was a baby. Besides, I am not as young as I once was."

"Then don't wear a kilt."

Sophronia continued. "But I am told that all of you do."

"I was not comfortable at first." The other three women smiled at Bianca's understatement, as she continued: "But that was for other reasons."

"Mainly to do with her not admitting that she loved Christopher," interjected Danelis.

Bianca tried unsuccessfully to deny that any such thing had happened before continuing. "I suppose that what I am trying to say is that your village will not expect you to be totally like them...after all, they are trying to be like you. Get yourself a kilt, and if one day you are comfortable with the idea, wear it...or don't...just keep it and wear it for Michael."

Then all of them grinned.

Olympias

After my experience with her at the Imperial wedding, I should have known better. Somewhat reluctantly, I asked Astrid to be my maid of honour. Now, I know why I was reluctant. I had thought to be married in my best clothes: the breeches, and coat, and ruffled shirt that I bought on the last trip. My sister will have none of that, and has dragged me off to see a woman that I have met briefly, but have never talked to before, apart from a passing word or two.

She is from Freehold, and it seems, has very set ideas on what a woman should wear to get married. My sister gives me no support whatsoever. She is encouraging the other woman and silencing any objections from me. It seems that in a few days I will actually own a real dress. It will be the first I have had for some time.

Unbeknownst to Olympias, her brother, who would be giving her away, was arranging a similar job for her groom and their bosun, Harnermêŝ, who would be his groomsman.

Christopher (22ⁿᵈ September)

I thought that after Aziz and Verily's wedding, I was all ready for another Hobgoblin ceremony until the bride and groom revealed that they want to be married in the unfinished basilica. Although it is not sanctified yet, they want to be the first couple married there. I cannot think of a problem with that, but we need to see.

When the pair left, he hastily ran out to the site to see what he needed. As he went, he gathered up Goditha and the other workers needed to make the area both safe and useable.

Now it is time for the wedding itself, and the drums are beating. The groom is attended by Aziz and Haytor, while the bride has Verily and Guk's daughter, Zumruud, and has the Princess Theodora giving her away. Of course, all are dressed in Hob fashion, even if Ariadne is used to a more conservative form of dress. He looked at how his new priests were taking this.

Father Michael

Well, it is a bit of a shock, particularly seeing the Princess mostly naked. I did have to blink a few times at the way everyone is clothed, but it is wise to stay silent. My Bishop-elect obviously approves, and I did make sure that I came down to talk to him about how much I should adapt the Church to abide by local custom. I am receiving a lot of that information very clearly just by watching.

I have to admit that it is distracting at first, but one quickly grows used to the custom. After all, I am already used to it among my own parishioners, few of whom wear more than a cloak on their tops, even in the coldest weather. For me it is a matter of my adapting to the whole mix of races among the Mice following the same custom.

Astrid

During the wedding, Astrid sat the Hobgoblin bard Pąrlakmugąni down. *Is anyone where they can hear? No, I don't think so, not with the music.* "I heard you tell a couple of stories when we were in Dhargev once. Now I want to hear from you all the tales that you may have…about the time of the last Age, or earlier."

He went to stand, and she pulled him back down. "No, I don't want you to tell everyone, and besides, I don't think that it will be a good idea for you to tell anyone when you go home, either, but I will let you know about that when I hear what you have to say."

Astrid (a fair bit later)

*I*t turns out that the legends of the Hobgoblins are both more complete, and very different to the tales that are heard in the West and the North, and even commonly in Darkreach.

According to Pąrlakmugąni's stories, at the end of the last age, the West invaded Darkreach and was thrown back to this side of the mountains. The Hobs fought on the side of the West. My old village is the only part of Darkreach that had stayed conquered by the West. It had not been the other way around. That, in itself, is very interesting.

The alliance of the West had fallen apart when it had failed in its goal. That first invasion was why Forest Watch was built where it was. It was not built to keep a watch on the wild tribes, as the other watch stations were, but to keep an eye on all the roads that could be used by an army and so to look out for the West coming to again invade Darkreach.

As for earlier tales, he had an interesting creation story to tell. According to his tradition, the Eldest Gods had made the world, but the Old Gods then arose and disputed with them over it. There were many of the Eldest Gods, and yet none of the Hobs knew their names. There were seven of the Old Gods, and they were bright and glorious, and terrible and cruel.

The Old Gods were gaining victory over the Eldest when one of them, whom he named as Hrqthnqrg, in a very guttural and harsh accent, took pity on what he saw, and rejected his race and its plans for the whole world, which he called Vhast. This weakened the power of the Old Gods, as Hrqthnqrg had been the strongest of them. This rebellion allowed the Eldest to survive, and since then the Eldest and the Old have battled for the hearts and souls of the people of the land.

His people can write the names of the other Old Gods down, but they are not allowed to say them. That was forbidden because it can summon them. He didn't know the real names of the Eldest, even though they are the ones that the Hobs worship under names that they know are newer than the Gods themselves are.

All the stories say that both sets of Gods are very rarely seen. The Eldest do not look like people; they are more like a harpy in some respects as they are winged. However, they act in the same way as people do. On the other hand, the Old Ones look just like people do, but do not act like us. Most of the stories insist that they feed on pain, and eat the souls of those who are sacrificed to them.

This is all sounding very familiar. We heard all of this from Skap on Neron. Some of the Hob stories even say that, in the end of all things, the Old Gods will even eat the souls of their worshippers to gain everything they want. One story, a tale supposedly told by a dying sacrifice, told of his soul being drunk by two golden orbs.

"I think that the Masters were servants of the Old Gods," she said.

Pạrlakmugạni nodded. "We thought the same, but they were too strong for us to resist, and the Eldest, who we used to worship, had given us no aid."

"I would not mention any of this to anyone. I would not even pass these stories on among your people again, until I tell you that it is safe. I have some questions to ask, but it may be dangerous bringing the subject up where it can be overheard until I have the answers. You will have to trust me on this, but what you have just said, if the wrong person heard you, could get you killed.

"Very few would have watched you before. If they did, it would not have mattered much when no people ever saw the Hobs, but now …" *To him these are just the stories of the past, ones that are no longer important now that his people are becoming Christian, so Pạrlakmugạni is a little puzzled, but at least he agrees to be silent on the matter.*

Rani (24th September)

I was right. Astrid was able to prevail upon the former Brotherhood slave girls to allow them to be tested as mages, that is, if prevail is the right word. To boot, she has them all treating it very seriously. I am not sure what Astrid said or did, but with her watching them like a mother supervising very young children, they are going through the testing as intently as any young Kshatya applying for the University ever did, although they keep looking at Astrid as they do so.

Yet, when they look at her, it is with a far more anxious look than even Kshatya applicants give to their parents, and they are all trying very hard to do what I want. It seems that, of the twenty-nine, eight show some degree of promise. It seems that I now have my second class of apprentices about to start.

It is an unexpectedly large number of successes, and once again I am left wondering what Haven is wasting among its people by holding so strongly to caste. These girls are all equivalent to being harijani and they would have been ignored and despised by the mages of my land, and they were to be killed out of hand in their old land...as if they had no value.

Olympias
25th September, the Feast Day of Saint Christopher

*T*he Feast Day of the patron of travellers, and also the saint whose *intervention is deemed to be efficacious against death from water, has been chosen as being the next suitable date for a wedding of a pair of sailors. I would have taken any day, but my sister is having none of that. It seems that having said yes, I have lost control of this side of my life.*

My sister says that we in the wedding party are dressed much as hers had been. It seems that the men and women are both fully clad in Freehold finery. I am nearly tripping over in the first real dress that I have owned since I was a child. At least she has a dress to wear already. She has not had to stand still while people pin things to her.

Denizkartal, with his crest of orange hair, was hard to change too much, but the slashed clothes that he wore showed off the breadth of his chest very well. Harnermêŝ was clad in leggings, and a puffed jerkin in dove-grey leather. Under it, he wore pale pink silk that set off his skin colour and had even the married women jostling for dances with him all night.

Jennifer

*M*y partner really is a very handsome man, as well as being rather vigor-*ous and long-lasting in bed. I can see how the other women are acting towards him. Could one of them lure him away? If he left me, I would be back to having an itch that would not be satisfied, wouldn't I?* She went to have a word with him, and then took him off by the hand to see Father Simeon.

"When they all come back from Darkreach, would you marry us, please?" *Simeon seems delighted with the idea that during the first marriage ceremony he has conducted, he is being asked to perform a second one.*

Chapter XVII

Theodora (30th September)

My husband decided that we are leaving for Darkreach tomorrow. Theodora Lígo's wedding to Candidas is set for the first of October and we want to be there for that. That date has allowed all the marriages and births to be put behind for a while and will, at the same time, leave a space of a few weeks before the next baby, Ayesha's, is due.

The date has also allowed me to finish the last of the new saddles that I wanted to complete for the moment. I want to have a try at repairing the Brotherhood devices, too. My lovely husband is nervous about that. She argued that the first enchantment nearly failed, and although the second time around is always easier, she does not want her pregnant wife, me, endangered.

I don't want to be hurt either, but I need to be firm. The first device has been worthwhile. This one will be also. "From what we saw, this will outrange the fire weapons on a dromond, and if we keep it as a surprise, combined with having the green-light box, the *River Dragon* will not have to even worry about that fearsome weapon," she told her husband.

This is the last thing that is to be worked on with magic before we leave. Again, Theodora looked at what they had gathered after Ariadne's explosive rocks had hit the chariots that these devices were on. *I think that I have the two sets of rubbish sorted into the right piles. The third, the one that Rani hit with her spell, is not damaged...it is a small pile of melted and charred junk. I think that there are even some bones fused into it.*

I am certain that, even if I had done this spell twenty times over, I would not be practiced enough to repair it. The other two are better off. They are both shattered, but I have chosen the most intact to do first. The second will have to wait until we return. These two are very similar to each other and each has some similarities to the insides of the green-light box.

Each of them has the same sort of box with wires as a part of the wreckage, although these two have thicker wires coming from the box and the box itself is bigger. They each have parts made of the smooth not-metal, including some of the green cards with metal lines on them and they each have the same sort of switch to turn them on. At least there is one part that I am sure of.

However, there are also many things that are different. These have a definite release trigger thing, just like a crossbow does. That will probably fire them. More importantly they have something like a wooden crossbow body that we will be able to mount on to the ballistae mounts on the River Dragon *just as they had been mounted on chariots. Galla and Norbert are already working on that.*

The crossbow-body part is split apart, and bent and twisted on both, but I am sure that this is what actually puts out the light that destroys.

One of the most interesting things, when we look closely, is that what looks to be almost the entire casing of both of them, apart from the wooden stock, is made of mithril. Who could afford to do that? Seeing that the stock and the post they are mounted on is made of oak, and they have mithril covers, I was certain that these were once a form of fire magic.

My feeling about this grew more certain as each has what Eleanor and Lakshmi are sure is at least one large ruby set into them, but no-one has been able to sense anything despite this use of correspondences. I wonder if it is possible to have a magic that works differently to the magic that I, and everyone else, uses. If it does though, why would it use the same correspondences? She sighed.

Neither of them is very large. In fact, these devices are a lot smaller, and far lighter than one of the repeating arbalests that Ariadne had returned with, even without counting the bolts that the repeaters are loaded with. Surely, to be as destructive as we know they are, that must mean that they use magic of some sort.

Again, the time came to cast the spell, and they went through the same preparations. *The way I worded it the first time, I need make no change to the enchantment, regardless of the nature of the device. This time at least, I am sure that the words, and the mental framework that I construct with them for the mana to flow through, work.*

She kissed her worried husband (who had Fear clutching her hand) and all of the priests in attendance (just in case) and went over to where the thing was, and began to chant the spell. *It is complete. I certainly felt more confident this time, and although it is just as draining channelling near twice my normal mana, this time I felt no uncertainty...there was no cusp that success teetered on.* She looked proudly at the compact device that was left in front of her after the casting.

Norbert has made an attachment to put it on the tripod that had first mounted the seeing part of the green-light box. It was very easy to do as it looked to be almost the same, if not the same, joint. It had been hard to tell exactly with the damage that had been done to it, but I am sure that he was right.

Ariadne

I watched it all...and I am impressed. Ariadne came over, picked up the light-thrower, and took it over to the tripod. *With a click and a few twists of knobs that are there waiting for me, the two objects are soon mated up as if they were made to do this by the same person, and this was a person who only knew one way to do things.*

The tripod had been lowered to make it come down to near her shoulder height, and Ariadne stood behind it and looked at the mages. "Do I try it?" she asked.

"Yes," said Rani, "but make sure that it is pointed to where it will not hurt anyone."

No, I am going to point it at my husband. Mages can lack common sense sometimes. Ariadne took up a position behind the light-thrower, and putting the bigger end of the wooden stock to her shoulder, where it seemed to be a proper fit, she did as she was told with the device pointed up the valley on the other side to the path.

I have seen how the green-light box works, and it has a switch just like this so I will start by pressing the switch on the side. Everyone may be holding their breath, but nothing is happening. She looked all over the machine. *There it is. That is what I want to see.* "A little green light has been lit on the left of the case."

Everyone rushed over to have a look. "I suppose that means that it is ready. Go away, and I will now see what happens if I push the switch the other way." She used her thumb to do that. *It looks like that is what is supposed to happen. It is in just the right position for a thumb to be used.*

"The light has gone out. I am pulling this trigger, and nothing is happening. I am pushing the switch...and the green light is blinking...now, it is on all the time and shining steadily. Now, I will pull the trigger."

A beam of light sprang out and hit the mountain to the left of the path. *It is the same sort of beam that the device had cast in the battle. It carves into the rock and starts a small landslide as it cuts away some of the support material.* Then, just as in the battle of One Tree Hill, the light went out. *It does not last long.*

"The light is blinking again…It started blinking when the beam went out… it is blinking for longer than last time…oh…I am still pulling the trigger…as soon as I stopped doing that, the light went steady…I am firing again." She did so with the same effect, only aiming right up the valley well out of the range of her ballista.

"It is not very accurate at that sort of range…maybe it takes a lot of practice… oh…" She leant over a bit, and looked along the length of the barrel, and pointed at what she had noticed there.

"See, here and here…you can line them up…I think that this is where it fires at…now…it is blinking again. I released the trigger this time when the beam stopped, and it has lit up quicker. I am turning it off now. I don't think that we need to do anything more. It works. Now, all we need is a dragon or a castle to test it on."

I like that idea. It cannot hit a saddle easily, as they are much too mobile and able to dodge, but it would work very well on a castle or anything that is fixed or that cannot move out of the way easily. She grinned in anticipation.

Chapter XVIII

Basil
31st September, the Feast Day of Saint Joseph of Aramathea

*O*nce again, we fly out from Mousehole towards Darkreach. This time *we are on the way to the wedding of our trader's daughter, Theodora Lígo, to Candidas, who is supposedly just an animal handler, but who is also working for the Antikataskopeía and assigned to us.*

Basil sighed. *From what I hear around me (and I have said nothing, and my wife tells me that she has not said anything) most of those going to the wedding seem to already know this. I am glad that my service is not this bad at keeping secrets inside Darkreach. At least our people seem not to care about his occupation. Indeed, some seem glad that we have such attention.*

Rani

*T*his time, for our second visit to Darkreach, a much larger party of *thirty-two are going. By leaving the far slower carpet behind, and only taking saddles with us, we are making a statement, not only to Darkreach, but also to anyone else who sees us. It is directed at any who look on the area with clairvoyance or another form of magical gaze.*

By taking so many people with us, we are advertising to them that the world has changed and is continuing to change. The stable but slow carpet, and the fast (but very unstable) broom of tradition are giving way to a new armada of the air that is far more suited to fast and mobile warfare that can strike and move away at will.

For those who have the wit to think ahead, it will be as if the Khitan are no longer constrained by the terrain on the borders of the plains, but now can operate anywhere they wish—over both land and water. She smiled. *Just wait and see how a battle will change even further if my wife and Ariadne can actually make the thing that Ariadne has excitedly described to us.*

The two women are debating what to put on a modified cart body and the design is nowhere near fixed yet. It might never even be made. They seem to be having too much fun making sketches and notes on a slate and then changing them again later. The Princess and the Insakharl make for an odd friendship, but they seem to have formed one out of a mutual love of new ideas and making new things. In one case it is out of magic, and in the other it is out of bits and pieces of mechanical things.

I am not even taking all the saddles with us. Two of the newly made ones have been left behind with the carpet for scouting, and to allow people to move between the valley and the ship...and for just flying around the area.

There are nine couples coming along: My wife and I, Christopher and Bianca, Astrid and Basil, Valeria and Nikephorus, Shilpa and Vishal, Olympias and Denizkartal, Bilqīs and Tariq, Ariadne and Krukurb, and Verily and Aziz.

Danelis, Sajāh and Hagar have all left their husbands behind, and are coming just to see the Imperial baby, while Lādi, the only one of the original women of Mousehole without a partner so far, is coming along partly to see the baby, but also to find out if she can have the same luck among the cooks that Valeria managed among the other servants.

Between us all there are a large number of children. Others are visibly pregnant. Some of those coming are there to be introduced to family; others are coming just to see their friend the Empress. In itself our lack of martial aspect is also a statement. It says, to any who care to look, that the Mice feel safe coming out of their valley without having to be equipped to fight all comers.

Ruth

I have brought along the five young girls from the school who are Mice. *It will be an adventure for Aelfgifu, Roxanna, Ruhayma, Gurinder, and Fear—and a good learning experience. It is about time they saw the world outside the valley and related it to what I am teaching them. They were all too young when they went in to remember much.*

For the first time, apart from training flights, the young girls of the village are being allowed to fly their own saddles instead of riding on the carpet. It is a skill that they will need as they get older. For the moment, they fly in the centre of the others, and the saddles are roped loosely to each other until Astrid is happy with how well they control them over a longer distance.

Apart from Fear, they have seen very little of the outside world since they had been brought in by the bandits. I have left my husband, Theodule, behind in charge of the other girls with strict instructions on their teaching for the week or so that we will be away, and I have language lessons for the girls while we are on the journey.

Astrid

*I*t is already chill when we set out. It gets even colder as we ascend. We are all glad that Rani has made enhanced cloaks to keep us warm with the same sort of speed her wife is making the saddles we are riding. If anyone incautiously flips their cloak back, or allows it to come open, the chill wind of our passage soon has them return to the enclosing warmth.

Without the carpet along to slow them down they were able to travel almost twice as fast as they had before, and Mouthguard was in sight well before it was time for lunch. Astrid went back to Rani and pointed west. "I notice that the people in Forest Watch have stopped lighting their beacons when we come out in numbers. I knew that it would be good to visit them. They see us now more than they see their own people…and they like their gifts. We should still stay high, however, so that we do not look like we are sneaking up on the fort."

Rani agreed, and with only minimal, and by now almost ritual, baiting of Mellitus from Astrid, they were given their entry papers and went on flying east up the Darkreach Gap. *I still manage to leave the man spluttering in my wake. It is his own fault that he is so easy to bait.*

Astrid (a little later)

*T*he chill winds of the lower slopes that we were flying above as we went north grow far colder once we head east and enter the long funnel of the gap. Freezing winds siphon down from the high peaks to the north and the south and spilled down into the Gap gathering speed as they tumble down its slopes. They came to the River's Head Inn before it was time for lunch.

Tokens of frost from the night before can be seen still lingering in sheltered spots out of the sun as we travel. Being on the end of the normal travel season, we have again descended on the Inn when it has a total lack of preparation for visitors. I suppose that normally the people there can see approaching travellers some way off and can predict roughly when they will be arriving. They cannot do this with us flyers.

"We will stretch our legs and freshen up, while you get some lunch ready." *You have to love Insakharl names. Our hotelier is Gorthang Taverner.* "We can wait. You will get used to us after a few more trips. This is the best time for us to travel as it is out of our campaign season." Astrid pointed at the five young girls hopping around and trying to make their legs work properly again.

"We need a break of an hour or so anyway. As you can see, the young ones are not yet used to being in the saddle for so long." Once again, they set up with the saddles in the main room of the inn and fed the littlest children with what they had packed while gradually drink and food started to arrive for the others.

Astrid (later in the afternoon)

They finally emerged from the chill of the Gap onto the Great Plain. *Now the wind blows from behind us, again tumbling out of the Gap, but this time headed east. It may start chill, but from here it will get hotter and hotter until we start to reach the environs of Ardlark and the ocean. It might officially be winter, but here winter seems to mean only that it is possible to work hard during the daylight hours without having the danger of falling over from the heat of the sun.*

It made for a short day, but they stayed overnight at Nameless Keep. *It is either that or keep flying until we reach Sasar, and no-one wants to overnight in the dust of that joyless town, even if it would have meant that we could have made Ardlark in one long flight the next day. There is little to do in this fortress town, although we have discovered that the baker, despite his young age, is excellent.*

Astrid tried to interest him in moving on with them, pointing out the beauty of some of the women in Mousehole as she did so, but she was unsure as to his reaction.

I really wouldn't mind if he moved. Zoë might be a good baker, but she is still learning. This man is excellent and can do much better pastries. However, he is unmoved by the idea of moving away from his comfort and safety. He is so unmoved by the idea of a possible beautiful bride and very good money that it might help explain why we have seen so very few, except for the damaged or those with no hopes, who come to us.

I suppose that, for most people, it takes something that is a lot more than a chance of a beautiful and rich bride to move away from their accustomed security, even with the prospect of perhaps gaining something very good being dangled in front of them. It seems that only a few are restless enough to want change.

Astrid (32nd September)

They left early the next day, and after a short stop at Deathguard Tower for a late lunch, they continued on to Dochra, where they intended to spend the night. *Even travelling during winter, the day has been hot and dry as we made the long flight across the plain. The greenery of the only large oasis on the Great Plain is a welcome sight.*

Ruth has spent the whole trip so far pointing out to the girls in her charge what it is that they are seeing. She speaks with such confidence about what is here that one would have thought that she has travelled this way many times before instead of having to rely on what she has read or has gleaned from the others.

I have let the young girls fly without a safety rope between them, but for the moment they must stay clustered around Ruth in a tight group. This lets her run through lessons for them as we go. That group flies along to the accompaniment of chanted-out practice recitation of Darkspeech words and the to and fro of stilted conversation in the same tongue.

They can get some formation practice later. In the meantime, I have the others all wheeling around in formation changes both for practice and to keep them awake. I rarely get the chance to make the mages take their places. They cannot avoid it here.

Basil

This little village on the edge of the salty lake ends up with all its beds spoken for tonight. *The people of a late arriving caravan of the Platys Dromos carrying ores from the mountains, even the caravan master, have to all sleep in the lesser, and more uncomfortable, of the two taverns in the village. Nothing is left spare in The Old Lobster. It is only right anyway. Theodora may think otherwise, but she is still an Imperial Princess.*

It is good to see that the garrison has no new information for me that will cause me to worry. I can have the night relaxing. I suppose that I get to play chess with the old shayk again.

As was rapidly becoming their practice, they entertained with the village that night. The musical Alat-kharl had already made himself a new dulcimer and seemed disappointed that he couldn't immediately sell it to Verily. She laughed and told him to make her a much better one, and once he had managed it, to send it on with Carausius on his next trip through to the valley.

For the rest of the night his playing is a little distracted. I am sure that he is trying to work out what he should do to improve his quality of work, working with timber in such a hot and dry place, and where he can get better timbers in the first place.

The Mice even left one of the small sausages made from the dragon that they had killed in the village to be tried. *No insult to our makers, but the smallgoods maker in Dochra makes some of best halal salami that that any of us have ever tasted but, good as he is, he has to admit that he has never had a try of a dragon sausage before.*

At least we can make more money here. Shilpa has had to promise to include some hot Gasparin on consignment as part of the load on the next trading trip to be delivered direct to him, rather than have it taken all the way into Ardlark, from where he will have to buy it back. I am sure that Carausius will not mind.

Chapter XIX

Astrid (33rd September)

It is only a short trip from here into Ardlark. The Mice took off straight over the saltiness of Nu-I Lake in the early morning light. *Its strange wading birds with their odd fat and curved beaks take off and fly low beneath us in a pink cloud. Even from up here you can hear their raucous cries as they are alarmed by the passage of our group rising and then flying over their heads.*

This time Astrid kept climbing, and flew them high enough above the road so that they could see both Jade Mountain far to their right and Metal Hill in the distance to their left. *Far below us, the way station villages on the road are only tiny dots. The only travellers that we can really pick out are large wagons, again as tiny dots, and we are finding it as hard to breathe as if we are on a high mountain. Why is that?*

They went so high up that, despite the growing heat at ground level, they were glad to wrap themselves once more in their warm cloaks. After allowing everyone to see the two very different mountains in the distance to the north and the south, Astrid brought them back down in a long sloping run towards the city.

Gradually, one-by-one as we descend, the cloaks are pushed back out of the way as we move down slowly into the growing warmth of the day. No more manoeuvres now. It is even far easier to breathe. Does that mean, if we go high enough, we will not be able to breathe? I need to ask someone about that.

Once again, they descended to fly along just above the head height of a rider as they approached the walls, and dropped down lower still when Astrid went up to the gate.

I was again prepared for a tussle with an officious guardsman, but I am to be disappointed in this. Not only is the guard ready for our arrival, but a servant is already waiting for us at the city gate to take us direct to an apartment in the Palace. Perhaps our reception when we arrived on our last visit was a test of some sort.

On arriving at the Palace balcony, they landed and settled in to refresh themselves, as they had been instructed to do.

There will not be an official audience until the next day, and servants appear to take charge of the littlest ones so that we can all relax after our travel and do as we want. If that meant we were supposed to just clean up and then sit in our rooms, then that expectation is never going to be met.

Except for Ruth, who first went in search of the Palace school with her charges, all the former slaves among the Mice have totally ignored the instruction to rest and have demanded to see the Empress right now. Word must have been left about this, as we have been quickly obliged in our demands, despite some shocked looks from the servants.

Ruth

*M**y charges and I stride through the corridors following our guide. I can see that we are causing no small sensation as we go. The mixed births of the girls, two from somewhere indeterminate in the west, in addition to one obvious Hindi girl, and two from the Caliphate, is very apparent from the way I have them dressed for this occasion. We must make an impression.*

Gurinder, who doesn't know any better, I have dressed as if she was born Kshatya. I saw that caused Rani to widen her eyes...but to say nothing...when she saw her. I am not sure that anyone here would know the differences, but someone must.

It is also evident that the staff of the Palace is not used to a small group of not-quite adults, but not quite children either, all armed as any Mouse would expect to be. The children only have small weapons about them, but they do wear several knives openly, as well as a shortsword each, and that almost counts as if it were a full sword for most of them.

Theodora made sure that I knew about Fear's previous experience, and I am not going to allow my students to take lightly any behaviour that I regard as untoward from Palace children. Before I go to see the Empress, I wanted to make sure that the girls are settled in and studying something that I approve of with a teacher that knows what they are talking about.

Olympias

*T*he others have dispersed around the Palace or the city to see the markets *or visit friends or family. It is very odd that my sister didn't want to come and visit our brother with me and watch me introduce Denizkartal as not only my Mate, but also as my mate. It is very unlike her not to extract the maximum amount of embarrassment from any situation.*

She insisted, however, that she had a few important things to do first in the Palace, and that she would come out to our brother's house when she could. She pointed out that Basil has already left on his business, and that she has hers, and we will all catch up later. What is she up to in the Palace? I don't trust her.

Theodora

*T*he others can disperse wherever they want. I am taking my husband to *see the Palace library. We need to start seriously looking at the maps there. There must be more that we can learn from them.*

We should be able to find much better ones of the Land, and indeed of Vhast itself, than I did the last time I was here. It will be so much easier now that I can actually ask the Librarian for help. I could not do that when I thought that I was trying to sneak un-noticed out of Darkreach.

Bianca

*C*hristopher is going to see the Metropolitan. I don't want to, but I suppose *that I should follow along. If I let him go on his own, he could get lost and not find his way back until the next day and miss the audience with this Emperor. I will see him installed with the Metropolitan, and then find something to do in the area, after I have given instructions to someone on his delivery back to me.*

Nikephorus

With a sigh, Nikephorus kissed his young wife as she left with the other former slaves and then headed off to visit friends around the Palace.

My family can wait until I have my wife with me, and for her, seeing them is a poor second to seeing the Empress' baby. Besides, I am quite sure that my family will completely agree with that.

I just need to show Tariq and Ariadne and the others how to get out of the building first. They are taking Vishal, Krukurb, and Aziz shopping in the largest city of The Land. I believe that they are all going straight to the street of the weaponsmiths. I need to go shopping, too, but not for that. We are running very low on cosmetics for my charges... and for my wife.

Chapter XX

Astrid
33rd September, after having taken her leave of Olympias

*F**irst things first.* Astrid went along with most of the women, and saw the new golden-eyed Imperial boy-child and his mother, and made sure that both were well and happy. *Theodora has a new uncle I suppose, and he is a lovely baby. Now, the others are all well-occupied, and I will not be missed by any of them.* She then quietly slipped out and returned to their suite.

Having made sure that Carausius was sent a message about their arrival and how many would be attending the wedding, and having set the servants to cleaning the saddles, there was something that Astrid felt that she had to do since she was here.

I don't really want to do it, but I know that I have to. If I put it off now, then I will never do it, and it will gnaw at me like a wolverine. Little things have been adding up in my head. You add one and one and you get two. You add another and you get three. You only must double that, and you have a full hand. Well, this full hand needs to be seen to…before it clenches and strikes me and my children.

None of the Mice are in the suite. *Basil is with his Strategos running over things, and the servants in the apartment will look after the children whether I am here or not.* There is no better time. She looked at her weapon, but reluctantly decided to leave it. Next, she considered and discarded the idea of leaving a note. *Neither will do much good if I have made a mistake in what I think.*

She then stood, and casting what might be a last look at Georgiou and Freya sleeping in their cots, she went out of the suite and into the main corridor. She simply accosted the first servant to come along. "Take me to Hrothnog's office." *The woman's eyes widen slightly at the unusual demand, but she is well trained and says nothing. She just inclines her head to acknowledge what I said, and then turns on her heel and heads off.*

Astrid

Astrid followed down the usual assortment of corridors. *It was a surprisingly short trip along a couple of corridors…down a set of stairs…back around and towards the sea again. In front of a pair of huge polished wooden doors the servant woman has halted and again bows her head. Without a single word she indicates the doors with her left hand.* Once that was done, she soundlessly brushed past Astrid and headed back the way that they had come without looking back. *She has neither offered comment nor asked anything of me during the whole trip.*

It is no use just staring at a brass handle. Astrid grasped the right hand one and pulled on it before slipping inside. She entered the room that Basil had described: *tall and square…thirty paces in each direction…a thick carpet on the floor and more carpets and tapestries on the cool white walls…three large glazed windows down one wall and a single, wide, and equally tall door at the other end of the room…there is the desk…the Islamic man with his cold expression, and the two messengers.*

Nervously, but trying not to show it, she went up to the man. *He looks blankly up at me.* She broke the silence that seemed to lie over everything like a thick blanket: "I want…" she faltered nervously, and then started again: "No…I need to see Hrothnog." Having spoken, she went silent and just looked down at the face in front of her.

A tiny flicker of emotion passes over the face of the man behind his beard and his professionally blank face. What I have just said is obviously something that he is not used to hearing. I guess that few people just wander in for a chat.

"The God-King does not see people who…just arrive," he said dismissively. "You have an appointment, or you are sent for, unless it is a matter of the highest priority…and you would not have that." *He is trying to emphasise his own importance…he is coolly inspecting me, as if I were an insect or something that clung to his shoe, before again looking down to his papers.*

Astrid smiled her sweetest smile. *One thing that I am sure of is the priority of what I have to say. I may not be sure about the reception that I will receive or of the answers, but I am absolutely certain of the priority.* "Are you sure about that?" *I hate to bring Basil into this visit, but it looks like I need to.*

"I am the Cat. You may remember me from our last visit. My husband is a special Tribune in the Antikataskopeía. You have no idea what I might have found out, and that I am unwilling to share with anyone else except him." Astrid nodded towards the door. *One thing that I need to try to do is look confident as I fold my arms.*

I must have succeeded in something, as the man in front of me suddenly looks a little shaken. I wonder what he thinks that I am here about. What has been happening here since our last visit? Abruptly he gestured, and the handsome seated youth came over and the official had a few words with him. *There must be magic used here. I am two paces away and I can hear nothing… and at that range I should hear every word.*

She interrupted the conversation to shocked looks from both: "Just tell him that the Cat has a few things that she needs to say privately to him, and some questions." The young man looked at the seated one who nodded, and the messenger went into the next room. *The seated man has not gone back to his work. He is just sitting and looking at me.*

Now the die is cast. Astrid took a few paces back, her toes in her soft hunting boots feeling the thickness of the huge rug covering the floor. She waited quietly, looking around at the tapestries covering the walls as she did so. *These are more than beautiful. They are works of art. I wonder how old they are.*

Astrid (several minutes later)

A head of her, the door opened, and Astrid found herself being ushered into Hrothnog's office without another word being said.

The desk, the chair, the window, and the low table and pair of chairs, are just as Basil said they are. On the low table is, from the rising smell, fresh kaf and sweet pastries. Behind me, I can hear the door softly closing and ahead of me, standing alone, is the Emperor dressed in purple and gold silks, a gold sash around his waist, purple boots, and with a jewelled collar around his neck like the one that Theodora uses.

One hand was extended to wave her towards a chair. "Come closer" she heard "Sit". Astrid suddenly felt terrified, and her knees were feeling weak. *His voice alone brings terror to any listener. I must speak up and say something before I freeze.*

She moved to sit by the window. "You can have me killed, or you can answer my questions…but this is something that I have to know…" She held up her hand. "I know that you can read it all in my mind, but it is all still unclear to me, and I need to know what I am asking so that the answers make sense when

I hear them. So, I want you to let me speak my questions out loud."

I am babbling instructions to an Emperor that most of the world fears, and who has probably not been given an instruction for very many cycles. She fell mute to collect her thoughts. *And that leaves a huge and overwhelming silence in the room. Hrothnog also stays unspeaking. Saint Kessog, my patron, please give me guidance in what I need to say.*

"When we have taken the Master's Patterns, we have often found these obsidian blades. They are made to prolong pain and agony while they withdraw the soul. I think perhaps for someone or something to feed on." She paused briefly. "When we took Skrice, we discovered that the Masters are not the end of our quest. There is something behind the Masters. Perhaps someone called the Old Gods or perhaps the Adversaries, although I cannot imagine that they call themselves that.

"There are six of them now, but when we destroyed the pattern on Gil-Gand, there were not six pyramids for them, there were seven." Again, she hesitated. "We now know a story about Zim Island, or perhaps it is really called Zim-Gand, and how something or someone that were called the Eldest and the Old Gods fell out, and how that falling out destroyed the city and left it twisted. If once there were seven and now there are six, that means there is one more. The bard that lives on Neron Island even had a name from their legends. He called him the Renegade."

"The Hobs have many old tales that others do not know, and their tales even give a name for the Renegade. They say that Hrąthnąrg…" Astrid pronounced the name as the Hob did, and with its drawn out 'a's, its harshness, and almost silent initial 'h', it sounded very little like 'Hrothnog' "…the most powerful of them all, rejected his race, took pity on the world and saved the Eldest, and indirectly the rest of us, from destruction.

"I would say that all of this is what happened when Zim-Gand was destroyed, but I have no proof, or stories about that. I will also say, in all honesty, that none apart from me, outside of Dhargev that is, know that name. Their legends do not name the other six. I can write them though, but we have found that naming them is a dangerous thing to do as it can start to summon them. Naming Hrąthnąrg, however, does not do this. So, unless the Renegade is dead, or otherwise no longer active in the same way…"

She stopped and sighed before continuing. "I do not know the exact arrangement between you and the Empress, nor do I wish to, I do know that you mean her no harm at all, as she is looking well and she is very happy…but remember that I know her special needs and you are looking…if you will pardon me saying it, both very well and quite young. You are looking far younger than when we were here last. Now you look almost the same age as the Empress."

She stopped for a short time while she nervously framed what she was about to say and finally the words came out all in a rush. *I know that there is almost a look of pleading on my face. I must ask, but I am not sure that I want the answer to be what I fear it is.* "Are you the seventh of the Old Gods? Are you the Renegade Hrąthnąrg, and if you are, then what do you want from us, and why haven't you stopped us, and what is it all about?"

For once, Astrid had completely run out of words and had nothing more to say. *I am without a quip or an idea of what to do next. All I can do is just nervously sit here and wait.* Unconsciously, she was playing with the edge of her jerkin.

I am so fucking nervous that I am close to tears. Have I just jeopardised the life of Basil and the children? Even of the village? Now that it is done, and the words are out, I am astounded at my own temerity in coming here to confront the dread Emperor with such questions. What is going to happen now?

At least it seems that it is now Hrothnog's turn to sit and consider what he is about to say. She felt a wave of relief. *He has done nothing to me, and this is a side of the feared Emperor that no-one ever sees. For once, he looks undecided and uncertain...I hesitate to think it, but he almost looks nervous.* Eventually, he spoke.

"In the reverse order to which you asked them," Hrothnog said slowly. "I cannot tell you what it is all about...all I can say is that I would if I could but one thing I am sure of is that you do not need to know the answers to act in the right way. You have done so up until now.

"I promise you that in time I will tell you everything when I can do so... although I admit I am also confident that you will have worked almost all of the answers out for yourself by then." *He even seems to smile a little at that.*

"I haven't stopped you," he continued, "because I approve of what you are doing...although I cannot help you any more without risking...but that is something that I cannot tell you now. Again, I will tell you when I can, but then you may already know the answer. Even I have limits placed upon me by circumstances." *He has limits? Is there someone more powerful than him?*

"As for what I want...I want you to do what you think you must do...I can do no more, and I can ask no more...and lastly, yes, you are right. I am the seventh, or more correctly, I was once the seventh. I was Hrąthnąrg of the Daveen, and when and why I stopped being him, and did what I did; well, I will tell you that when, or if, I can. It is all bound up together, and a part of the same answer. I am now not like the others are, and that is one reason why I am not him anymore.

"We argued...and I reached a decision. I went one way, and they went another...I cannot say more than that. Over time, we have gone down very different paths. We are now far further apart than we were then. The relationship between the Empress and I is as you have surmised. It is essential for me in more ways than one, but who I am now will do her no harm that she does not welcome."

They sat in silence as Astrid thought on what had been said for a little while. *I sort of have at least a part of the answer. Most likely it is all that I am going to get, and I am still alive.* She decided to continue. *There is more I need to know.*

"One more question," Astrid said. "Are these...Adversaries, or should I say Daveen, the last? If we get rid of them, are there any more enemies that we have to face, or can we have lives of our own? I have children now, and I have more on the way, and I am likely to become pregnant again, and have many more of them. Is this affair ever going to finish, or do I have to risk my life and then the lives of my children over and over, again and again?"

"That is one thing that I can tell you," said Hrothnog without hesitation. "If you conquer this set of foes, you should have no more to face like them. You will only have the normal and everyday evil to deal with that others face.

"Knowing you, I am sure you will keep finding other beings that you will combat, but never again will it be anything like them. It may only be a Kingdom you face on your own, or a dragon, or something like that. It will be just something little for you to keep your hand in. One thing that I will do is that I have arranged to get someone to train you in your new weapon while you are here."

He has just casually revealed that he keeps a watch on us. Hrothnog stopped, and smiled, and then passed his hand over the kaf where it sat cooling in its brass ibrik. It started steaming again as the froth rose briefly up its sides, and when it had settled again, Hrothnog poured some out into a small porcelain cup and handed it to Astrid, before pouring one out for himself.

The sheer normality of such a gesture, under such circumstances, from a being whom I have been brought up to fear and had almost lost my fear of, and now fear again...almost made me break into hysterical laughter.

She controlled her face, but it was obvious that Hrothnog had caught her thought, and he smiled. "You, along with my wife, of course, you two alone can stop fearing me. She has my love, and you, I treasure...you and your insight. However, I must ask that you tell no-one else what you have worked out. In particular, you must say nothing to my grand-daughter.

"There are others in the world who are as old as I am, or very nearly so, but you are the only creature in many millennia who has managed both to see inside me and my plots, and who has had the courage or temerity to ask me about them. I really do cherish you, and would do nothing to change or harm you."

Hrothnog changed his tone and indicated the table. "Now, finish this kaf and these excellent pieces of food. As you and your husband have thought before, I do have someone working nearby here in the Palace, who stands there all day preparing things and hoping that someone will use and appreciate what he does.

"He is far too often disappointed in this, and the food is sent away unwanted by me to the servants. It is nice to send him empty plates sometimes, so make him feel needed by eating these. I promise that I will tell you the rest of what you ask when I am able to.

"In the meantime, talk to me of normal things and simple pleasures. How is my Tribune whom I have lent you? Tell me about your children, and your little valley that I cannot see into, and what happens there from your point of view. I want you to tell me what you need."

To Astrid's surprise, they sat and chatted about such mundane matters for a goodly while and she actually enjoyed the rest of the visit that had started out so dire.

Despite the change in the outside light streaming through the window, it seemed like only a short while before it was time for her to go. *The food has been replaced once and is all eaten again, the cook will be pleased, and a quiet servant has refreshed the kaf several times...* As they moved towards the door, Hrothnog paused and then spoke:

"Please destroy my lost dromond, if you get the chance. They have hidden it from my gaze and protected it from my actions. I think it may be at another land at present, but that is all I can say for sure, and I know not even which one it is at." He stopped speaking for a moment as if judging what to say next.

"I am also asking you to tell the woman husband of my granddaughter that the spell she used against the Lamia, and extended for the Brotherhood machine, the one she used against the so-called Master, it needs to have a far, far, longer range and as much power as she can give it, even if it drains her totally and she can never cast again in her life.

"And if it is possible, she needs to practice it over and over, until she has it perfect. It is very likely that she may need it, or something like it, to bring everything you are working towards to an end. What I am sure is that what you have repaired may be useful for you, and more useful if you keep it hidden, as you have so far done, but it will not be enough."

It is now his turn to hold up a hand to forestall the many new questions that I suddenly have. What does he mean? The light-thrower, I presume. Is he giving a hint about what we will face? How do I convince Rani to make a more powerful spell?

"Moreover, you cannot tell her how you know that, or that I said it. I ask that you trust me on this, but I am confident that you will find a way." With that he ushered Astrid out of the door ahead of him, and then turned to the man at the desk. *He seems shocked to see Hrothnog himself opening the door:*

"Mūsã…as you know, this is Astrid the Cat. She…or anyone who comes to me in her name…has the same right to see me as the Strategos Panterius does." *The seated man, and even the two messengers look even more shocked than they did before. I could almost laugh at the expressions on their faces.* It did not take Astrid long to realise that this was a rare, perhaps even a unique, favour.

Hrothnog was about to turn and go. *I will take another chance. Let us add to the confusion of the situation.* She leant forward and gave Hrothnog a kiss on the cheek. "I will see you again for those answers that you promised to give to me," she said lightly. She quickly glanced around at the other three people in the room.

From the expression on their faces, their trained composure is now completely shattered. I wonder what the gossip will be in the messenger barracks tonight. Astrid then turned to the three of them and smiled.

"May your day be enjoyable and profitable." She turned on her heel and left the room without looking back. There was a grin on her face. She turned and closed the door behind her instead of letting it close itself. Astrid glanced back into the room. *Hrothnog has returned to his office and none of the people in the outer room have even moved yet.*

She spun around, and headed back to their rooms unconsciously singing a silly little song to herself about bells and returning safe and alive from Hell that, by custom, the Rangers of Wolfneck sang when they were returning from something dangerous.

I have all the servants I pass looking at me with strange expressions on their faces and moving away from me. Oh, I am singing that song. She smiled back at them, and as they moved away, she kept singing, only now she sang a little louder and more clearly enunciating the words so that they could hear more about the bells of hell.

A strid came into the suite, still singing to herself. *Basil is already back. She looked at the sky. I was away for a while, wasn't I?* She came out to where he sat on the balcony, reading a book placed on a table in front of him. *Beside him, and looking ignored, is another table with a tray of kaf and sweet things on it. He has a frown of concentration on his face as he looks at what lies before him. He has not even noticed my approach.*

"Interesting?" She bent over and gave him a kiss on top of the head.

He gave a start and then waved her to sit beside him in another chair. He took a sip of the kaf. *From the face he pulls it is cold.* "Very," said Basil. "It is a record of the interrogations of the agents of the Masters that were picked up both here, at Nameless, and in Antdrudge. They seem to have expected some of their people to be discovered and to have planned for it.

"Apart from a couple of other people, each of them knew very little about any others. My sister didn't mention it, but she discovered one of them when she was here who had been in place for years. The woman that she discovered didn't even know who she worked for, but absolutely everything that happened in the two ports of Ardlark was known to the Masters within a few days, and that official was very wealthy.

"All the woman did was to leave a message somewhere and come back the next day and money, and sometimes instructions, would be in the same place instead. The money varied depending on what she had told them. We picked up the ones she reported to as well, but not from what she said. We can go and see her if you want. She was sentenced to the arena, and is apparently still going, but she has only fought a few combats and has about forty bouts to go, so she probably will not survive for long.

"There is a bout on the thirty-sixth. I will be going. There are several people in combats because of what we have revealed about the Masters and their patterns. Olympias will be going when she knows about her woman. We consider it is right that you see your accuser before you die, if it is possible. It is considered to be polite on the part of the accuser...now, where have you been for so long?"

"I went to see Fatima and the baby." *Was I casual enough?*

"And ...?" asked Basil quickly and curiously. *Damn. He is used to reading such evasions from those who are trying to hide something, and I think that all I have done by attempting not to answer is to intrigue him.*

"He is a baby...not as good looking as ours are. There is no doubt as to who the father is. He has golden eyes and both he, and his mother, look to be both happy and healthy."

As if casually, he turns in his chair and looks behind us through the open door into the main room of the suite. He is enjoying this. "So, Puss, I notice that none of the others who went on that visit have returned ..." He turned back and relaxed. *He really is having fun with me.*

Basil picked up a pastry and nibbled at it, his eyes locked on his wife, with an eyebrow raised. *For once, he has found me being devious about something, and he is now getting a chance to watch me twist and turn in an attempt to keep things hidden from him. I am not very good at it.*

"And then I went for a walk."

"Which took you to ...?"

My attempts to tell only part of the truth are not of much avail. I should stop trying to dodge. Hrothnog only said what I cannot talk about. I should be able to at least tell Basil where I have been. I haven't been told to hide that much. "I went to see Hrothnog to get some questions answered."

Even Basil's usually well-trained face shows a tinge of surprise at what my answer was. "And that means …?"

"It means that he answered some questions and told me that he couldn't answer others yet. He asked me not to say much about what we talked about…I can say that we talked about you, and we have come to an agreement on our children. They get the choice of whether or not they want to follow you when they grow up, and if they decide to, they must come back here to be fully trained before they take over your job. They do not just inherit it."

"But that wasn't the main thing you discussed, was it?" Astrid shook her head. *I wish I could say more and ask his opinion…but I cannot.* "I suppose that if I offered to share this book with you that would not be enough for you to share with me, would it?" *Damn him for enjoying this.*

"I still cannot read it anyway. When we first met, you told me that there were things about yourself that you could not tell me. I now have things that I cannot tell you. Just trust me. I will tell you what was said if I decide that you need to know. Just be prepared to back me up if I propose anything to our Princesses…or if I am trying to head them off from asking certain questions.

"We started out with you not being able to tell me things about yourself, now the shoe is on the other foot. I have things that I have been asked to keep secret. The Emperor asked this of me. As a favour, you understand, not as an order.

"I think that I can say that a lot of my guesses have been right, and that your Emperor is no threat to us." She thought for a moment. "Yes, I can say that much…now stop probing…how about you put that book away and we go and see how your sister is getting on introducing her Boyuk-kharl to the rest of your family."

When they got there, the answer was apparently very well. *Both of Basil's nephews are already trying to make their hair stand up in a crest like Denizkartal's does. They are not very successful at this as their soft black hair lacks the texture of his orange crest, and I will bet that he didn't tell them about the aromatic wax that he uses and how he carefully rubs it through his hair each morning. I will also bet that his wife has not mentioned to them the way it looks every morning before he does this or what it does to his pillow.*

Chapter XXI

Astrid (34th September)

The next day, the Mice were to be formally taken to see the Emperor. Luckily, it would be a late afternoon audience. Astrid and Basil were the first to be woken early in the morning. A servant brought the news of the audience to them.

Much to my chagrin, I have never had a chance to learn the nonchalance towards such matters that the Princesses seem to have. I find that having a person waking me from beside where I sleep naked to be disconcerting in the extreme. Once the woman had recovered from nearly being throttled, she let Astrid know that it would be a formal audience, and that they would be expected to come in what she called "full regalia."

I think I am allowed to grumble at having been woken up. I don't see why anyone else should now sleep in. "In that case, you can have the rest of us stirred awake and brought out here. For God's sake though, get those that do it to be more cautious about how they do it than you were."

Grumbling people began to appear to eat, and to be told to wear uniforms or armour, and that it was to be a formal audience. *At least I can just tell the Princesses what I have been told, and leave it up to Theodora to get her husband ready.*

Obviously, this is to be a production, as she has grabbed Rani by the hand and immediately retired back into their rooms, without having eaten. She is calling for servants as she goes. After that, there is a continual stream in and out of those chambers, and instructions start to be passed to the others about what they should wear and how they should behave.

I am just going to ignore most of them. From their frequency, and the fact that some messages are coming out more than once, it is easy to see that Theodora is more than a little flustered by all of this. I have decided that, if we must go through all this fuss, then we are also going to make a statement.

Without consulting, or as she put it, 'worrying' the Princesses, she organised the others.

Astrid (some time later)

*I*t is too late for the Princesses to object and Theodora is hushing her *husband's attempts to do so.* Instead of them all walking, Astrid reviewed everyone as she got ready to fly along in the lead with her bardiche upright and resting on the small, cupped, shelf at the foot of the saddle, one that was meant for a lance.

Although it is far smaller in relation to the body for the larger Insak-div that it was meant for, for me it is near as tall as my long hunting spear was. Behind me, the others line up as I want them to. Most of them will also be flying as we go through the corridors.

Firstly, directly behind me, I have Vishal. He is dressed as in the old days in pyjamas, worn as usual without a shirt but now his pyjamas are made of silk instead of cotton, and with his long bamboo bow slung over his naked back alongside a quiver of arrows. He wears golden torcs on his arms, and carries his two-handed sword slanted across his back the other way to the bow. His well-muscled body and long bound-back hair are oiled in the fashion of his people with scented oils.

Something long was wrapped up and attached to his saddle.

Behind him fly the two Hobs, painted for peace and discussion, not that anyone will know that. Next, the only ones who are actually walking, we have the Princesses' party. Behind the Princesses, walk Valeria and Nikephorus, and then Christopher and Bianca. In a splendid blend of cultures, Nikephorus holds a huge silk umbrella over the heads of the two women in front of him while Valeria carries a small box. Where did that come from?

Where they found a Havenite umbrella of rank, I don't know, but it works well. I wonder if it has the symbols of the right status on it. Mind you, I wouldn't know, and it would be unlikely that any apart from Rani will have a clue if it is wrong. The two are both dressed as high Darkreach servants, but with a Mouse embroidered on the chest of their robes over the heart. That must have been quickly added to clothes obtained here.

Despite the umbrella, the Princesses are both dressed in Darkreach court finery with circular crowns covered in gems. Theodora must have had things brought from her old room, and somehow gotten the servants to make something for Rani, or else modify something that had been made for her so that it would fit her taller partner. They are clad in dresses, one of gold cloth and the other of heavy red silk, both had so much embroidery and jewels on them that they were almost stiff.

They walked with one hand held above their waists, palm down and horizontal, with Theodora's placed on the bottom and Rani's on top.

Christopher and Bianca are in formal ecclesiastic wear. After them come the schoolgirls, dressed as alike as possible, fully armed, and following behind Ruth. Fear flies in the lead, and then the others come behind in pairs. Each carries a recurve bow and a quiver on their saddles, the servants did a good job on them, and they wear their blades.

After the girls are the two sailors, Olympias and Denizkartal, in their Darkreach uniforms, but flying on saddles. The rest of the Mice bring up the rear. They are armed either with a close combat weapon or a recurve bow, as they prefer. Their armour has also been cleaned and polished by the servants. They fly along in pairs.

In this procession, and following a servant, they flew and walked, armed and armoured, through the vast halls towards a grand reception hall. As the Mice passed down the corridors, all the servants that they passed stood back against the walls to allow them passage.

*W*e *go down two sets of stairs and then along a corridor. It is much further than I travelled the previous day. The second set of stairs went down, and turned back on itself twice before reaching the level of the corridor we want. Our servant kept turning around to see if I was going to run her down as we descended.*

She looked around when they were again level. *The corridors are much larger on this floor than any we have seen before. It is as if large groups, such as this one or larger, are expected to travel along them regularly. A Brotherhood four-horse chariot would have had ample room to travel along them and it could even turn the corners easily.*

The walls of the passage are covered with lush carpets. Light comes from crystals hanging from the tall and imposing ceilings, fifteen ells or more high. The floor underfoot is bare stone.. marble or something similar. Basil is right. It is meant to echo under hob-nailed boots. They glided around a corner, and ahead of them by a hundred paces or more, Astrid could see groups of people hurrying through a large set of open doors.

The servant who was leading them slowed down so that they were only just moving ahead. *They are obviously waiting until all the people ahead of us have entered the room. Looking ahead, it is easy to see that the servants at the door have seen us approach and are trying to hurry the people at the end of the crowd through the doors.*

Astrid grinned. *So, this is what formal means. No wonder Theodora was in so much of a fuss. I guess it was too much to hope for a quiet audience with just the Emperor and us. It is just as well that I had a chance to have my chat yesterday. It would not be happening today.*

All the people are now inside, and the doors are being closed, but still our guide walks slowly. She realised why when, as they approached the doors, she heard a roaring noise from inside the room. *That must be Hrothnog arriving. I wonder how many people are in there, to make that much noise through the stone walls and the thick doors.* She thought hard as she hovered in place.

If he is doing this, he expects me to manage my end of it on my own...or it is a test. What does he want me to do? I guess that we will have to wait and see what is revealed inside. She turned to the rest of the Mice. "Follow what I do...and watch my hands".

The doors were flung open, and a silence filled the room. The servant stood aside. *It is time to enter.* Astrid tried to look confident as she saw the number of people standing inside and looking at the doors. She gestured to Vishal to stop, hoping that he picked up her hand signal, and glided forward into the room trying to look around without seeming to.

I can hear a gasp, as people see that I am entering fully armed, and I am not walking. Now a murmur as the news spreads to those who cannot see. Perhaps I should rise a little.

An awful lot of the people here have golden eyes. I guess that they have been brought along to the audience in order to be shaken up a little. Theodora had said she had lots of relations, and it seems she has not exaggerated. The wide corridor that I fly down has a row of soldiers, spaced well apart, down each side. They are there for decoration, not for battle.

Those on the left are Isci-kharl. Those on the right are Humans. Both sides carry a sword and a large shield, but slight differences in armour and tassels and flashes from one side to the other show that they are of two different units, at least four patrols from each. Ahead, I can see two people on huge thrones on a dais of about six steps high, enough to make the people seated there visible to all of those in front.

The thrones appear to be made of stone, but there is so much gold and gems worked into them that even a Dwarf would not be sure from here. Although it is a different shape, more like a quarter of a circle, the room is nearly as big as the vast hall in the centre of Dwarvenholme. Looking up and around, while still trying to keep her head still, she could see ranks of balconies, with more people on them, going up the walls.

The very top balcony, the smallest, one that is probably only a walkway, has a spread-out group of soldiers standing to attention around it. I presume it is the same behind me, but I am not going to look back. She flew alone towards the front with the saddle at around eye level and grinned inside herself. *This will shock them. They can all see me...and just me.*

She eventually reached the clear space at the front. *To the right are a block of two patrols of Insak-div. Each has the same sort of weapon that I carry, and although their bodies make no move, I can see the eyes of several of them are looking at me and at my weapon. To the left is a block of at least four times as many Kichic-kharl taking up the same amount of space.* She brought herself to a halt to the right of the corridor.

Astrid brought the loud talker up, but not right up to her lips. *It is good that I have done some playing around and have finally learnt how to control the volume on the device. It all depends on how far it is from your lips when you speak.*

"Your Imperial Majesties..." *My voice echoes around the room and out of the corner of my eye I can see startled looks on the faces of many of the ones at the front.* "I bring you the greetings of the proud and independent village of Mousehole, and present to you our beloved Princesses, Rani and Theodora."

She went silent and motioned with one hand. *I didn't organise this, but Vishal is proving quick on the uptake. It could have been awkward.* He led the Mice in. Once he was nearly down to where she waited, her left hand began to make signals. *I need to attempt to use the hand motions I use when we are aloft in a subtle fashion. Luckily, most people have turned to watch the entry of our people. They no longer look at me. The hand signals must have worked.* Vishal stopped on the other side of the entrance from her.

The Hobs split and one went left and the other came right. The Princesses and those on foot went straight ahead, and the others began to split up. Ruth led the little girls to the right and Olympias and Denizkartal went left and the two files behind them split. *Good.* Once they were all past, she nodded to Vishal and gestured, and they closed to hover behind the Princesses.

Hrothnog has made a small nod at me that would be unlikely to be noticed, even by the first rank of the audience behind me. I think that we did good.

Only then did she notice Mūsā. He stepped forward and spoke. "Their Imperial Majesties welcome the visitors from the village of Mousehole." *His words came out near as loud as mine did. There must be an enchantment in place to affect that.*

"They are pleased to see those who have found Dwarvenholme, destroyed the great dragon of the South, and removed that noxious nest of evil that called themselves the Brotherhood from this Land. They wish you felicitation and good fortune on completing the rest of your destiny on behalf of all of those with sense." He looked in Vishal's direction. "You have a presentation."

I mentioned this to Hrothnog yesterday. Astrid nodded and brought her saddle down and walked over to Vishal. *This will be a surprise to the Princesses. I have never actually told them what Thord and I had found concealed in Greatkin and they have probably forgotten about it.* Vishal handed her the contents of the bundle. *It is obviously a two-handed sword.*

With her blade in one hand and the sword in the other, she moved around the Princesses and towards the front. She climbed up the stairs, and noticed that there was enough space up front that anyone standing or even kneeling up there would also be seen by the room. *With both hands occupied I will have to rely on my own lungs.* Astrid half turned at the head of the steps to address the crowd. *It looks even larger from up here. I will bet that the spell that covered Mūsā will cover me when I speak. That is how I would build it.* It did.

"The forces of the North and of the Khitan, united and fighting under the direction of the Princesses of Mousehole, recovered this from the ruins of the Brotherhood in a secret chamber under their head temple. Our bards told us that it belonged here, and so their Highnesses deliver it back to the Emperor."

Out of the corner of my eye, I can see that Rani is bursting to say something, and Theodora is looking up at her, and tugging at her arm, shaking her head.

"From the writing on the blade, it appears to be His Imperial Majesty's blade that is called Doom of Nations, of which tales are told. It was lost at Nameless at the end of the last Age and is now being restored by us to you at what may be the end of this one. Let the return of this blade to its rightful owner symbolise the turning of a full circle and a completion."

She moved further forward and closer, and Hrothnog stood and took the weapon from her hands. He drew the blade, discarding the sheath to a servant, and holding the massive weapon aloft with two hands by its hilt, which was itself nearly an ell long. *Seeing that the weapon is longer by several hands than I am tall, it is an impressive sight. I hope that he is careful with it if the legends are right.* Behind her, Astrid could hear a collective intake of breath. She made a nod, and returned down the steps to her saddle.

"We thank our daughters for this welcome gift." *Hrothnog's voice seems to scarce need the amplification of the magic as its deep tones echo through the huge chamber.*

"Only once in this Age have I sensed its presence. When I was able to reach where it had appeared, there was just a scene of recent battle and it had disappeared again. The magic of hiding and concealment has become more and more widespread across the Land," he said ruefully. He sat down again, handing the blade to a servant, and looked at the Princesses.

Theodora is thinking more quickly than Rani, and spoke up next as Astrid took a place near the edge of the platform. "We have also brought a gift for our Ambassador, the Empress, as a token of the affection of our people for Her." *Damn. I should have passed her the Speaker. Only a few will hear her.* She waved behind her, and Valeria came forward and climbed the steps to kneel in front of Fatima.

She presented the box with both of her hands as she bowed her head. Fatima took the box, and placing it on her lap, opened it. She let out a cry of happiness, and picked out something with a huge smile on her face. *I guess this is what Eleanor had been working on in secret.* A servant appeared and started to help her put it around her neck.

For the benefit of those who could not see what the item was, in other words almost everyone present in the room, Mūsã made an announcement. "The Empress has been presented with a very large carved and mounted garnet ..." he stopped as he could see Theodora was shaking her head at him, and his eyes widened.

He paused, and then, still looking at her to see if he was right this time, he continued as a tone of awe entered his voice, "I am sorry...a carved and mounted dark ruby...a ruby near a hand across...in the shape of a mouse." *Theodora is nodding. It is good to have the supply of them in our valley.*

Attendants moved aside, and two more thrones were brought forward to the left of the Imperial couple. *They are nearly the same size as the first two but made of timber, and not as elaborately carved and embellished. From the murmurs that I can hear rising behind me, I guess that few have ever been invited to not only sit in the Imperial presence in such a gathering, but also at nearly the same level.*

Again, we are being used to shake them up. Hrothnog spoke again. "We invite our daughters," *there is a slight stress placed on that word,* "to take a place beside us." He motioned with his hand and Rani and Theodora, again with their hands horizontal climbed up the stairs. *They are followed by Nikephorus and Valeria. He had to tug at her sleeve to get her to follow. Finally, Christopher and Bianca go up, even if I must prompt them with a jerk of the head.*

Once they were seated, Hrothnog looked over the throng. "There is little that I can give my daughters that they lack. As can be seen by their gifts, the wealth of their small village is already beyond that of most of the nations beyond the mountains. Their valley produces most of what they need, and as these, their mounts, show so well, they are more capable of making useful enchantments than any I have seen, apart from myself."

"Besides, as they have already made clear to me, their independence is important to them and to their position in the world." He paused and looked along the row of Mice below. "Each of you has a gift waiting in your rooms, but these are trivial and not worth showing here." He held his hand out and someone behind the thrones placed something in it.

He held it up. *Those of us who are close can see that it is a small statue of a horse. Our Khitan will be pleased. It is made of gold, and it has emerald eyes. Somehow though, I do not think that it is just a piece of art.*

"The Empress and I have thought hard about a suitable gift for the whole valley. This is it. It is up to the Mice to keep this statue safe, but while it exists, wherever they may be in the world, they will find that luck will always favour them just a little bit more than it does others."

He stopped and the statue was handed over. *I suppose that the mages among the crowd are starting to work out for themselves how much mana might be needed to construct such an item. That would cause the murmuring, the series of audible intakes of breath, and the soft cries of astonishment. I guess that the answer is many lots.*

"We want you all, and any others to whom this news may come, to know that the people of this little valley have been of great aid to the Realm and to Us, and that they have Our full support and encouragement should they need it and want it, whatever they choose to do. If, while they are in Our realm, they happen to ask for your co-operation then, whatever your station or rank and whatever theirs may be, you are to treat their request as if it comes from Us." He looked significantly out over the crowd and then nodded at Mūsā.

"Their Imperial Majesties will consult with their Highnesses privately," he said. "This audience is ended. Good fortune to Their Imperial Majesties. Good health and long life to Their Highnesses." Hrothnog and Fatima stood, and Astrid heard a rustle behind her as Theodora and Rani also rose and fell in behind them. *The whole chamber, except for the soldiers, is kneeling. The soldiers are saluting.*

I think that the Mice are soldiers. It is hard to quickly kneel when you are seated on a saddle. She saluted as she used an urgent whisper to alert the other Mice. Eventually all, even the little girls, copied her gesture of a fist over the heart that she had seen her husband do. She moved around and climbed back onto her mount, and once the dais was cleared, Astrid rose and wheeled her saddle around. "Follow me." *The noise of the crowd is increasing. The soldiers are still holding the corridor open.* Astrid led the Mice out through the crowd, out of the door above the heads of the servants there, and into the corridor. *Our servant is already waiting to take us back to our rooms.* Astrid brought the saddle down to her. "Hop onto my lap." *The girl looks astonished. It will be fine. She is only tiny.* "It will be much quicker."

Chapter XXII

Astrid

Now we are back to the suite, we are all discovering that there are people waiting for us and that there are gifts of various sorts tailored to the recipient according to what I talked about with Hrothnog yesterday. In our reception room, on tables, are many items with names written on them.

Ruth found a large book entitled *On Understanding the Secrets of Design and Construction* with a note that this was a magical tome. *It is one of those items that will only need to be read once for her to have all the knowledge that it contains. I just said that she needed to know more to finish our Basilica. I am told that, as with all such works, it will be spent once it is read.*

On another table, also with her name on it, is the main gift for the children and others back in Mousehole. It is a box containing many small identical volumes of the same type, all of them on how to speak and write Darkspeech. It seems that we will now be able to concentrate on learning other tongues as there are more than enough copies in the box to make sure that anyone who doesn't have that language will now be able to have it.

Many of the others are already talking to people who are waiting to measure them for new sets of armour, others have new bows. There really are gifts for everyone. They are often based on what I said the previous day, but sometimes they just prove that Hrothnog keeps an eye on us and has worked it out for himself. Ariadne has, not only someone measuring her, but also a book similar to Ruth's simply called On Sieges.

She didn't wait to get home to read it, but as soon as she had been measured, disappeared. *Hrothnog may have called the gifts trivial, but to most people they would be regarded as very lavish indeed.*

I have an idea what is about to happen with me. She kissed her husband goodbye with a vague comment about 'going to have a look at something.' *I am being asked to follow a servant.* When she arrived, it was in a large room somewhere in the Palace. *I have turned so many times getting there that I am completely lost. It is far easier to get lost in a building than in the forest.*

It is obviously a practice room for weapons training, and there is a huge Insak-div waiting for me there. He started by making her tell how she came by her new weapons, and grunted in approval when she had finished. *He obviously does not approve of traitors. He has a padded wooden practice bardiche for each of us. I have a feeling that I will soon be glad that it is not him that I faced in serious combat when I gained my weapons.*

"You only got short time, me told. Me, Sergeant Rhaldraht. Me must teach much in few days. Me good teacher. You learn." *He makes that sound as much of a threat as a promise.* "Other things here to help. You work here all time when not busy," he said. "We not need sleep." He pointed at a shelf covered with bottles of different sorts. *I hope I don't get addicted. I am willing to bet that at least one of them will be a Sleepwell potion. I wonder what the others do.*

He indicated some servants standing there. *We even have servants.* They first sat her down and gave her a small book that she quickly looked at and ended up reading while people handed her things to eat and drink. It would have only taken an hour, but by the time she looked up again, she realised that she could now read the labels on the bottles on the shelf. *It seems that I can now read the new form of Darkspeech.*

The servants quickly helped her undress and change into sturdy practice clothes, and then handed her a padded helmet, and a padded vest that covered and held her breasts. She had another drink, and then the Sergeant proceeded to put her through a very intensive session that lasted all night with brief pauses to eat, and even more frequently, drink.

The drinking includes curative potions to remove the remarkable number of bruises, strains, and sprains that I am accumulating as we go. Those potions, by the taste, are nearly the only things that I can identify. So much for some relaxing time off. She picked herself up with a grimace from a particularly hard fall against a carpeted and seemingly padded wall and reached for a drink that a servant was handing her.

I hope that someone tells Basil where I am, and I hope that my baby will be kept safe through all of this. At this rate, it will be born knowing how to use one of these things. I think that I have at least another day of this.

At least my instructor is being quite solicitous of my pregnancy, and although he hits me in the stomach, they are comparatively light taps, and no hard blows land on that area of my body. He makes up for that by thumping my head, shoulders, and limbs all the harder.

When she stopped to eat in one of the chairs, she had another one of those magical books to read, and then, when she returned to her classes, her brain knew some new techniques to try. *I wonder just how much this forced method of learning will leave me with. If it works, why doesn't everyone do it? Is it that expensive? Ouch!… Pay attention.* It turned out that her only break from learning was when she was in the attached garderobe using its facilities.

Chapter XXIII

Basil (35th September)

A strid is tied up in what I have been told is some 'beneficial training.'
*Knowing my wife, that phrase worries me more than a trifle. I have
been trying to find out more about what she is doing, but it is proving to be
impossible.*

*Mind you, it is quite likely that the people I am asking have no idea where
she is and what she is doing themselves. I am not going to simply charge off and
ask the Emperor where my wife is. At least she is well aware of her pregnancy,
and so she will not be likely to do anything too active that might injure the baby.*

*I was hoping to show the games to Astrid, but that does not seem to be
possible now and it will have to wait for another visit. I will go with my sister
instead. I hope that we have good seats for the event. You can see very little
from the top rows unaided, and many people, even those who have lower seats,
bring some sort of vision enhancement with them.*

*There are even mages who make their whole living from selling such items.
At least I don't have to organise tickets myself for once. It is a nice change to
just let it be known to the servants that we want to go, and then let the Palace
staff organise the whole thing.*

*I let others know also, and in this fine and clear weather, it seems that
most of our people will be there. Ruth is even making sure the girls go. She
has apparently had a special lesson to make them think about crime and
punishment...and how it works in other lands.*

*In Mousehole, so far, we have only ever had capital crimes, and punishment
is invariably swift, and to be honest, fairly brutal. One day, we will find that
we have more trivial crimes and we have no framework to deal with them.*

*While we wait, she is still talking of how the system in Darkreach is bloody,
but a much more merciful system as it allows the possibility of redemption. She*

is running over systems of kaffāra, or blood money, and of outlawry, of a geas, and of imprisonment or slavery. As long as they understand that here it is not just the arena and possible death. There is also working for the community for minor crimes and enslavement for the most venal.

When they get home, I am sure that they will be getting all of the other children in the school to talk about the systems that are used in their own villages. It is good learning for children to have, who I am sure, will go on to become leaders in their own homes.

As we gather to go, it seems that the Princesses and Astrid will be the only ones to miss out. I wonder where the Princesses are, but here they are not my problem. Others of the Antikataskopeía have that task while we are in Ardlark, and a whole temporary small kentarkhion apparently exists just for us. I saw my old Praetor hovering around the other day near the rear of the crowd at the audience.

Upon leaving their suite to walk to the arena, they are confronted with a train of sedan chairs. *It seems that walking any distance is considered to be beneath us. I am starting to really worry about what seats we are going to get, not in terms of how distant from the front they are, but more in terms of how close.*

Upon them arriving at the arena, they are whisked inside via the private entrances straight into one of the special areas. *I didn't even have to look out to know which seats we were headed to. It was obvious once our porters only brought us up a short ramp from the private entrance before stopping to unload us.*

With servants holding a door open and ushering them inside, they entered one of the areas along the front of the stands, only a few paces above the ground. *We are placed in an area that is reserved for the specially favoured. It is one of those boxes that are usually left empty when there are none present who are deemed suitable in rank or favour to sit here.*

He looked around and up. *As far as I can work out, we are directly below the Imperial box at the lowest level. We have the most favoured seats in the whole arena. We are just high enough that, barring accidents, we are safe from the action; however, we will be able to clearly see everything from our seats.*

Looking around in the box that we are in, I can see comfortable chairs, rather than benches. Servants stand to the rear with tables of food and drink in case anyone wants anything. The schoolgirls are already being handed bowls of flavoured milk sorbets and sharbats. They are all giggling and having a great time.

I wonder who the officiating nobles will be, and if the Emperor will be attending. A flourish from the trumpets of the Bucinators and a roar from the crowd are announcing someone's arrival. It is impossible to see from here, but from the volume, it must be the Emperor. Ironically, the most favoured position in the stands has the worst view of the Imperial box. It is impossible to see through the awning that is placed above us to provide shade from the sun. The announcer let everyone know that he was correct, and that the Princesses were also in attendance.

The ceremonies began with those fighting their last bouts announced. Today, there was only one man, a merchant sentenced to five bouts for repeated short weighting of his goods. No special activities were scheduled.

The first bout is called. "That woman is mine," said Olympias, as the woman's name and her crime were called out. She stood and moved to the front of the box. When she was standing there, the announcer let everyone know that the accuser was present and there was applause from the crowd.

Below her, the woman looked up at Olympias, and then spat onto the ground. *Except for the fact that, unless something unusual happens, only one of them will be leaving the arena alive, it could almost be thought that she and her female opponent are there as comedy. Both wear just a loincloth and a headscarf and it is not a flattering look for either of them.*

The former ploi̱gós wears blue, and the other woman, a long-time thief who was finally caught, wears red, and they are each armed with one of the bardiche that Astrid has, only scaled down to be used by a normal-sized human. It is still a large and heavy weapon for both of them, and it is obvious that neither of the women has any idea how to use one, apart from what they may have incidentally seen in the arena. At least that makes it even. Neither knows their weapon. Everyone is waiting tensely.

"Begin." Theodora's voice echoed through the arena. The two women looked at each other cautiously. They took their weapons in hand and began to close, and then circle each other out of range of the other's weapon. This went on for some time and loud cries started to come from the stands.

"Teacher, what happens if they will not fight?" Gemma asked Ruth.

"Basil?" Ruth asked in return, passing the question on to where he sat.

"Lots of things could happen. Sometimes they are just both killed by archers, but this time I would say that they will both probably be taken out, and then brought back later unarmed or more likely given just a knife, and let loose with a fast and hungry animal to chase them and eat them. That sometimes happens, but when it does, it is usually not needed to be done again for a very long time."

The thief looked up at the jeering stands, and seemed to realise the danger she was in. Suddenly, she stopped circling and charged, swinging wildly as she ran forward. The ploi_gós countered with a wild swing that seemed to be an attempt to block the blow. Both missed their opponent, and the ploi_gós turned around in a circle and nearly fell over, as the thief kept going straight ahead.

From the jeering that had started at their inaction, the arena now erupted in laughter. Again, the thief came back. This time she was walking and swinging her blade back and forth, as if she were cutting long grass ahead of her. The ploi_gós had no difficulty blocking that, and both women ended up glaring at each other with the blades locked together as they pushed and shoved. The ploi_gós brought her foot down on that of the thief, but seeing that both were barefoot it had no real effect.

How humiliating it would be for the loser to die showing so little skill or nous, and to be laughed at while doing so.

They broke apart, and then they started trying to use the weapons as spears. *It is an improvement, but their parries are so poor that the only reason neither succeeds is that the thrusts are worse. They have their blades locked together, and they have to stop, and push and shove, as they disentangle them.*

The crowd are laughing almost continuously now. They backed up. Again, they swung hard at each other, missing as they did so. This time, the thief recovered quicker and brought her blade up backwards, and the point scored a shallow line across the body of the ploi_gós. It was not a serious wound, but it immediately started to bleed profusely. The woman shrieked in pain and fear and began to swing her blade wildly.

She is swinging so hard and quickly it seems the thief will be overwhelmed. She is forced onto the defence, and has no chance to attack. All she can do is defend and back up around the arena. It is fortunate for her it is a very large arena. However, the blows are very wild. One miss left…the ploi_gós again spinning around in a circle, following the mass of her weapon.

This time, the thief is quick to seize the opportunity, and she leaps in and thrusts hard. She still nearly missed, but there is a scream, and the ploi_gós has dropped her weapon and fallen onto the ground. She lay writhing and crying for mercy. She clutches at the gaping stomach wound she has been dealt.

It is not necessarily a fatal wound, even if it would be very painful. She could probably still fight on without much difficulty. The thief is giving her no chance to realise this. Without even looking up for instructions from the box, she stepped up, and holding the blade in two hands as if it were an axe, quickly brought it down and chopped deep into the ploi_gós's body as she groped beside her to try and find her weapon.

Still screaming and crying, she only then tried to scrabble clear of another blow, to where she now realised she dropped her weapon. The thief again raises her weapon and steps quickly after her opponent, ending the woman's suffering as she brings it down on her head.

It was only then that the thief looks up, and obviously exhausted, after making a sketchy salute to the Imperial box begins trudging back to where she entered the field, dragging her weapon behind her in the sand. She now has only one more bout to survive before being freed.

Attendants come out and remove the body of the ploi_gós. Olympias turned from where she had stayed standing and said to the girls.

"That was brutal, but in Mousehole we would have just killed her. Here, she had a chance to confess her sins to God first, and then had a chance to earn redemption for her body, and although I could not bet on her fate, others did, and we all got to see justice happen. Seeing justice happen in front of you like that makes you less likely to be a thief or a traitor. I am sure that the other woman who won is already contemplating what to do in her new life, if she survives her next fight."

The rest of the day varied. Interspersed through the rest of the program were several private bouts, as people fought to first blood to show their skill to themselves and their friends, or on a bet, or once, over a grievance with someone. There was even a training battle between two double-patrols of Isci-kharl armed with wooden weapons.

That is a lot of fun for everyone, both those on the ground and those in the stands. As usual, some of the combatants do not want to take their blows, and referees have to step in a few times. The crowd love it.

Even with the cane weapons that they use, there are several broken bones, and the attendants have to carry several of the combatants out to be cured. Those who are still walking as they leave are heartily cheered as they wave to the spectators. That was good entertainment for people who know their weapons.

The merchant won his bout, and is presented with his certificate of pardon. He bowed to the Emperor, and then all quarters of the crowd, and loudly vowed that they would not see him again except as an honest merchant. There was a bout where one of the naked Deodanth creatures that Ayesha had faced when she had first set out was pitted against a man, a murderer, who quickly showed that he was a skilled swordsman.

Ayesha has always said that she was lucky to beat the two she had met. She was. The snarling creature, a male, has simply demolished his opponent. He has to be stunned with a wand to be taken out after his victory, when he tried to start eating his victim as he lay there dying and screaming.

There is even an animal bout as four black wolves, the same sort of beast that Astrid and Christopher met, faced four Kichic-kharl who had been involved in a rape together.

Despite co-operating, and having both martobulli and spears, and being fleet of foot, the Kichic-kharl died together. *Only one of the wolves died, although once the other three had been forced to sleep by another wand, they will all have to be healed before they can be returned to the vast menagerie that they, and indeed the Deodanth, have been brought from for the occasion.*

The last fight of the day is between two of the giant Insak-div. *This was good placement as a last bout. They show everyone how the bardiche should be used. Both were caught in the round up that followed the discovery of the Patterns, and both Christopher and I are among the several people who are standing during their fight. Each of the giants blames the other for their predicament, and it is a hard-fought bout. Both are severely injured, before one of them finally lost and died.*

Those who did not see my wife fight against one of these giants can wonder how she can have killed two of them on her own now. I still don't know myself. I think that she is just more stubborn than them. Even those of us who were there did not have the leisure to just sit back and watch. I think that everyone is impressed by what they see.

It was a fitting bout to end the day, and the Mice returned to the Palace excitedly talking about all they had seen.

Christopher

I suppose that, like our little girls, I am left pondering on crime and punish- *ment after the arena visit. They may have been distracted by the ices though. I take the point that Basil and I have been debating all day that it is best for everyone to publicly see justice done. No-one should hide from the consequences of their decisions. I also understand the importance of deterrence, but I still wonder if there is a better way to achieve the same effect without the loss of a person's life.*

Just locking a person up, as is sometimes done in Freehold, I dismiss out of hand. It will just let the evil ferment and spread among the prisoners, rotting their souls further as they learn villainy from each other. Could there perhaps be a miracle cast that might change a person…so that they will be of a better character? If the person who it is cast on is not complicit in the casting, will it be better or will it be worse?

If they do not consent, would it not be the same as killing them, without allowing them the chance of redemption? Except that he had wanted to die, and would have probably killed himself if he had been set free, could there have been another way of punishing Skap? Would letting him live with the knowledge of what he had done eating at him have been crueller? How about making him forget what he had done under the influence of evil? The drawback of that would be that those around him would still know his deeds, and would, even if they did not mean to, inevitably remind him or ostracise him.

When Christopher was back at the University next, the guest lectures he was supposed to give on theology turned out not to be lectures at all. As he had done when he brought up the actions of his wife in questioning the Khitan on his first visit, he opened a vigorous debate on the ethics and morality of punishment among both staff and students.

I do not have any answers...yet...but I certainly do have some interesting questions to pose to the students that will, I am sure, be debated long after our visit finishes. Indeed, unbeknownst to Christopher, the whole talk had been written down, and his questions would end up being debated among students of law and religion throughout the Empire for some time.

Chapter XXIV

Astrid (1st October)

I am not even sure how to describe the next book they gave me to read. The first gave me reading of the new Darkspeech, the second one was some sort of arms manual, a magical one admittedly, but still one that told me ways of fighting and even of moving. I had to run around and jump. He even made me throw axes...and that felt right.

The third book talked of many things, and all of them had been interesting at the time, but already I cannot remember even one of them in detail. I am sure it sometimes talked about bone and sinew and spirit. All I know is I have finished the book feeling...more complete may perhaps be the best description.

When that was finished, servants were there to usher her away. *It seems that I temporarily say thanks and goodbye to my instructor, so that I can go to a wedding.* She realised in their last bout how far his instruction, combined with what she had drunk and read, had brought her in only a few days.

In my body, I am tired down to my bones. My joints and my muscles ache with the effort I am putting in. She had a bath in an attached room before going back upstairs. *Such a huge bath, and so much luxury...there is even a big mirror.* She looked at herself naked in it as her servants waited with towels to dry her. *I am sure that my arms and legs are larger and firmer.*

As she was being dried off by a servant (one of the ones who seemed to have been hovering the whole time she was here, attending to her needs) she reached out, and grasping her around the waist with her hands, casually lifted the surprised woman off the ground.

I can do it easily and without strain. I am naked and without my charms at the moment, but I think that I am near as strong now as I am with them on, plus gaining skill with my weapon. She began dressing. *I wonder what Hrothnog has done to me. More importantly, what effect will all of this have on my baby?*

Basil

I am more than a little worried. Everyone is starting to dress for the wedding and there is still no sign of Puss. It was only once a servant came in with something that looked somewhat like a fuller version of her good dress and hung it up that he started to calm down a little. *She very reluctantly left her dress behind in Mousehole, as it didn't fit her pregnant figure, and there was no way it could be made to fit her new shape without taking it to pieces and she was not having that happen.*

She is obviously not meaning to miss the wedding and has made provision. She came in only a few minutes later looking a little tired, but already bathed. *Evidently, she knows about the dress, but has not had a chance to try it on.*

Despite my probing, she is neither reticent nor evasive about where she has been. She just flat out refuses to say anything, except that she has two more days to go before she can leave. He sighed deeply. *I know that I have no chance of out-stubborning my wife. I will just have to let it go, and I am sure that she will tell me when it suits her.*

I cannot follow it up anyway as I have to leave straight away, leaving Astrid to follow with the others. I have to get there earlier. It seems that I have a place in the wedding party as a groomsman. Although we were not able to confirm that we Mice would all be at the wedding, Candidas had hoped that I, at least, would be able to come. Almost as soon as my wife appears, I have to fly to get there. At least in my case, the flight is actually both literal and fast.

Theodora (an hour or so later)

I am sure I am getting to see more of Ardlark than I saw in all the time I lived here. We can go now. Astrid has arrived back. For her, the sedan chairs that are waiting for us may be a novelty, but she is apparently asleep before we leave the Palace. Where has she been? It seems that the rest of our people are rapidly getting used to the idea of arriving somewhere fresh and without having to worry where it is.

The wedding is to take place in the Church of Saint Menna, the patron of traders and merchants. Even I know that, although Ardlark is a large enough city, even if they had to travel across it to get to the right one, most people have a church that is devoted to their own trade, and that is usually the one that they go to if they can, at least for a Krondag service. Moreover, it is always the one used by them for important matters…like weddings and funerals.

Mind you, I have mainly been to the Basilica of Saint Thomaïs. From the sound, the arrival of our train of sedan chairs, from the way they are decorated, ones that obviously come from the Palace, seems to be causing a sensation among the rest of the merchants and their families, who are waiting even before we get out. As soon as we set foot outside, and the rest of the Mice follow, you would think that there was a major chariot race on at the Hippodrome that involves every colour.

It seems it did not take long for people to hear of us. I am sure that the rumour mill of the city has been in full flight ever since our appearance in Court, and some of the assembled attendees are perhaps a little disappointed that most of our Mice seem to be built on a human scale, and are not a cubit or two taller and built more like Astrid. The women seem, at least, to be generally more than gratified to see what we wear in clothes, and in particular in the way of jewels. Good luck to them in copying Astrid's rubies, even in garnet.

Our gift was sent on ahead, and Theodora Lígo and Candidas each wear a gold armlet a hand wide that Eleanor had been making, or more correctly repairing in her spare time, since my husband and I asked her to. They were taken from the dragon's treasure and are from a time that was probably very long ago. They were crushed flat and had lost some of their adornment when she started repairing them.

Apparently, getting arm measurements for the pair was interesting, but somehow Astrid managed it. Now, the bands are circular again and seem to fit well. The gaps are filled, so that they are once again encrusted with crystals, pearls, and mainly semi-precious gems. The sight of such lavish and old-fashioned jewellery is causing a sensation.

Father Gennadius

I *may only be the Parish priest of Saint Menna, but I thought I knew most of the clergy in Ardlark. Who is this young one in unfamiliar regalia among the congregation? He is someone senior I am sure, despite his age, by what he and his wife are wearing. Is that a member of the Imperial Family beside them? There are even Kharl here and of a race I have never seen before. Many people are armed and in my Church. I am marrying a merchant's daughter and her guard, aren't I?*

He became even more nervous when his enquiries told him who it was that was waiting, but Christopher saw what was happening and hastened up to talk with him before resuming his seat and the two ended up at the wedding feast deep in conversation.

Shilpa

*T*o the surprise of some of the guests from Darkreach, they already have met some of us Mice. My face was a shock to them. They did not make the connection between the legendary mountain valley of the Empress and the River Dragon *before, but it looks like I will be spending a good part of the wedding feast discussing possible items of trade that might be of interest. They want to be sure that I know of products that I can bring in from the far north… or from Haven…or from wherever else we might sail.*

I was careful to not be specific about this, but I did start to imply that there is a lot more to the world than they knew about. It was only after I spoke that I realised what I said. I hope that my eagerness to trade did not let a secret out. I hope that the existence of other lands isn't supposed to stay secret, but by then the cat was well and truly out of the bag.

Mind you, apparently there has already been a ship come in from Freehold to conduct trade. It is the first that anyone can remember arriving. Do the Princesses know of that?

Basil

*T*he surprises keep coming. I expected her to be here, but Olympias is chatting to Procopia Ampelina as if they are old friends. She neglected *to mention their acquaintance. I have recognised quite a few of the guests, actually a large number of them. Given that Candidas is Antikataskopeía, you would expect many familiar faces.*

Most seem to be here in a social capacity, but seeing we are all keeping an eye out from habit, it must be the most secure wedding that has been seen in Ardlark for some time…at least since the Imperial marriage. Even our Strategos is quietly here. I am not sure that our Theodora has realised who she was just talking to. We seem to have all the Foreign Service people here in one place.

Lādi

*U*sually, *it is the mother of the bride who spends the most time in and out of the kitchen annoying the people working here and getting in their way, but at this feast it is one of the guests...me. I have high standards, as do my people, and...I really am not used to not being in the kitchen. Perhaps, I need to get out of the valley more often.*

Lādi had already been to visit the cooks before the wedding with some 'suggestions' about favoured foods of some of the guests. *I made some baklava for today, also. I do mine differently to what they do here in Ardlark.* Now, she was following it up on the night by ducking in and out with comments, criticisms, and aid. *At least I am fairly satisfied with their efforts. I think I need to spread a few small purses around. They are to encourage them and their work.*

Theodora Ligo

*H*aving *been to their valley, I am not really surprised, but many of my father's more normal guests are scandalised by the behaviour of the people from the Palace. There are so many minor changes to what is considered 'proper' by the matrons of the capital, I am sure that they are having difficulty listing them all.*

Even more shocking than the torrent of little ones are the major breaches of propriety. I have not seen that wedding dance before, for a start. The obvious closeness of the Princesses as a couple has some of the matrons and our priest frowning, and my namesake is even heavily pregnant. I am not sure how she managed that, but she is Imperial family. I suppose the biggest shock is that most of them are armed at a wedding, even the children.

When they insisted on entertaining, even if it was better entertainment than people are used to, it has been almost too much. The gossips are having a marvellous time being scandalised. Having seen the Mice at home, only my father, Candidas, and I are completely calm, or in my new husband's case as calm as any groom is on his wedding day.

I suppose that I am a little in shock with everything, despite or perhaps because of, Astrid's best efforts. Her sister Olympias is near as bad at giving cause for gossip, with everything from her wearing man's clothes, to her jokes, and her man.

As for my mother, Theodora, she has spent most of the night stunned over the fact that the woman our entire line is named after is not only present in the hall with her at my wedding, but also dancing around in it, clad as if she were a Muslim dancing woman of the taverns, even more scandalously displaying her pregnancy to all.

Astrid

I *am aching all over from the changes that my body has undergone over the last few days, and that on top of the effects of my pregnancy. I have tried to keep Theodora Lígo company, but I have had to spend much of the wedding seated, watching what is going on, and the effect of the Mice on the assembled crowd.*

She paused and inhaled the aroma of the sweet kaf she had just been handed. *It is hard not to note that, despite what Basil has said about all of the races of Darkreach being regarded as the same, apart from the Mice there are few who are present at the wedding from outside the Orthodox community.*

Even though, on my last visit when I had had more time to look around, I saw many Islamic and Greenskin merchants, there are only a couple of them present at the wedding. Most of them are those who work their trade outside Darkreach.

I do admit to having been amused though to see the expression on the face of one of the few Islamic traders present, Habib Asen (who has come down from Antdrudge especially for the occasion) when he discovered that his former guards on his first trip out of Darkreach were actually a Princess and a tribune of the Antikataskopeía.

The matrons present never did have enough of a chance to work out how to treat Denizkartal the Boyuk-kharl, Aziz and Krukurb, the Hobgoblins, and Ariadne, the part Alat-kharl woman…she is enjoying herself. Even Basil and I manage to confuse the women slightly. It is obvious that they have little to do with other races in their normal life, and the casual inter-race relations of the Mice are far beyond them.

Procopia Ampelina

O *verall, my Mice seem to have regarded that wedding as a successful social event. Despite the gossip that followed the wedding about its 'innovations', a keen observer of the social life in Ardlark (and it is my job to be that) would have noticed that little bits of what happened at either the wedding or the feast, in terms of its innovations, started very quickly to appear in similar occasions among the merchants and traders of Ardlark...and then to spread further afield.*

The first to appear were cheaper copies of the wedding armlets, but even the idea of guests joining in on the entertainment is seen sometimes. I hear that entertainers are even hired to teach their skills...and singing teachers, in particular, are suddenly in demand. After all, for any hostess who has any degree of social pretension—and most do—if it is a good enough custom for a Princess of the Blood...

Chapter XXV

Theodora
2nd October, the Feast Day of Saint Nicodemus

Something is happening. I know that we were planning on heading back today. Now a series of things seem to be conspiring to keep us in Ardlark. Furthermore, Astrid, even though she knew when we wanted to leave, has disappeared again. It may be Saint Nicodemus' Day, and he patron of the curious, but my curiosity is not being satisfied.

Theodora
4th October, the Feast Day of Saint Francis

Only now are we finally setting out for home after having been seen off again by the Imperial couple. Our saddles are hung with boxes, weapons, and armour. Astrid has even found a practice version of her Insak-div weapon from somewhere, and has perhaps swapped her old weapon for another. It is perhaps an odd gift for her to have been given, or perhaps not. Astrid will admit to no other.

The first leg of the trip will be to Deathguard Tower, an easy and short day's travel. I know the garrison there will be keen to be filled in on the progress of the quest of the Mice. The lunch stay on the way to Ardlark did not give us time for that. Of all the people of Darkreach, they are the ones with the most reasons to see our task successfully concluded.

I am sure that most of the others who hear the tale feel it is a great story. They think that the people who take part in it must be the stuff of legend, even when we are telling them the tale. I can see it has little relevance to the normal daily existence of most people. For the men and women who every day tend the tombs of the unquiet dead, such matters are the very stuff of their normal life and their interest in us centres on what is happening.

One whole file of the Basilica Anthropoi, the ones who are newly arrived in the west and who helped in conquering the Brotherhood, have come from a retiring age cohort from among the troops here. Their former colleagues are very pleased to hear of their arrival and their presence in the battles.

Basil tells me he thinks that over the years, more of these men and even the women, might find their way west over the mountains. He says that the troops who stay here for a while are those people whose life lacks a safe rut to run in anyway. They might find their own form of peace and quiet in a trip to the West.

Basil (5th October)

W e left Deathguard very early, and now we fly the longest leg of our trip going direct to the River's Head Inn in the Gap. Although we are arriving two days later than we expected, there are still rooms prepared and ready for us, and we are able to eat and then fall almost straight into bed. I still have no answers from my wife about her time in Ardlark.

To Basil's great surprise, his wife was the first among the whole party to head off to go straight to bed, and that was after she had nearly fallen asleep over the food. When he had retired to sleep, he did not disturb her slumber at all, which was also unusual. She has gone to bed even before the little girls, who are also exhausted from the long day's flight.

Basil (6th October, the Feast Day of Saint Clare)

T he last leg, apart from a side trip to Mouthguard to register that we are going out of Darkreach, is direct back to the valley. We arrive there on a chill, and indeed bleak, winter day. I suppose that we were lucky in that winter chose to wait until our return to settle in fully. Now that we are back in our valley, it settles in with glee.

As night falls, it is already snowing heavily through the village and on the hills above us. Unlike every other year, Puss is totally ignoring it. She is not interested in making plans to play in the snow, not even when I mention skiing. Nor is she interested in the casual small talk and gossip. Once again, she has headed straight towards our bed and sleep.

Chapter XXVI

Goditha (8ᵗʰ October)

*T*he arrival of winter may give us Mice time to keep working on our own projects, but I have to admit that my normal work clothes are not suitable for the weather. Either I am getting soft, or it is even colder than it was last year.

I really don't like my nipples nearly freezing off or having to rub lanolin on them to stop them cracking. I am forced to work in several layers of northern clothes. At least I don't have to wear a dress.

With the wind whistling around my ears, I was even considering re-growing my hair. Then Astrid took pity on me, and quickly sewed me up one of the fur hats of the north that has flaps coming down to cover the ears, and which can be tied fast under the chin with a njal-bound arming cap under it all to make up for not having a beard.

All I can do is cut, shape, and dry-stone anyway. It is useless to try to use any mortar in this weather. It would not set at all.

Rani

*N*ow we are home, tales of the trip are told to those who stayed behind. The gift of the Emperor, the Horse that will give us luck, is displayed to everyone. The Khitan approve of this and have called it Az. They have also insisted on hanging around its neck a small bag that has an...aromatic and interesting smell.

Once all have seen and admired it, we get to hide it away from danger. Like the statue of the Mouse, the one that contains the spell that hides the

*valley from outside gazes, it will now only come out on ceremonial occasions.
I hope that no-one can follow the smell to where they both are hidden. It is
worse than a funereal Ghāt for the poor.*

With nothing urgent on the horizon, Rani returned to making wands for
when they went out again and Theodora went back, with her collaborators, to
making saddles.

*By the end of winter, my wife wants to have at least another thirty of them
done. That will enable most of the people in the village to be mounted if we
need them to be. I am sure that she can then just keep on making more of them
each winter until she is happy with what we have, if she ever is, that is.*

Ayesha
15th October, the feast of Laylatul-Baraʾah

*T*he normal life of Mousehole resumes, and we Muslims celebrate the
Night of Record. I wonder what deeds will be recorded for the next year
for me. I am fairly certain what the first will be. Fear has told me to expect a
healthy son.

Aziz
16th October, the feast of Saint Cyricus

*G*uk and Haytor have arrived, for once wearing cloaks. They have with
them some well-laden and very shaggy packhorses due to their long
winter coats. Like me, they think this is mild weather. Being used to living in a
village much higher up in the mountains, as they do, winter down here on the
slopes is only a minor thing as far as we Hobs are all concerned. Besides, we
all have thick skin.

*I am glad to see them again. They will be coming around every five or six
weeks from now on with at least one horse. It seems that Haytor is already
enjoying his new life of constant travel and being the bearer of news as he
shares a drink with Krukub, and I while we catch up on the gossip of the
mountains and news from home.*

Ruth
18th October, the Feast Day of Saint Luke

*M*y life has been all about teaching and drawing plans. I have been seen very little out and about in the village. It has taken me two weeks to come out with a new set of plans for the basilica. I need to apologise to Goditha, in particular. Her face fell when I showed everyone that some sections of what we have done so far have to be torn down and re-laid.

Luckily, there are really only a few corrections that have to be made to what has been done so far, but what I have learnt from my magical tome in Ardlark has been most valuable. I want this building to be perfect when it is complete. It is a legacy that Goditha and I will be known by forever.

When it is finished, it will be a smaller version of Sancta Thomaïs with the same sort of open spaces that make the cathedrals I grew up with in Freehold, with their forest of pillars standing among the worshippers, seem cramped. It will perhaps end up as one of the largest open enclosed spaces west of the mountains that is not under a Dwarven mountain.

Rani (20th October)

*W*hen this temple and the school are finished, there will be very little spare space left outside the wall in the lower valley, space that is not occupied by the practice areas, our old and new buildings, or our walled-off and established fields.

It seems that we have no choice now. It has become obligatory for the new farms we need to be set up outside the valley, at least until we repair the downed inside bridge across our river and can easily work the other bank that we can only access now with saddles. I have decided that this will not happen until after this temple is done, at least.

By accident, it is Ruth who has given our temple its name. When she allowed others to see her drawings, she had idly labelled them as being for the Basilica of Saint George. It was not long before the idea of adopting as their patron the Saint responsible both for combat against dragons and having patronage over cavalry spread through the village. It is a good name for us.

The name was confirmed when Ayesha revealed that her people also tend to regard him as a holy figure, but they attribute to him not only his victory over the dragon of evil, but also an efficacy against madness. As soon as *he heard that the saint would appeal to both village's two major religions, Christopher would hear no more ideas. His mind is made up.*

Ayesha

*H*āritha is to be named after my father. I was surprised by how easy the birth was. Based on what I have seen so far from the women having their first children, I had been expecting it to be both harder on my body, and for it to take far longer. Despite having to take a little opium, and having to have some healing afterwards, it was not as horrendous an experience as I had feared. I am able to quickly return to my exercises.

For the first time in my life, ever since I was ill as a child one year, I will not be undergoing the fast of Ramadan that is due after mid-winter as the strictures are very firm about who should and who should not fast, and just as they are for the Christians during their fasts, nursing mothers are very firmly on the second list.

Christopher

I have secretly written my note and handed it to Stefan, with a small bag and a whispered conversation, and while one wife is on watch seeing him out, and the other has the watch that sees him return, Stefan has quickly flown north with a message to be delivered to Mouthguard. It will then need to be delivered on to Ardlark.

I have to admit a small sin to myself. I am now, I admit rather smugly, looking forward to my next arrival to come from that city.

Astrid

*T*he effect of the visit on others of the Mice is varied. My brother Thorstein is most delighted with the magical teaching books that we have returned home with. At least now his girls have only two languages to learn.

Perhaps even more importantly, Fire now has a list of wages and prices to work with that Rani has brought back for her. She has only just finished listing the wealth of the village, now she can try and work out who is owed what.

It seems that we are the only ones to see her now: because of her work she hides herself away, and is rarely seen by most of the Mice. She has taken over one of the houses beside ours. She is the only single person to take a house on her own. She needs to have it though.

While most of the house is still derelict and people work on it around her, she works and sleeps in the one room that is wind-and-waterproof. It is her office and the largest room in the house. It has a desk at one end, with a shelf for ledgers beside it, and a small cot in the centre. On one white wall, where she can see it clearly, she has painted the wages for different types of work. It is written in sections and covers a large part of the wall behind her desk.

She sleeps there, but she still comes to us to eat, and even to help with the house and children. She still avoids the common meals and the other women as much as she can, and she shares the table with Basil, Thorstein, and me. I really cannot see how anyone can take a dislike to the young girl. Apart from being so bookish, she is a very sweet child.

I refuse to think of her as a woman. Not only is she over three and a half hands shorter than I am, but she seems so fragile and delicate next to me. As she works, she often sings or hums distractedly in the soft and innocent voice of a little girl. She doesn't even seem to be aware of this when she does it, and blushes if it is pointed out. When she knows she is singing, her voice has a much more mature tone.

Lādi

I am now much happier with my lot. I may not have found a lover, as Valeria did on her first visit, but I am quietly entertaining some hopes about the older widower who made the pastries for the wedding. He might be a Christian, but he certainly seemed interested in me, and he makes things that I haven't seen before. Ayesha may be disappointed that he is Christian, but I just want someone who wants me.

After the event, he even shyly visited me in the Palace under the pretext of gaining a recipe from me. Nothing else happened, but had he really needed the recipe so badly? At any rate, I have some aspirations for summer, and am already looking at which of the houses to perhaps claim before we run out of the best ones near my kitchen.

Chapter XXVII

Rani (22nd October)

*T*he River Dragon *is re-launched but, after a trial cruise, we are only keeping a skeleton crew aboard her to watch over her. I know that* Olympias *is disappointed, but that is all that will be there until we need her to sail again. In rotation, four of the crew will stay on board for a week at a time, as the ship is tied up next to the wharf at Evilhalt.*

Except for when they all go out for a practice sail to keep their hands in, I don't want them to stay away for longer than that. I have decided that, if they spend all their time on board, they might drift too far away from the village, and think of themselves as belonging to the boat itself and not as being a part of the village. We are too small to afford a fragmentation of our loyalties.

Christopher
24th October, the feast of All Souls

*W*ith Ayesha's delivery, and now Jennifer's, I am having my suspicions *about the effect of Fear on the newborn confirmed. I eagerly wait on the other births that are due soon, those of Astrid and Theodora, to see if the same trend of easier deliveries continues. If Fear is accurate in what she has heard, Astrid's birth could be very interesting indeed.*

Jennifer was delivered of her girl on All Souls. It seems that she has been listening to the village bards, and has decided that her baby will be different. She has one name from her godmother and a second to distinguish her past. Under Fear's apparent coaching, the birth of Goditha Atalante was also far quicker than most first births seem to be.

Basil (36th October)

*T*his year the mid-winter fire must be set up and run by someone else, and Puss has to agree to allow her brother to use her skis. I refuse to even try. While my wife still gives plenty of directions, she does so largely from a seated position. She has chosen her brother to get things set up as she wants. I get to take directions to him.

Fear has confirmed what any can easily guess from Puss' size. Once again, we will be having twins. This time, it is known that they will again be a boy and a girl. We have already chosen the names Anna and Thorstein for them, but her brother is not to find that out until after the actual birth has taken place.

Christopher (2nd November)

*T*horstein found out nearly straight away, as despite his embarrassment at being at his own sister's delivery, he had to be present when they were born. *He needs to understand that he has to be there as a part of his learning. Even Aziz, as the first novice to be taken on in our parish, must be there and learn what needs to be done.*

"At this rate of adding people to our valley, priesthood and healers, the mother will soon have to be outside the room." *Oh well, I tried to lighten the mood. From what Fear has said privately to me, and the look on Astrid's face, I think that we need to have some levity.*

Although the births were quick, they were not painless, and Astrid has had to take opium. She has also needed healing after she started to bleed badly. It seems that, Astrid was expecting her babies to be different, for some reason. Fear realised something was happening and she told me. At least we were ready for this.

Both babies are very well developed and healthy, and indeed, despite being a twin, Thorstein is the largest baby that has been delivered so far in the valley...and his sister is not much smaller. Not even the part-Hob children are as big.

Fear said that the babies were large and healthy and very strong...and that they are. The lack of surprise that Astrid is displaying over all these events leaves me wondering about where she had been in Ardlark and what she did there. When I consulted him, Basil said that he was not sure what happened either.

Basil

*O*nly now that the babies have been introduced to their sibs and are happily, and very greedily, nursing will Puss admit to me what happened to her in Ardlark.

"I was not concerned much," she said. "Everything was laid out. It all seemed to have been carefully planned, and there were servants stopping us, and making me eat and drink according to their own schedule…even if I was not sure exactly what I was drinking all the time. From the taste, several were potions, and no, I am not addicted to anything even though one was very definitely Sleepwell.

"The way it was done, I am sure it has all been done before. I am also sure that Hrothnog would not have arranged it if he were not sure about the results. I thought that it might have some effect on the children. I just didn't want any of you to worry, so I didn't tell you. Now, I haven't been able to show you this, in case you guessed…but feel my arm…I am going to recover soon and be up and about well before you expect me to, and just wait until you see what I can do with my bardiche."

At least she is back to smiling again. The healing has taken effect.

"Those two I killed were really not all that good…thankfully. They were just big and strong. My instructor could have beaten them both at the same time, and I think that I can now use my bardiche to better effect than I can use my spear."

Basil (3ʳᵈ November)

*D*espite some tenderness from her stitches, Astrid was up and doing some exercises that she had learnt. *She is still vague about how she learnt them, and she insists that anyone else who is in our house will be doing them along with her. Currently, this means just Fire and me. I have seen these exercises done before by the Imperial Guard, but I have known no-one else who knew how to do them.*

I wonder exactly who has been teaching her. She still refuses to say. We have done one of the opposed exercises, and despite her long inactivity, it is hard not to notice the increase in her strength. Despite the difference in our size, we have always been just as strong as each other, now the difference in our size is matched by the difference in our strength.

Basil (4th November)

*I*t is almost as if my wife has only just now reached her potential. She was delivered only two days ago, and Puss is already up and waving her practice weapon around her like a long-bladed quarterstaff, as lightly as if it were a wand, and complaining that she has slowed down far too much and that she is rusty from a lack of practice.

Goditha

*R*ani is indignant at being excluded from the delivery room as Theodora gives birth, and she is not mollified by having me among the other husbands there to share the experience with her. She wants to be with her wife. I wanted to as well. It would not have been a good idea.

Goditha shared with her what Robin pointed out to her when Melissa was born: "But if you listen, she doesn't seem to want you there at present." A moment's silence in the waiting room confirmed this. "Actually," Goditha continued, "she is doing fairly well, and is much quieter than many of the other women have been." Several of the other men waiting there in sympathy nodded.

Christopher

*I*nside the room, I am thinking the same as what Goditha has just said outside. I even suspect that a lot of the noise that is being heard is just Theodora acting the part of a pampered Princess, as she sometimes still is. As far as I can see, the delivery is a quick and straightforward one, and Aikaterine has not damaged her mother at all. Astrid was in far worse condition and made less noise.

Once mother and daughter had both been cleaned up and moved to a chair, Rani was let in.

I am surprised to see her clutching Goditha's hand and dragging her in.

Goditha seems surprised at that, too, but I am guessing that holding onto the hand of another woman husband for support is better for Rani than holding the hand of a real father. From the expression on her face, one thing that a more than slightly bewildered Goditha is very sure of is that, although they both love other women, they are very different in their approach to the matter.

Unlike Astrid, it would be some time before Theodora was up and about.

Christopher (6ᵗʰ November)

Dulcie's baby was not due for some time, but during the weekly check Fear registered that there was something "not right...I don't know what it is," she said. She cocked her head to the side, as if listening and thinking.

"Her baby feels healthy, but she is worried about something. Does it make sense that she feels like she is choking?" Christopher and Lakshmi looked at each other. *Her cord is around her neck? That makes sense.* Christopher thought about his new prayer. *Will it do as it is, or will I have to change the wording?*

By the time Jordan had been fetched from his wheel, Christopher was writing out the adaptation. While Theodule explained the situation to Jordan, and Aziz and Thorstein got things ready to proceed, Christopher ran over what he had to do in his mind. *I hope that I have written this adaptation so that it can be used in several situations where there is not actually something wrong with the baby itself, but just with its positioning.*

I guess that we will soon find out. I hope that I am right, otherwise we will have to try something else and that will perhaps be riskier. Now it is time to see if it works. Lakshmi stood ready beside Fear, in case they had to do something more drastic than just prayer to save the life of the baby.

After the normal everyday prayers were said, they launched into the ritual. *Again, we see movement happening within the body of the mother. Once again, Fear pronounces herself happy with the results, but I want her to check Dulcie every day to make sure the problem does not come back.*

He thought a bit more and turned to Lakshmi. "As a matter of fact, I wrote that one so that it should cover a baby that is around the wrong way, and a variety of other problems that can happen with position. I think we should get her to check all the women every day, for the last week or so before we think they are due." Laksmi nodded.

Lakshmi

*I*t does not take me long to think about that. I agree. After all, I am the next one due to deliver. According to Fear, it is another son, and I want everything to be as easy for me as possible. I am quite clear that, as far as I am concerned, pain and mortification are not something to be cultivated as a religious virtue, but only something to be endured if they cannot be avoided.

One thing that her question about choking reveals is that we need to sit down with Fear. She needs to learn about the body and how it works. Not only that, but Fear needs to start learning some herb lore and alchemy. She is going to find herself very busy on her practical afternoon away from school.

At the time that they were executed, Ayesha had suggested using one of the slaver's bodies for dissection, so that we could start to show some of the people being taught to physic how the body works. I thought that it was wrong to do so, and they were male after all, but I am now regretting that we didn't follow her advice.

Chapter XXVIII

Christopher
13th November, the joint feast day of Saint Homobonus and Saint John Crysostum

Today's Feast Day is shared by Saint Homobonus, the patron of cloth workers, and so a favourite of many of the women in the village, and by Saint John Chrysostum. I will share the day out for the saints with two main services. The cloth workers can have Orthros, before work commences, and the latter, the patron of priests, peacemakers and those who seek to live a simple life, getting Hesperinos the day before.

Even though I have read his Life many times, I can never meaningfully work out how the patronage of a simple life ever came to be conflated with the other two areas. I have certainly noticed that, ever since I became a priest, instead of being a simple monk, my life has become a lot more complex.

Astrid

After the evening service, when they were back at the house and Fire was, as she usually did, helping her put the four babies to bed, Astrid came in for a surprise.

In her normal quiet voice, and showing even more reticence than usual, Fire, after having made a few 'umm' and 'ahh' sounds, finally admitted what was on her mind. "Would you mind if I asked your brother to marry me?" she finally blurted out. Astrid nearly dropped Anna onto the floor. She gawped at the girl.

I have been trying unsuccessfully to get Thorstein interested in several of the girls ever since I arrived home. Now one girl that I did not even have on my list to be considered has been...refreshingly...direct. She thought for a moment, looking the little girl up and down. *I should not do that. It makes Fire very nervous.*

Astrid thought about it for a little while longer. *The two younger people get on well. My brother is three years older than her, but that is no difference. Fire has been brought up to think of herself as a priest's wife and she will make a good one. She is nearly as quiet as my brother is, and almost up to the standards of the original inhabitants of the valley in terms of her beauty. That is a bonus for Thorstein. She brings some good skills to the union, and even though she is not strong nor will she ever be, she can at least use a crossbow, sword and shield competently, if not well.*

Astrid was just about to agree when Fire spoke again. "If you agree, I am going to change my name. I am no longer going to be called Fire. It is a name that shows my past, not my future. It is not a suitable name for the wife of a Christian priest. I am going to get myself properly christened...and then I will be known as Kaliope."

Astrid smiled at the reference to the girl's superb voice and finally nodded. "I think that you will do very well for him. Let us get the children put to bed. Thorstein will soon be back from his duties with Christopher, so before one of the children wants feeding or changing, I can make sure that he sits still while you ask him."

Astrid (a short while later)

Thorstein came back to his sister's house to see the other three adults all seated at the smaller kitchen table with kaf in front of them, but no food visible. A fourth chair stood a little way from the table, inviting someone to sit in it. "Brother, dear," said Astrid, pointing at the vacant chair. "I would like you to take a seat."

Looking dubiously at his sister, Thorstein did as he was bid, sitting at the table in the empty spot between Astrid and Basil, and across the shorter length from Fire. As he sat, he looked sidewise at his sister worriedly.

He is remembering that voice of mine from our home in Wolfneck. I used that voice when someone had stolen biscuits fresh from the baking, or when some other similar serious matter had come up. I can see him running his mind over what he has done that could cause such a serious tone. Once she deemed him ready, his sister nodded to Fire.

Fire then cleared her throat, and Thorstein changed his attention to her. *She is already copying the look that I had, and his face stays worried about what he has done.* "I don't have anyone to speak for me or make arrangements," she said. *She is speaking in a firmer tone to the one she asked me in.* "But I have asked your sister and she has consented so...will you marry me?" *Her voice is growing a little shakier as she draws closer to the end of what she asks.*

Thorstein's face showed his astonishment, and he could not speak. She continued. "You are a priest, and I know that it is wrong for a priest not to be married. Your sister has tried to interest you in other women, and you have shown no attraction towards any of them, but I have seen you trying to avoid looking at us women when we are just dressed in kilts...and so I am sure that you are not interested in boys."

I did not even consider that as a possible reason for my failure. That was silly of me. Given the number of our women who like women, I should have thought of that.

"I was trained to be a priest's wife, and I think that I will make a good one. I know that I am not a virgin, but I do not think that you are someone who would be concerned over such a matter. And besides, I have made sure that you have seen me when I was working in just a kilt, so you know I am not unattractive, so I think I will suit you very well.

"I have developed...feelings for you, as the one who has looked after me and protected me here. You may not love me now, but I am sure that, if I am given time, I can get you to learn to." She stopped, and looked down at the table and the kaf cup clutched between her tiny hands.

Thorstein looked at her, then he looked at his sister, and then at Basil. *Fire keeps looking down, but Basil and I are both looking at him. There is hardly even the sound of breathing. Surely, he will say something...no? I think that I need to then.* "Close your mouth, dear brother, before you catch a fly. You don't want her to change her mind when she sees you looking so much like a frog."

"Stop teasing him," said Basil to his wife and turned to Thorstein. "It may come as a shock to you, but we think that you will make a good match for each other. If you need to think or pray about it, you can take some time. We can all leave you alone, or your sister and I can leave just the two of you together to talk about it."

Thorstein still had not spoken. His mouth had worked a few times, but nothing had come out. *The bravery has seeped out of Fire, and now she thinks that, after having laid herself bare like that, she will be rejected. She thinks that perhaps her past will never leave her. A tear is beginning to leak out of an eye.* Astrid reached across to take her hand.

Finally, Thorstein spoke. He sounded both nervous and hesitant. "I don't know what to say...I will?" *Fire's face has lit up and she has let go her kaf cup, which is rolling around the table.* Basil grabbed at it and just stopped it in time from dropping onto the floor.

The two just stared at each other across the table. "Go on," said Astrid. "I am sure that even a priest can kiss his betrothed without breaching any vows. Then, once you have done that satisfactorily, then you can both go to see Christopher and start making arrangements."

The two kissed, tentatively at first, but gradually with more vigour and then began to hold each other tight as first one hand, and then another moved from where they hung over to the other person. When they finished, it was actually Fire who broke away blushing as Thorstein gazed at her with a slightly stunned look. *Somehow, I think we need to get them married soon.*

In the end, it was decided that Fire would be baptised on the feast day of Saint Matthew. Seeing that she was now, more or less, their banker, it seemed appropriate to seek the approval of the patron of that profession. They would be married three weeks later on Tetarti. Unless there was an emergency, the calendar appeared to be free and clear of other matters, such as impending births.

Rani (14ᵗʰ November)

T *he marriage of the priest and our banker will only be a brief pause in the rhythm of new life as nine women are due to deliver children in the four weeks after that. Then we have to be in Greensin for Metropolitan Basil's Conclave of the North.*

To that end, I need to decide as soon as possible how many people to take or send. How do we approach it? Should we send only a peaceful group? Just our warriors? Just my wife and I? It is important that we get it right. Although we are not of the North ourselves, I am determined that we should be well represented at this meeting.

We still have Freehold as an unknown threat, and it is in the best interests of us Mice to have the North strong and united against any threats that may present themselves. In addition, the Mice should have a fair amount of moral authority at such a meeting. After all, we are the ones who provided the impetus towards crushing the Brotherhood and freeing the slaves there.

For a start, with the snow lying thick on the ground, the farmers can do other work. Rani decided to send Arthur, and a purse of money, to Greensin on a saddle to book and pay for all of one of the taverns for a week, with an option of taking a further week if needed.

I want him to get the best accommodation that he can. I am betting that few people will be thinking that far ahead, and whereas the men of other villages can stay in the monastery if they need somewhere to sleep, that will not do for us with the number of women we will have there. Besides, I suspect that the Metropolitan's guest house will fill up rather quickly.

Chapter XXIX

Theodora (19th November)

*I nearly managed to forget that we are hosting this conclave of prelates
when Father Christopher will be installed as a Bishop. The word has come
through that the Metropolitan has set the date for it to start the first of Primus.
New Year's Day would normally be a secular festival, but it is easy to see that
it will be a more religious affair this year.*

*Having announced the date of this conclave far and wide, and not just to
us, the imminence of the installation of our own Bishop, and the Synod that it
occasions, need to be brought home to our village. We have a lot to do to be
ready.* She sat back and started to think about the tasks ahead of them, making
notes on a wax tablet as she did.

*For a start, this means we will have arrivals for at least a week beforehand…
and we still don't know how many. Although, with the tools that we have to aid
us (only one of the short walls of the Basilica is at last nearing completion) it
will be impossible to have the building anywhere near complete by then.*

*I think we need to abandon work on the Basilica for now, in an effort to
get every house in the village repaired to at least a basic level. That way we
should be able to house all of those who might come. We need to keep working
on the school also, as it is unsure how many meeting areas we will need.*

*My husband can worry about the meeting in the north, but this is my job to
organise the valley. Now, what else? Perhaps, if the weather permits, most of
the horses of the Mice can be moved to the Upper Pasture, along with all the
sheep, and most of the cattle and goats. We will just leave the ones we need
for milk down here.*

*Naeve has already told me that if we do move them around like that, the
large stables and the enclosed field for livestock that is close to the village will
be enough for the mounts of those who come. I hope she is right.*

Theodule

*F*ire's baptism as Kaliope and the announcement of her impending marriage has led to a little more acceptance of her from the other Brotherhood women. They can see now that she is deliberately cutting herself off from her past, as if her working in an office in a kilt, when some of them still do not do that, even when they are alone in the fields, is not proof enough of that.

The fact that they respect Father Thorstein helps, and I have even heard several mutter regrets about not having had the forethought to ask him themselves.

Kaliope's re-naming has sent an urgent flurry of converted women to us priests with enquiries. They all have the same question...should they change their names? We have given them all the same answer: only if you feel that you need to.

With all the fuss, the arrival of Guk with trade items is almost passing unremarked and unnoticed, although he seems to have sold a lot while he was here. A routine visit from a travelling Hobgoblin trader, and his man with goods from all around the mountain slopes, is now just a part of our normal life. Once it would have dominated conversation for a week.

Lakshmi (19th November)

*A*s it was supposed to happen, I was the next to deliver and Henry Pitt can now join George in our home. Who would have thought that I would have two healthy and happy sons? She smiled to herself.

After the birth, Lakshmi confided to Christopher that now she was sure that whatever Fear was doing with the babies, they needed to make sure that she kept doing it. *My delivery was so much easier this time around, and knowing what I am looking for in a birth, in my opinion Fear is both calming the baby and helping my body push at the right time.*

"No wonder she is exhausted after some of the deliveries," she said. "She may not know exactly what she is doing, but I think she works near as hard as the mothers do. Perhaps she combines some degree of telekinesis with her telepathy. In time, she may learn how to make it easier on herself...or else, perhaps, she will grow stronger."

Lakshmi (21st November)

*A*ine and Verily are now both in labour. I am moving slowly from one to the other, with a baby at my breast, as Fear alternates at a faster pace back and forth. Christopher took Thorstein and cared for Verily, while Theodule and Simeon cared for Aine. Aziz was banished to the waiting room for both deliveries.

Aine's delivery came to a conclusion first. *Verily, according to Fear, is not yet ready to deliver. We are starting to rely on what she feels, and so our main attention can be given to Aine.* It was a smooth delivery, and her son Abel was over an hour old and had already been presented to his father, Aaron, when Fear called them all to Verily's side.

The identical twin girls, Qvavili, or Flower, and Fear, were a much easier delivery than her sons were, and although she has received opium and required healing, and indeed will probably always require them when she gives birth, there is not the crisis that we had the last time she delivered. I thank God and Our Lady for that.

Despite a close examination by the priests and me, the infant Fear shows no sign of what had been wrong with her. I guess that we will never know. To all appearances, she is as fit as her sister is. She is a trifle smaller than Qvavili, but that is all.

Aziz is very relieved, and he has hugged everyone present…going around them all several times as he moves in a distracted fashion. He does so love his wife.

Lakshmi (23rd November)

*I*t is a busy time for us. It is just two days later, and already we are back in our medical chapel for Dulcie's delivery. She has been delivered of Rebecca. Despite everyone being prepared in case the delivery presented problems at the last moment, it was a healthy and easy birth. *I like births that are without any complication. Mother and daughter are now resting and happy.*

Lakshmi (25th November)

*I*t *is only two more days, the next Firstday, and it is Adara's turn to be delivered. While Bryony holds her hand, she is delivered of the identical twin girls, Finnabhair and Sinech. We really do need to stop the priests from seeking blessings of fertility during the marriages here. They are too good at gaining them. I am lucky to have single births, but I seem to be unusual that way.*

Astrid (28th November)

*U*nlike *when Bianca's marriage happened, in what already seems to me to be the distant past, there is now a group of Presbyteras to sustain each other, and so Kaliope does not go unsupported into the role she has chosen.*

To show her faith in the girl, or at least because her wife told her to, Rani acts in the place of her father, while Basil and I get to take the roles of the two attendants. At least we can throw the groom out of our house, and he can move the whole way next door across the village stairs into the bride's house.

Mind you, it still doesn't have a working kitchen or any other amenities. At least a second room, for them to sleep in, has been finished and they have a bed. There is now a front door, even if the roof still has large sections of it missing and the other rooms, and indeed the corridor, are still in ruins. If it rains, they can get wet going from the office to their bed.

Ariadne promises tiles as soon as the weather lets her go out to collect clay and enough timber to fire them with. She has, however, also explained that there is not enough cured timber for the beams either, so having the tiles really will not help. In the meantime, she is making more moulds for tiles, shaped to hold on to each other, so that her work will go quicker when she can proceed.

The timber for the beams has been felled and has been largely sawn, but it will not dry out enough to be used in the snow and damp. If it is used green, it will warp and the tiles will lift. The apologetic builders are being assured that the newlyweds don't mind. I am sure that, with an office and a bedroom they have all that they need and can wait for the rest. As a house, it is a bit of a disaster, but I am not sure that either of them notices.

Lakshmi (2nd December)

*T*he night after the feast of Saint Eloi, and the feast of the Muslims for Eid, *it is the turn of both Bianca and Naeve to come to term. This time it was the turn of the woman who will be having twins to give birth first and I get to expel Christopher from the room.*

Bianca gave birth to Diogenes and Rhodē. As Bianca had promised, they were given the names of Christopher's deceased parents, even if this would forever lead to family confusion as to whether the older Latin-named Rose, or her younger Greek-named sister was being called for.

Naeve had her daughter Beth quietly and without any fuss at all. "It is one thing we milkmaids are always known to be good at," she said. "We are so used to deliveries we can even do our own if you let us, and we are well capable of feeding them…one way or another."

Astrid

*T*hord has a saddle and cloak of his own permanently now and has been *keeping in contact with the Dwarves all through the winter. I am not sure that I have seen as big a grin on his ugly face as now. He has arrived back from Kharlsbane and cannot stop smiling as he shakes the snow off his cloak.*

"I am getting married," the Dwarf announced in a very proud voice. "My mother has culled through the eligible partners, and she has made her mind up on the matter. I think that she has made a very good choice."

"Have you even met her?" Astrid asked.

"You have even met her," was the reply. "She is Ragnilde, the eldest daughter of Baron Hrolfr Strongarm of Oldike. You would have seen her when we were on the way to and from Freehold." *I think that I can remember being introduced to a young Dwarf of that name. I just hadn't realised that it was a female. That would not be diplomatic to mention just now. I will just nod.*

He nods back and his smile is fixed in place. "The date is not set yet, and there is some visiting back and forward to do. I have to go there and give her something to impress her, and she then has to come here and give me some— thing back. We then decide on a date. We Dwarves do not rush these things like some do." *He chides me over my hasty marriage whenever he can.*

Now he is rubbing his hands together, and I can see a light appear in his eyes as he thinks about what the village has in its stores of gems and jewellery that may be suitable as a gift. "I have to work out what will impress the daughter of a Baron who mines diamonds." *I knew that his mind was going to go there.*

Lakshmi (4ᵗʰ December)

*H*agar and Umm were delivered of their children three days after Eid ul-Fitr, but what I had to say was not enough. Both needed stern words from Ayesha to force them to have the Christian priests near them for the delivery. It is not the religion, they protested, it is because they are men. In return, Ayesha pointed out that she had allowed the priests to be present when she gave birth. It didn't work fully.

Eventually, there was a compromise. Fear, Ayesha, and I will be in close attendance on them, but, if there is the slightest sign of problems, the priests will be called from outside the room straight away.

I can see that Christopher is not happy with this. He says that it is harder asking for miracles for a person who is not of your faith already, even if you do regard them as being one of those who are under your pastoral care. Add that to any more delay and it could be fatal. He needs to live with it. It is the best he will get.

Wisely, he doesn't voice these concerns to the women, but he says that he is putting his faith in Fear reassuring him that all is well, and that she will be able to give him notice if something starts to go wrong.

In the end, under Fear's baby coaching, Hagar gave birth to her daughter, Alia. To Umm was born a son, Achmed. *If Asad would have preferred a son, he hid it well.* Atã joined him in celebration as they both started their new families.

Lakshmi (7ᵗʰ December)

*O*ur next set of births on the same day, and Bryony has given Aneurin a full brother in Trystan. He is named after her murdered little brother. This time it is Adara's turn to be held onto, but it is somewhat disrupted as she feeds her two girls. At least I have no fuss being made over priests this time.

Danelis has named her two in Khitan. I am not sure why. I think that it is just to be different. She and Simeon have a son. Epanxer, or Brave and a daughter, Mehre, or Silver. She is already showing that she will also bear her mother's distinctive hair. "And the only silver allowed in our house," said the shape-changing priest jovially when he was finally allowed in.

Lakshmi (8th December)

They come now thick and fast. I suppose our celebrations let us know when the births are to be expected. Parminder had her second child, Daniel. *Although it is an easier birth than her first, again the tiny mage needs healing afterwards, and this time she takes the opium that is offered eagerly. Daniel is indeed a big baby for her small frame.*

I may think that it is too soon to be sure about such things, but after Parminder had been healed and her husband allowed back in, Goditha has already started planning how and when to put him to work to train him in her trade. I doubt that he will have much choice. Fathers can be like that it seems, even when they are women.

Lakshmi
18th December, the Feast Day of Saint Sebastian

It seems so long to have a break of nearly two weeks in the births. We have had time for our Hobgoblin traders to come and go again. They are regular now. It seems that Eleanor and Fortunata are more than making up for the pause. Both have been delivered of twins. Eleanor has Michael and Sara, while Fortunata has Bryan and Alice.

The waiting area is crowded with husbands, siblings, stepsiblings, adopted siblings, a sister-wife and two half-brothers. There is scarce room for anyone else except in brief visits. Eleanor and Robin now have six young in their house. Our old village of pain is now full of the sounds of small children. They mark our rebirth.

"Just as well neither of us likes too much quiet," said Robin. He turned to Norbert: "You need to get to work. There are only five of them in your house and you have the advantage of an extra wife." *I think that it was his own wife who threw the first cushion at him.*

Chapter XXX

Rani
19th December, the 1st day of Spring

*W*e all have our saddles loaded as heavily as we can with supplies, now it is time for us to start off to Greensin. I hope that I have prepared properly for all that can take place, or rather I should say, I hope that my wife and Astrid have prepared properly, once I said who was going. It is not yet light, but Astrid says we need to leave now.

It seems that my people are counting on having supplies of our own food with us in case the town runs low due to the number of people going. No-one knows how long this meeting will last, and winter always exhausts stores even in the best prepared village and this year the war has badly interfered with any preparations.

I have decided that my wife and I will go, along with Father Christopher and Bianca, Astrid and Basil, Nikephorus, Stefan and his wives, Hulagu and all three of his wives, Aziz and Verily, and Dobun and Thord. I did worry about the new mothers travelling, but none wants to be left out, and all assure me that the wool-lined baby quivers and the cloaks will be enough. After all, there is now no need for us to fly high out of secrecy.

Only the new-born babies will be coming. The rest of the children will be staying at home. It will still be a lot of children, but we will fly there directly, except for change stops. By leaving early, we should still be there by night-time, but I have allowed an extra day just in case.

Who will be going along on this trip has been carefully considered. We Princesses speak for our village, and Christopher for its church. Hulagu, his wives and Dobun must be there in case the Khitan send someone along. Stefan is known to all the villages for his Captaincy, while Aziz would be there for the prestige accruing from the artillery of the Devartetilcu Yamyam. Ariadne has declared that she cannot be spared from repairs, and he can stand in for her.

Aziz is also a very impressive figure in his own right, and he would also be there as a trainee priest to meet the Metropolitan. Astrid will be going to look after the people from Wolfneck, and Verily will go along to make contact with any women of the old Brotherhood who might be there. Basil is coming to be Basil, and keep an eye on the behaviour of the other attendees, and lastly Nikephorus is coming to look after the rest of us, and to make sure that we are fed. That should be enough.

When she had outlined these plans to the Mice, she had not reckoned on Ruth. "We promised their parents that the students would learn about the world and the cultures in it and not just our little village," she said. "We are going to something…a meeting. It is one that will shape the North…probably for hands of cycles to come. The children deserve to see it as it happens. Then they can compare that with the Synod in a few months' time.

"You have booked a whole inn. We only need a small room for the boys and a large one for all the girls. They will take bedrolls with them, and then they can all see what happens. It will also add to the prestige of our school." Rani had sighed.

It seems that the children will be coming. Not only is she right, but I have no chance of budging Ruth from a path once she has taken a stand like that. In her own way, she is as stubborn as Astrid. At least there are now enough saddles. I suppose that showing the number of different cultures the children come from also makes a strong point about Mousehole. We should emphasise that.

Astrid

It was a long flight, and we had to stop and land several times to feed and change babies. I am reminded of the frustrations of the last time I came this way with children. Much of the frustration, and indeed more, was repeated this time. At least we do not have the far slower carpet to hold us up and that is a big improvement.

Now that we have arrived, it looks like the frustration will get worse. Arthur booked the Wolf's Warning, but now we have arrived, we have discovered that Greensin is starting to fill up and some of the best rooms of the inn already have people in them. The innkeeper does not want to remove them. Rani is about to storm in there. It is time that I intervened.

"You are a Princess. You sit and look…like a Princess." *See, even Theodora is nodding and pulling at her husband's sleeve.* "That is why you have people like me and Basil. He can go and be diplomatic and I will go and loom in the background and look threatening." Making sure the babies were asleep they headed off.

Astrid, naturally, had her outsized weapon in her hand. *I must admit that it almost looks like a sort of scythe, and seeing that I may have accidentally left my black travel cloak on, there have already been several comments about a visit from the Reaper. I suppose that my smiling in the direction of the comments may have helped spread the notion and add fuel to the fire, all accidental of course.*

It took only a few minutes before people were seen leaving the building, and Astrid was waving the rest of the Mice in. "Basil went and explained things to the innkeeper about honesty and getting money back and having to pay for us to stay elsewhere while I went and visited people in rooms and explained the situation gently. They were all merchants here to peacefully sell things when it starts, and they all understood when I smiled at them."

She grinned. "They hadn't realised whose rooms they were taking when they offered more money to the innkeeper." She leant closer to the Princesses. "You probably cannot do one, but Basil implied that you would be putting a spell up to keep an eye on everything done in the inn while we are here…so say something along those lines if you can."

"I could do that if I wanted," said a puzzled Theodora, "but why would I want to?"

Resignedly, Astrid explained about how it was so important not to upset the people who were going to prepare your food. "I think that Basil is off talking to the people in the kitchen and making friends with them so it should all be fine anyway."

Astrid (20th December)

*W*e have had a quiet night, and The Conclave is not supposed to start until tomorrow, but I hear that we are nearly all here already. There is still plenty of time to move around the village and to meet others who are here. Some attendees have been here for days, but others are still on the way. Even they are supposed to arrive here tonight.

Adara, Bryony, and Hulagu's wives have been left caring for the babies to allow the rest of us to move freely around. We all get to split up and talk to the people who are like us. Hulagu and Dobun are off to where the Khitan are camped outside town, while Christopher has obviously taken Aziz off to see the Metropolitan as he should.

Bianca is headed first to the Church of Saint Nicholas, just beside our tavern, and then to the Basilica of Our Lady of the Sorrows to see if she can find some of the local Presbyteras. She wants to tap into what she has already found is a useful source of information wherever she has visited. Thord has already heard there are other Dwarves who have arrived in town. He is seeking them.

As a Captain of the Army, Stefan is going the rounds of the taprooms to see if he can see any other leaders of the troops. Basil is following behind him to talk to the servants and the lower-level men. I suppose that, between them and their full purses, there will be a fair number of drinks bought through the taverns.

For once, the Princesses are doing as they have been told and are secluded upstairs waiting to see if anyone comes to our hotel on the edge of town to visit them. Our arrival was not inconspicuous, but Nikephorus has still taken a note to Andronicus to say that the Princesses are available to the Metropolitan whenever he was free if he wished to see them.

Now that they had put all their stuff away, Ruth is walking her charges around the village. With less than a month before she is due, she is not walking quickly, but it is obvious that the children are all together as, unless they are stopped, they stay in pairs behind her with Cadfael, as the oldest, bringing up the rear. Looks of wonder came from all sides about the unusual group.

While the paleness of the blonde Neronese Groa is unusual, most have never seen anyone with skin as black as that of the twin girls from Gil-Gand-Rask, and to almost all of them, Hobgoblins are legendary. Although many have seen Aziz and the other men by now, their young have never been seen by anyone away from the mountains, and Zumruud stands out.

The children have all been dressed in the clothes of their homes, except for Zumruud who wears a dress today. Her kilt may shock too many. Gurinder is again in higher status wear, and Fear is in Khitan clothes today. As usual, they bear their blades, and some have horse bows in quivers at their side. A small group of local children follow them around curiously.

Between all our people, they are fairly busy. Verily and I just get to sit outside the inn on the porch under the small awning that covers the area near the door watching what goes on in our square and making sure that the inn is safe. We have our weapons conspicuously beside us. We have heard of no-one from the far west being here yet. If they are here, hopefully they will find us.

Astrid (towards lunch)

I will hazard that these are the ones from the old Brotherhood. Moving towards her down the broad street were a number of women. *What they wear looks like Brotherhood clothes, except that I can see at least some hair on all of them, and several have no scarf on their heads at all. There are no men at all with them...and they are armed.*

They came up to the two women sitting outside the hotel and came to a halt. One stood in front of the others with her arms crossed. *She is obviously one of their leaders.*

"We are some of the women from the villages of Amity," she said assertively, as if someone were about to question the obvious fact that they came from the North-West. "You won't remember me, but the name I am called is I am Now Come Forth and I am now the village leader of Baloo. You can call me Forth." *She speaks with the obvious confidence of a person who is used to getting things done as she wants them to be done. I use that tone a lot myself.*

Astrid had been peering at her as she approached. *I know that the woman's face is familiar somehow. I don't know why, but I have seen her before...and I am sure that it was in a memorable way.* In the growing silence, she looked at the woman as she stood there and thought hard and then she realised who she was.

"You are the frying pan woman!" *Several women behind the speaker have started to laugh at this, and even the woman I have addressed has had to break the sternness of her features a little.*

"I suppose that will be how you remember me always," she said ruefully.

"Suppose? You have a famous part in our stories. You single-handedly... actually you had it in a two-handed grip if I remember it rightly...saved most of your village either from death or slavery. Of course, I would remember you. I am glad to meet you at last. I am Astrid the Cat, and this is Verily. We are from Mousehole. I am glad to see that you have no frying pan with you, and that I am safe for now." She grinned, as did most of the women. *The ice has been broken.*

It turned out that these women came from many of the villages of the former Brotherhood and that they represented the rest of the settlements as well as their own.

So, the people of the area are now calling it Amity after the forest that lies between the settlements. The men who have moved in after the conquest have not been allowed to take over and run everything. Seeing that most of the women are former slaves, the women have been on the wrong end of men running everything all their lives. They need to know what to do to stay free.

It is obvious why they need to see us. She looked at Verily, who took the hint.

"You are here to talk to our leaders," said Verily, "and although you do not know it, to see me. I was born in the Brotherhood, but I cannot remember what village I am from. Any of you older women might be my mother. I was sold when I was too young to know where I came from. If you look at our children out there," she waved towards where Ruth had them talking to a passing file of the Basilica Anthropoi, "Repent and Fear are also from the…from Amity."

I now get to keep the women engaged, while Verily goes to see if the Princesses can move to a room where there will be enough room to see them all at once.

Astrid (later in the day)

*A*nd now there is just me sitting and enjoying the sun. The wind is coming soft from the west and although this time of year is when a lot of the rain falls for this area, the weather looks to be holding fine for the Conclave. That can change at any time and the locals know it. There are mages running around setting up equipment and looking up at the sky.

From where I am sitting, they must be getting prepared for a major conjuration if it is needed. I doubt that they can stop the rain if it is a major storm, so I wonder what they are up to. We have rows of houses and the Basilica between us and the major meeting area, but I suppose that they could shield the whole town like an umbrella if they had to. We Mice are used to seeing powerful magic at work, but that would still be an impressive conjuration to see cast. I am starting to hope that it will start to rain.

Astrid (late afternoon)

Much later Bianca came back to check on the children, and briefly looked around fruitlessly for her husband. Once she had the children fed, she went on to see the Princesses, but they were still busy. Astrid was feeding her two when she returned outside.

She is still looking around for Christopher. She looks concerned. "Don't worry," said Astrid, "you know exactly where he will be, and this is one place where he knows his way around without help and without getting lost. Where have you been?"

Bianca sat down with a sigh. "In Mousehole, Ruth and I started having tea together, and keeping track of what our husbands are up to and what the other women had come to talk to us about before they might talk to our husbands. We have found it useful, even if we haven't told our husbands. When she married Simeon, we added Danelis…and now we have Verily and F…Kaliope.

"I thought that if it was useful for us, it would also be found to be useful elsewhere and I was right. There is quite a circle of wives. I have been talking with the Presbyteras here…and some from elsewhere who have come here with their husbands." She paused and sighed before continuing.

"They need our help. They believe, from what they have heard talking to the women of their villages, that some among the men will push for the North to become a Kingdom, and some of the men think that we will help them do this. As I think you and I both realise, the Khitan will not like that at all. All of us think that, without the Mice, the North is far too weak to do anything without the help of the tribes.

"The same ones want to make the former Brotherhood areas join them, so that there is one Kingdom that stretches from the mountains to the western sea right across the north. The women who run that area now are helpless without aid.

"It seems that some in the North even want to see Freehold being conquered so that, as they say, the Faith can be re-united. To do that would mean adding the south, and then the Khitan would be surrounded. Even if the tribes allowed the North to join together, they would not sit still for that." *She looks glum.*

Astrid nodded. "The women from there are calling the old Brotherhood area Amity…after the forest. I really don't think they want to be part of something else apart from that, and I am very sure that they do not want to go to war. They are with the Princesses now, working out how to stay independent, and have been there almost since we arrived."

Bianca thought briefly. "Amity…that is a good name. However, even if they just combine the villages of the north, these other ideas will lead to war. They will not lead to peace. None of the women want the Princesses to directly interfere the same way that the Princesses do not want to directly ask Hrothnog for anything. But something needs to be done.

"Of course, just as he sent us Olympias, and the priests have sent us other people, we can arrange to see that things just happen as we want. So, it is up to us to make sure that people say the right thing, seemingly on their own and not as a part of a plan. Theodora is better at this sort of thing than her husband is…I mean to say…even I can read Rani like a book. She is as bad at dissembling as most men are." She grinned. Astrid returned the smile.

"Apparently, the way these things work is that the men, without knowing what they are doing, talk to their wives. Their wives want someone to talk to with a level head, and they talk to their Presbytera. She brings it to the attention of the Metropolitan's wife, who realises that something has to be done and has a word with the wife of the highest-ranked local priest, who then has a word with her husband, and she gets her people to talk to the women who talk to their men. Apparently, this is normal...I never realised it when I was working in a tavern, but this seems to be the way the world works." Both women shook their heads at this.

Rather than talk directly with them, we need to just steer the Princesses instead of worrying them with all that we know. "They are very busy looking after the questions from the Amity women, after all," she offered. *Now we need to try to work out what needs to be said, and who to get to say it to stop this silly idea.*

Astrid (a little later)

Hulagu returned a little drunk. "Dobun is staying with the shamen. They should all be back with us tomorrow, but they are going into the real world tonight. Both the Ünee Gürvel and the Bagts Anchin are here, but I doubt that anyone will say anything unless they have to. They are here to watch and listen. They have a lot of listening to do. If anyone gets to say anything, it is me. They have heard things that may lead to the breaking of what we agreed before One Tree Hill, and they are not pleased..."

Astrid looked at Bianca. *Although we both suspect what is being feared, if this is a tribal matter, it is up to Bianca to find out the details, and to fit this in with what we are discussing. She has taken my meaning and is taking her brother aside for a walk. He is still talking when she begins nodding towards where I am watching them intently. It seems that the tribes have heard the same as us. This is getting very important, very quickly.*

Astrid (still later)

Thord came back fairly late and sat down beside Astrid. "There are Dwarves here. They are from the Northern Hills," he said. "Duke Thorfinn is getting lazy. First, he sends Snorri off to the re-occupation of Dwarvenholme...and he still hasn't been there for a visit himself...now he sends him here to see what is happening, when he could end up like my betrothed's people and surrounded by a Kingdom." He shook his head.

"I wouldn't be surprised if he is the last of his line. He is apparently trying to stop the Dwarves who live in the hills from heading home to the mountains and they are not happy with him at all. I can see, after I have visited my betrothed, that I am going to have to go there and Say a Few Things." *I can hear the capital letters being added to the words as he speaks.* He shook his head again.

"And you were such a quiet and shy Dwarf when you came to us. You just wanted to see the world outside Kharlsbane. Now who wants to shake it just to see what happens?" Thord grinned back and went to get them some beer.

Astrid (shortly afterwards)

Christopher and Aziz were the next to return. *It seems that the politics that are washing through the village seem to have steered clear of where they have been. They are only concerned with the upcoming Synod of the Faith and to ensure that the two halves of the Church were still communicate with each other. I suppose that is natural. The Metropolitan was a party to the agreement at One Tree Hill. He may not like this new idea.*

Bianca is shaking her head at me. I will bet that she has decided that it is perhaps best to let him keep worrying about those Church matters and not worry her husband with the other concerns that have been raised until we women have worked out what he must do. After a few words, Bianca has sent him inside to rest.

Astrid (a little later)

The babies are upstairs again and asleep, and Stefan is nearly the last to return. He has a very worried expression on his face. The two women were still sitting outside in the growing dark with a pair of lanterns flickering their light around the veranda. *Moths are everywhere.* Astrid grinned to herself. *Let me see if I can get a rise from him.*

"I hope you had fun or at least a good excuse. Your wives are nearly ready to divorce you and run off together with all the children. We have had them looking after all the babies most of the day." *Stefan must be worried. He didn't rise in the least bit to what I just said. Although it is hard to tell in the dark, he didn't even seem to blush at the reference to his family's domestic arrangements.*

"I am worried…this is not going as I had hoped…I need to see the Princesses before tomorrow…are they still awake?" he asked.

"They have been busy all day and are still deep in a serious matter," said Bianca. "Why don't you tell us the problem and we will see if we can help you first." Astrid nodded brightly and helpfully. *I am just innocently and casually agreeing.*

Stefan looked at them and sat on the steps. "The world is full of idiots," he said. "We have no sooner stopped a war than others want to start a new one. I have been talking with three prize fools today: Laurence Woolmonger, John Hyde, and David Granger. Bianca, you will remember John and David riding with us with David's friend, Mark...they were some of the few who are rich enough to equip himself to fight as kataphractoi. These three are the Mayors of Bidvictor, Bulga, and Outville, and you will never believe what they want to do ..."

You are taking too long to explain things. "They want to form a new Kingdom."

"They want to...how do you know that?" he asked curiously and having to deflate as his thunder was stolen.

"We have been hearing things as we sit here. We didn't have names to go with what we heard, but that makes sense."

"David is very full of his own importance," said Bianca. "And his friend Mark encourages him. Between them, they own half of the land that is around Outville, and they are starting to think that they are really Barons—just like in Freehold. It makes sense that it is him. If anyone would, he would want to be the King. I suppose that the other two are to be Barons?"

Stefan nodded. "And I am to be the Baron here. He has gotten the other two to agree with the idea. He has told them that the compact that we made at One Tree Hill only binds the Metropolitan, and that the Metropolitan should not be running a town anyway. They are saying that the Church should only run the Church.

"He wants me to convince the Princesses to back him, to help him talk to the Basilica Anthropoi, and to convince those in his village who don't like the idea. He thinks that the Basilica Anthropoi, seeing that now half of them are from Darkreach, would prefer a King to not having a real ruler." He shook his head.

Just then Nikephorus came out to them, as they sat there, with kaf and pastries, and they sat for a while in silence as they ate and sipped. Soon Basil arrived to join them.

"Hello, dear. Are you going to tell us what *you* have heard about the new Kingdom of the North, or do we have to guess?"

"I am." *His voice shows no surprise at what I asked. His eyebrows may have raised a fraction, but it is hard to tell in the dark.* "The main point is that it is not a certain and established thing yet. A lot have not yet heard of the idea. Of those that have, some want it, mainly the wealthy ones, and some don't, mainly the poorer ones. Most of the traders, servants, and farmers see it as meaning they will get taxed more, and end up fighting wars for whoever ends up as King. They see nothing in it for them."

Time we got things moving to stop it. We just need to work out what they are. She looked at her husband. "Husband, get some kaf, get Nikephorus to bring more out for us, and then we will talk." Basil went inside and the others sat in silence again, waiting.

He came back out grumbling. "In Darkreach, all I have to do is report things like this. I don't have to fix them myself." He sat down and they started talking quietly, working out what needed to be done.

Suddenly, Astrid spoke up brightly. "I am sooo good. No wonder Hrothnog loves me." She briefly grinned up at the sky as if expecting to see some sort of confirmation there. "I have a solution," she said, and as the other three listened, she laid out her ideas and they refined them. Once they were all satisfied with what they had wrought, they headed off to their beds leaving instructions behind them for an early rise. *We have a lot to do in the morning to set things in place before the meeting.*

Before she went to bed, Astrid went to where the Princesses were still talking to the Amity women. She excused herself and asked if she could borrow Verily and Forth for a few minutes. It did not take long for her to have Forth's full co-operation with what she wanted to do. *As soon as the Amity woman was given the details of what has been planned for her by a few men, she didn't like the idea, either.*

Before she went to sleep Bianca innocently asked her husband if it would be possible to arrange a few things with Andronicus for the next day as a favour for some of the guests. He was happy to agree.

Chapter XXXI

Bianca (21ˢᵗ December)

The morning has dawned bright, and it shows the promise of being a nice day. The threatened rain has blown away without troubling us. Even among the Mice, most are lingering over their breakfast, talking to others about what they want, or at least expect, from the Conclave. Most of what we want is in place, in other cases we still have to talk to people. I am sure that in some other places around town there is a lot more activity.

As they were headed for the Orthros service, Bianca reminded her husband what he needed to talk to the Metropolitan's Secretary, Andronicus, about.

Once she was sure that he had it firm in his mind, and she had pointed him in the right direction, she left him. "I see a woman that I would like to talk to. I will get back to you soon…look there is Andronicus." *Now, the Mayor of Glengate…it looks like I don't need to. I think that Astrid has talked to her from the way that she is grinning at me.* Astrid joined her at the door of the Basilica of Our Lady as they hurried inside.

"Done," she said. "She was very easy to convince. I haven't seen Basil since he left to have his own word with Andronicus…I suppose that I will be lucky to see him at all today." Together they went inside. *Now that we have made those arrangements, we just have to wait to see if everything can come together as we need it to.*

As they walked into the multi-coloured light from the stained-glass, Bianca made sure that she passed a certain area where a particular group of Presbyteras stood, and stopped to have a few words there before the service began.

Metropolitan Basil Tornikes

*G*iven *the importance of the day, I will lead the service myself. Greensin might be a church town, but it rarely has as many people in attendance at a service as it does today. I am filled with hope that my prayers of peace and co-operation across the north are about to be fulfilled. A nice homily on the Beatitudes will do very well to set the theme.*

In a way, it is a pity there is no important Saint for me to talk about today. Maybe I should have set the date of this for a little later...no, Saint Constantine is the patron of rulers...his Holy Day might have set the wrong tone for this event. This is a meeting where we wish to confirm the ideas of peace and co-operation that we flagged at One Tree Hill, not ideas of war and conflict and domination.

Astrid (mid-morning)

*E*veryone *is starting to drift into the centre of town and gather together. There is no hall large enough to hold them all, apart from perhaps in the monastery and there are many women present, so that is not going to be possible as a venue. At least the mages are ready with their shield spell in case of rain, but that now looks unlikely.*

In front of us is the Metropolitan's house, taller and grander than The Pious Smith, the tavern beside us. On the other side, the Basilica looms large, and then, making up the rest of the huge square we have rows of shops and houses. The two bakers are doing a great trade, I already have a supply of boiled sweets from the confectioner, and I am not the only one of us.

Chairs had originally been set out in a large circle in the square, but a little while ago Andronicus came out of the house with servants, and had them brought up onto the veranda. He re-arranged the chairs into almost a straight line that is facing the square. On the ground to one side there are three large carpets laid out. Each has a divan and a large number of cushions. That means he has listened to Christopher.

On the other side of the veranda was another carpet, and next to it were some more cushions and some chairs. I have most of the Mice in position in one of these areas already, and people are doing what they have been told. Most of them sit on their saddles, and again Adara and Bryony have to deal with my babies in addition to their own.

The Princesses have not mentioned anyone of our people who is still not with us. *Only a few people are fully armed here, but I am one of them. I stand ready beside the Princesses, just as Hrothnog's Guard did for him. Not only do I have my armour, all repaired and looking as good as new, but now also with my new bardiche in hand and helmet on.*

Early this morning, I made sure that others in the village saw me doing my exercises. She grinned. *In deference to those from outside Mousehole, I did the moves fully dressed for once.* How easily she had moved her over-sized weapon around had attracted watchers. *They seemed to be impressed. It was good to have found a pole to practice against. It was kindling in a few blows.*

As a part of what we are doing today, my husband, and this morning Ayesha and even Stefan, have been spreading stories about how I got my first weapon, and although the Princesses, sitting there in more formal attire, do not seem to realise it, I am standing here representing the military might of our small village.

Basil has obviously had his chat with the servants that Andronicus has put in charge, and as people arrive, they are shepherded either into a seat, or out into the open space of the square. Those in the seats on the veranda are only allowed to have one or two people behind them due to the lack of space there.

As the Khitan arrive, Alaine meets the Cow-lizards, and Aigiarn greets the Pack-hunters, and they show them each to a carpet. Hulagu, Dobun, Bianca and Ayesha are already installed on the third carpet, where the other Mori join them when they are finished with their duties. The stage is being set up just as we want.

Metropolitan Basil

I wish that my wife would stop fussing, and let me go out and make sure that it is all set up right. It is past time for me to go out to take my place. I have great hopes for today, particularly after this morning. If I speak well enough, perhaps we can form a peaceful alliance that stretches across the north, each village or totem with independence, but pledged to defend the others if any are attacked...all trading together, and peacefully.

He emerged and looked around, slightly puzzled at the scene in front of him. *I was sure that I asked Andronicus to arrange the seating differently...in a circle to show equality, and to allow leaders to have their people with them. Oh well...they are all in place now, and at least this way the large number of villagers from all over the north can see what is happening better.*

He looked out over what seemed like a sea of faces. *All are looking back at me in expectation. It looks like I am the last to arrive and that everyone is here already.* He motioned to Andronicus. *He has been around the people here and supposedly has a list of who will speak when. All I know is that I will be speaking first with my welcome.*

He rose to greet everyone and pronounce his blessings on the gathering. *Such formal words tend to bore people. I will try hard to be brief in what I say.*

Astrid (a few minutes later)

I *get to have a good view from here. Now we see if everything works out as we want it to, or if we must follow someone else's agenda.* The Metropolitan had just sat down, and John Hyde had started to rise when Andronicus called for Mayor Forth of Baloo to speak. *It is as well that, for a small man, he has a strong voice to be heard with this many people gathered.*

The mayor of Bulga looks more than a trifle vexed, but at least he sat back down again. It looks like the script to be followed today is the one that we want. I thought that Basil could speak so that Andronicus understood the issues that we are facing.

Forth and the women (and some men) from Amity are seated on the cushions and chairs at the other end from the Khitan and beside us Mice. This morning the women seemed to be wearing lighter garb than the ground length heavy wools that they had been forced to wear in the past. Forth stood at the corner of the veranda, and looked along it before turning to face the crowd and speaking.

"My name is Forth, and for the many who do not know me, I am the Mayor of Baloo. However, here I am speaking not just for my little village, but for all of the women and men who now live in the area that used to be called the Brotherhood. We wish to wash that away, and if you have not heard this before, we are telling you now that we want the area to be called Amity.

"I wanted to speak first because this is the first occasion for us to properly thank the people of the North for fighting for us and freeing us from what we have had to endure for so many generations. Although some of us have come from outside Amity, most of us that are living there now were born slaves, and until recently we expected to die that way.

"Our land has been apart from all of the other realms for a long time. We are not part of the North, and never will be ..." Astrid looked intently. *Those words are getting a reaction from a few of the right people.* "But we will always owe you a great debt. We hope that today you are able to carry on with what was set out in the Agreement that was made at One Tree Hill.

"I have spoken with our other village leaders, and we are going to form a loose confederation, perhaps a little bit like that they have in the Swamp, but I think that it will be a little more orderly." *There is some laughter at the slightly prim way she made that last comment. I think that Amity will always have a reputation for a lack of.. fun.*

"We have spoken together, and have agreed that we would like to join that agreement as a full party, if the tribes…" *She has looked at the other end of the row and Janibeg may have inclined his head just a trifle.* "and the North…" *She smiles at the Metropolitan, and he very openly smiles back.* "…can agree on it.

"What you agree among yourselves is your own business, but I hope that we can work with you. Of course, any who want to move to our area are still welcome to do so. I believe that, just like the village of Mousehole does, we will have more women than we have men for quite a while. Also, of course, unlike our former masters, we will always welcome your trade, whatever your faith.

"It will be many years before we are able to produce everything we need, and our free growth should make the North prosperous, as well. We need so many things, and our crops of herbs are at least coming on well, and we need people to come and buy them." She nodded to the Metropolitan and sat down with the rest of the people from Amity to a fair amount of spontaneous applause from the crowd.

Again, the Mayor of Bulga went to rise, but Andronicus seemed to not notice him as, consulting his notes, he called on Theodora to speak. *She looks surprised but stands up. Nobles respond well to prompts. I know that she had not asked to speak. She had expected to only be an observer here or at most to say something later.*

Astrid moved quickly and handed her the loud talker. Theodora looked at it and then at Astrid suspiciously. *She is not slow. She fully realises that the quick way that this has been done suggests that something is happening that she is not aware of.* Astrid smiled at her innocently. *From the look I got, that innocence was wasted. At least Rani looks puzzled.*

"Your Eminence, people, hello," she said to the crowd far too loudly, and Astrid leant forward again and adjusted where her hand was. She just looked at the loud talker as if it would bite her. She continued in a more normal tone: "I am the Princess Theodora, of Mousehole, and this is my husband, the Princess Rani. Many of you will have seen us during the fight against the Brotherhood. Our village is in the mountains, and our fight is with the Masters, their servants, and those who stand behind them.

"We fought against the Brotherhood and for your freedom, not only because it was right, but also because they were controlled by evil masters who wanted to enslave you all. We didn't like that then, and we will always fight that evil, until it is banished from this world. Like Forth, we wish you well and we hope to co-operate with you in the future. You may have noticed one of our teachers here with her class." She waved out at where Ruth had the children.

"I want to remind people that we are offering to teach any of your children as well as we can, including as mages, partly so that you can stay free and independent from tyranny in the North, as unbound villages, in the same fashion that we are in the mountains. I hope that we see you all often and in peace and prosperity through trade."

It is obvious that she has run out of extemporaneous comment and so she just nods to the front and also sits down to cheers. She can give me that look, but I am happy, Theodora has said pretty much as Bianca, and I thought that she would, when she had not been given a chance to write down a formal speech.

Once again, the Mayor of Bulga tries to get Andronicus' attention, but he has been seated down at the end of the row beside the people from Amity and us deliberately, and Andronicus seems not to be seeing him very well. At the other end, at the far end, near the Khitan, the Mayor of Outville is having a similar lack of success. Andronicus did not notice either as he called on Hulagu. He stood.

"I am the Tar-Khan Hulagu of the Clan of the Horse, and I speak for the Emeel Amidarch Baigaa Khümüüs, the Kara-Khitan. I speak not just for those who are here today, but with the agreement of all eleven of the Clans.

"We are also here to just watch today, and to make sure that what was agreed upon once stays agreed now. We are here to affirm the compact made at One Tree Hill, and hope that you will agree to continue to be in peace with us. We will need to discuss this further at another time, but I believe it likely that we can add Amity to our compact."

He looked at the other two as if asking if there was anything else. *Both faintly incline their heads.* "That is all." He sat down to sustained applause. *The people around the plains have always had an odd relationship with the Khitan, and the idea of continued peace with them is very appealing to most of them...very, very appealing.*

During that short speech Astrid finally managed to locate her husband in the press. *As I thought, he is moving through the crowd and appears to occasionally stop and have a word with a person or two.*

Again, the two men at the far ends of the row try to get Andronicus' attention, but this time he calls on Siglunda. She needs to pull her weight now, but I think that she will. She stood up from where she sat on the left. "I am Captain Siglunda of the village of Wolfneck. We did not contribute to your battle against the Brotherhood, but we almost fell to the same foe that stood behind them and we had our own battles later.

"I have to say that we also do not think of ourselves as being a part of your North. Our kinship is with the people of Neron Island, and the north of the mountains and the Dwarves there, and even perhaps with the north of Darkreach. Neron Island fell to the quiet evil of ambitious men, and we nearly did the same. I am glad that you seem to be taking a different and freer path, but we are also here just to watch what you decide.

"Our village has consulted on this matter with Captain Kadlin of Skrice, and she agrees with us, and I speak today for her also. We wish you well and we invite your trade. Thank you for this opportunity to speak to you." She sat down to applause and cheers. *The applause is starting from the areas where Basil has been.*

Andronicus next calls on Mayor Aimee Tate of Glengate, again ignoring the two men at the ends, whose attempts to speak are getting feebler. She is seated on the right. She stands and introduces herself. "My village is in the same position as Wolfneck, but even more so. We are very isolated from both the north and the south, and we rely on trade and good relations with the Kara-Khitan to survive.

"We have no sea on one side to defend us. We hope that the Compact that has been spoken of applies to us, too ..." *She pauses as if she is hoping for one among the Khitan to say something, but it seems that Hulagu has said all that they are going to say here, so she continues. All three of the Tar-Khan now look stone-faced and stay silent.*

"We were untouched by any direct action from the war, although we lost some traders before it started. We are glad that we avoided the war that you had. Even if we will fight to stay free of others, we wish to stay away from all wars if we can. I hope that you stay in peace, and like Wolfneck, we welcome your trade." *It is now her turn to sit and be cheered.*

Andronicus now turned towards the left and started to call on the Mayor of Bulga, but on the right Joachim Caster, from Warkworth, jumped to his feet and interjected. Stefan also started to rise, but Astrid signalled frantically to him to sit when she saw who else had stood. *This is one man who we did not speak to, as we could not work out which way his village would want to go.*

"If I may," Joachim said. "You have heard from all of the others here who are not from the North. Before you hear from the North, can our village be heard?"

He is looking at the Metropolitan for permission who is nodding in blissful ignorance. He thinks that he is running the meeting. Andronicus has waved at John Hyde to sit and grumpily he does. For a moment, he had nearly gained the floor, but that was a false hope. Stefan will speak before you, my would-be Lord.

Joachim introduced himself. "We also have little in common with the rest of the North," he said. "Like Glengate, we need the help of the Kara-Khitan to survive, and are glad that it is not just our local Clan, but also the other Clans that are guarantors of our freedom." *A keen observer might have noticed a few faint smiles being shared among the Khitan at that comment. I certainly did. It seems that they share in the general opinion of Tar-Khan Mongka.*

"We have lived in fear of the Brotherhood since they broke away from Freehold. That is a long time. Since the Great Schism, we have also lived in fear of Freehold. Although Amity has only just gained its freedom, we have already heard rumours about what they wished to do and the elders of Warkworth have met and have asked me to start talks with the people of Amity about the possibility, if it suits all parties, of us joining with them, at least loosely."

He nodded to the Metropolitan and sat down to loud cheers and applause. *The group of women at the other end are nodding and talking among themselves. They seem happy with the idea. Well, that part was not in our script, but if we had seen it coming, it would have been.*

Again, Andronicus turned to the left but this time he didn't even get a word out. Stefan, who was seated a little away from the Mice, and could have been seen as more a part of the crowd than a part of his actual home, leapt to his feet and strode into the open area. *It is time for our impromptu interruption. He is quicker to his feet this time.*

"I also am sorry to interrupt," he said loudly, turning so that all could hear him. "But all of you have probably heard of me. I am Stefan, Dragon-slayer, and I think that my deeds as your Captain in the recent war allow me the right to be heard, and what I have to say needs to be said, even if I do not talk for a village."

Astrid looked at David Granger where he sat on their end of the row. *He looks surprised but pleased. He thinks that something is finally about to go his way.* Stefan did not wait for approval before he continued. "Several men have approached me with an idea for the North, and to start with, it sounded a good one and I am sure that they had the best interests of the North in their hearts when they spoke." *Lay it on thick.*

"However, since we have started this morning, I have heard village after village and group after group speak of freedom, of independence, and of mutual respect and trade. I no longer think that this idea is a good one. I urge all of you to continue on the path that was set out and started on earlier during the war." *He is pausing and looking around at the leaders on the veranda and then turning back to the crowd.*

"If any try to set up a King of the North, then it will end up taking away from your freedom, it will lead to war with the Khitan…and it will not be a war that I will lead you to battle in…more importantly, it will not be, in the long run, good for trade. It will also probably mean war with Freehold and higher taxes. So…again I urge you…if you hear about such an idea…shout it down." He turned towards the Metropolitan.

The poor innocent dear has a stunned look on his face. My two have the same look. In all of their minds you can see questions running around: What has just happened? What idea? What King? "Thank you for your indulgence in listening to me." He walked back to where he had been and sat down again. *The applause that comes after his words is the longest yet and I am sure now that Basil's plants are leading it, but this time it is very quickly taken up by others and it seems to be very heartfelt.*

It was some time before Andronicus could make himself heard. *He is trying to call on John Hyde, but John Hyde now does not want to speak. He turned to try to get David Granger to speak, but he also seems to have lost any will to be heard. They both look quite deflated. So do some of those around them. They can see their plans in ashes.* He turns back to the Metropolitan. *With any luck, the meeting has scarcely begun and yet it may already be over.*

The Metropolitan stood. *For a while he is lost for words.* Astrid looked at his wife. *She is smiling towards Bianca, and I can see Bianca smiling back.* Eventually, the Metropolitan spoke and thanked the previous speakers before proposing a similar loose confederation to that of the Confederation of the Free. *He has thought it out well and goes into some detail outlining his ideas.*

In every area, he wants each settlement of over three hands filled of adults to send a person to form a local court to pass local laws and judge local matters. They will select their area leader between them. He wants them to meet every month. He also wants each of those local groups to elect another person, who is not their local leader to, once a quarter, come to Greensin to form a similar body to regulate matters between the areas. Once he had finished, he sat down, as if waiting for a response. *Everyone just sits on the veranda looking at each other and no-one is saying anything.*

From the crowd in front someone, a person with a strong northern accent, yelled out "No rulers? We get to have the say? Then we like it."

After some laughter, there are some more shouts of approval to be heard. Once again, they are from ones that I have seen Basil talking to. Still, none of the leaders up front seem to want to say anything, but I can see several looking out over the crowd and gauging their reaction. It seems that the crowd generally likes what they have heard and there are few, if any, who would be willing to comment against it.

Eventually the Metropolitan stood again and nodded to Andronicus. *He is waving into the building.* "I cannot see any objections," said Metropolitan Basil in a surprised voice. "I have taken the liberty to have it all written up… just in case. I mean…if you all agree we can sign it now and the observers can also sign it and we can have a celebration. This will be a much shorter meeting than I had thought that it would be. We can do copies for everyone later."

That declaration is greeted by the loudest cheer of all from the crowd. Astrid kept watching. The thwarted leaders are going to be signing, but it is easy to see that they are not happy. Such a structure as they will be putting their names to so openly will make it nearly impossible for them to ever achieve what they want.

Astrid (a good while later)

A s the crowd started to break up, Theodora turned to Astrid. "What just happened there?" Astrid tried to look innocent, but quickly gave up. *As my husband has pointed out more than once to me, I am not very good at dissembling. I suppose that being too honest could be seen as a disadvantage in this case.*

"The Metropolitan got what he wanted, other people didn't, and you two didn't have to interfere, and so make people on one side or another dislike us. You two can now keep on being regal and Princessy and independent. The North got what it needed, and no-one can trace anything back to anyone…and it all seemed to happen naturally." She grinned openly.

Theodora gave Astrid a very long hard look before turning to her husband. *She may be good in battle, but she is a complete political innocent. She is looking even more bemused than Theodora, even if she has just signed the Compact as a witness, and is looking at an ink stain on her finger and then trying to check to see if she has managed to somehow also get the ink on her silk.*

Astrid (23rd December)

A lthough the main business is done, many have stayed for several more days as an impromptu market has been set up and the gathered leaders, and their people, are all taking the opportunity to discuss things of interest with their neighbours, and those who are further away, before they head home. The women of Amity are often to be seen talking to the Princesses or to Verily.

When I don't have to look after the babies, I get to just look around and shop. I am still not seeing much of my husband, but when I do see him, he is often chatting with ones that I have seen him with before, traders and guards, and all sorts of people.

Astrid

23rd December, the Feast Say of Saint Thomaïs

It was on the last day of their stay in Greensin, that two young girls of at most fifteen years came to see Astrid. *Both of them look dusty, travel-worn, and hungry, and they are determinedly holding each other's hand.* "We seem to have made it in time," said the taller of the two firmly. "Is your woman with the short hair and the dark-skinned wife with you? We need to see her. We met her in Warkworth." *She is looking around and sounds very anxious.*

"Do you mean Goditha?" *I can somehow see where this is going.* She received nods in return from the two. "No, she didn't come on this trip. Can I help you instead?" *The two girls have an unhappy look on their faces now as they look at each other. They have deflated like a stranded jellyfish that is unable to move any further forward or retreat.*

"I don't know." *The girl now seems to be nearly in tears. They have obviously pinned all of their hopes on seeing Goditha. I can see it written in their faces. I may be dressed as Goditha was, but I have babies in slings. I may even be hostile to them, as others in their village had been.*

"Let me see that you are fed and then we can talk. I think I know what you may want." *Do I sound motherly and sympathetic enough? The girls are determined. They may be hungry and very travel worn, but they have somehow managed to have worked their way right across the northern plains during the upheaval and have indeed come all of the way from Warkworth.*

In the end, after taking them to see the Princesses, Nadia and Erika came back to Mousehole with the Mice. They were conditionally allowed to join the village.

Chapter XXXII

Theodora (26th December)

*W*e were only away for a few days at the Conclave and yet two men from the south, one from Saltbeach on Arden Creek, hard by Freehold, and the other from Ooshz, had managed to make their way to the village. I need to learn more about where these places are. It is sad that I had to look at our maps before I talked to them. It falls to me to see if they are suitable, and I think that they are already.

Adrian Digge tells me that he left Saltbeach for three reasons. Firstly, in the same way that Stefan had to leave Evilhalt, his village didn't have the work to keep another journeyman miner busy and he wanted to keep working at his trade.

Secondly, he was getting very nervous about Freehold, and the elders of his village were, at least publicly, dismissing the concerns that many of the local people were expressing. They believed that it was posing no more risk that it normally did. I think we need to talk to him more about that. Perhaps it is Basil who should do it. He will know what to ask.

The third reason is, however, as far as he is concerned, the more important one. Rumours of Mousehole, its wealth, and the beauty of its women, are beginning to appear even as far away as his old home…and that is as far away as you can get. The tales could have been carried by traders or the Khitan. While he expected to be disappointed, the rumours at least gave him a place to head towards when he left home. It seems that no-one along the way had needed a journeyman miner, so he has not been tempted by elsewhere.

Their loss is our gain. Already he has Harald speaking for him. Apparently, we are a village that does need more miners. With our changes and our growth, Harald has been hard pressed to keep doing what he wants to do.

He wants to keep the established mine going and producing, and yet still *pan the antimony, and find its source. He cannot do this on his own and without some labourers. He badly needs help with the mine, and none of the Brotherhood girls are interested in it as a career. Seeing that Adrian is also happy to help Tãriq with quarrying stone, he is being made doubly welcome.*

She turned to the next man. *Denny Pollard also found himself without steady work. A small village only needs so many shearers, even if there are a lot of sheep in the area and his home village had one of the best...his teacher, and others in the trade. When Adrian worked his way eastwards along the south coast and talked of where he was going, Denny decided to join him.*

It had been hard work for him getting here, but he is here now, and hoping that he will be needed. Giles says that he is. He has too much work to do ploughing and working the farms to spend time keeping the increasing herds shorn and none of the women have shown any aptitude for the back-breaking work.

Moreover, as shearing is always a seasonal trade, Denny has worked at other things all his life. Although he is not a full journeyman, he has some experience in working with plaster on walls and ceilings.

He says that he does not have much skill, but admitting that he has some is more than anyone else in the village has. He is willing to try his hand at that until his shearing is needed. Up until now, the stone and brick walls of the village houses are generally just being painted, rather than plastered, even though a proper plastering and whitewashing will make them much warmer and less dusty.

It will do even better at keeping out mice, as no-one has yet had time to cast enough spells to keep all of the inevitable rodents away. I must think about how to do that. No-one has even mentioned it to me until now.

While looking for her clay, Ariadne has already found an old gypsum mine a couple of days walk to the north, but she doesn't know enough to be able to make plaster from it. It does seem that Denny has several people speaking for him as well.

Both men have said that they were more than happy with the financial arrangements. Astrid has quietly pointed out that they should be. Just like the two new girls from Warkworth, the men were both looking more than a trifle hungry by the time they reached us. It is a long way up from the south with vague directions and few chances to work for food.

I am very happy with the way they have set straight to work and tried to fit in, even before I have approved them. They were both in work clothes and brought in from tasks when I saw them. Denny has, in a week, even been out and collected supplies, made some plaster as a test and applied it. I think we now need to see which of our many single women will attract their attention or, more likely, the other way around.

As for the two new girls, Nadia already wants to work alongside Goditha as a mason and stoneworker. It seems that many who live in Warkworth, between their wall and the new wharf being built, have some experience at that. She lacks the strength that Goditha has.

"It took me a while to gain that, and I am still gaining it," said Goditha. "She is young. I will work on building her up." *In a day, she has already had her hair cut like a boy and is hard at work half naked in a full leather apron. She came to me with rock dust smeared all over her face where she has tried to wipe it off.*

Her lover's father is the moneychanger and lender in Warkworth. Seeing that she has some training there, Erika can help Kaliope with our increasingly complex village accounts. Astrid is already giving me hints about her new sister not sleeping enough…actually, it was more about not having enough time in bed, but she could have been talking about sleep.

Theodora (30ᵗʰ December)

*C*arausius, his newly wed daughter, and her husband, and their guards *are now here. Of more import, he has supposedly brought an older man with him, but I have yet to see him. Furthermore, there is the usual supply of metals that our village has a constant need for, boxes of nails, and sheet lead, in particular.*

It also seems that Astrid ordered an icon of Saint Kessog in Ardlark, and others have arranged for other things. Apparently, we now have a small flock of fat-tailed sheep grazing happily in a paddock somewhere. I am not sure who arranged to have them bought, but it seems that they are welcome. It is a big load they brought. There are also our gifts from Hrothnog, such as the armour that people were measured for. Except for the sheep, all those goods were laden on the three carts.

All the packhorses share the same load of carefully packed small sheets of plain and coloured glass, set in frames of lead and timber. It is the first glass to arrive at the village. Now the task of replacing the oilskin in people's windows can begin. I don't care who ordered this, but I am very pleased to have more light to work by.

On one of the carts there is a large and heavy package that none are allowed to touch. Karas and Festus carried it in carefully. Carausius insisted that as many as possible should gather around when the package was unloaded into the hall and then unwrapped.

It proved to be a large triptych meant for the wall of the Basilica when it was complete. It depicted Saint George in the centre panel, the stylised village of Mousehole on the left and a dragon surrounded by riders on flying saddles on the right.

I am sure that we are all glad to see it. This is what Christopher sent back to Ardlark for. He told me afterwards that he had ordered something, but not what. He is beside himself with the result. The whole village are in awe. We have this, for now, to indicate to us that a major service is about to begin, and that the communal hall is about to become a church.

Theodora (an hour later)

A part from those on watch, nearly the only people not present when the *triptych was unwrapped are Lādi and the new man. I wanted to find out about him, but he disappeared before I got the chance. Astrid apparently saw them leave, but it was a while before they have returned to us.* When they did so, they discovered that most of the older Mice had found excuses to stay around.

The man is introduced as Nathanael Ktenas, the pastry cook that Lādi had met at the wedding. He looks to be an older man, slightly overweight, and balding to go with it. Despite that, he is not unattractive. From his speech, he has a soft and gentle manner, and he has travelled a long way on his quest. It seems that he had despaired of ever finding someone to be his partner.

He is explaining this to me as he stands there nervously wringing his felt hat in his hands and kneading it into shapelessness. I am sure that explaining his love life to a Princess of the Blood had not figured in his mind when he had left Ardlark. However, it does appear that the last of our original women of the valley is about to get married.

Carausius was apparently initially disappointed to hear about Guk and his travels around his circuit. However, Astrid tells me that she has had a quiet word with him. He apparently thought for a moment and then was quick to find a pen and paper, and to leave a note for the Hob with his daughter, which Guk will have to have read to him.

His children may be learning the scripts of other languages, but it is a skill that, bar his name and a few other words like the names of items that he trades in, he seems to try and avoid. Astrid suggested to Carausius that there will be many items made in the area that will not find a market on Guk's circuit, but that might be welcomed in Darkreach.

These can be left here in Mousehole on consignment for Carausius to take back into Drakreach. In return, Guk can leave orders for rare luxury items for Carausius to bring back from Ardlark. Between them they have the jump on any other traders, and can almost corner the market for this part of the mountains.

I am sure that Astrid is right. That idea will well appeal to the men as both of them should reap a good profit from the trade. I like it a lot...as it helps bind our area together. Now, how much do we charge them for storage of goods? Shilpa can deal with that, I think. I am certain that the three of them can argue happily for days on the subject.

Theodora (31st December)

When the village started to see Nathanael's work appearing to be eaten on the next day, Zoë swore that she was happy to confine herself to working just with breads, and the Mice were well pleased.

He is a master at his trade, and while my husband may like fruits, I do enjoy pastries for breakfast with my kaf. While he and Zoë can share an oven at present, it appears that Mousehole must originally have had more than one person who baked, as there is a second workshop that has an oven that still has not yet been renovated.

It is just luck that he has arrived when he did. We had started to have debates as to whether this was a waste of space and whether the oven should come out. If it were not needed for its proper purpose, then that would have left another workshop free. I still do not think that we need more workshops yet anyway.

Atā (34th December)

Outside the valley, more land is being cleared of trees and scrub, and the timber is being put aside in huge stacks to dry. Some low stone walls are even starting to be built...at least enough to outline fields for Asad and Arthur. Next winter, Inshallah, some of the flocks can probably be driven out here to be pastured during the day, if the snows allow it and we have a shepherd to guard them from mountain lions.

With the clearing that is going on, too much timber is having to be cut down for me to process immediately on my own, and for lack of having an assistant working for me full-time, I have tried to show some of the former Brotherhood girls how to use the long saws of the profession. I work on one end the whole time, but six of them must take it in turns to help me.

They are not very strong, and have difficulty working in the pit, but it is better than having no help at all. Luckily, young Cadfael, the student from the Swamp, is growing to be a strong boy, and on his half day of work has settled on my work as his trade to learn. I give praise to Allah that, like me, he has come to love that smell of fresh sawn timber.

Lakshmi
7th of Undecim, it is the third day of Deepavali

*S*hilpa has come to term, and her younger lover is near beside himself over the lack of the right priest and...well...nearly everything that he is used to. I am sure that we did not need Devi's adherents here. Too many women die in childbirth in Haven. In the end, the boy Abhaidev, which means Free of Fear, is happy and healthy, and the birth went well.*

I do admit to some worry myself about this pregnancy, as Shilpa is nearly thirty years of age. She is near to the age when many women of Haven are grandmothers, and so is very old to be having her first child. Although she is exhausted, she has declared that the wait is worth it. More and more, I praise God for giving us Fear and her gifts.

Olympias (13th Undecim)

*I*t is good to be back on board and being a sailor, even if my pregnancy restricts what I can do. She handles so much better with the copper sheathing, and we get to use the* River Dragon *to make a much more leisurely trip than on its previous transits to and from Sacred Gate. We can spend the time just for the purposes of better mapping the channel.*

This is our second day of travel, and I am pleased to see that the changes in the channel are not rapid on this river. It seems that there is too high a flow, down too narrow a channel, to get the lazy drifting that we could see, and often do in Darkreach.

In addition, I get to trial six of the former slave girls to see how they will perform as a part of my crew. They are the six girls who were in the brothel in Warkworth. Whatever they do, they have insisted on staying together. So, they go on my ship together, or they farm together, or they work on houses together.

I think that I agree with the Princess on this. If they can turn their hand to the work, being on my ship sounds like the best option for them. I have had groups enlist on my ships before like that. If they can be proper sailors, they will never really need to be apart for long again.

Lakshmi
15th of Undecim, it is the Feast Day of Saint Swithun

*I*t seems that winter is when many of our women will give birth. Ruth went into labour late last night, but it is not until well into today that she gave birth to Isaac. Ruth is nearly as old as Shilpa, and far smaller in frame, but she rejoices both in having Fear's help, and the fact that, at least, she is only having one child this time.

Theodora
16th of Undecim, the Feast Day of Saint Jude

*T*hat was nice. Guk has brought Ruth a present of baby clothes from the Presbytera's among the Cenubarkincilari. Now he is about to leave with two half packs of cloth to sell to the Dwarves. With all the new girls that we have now living here, my village is finally starting to produce a small surplus of plain woollen cloth.

I am told that our greatest limitation now is the number of available wheels to keep even one loom fed. Apparently, it takes twelve spinners for each loom, and many have fallen back on using drop spindles to do their spinning for lack of an alternative. The cloth is not of the highest quality, but it is serviceable, and like in Mousehole itself, that is more important for our uphill neighbours than fine cloth, which can be imported from further afield until they establish their own flocks.

Theodora (17th of Undecim)

I get dragged out to inspect everything and tell people that they have done well. We have been back a few weeks now, and work keeps being done on buildings. *Soon, almost the entire village will be brought back to being at least minimally habitable in time for this Synod. It is only rough work, but the guards and horse handlers will at least have dry places to sleep in.*

In the far future, once the Basilica is finished, I am told that workers will probably go back and re-do large sections of the village, particularly their earlier work. As they go on, they are getting better, and some are almost ashamed of the standard of what they did when they started out. All are sure that it will be many years before every old building is refurbished to a standard that everyone is happy with. We have plaster walls and glass in our house now though. It is almost cosy.

Astrid is escorting Christopher out most days. He is using the time to start visiting all the local settlements of any size to check and to make sure that no Patterns have appeared anywhere. Some areas have never been checked before, but some places, such as Evilhalt and its hamlets and assarts, are being checked again as a re-affirmation that all is still well.

My husband and I can use the visits to the larger places to talk to the village leaders. It has become quite common now for flights of saddles to head out of Mousehole on almost any fine day. I am sure that it would be hard to sneak up on us now with any large force, or even quite a small one. It is nice to start feeling safer.

Shilpa (24ᵗʰ Undecim)

*I*t may be just a surveying trip, although I am busy enough writing down the *readings, but I get to take my baby with me, and trade as we go out of habit. At least, while we were in Haven, I started to sound out the possibilities of lending large sums of our spare money to some of the moneylenders there for a year or two. I still have some contacts from my old days it seems, and some of them even seem to be respectable to the rest of Haven.*

On the next trip, I will be returning with cash, and with Zeenat and some guards along. It was nice seeing Gupta ke Dvīpa and Vyāpārī Dvīpa again, but although she does not want to return to Pavitra Phāṭaka and its memories, Zeenat has more familiarity with the people that we need to deal with than I do. A former client of hers knows a man whom she insists is an honest lawyer. We need him to draw up the contracts for us.

Shilpa also suggested to Olympias that, on that trip, they explore the idea of a transit along the length of the south coast for trade.

I have dangled the carrot of learning the currents, hazards, and winds of the area in front of the captain...an irresistible lure to that woman as I well know. Combined with what we have found in books from various places, and the maps from Darkreach, we will soon have at least rough charts of most of the coast of The Land.

To our surprise, although the Brotherhood ignored the sea, at least one of its people must not have done so in the past, as we recovered an excellent volume of charts of the north to Wolfneck and part of the west down into Freehold from the library in Greatkin and written in their language.

The book of charts must have dated from before The Burning, as it mentions settlements that are now not even memories. It was now only the south and a little of the west along the coast of Freehold that we lack any real detail on. It is a lure Olympias will not be able to resist.

Lakshmi (6th Duodecimus)

*S*aints' days come and go before this next birth, but now Ariadne has gone into labour. Her child is the most mixed-race birth that the village has seen, or is likely to see for some time. While the mother is half Human, she is also half Alat-kharl, and her child is half-Hob and none of us are familiar with how that combination might affect the birth.

As it is, she required less opium than Verily did, although she still needed a fair amount of healing. It seems that all Hobgoblin babies, or at least part Hob babies, are born with a far larger head than those of the other races. She and Krukurb are, however, quite besotted with their daughter, Nikê, despite her unusual, shaded tri-colour appearance of grey, green, and brown skin.

Lakshmi (12th Duodecimus)

*O*lympias was also grateful for the presence of Fear and the healers. She took opium. She is, like a lot of sailors, small…smaller even than her brother, and in addition, Denizkartal is both nearly as large as Astrid and a Boyuk-kharl. Their daughter, Thalassa, takes after her mother in looks, except for the already evident, and striking, bright orange hair of her father, and her size.

Chapter XXXIII

Astrid (34th Duodecimus)

*N*ow we get to transport wandering Metropolitans. The first of the Metropolitans to arrive for the Synod—indeed, more than a week before it is due to begin—is the one who had the furthest distance to travel to reach Mousehole. Kyrillus Dabatenus, Metropolitan for Beneen and the South, lives in Garthcurr, on the southern edge of the Beneen Plain. He also proves to be the only one who planned on arriving in our area by water.

He took the opportunity to sail down the coast, visiting his churches in Mistledross and Southpoint, before sailing across Iba Bay to Sacred Gate. He apparently made no fuss there, and did not even try to speak to their rulers. Probably for the better, really. Customs visited him and found little to levy tax on, bar the fact of transit. Apparently, on the way back he is not even bothering to stop. He sees no reason to.

Metropolitan Kyrillus had, while he was in Sacred Gate, been approached by and picked up some passengers who were running late. Demetrios Choumnos, the Metropolitan of the South Plains, had experienced problems with his horses. This pair of prelates are the first from east and west of the mountains to start talking. There is going to be a lot of that.

He left his animal handlers to travel to Erave Town by land as quickly as they could, and accepted a ride with Kyrillus as his ship felt its way up the river to Evilhalt. Their vessel took far longer than the River Dragon to make the passage. It probably travelled barely faster than the horses due to feeling its way as it went. We need to see if Olympias can help them on the way back down.

Like the River Dragon, Kyrillus' dromond is also provided with its own wind, although it has also kept its oars. It was borrowed from the navy, and is one of their smaller ones, even if it does have two masts. He visited the Basilica in Erave Town before leaving his vessel behind in Evilhalt.

There it provides even more of a sensation than the River Dragon does. Not only does it have a part-Kharl crew, who are now relaxing in the village, but also it is of an even more unfamiliar, and larger, construction than the ship of Mousehole that is docked upstream of it.

Kyrillus was planning on getting horses and riding up to Mousehole from there, but once we saw them, he and his party, along with Demetrios and his smaller group, arrived up here by carpet and as pillion on saddles. Cosmas set out the same day that Kyrillus and the others started to leave Erave Town, but he had to come all the way into the mountains by horse, and so takes longer to arrive, even riding hard.

Metropolitan Basil has arrived with Abbot Theophilus and Basil Phocas, the Consiliarius of the Basilica Anthropoi and an escort. It seems that all the senior ecclesiastics in The Land are coming. Even my brother, Thorstein, the most junior of the priests, and the trainee priest, Aziz, end up guiding Metropolitans around and showing them what is happening in the village.

Out of deference to the visitors, none of us women wear just a kilt, although Verily very nearly did. She admits to leaving the doorway of her house, and that only a sight of all the unfamiliar faces in the village courtyard near the water fountain made her remember. She quickly ducked back into her house and changed into something that the visitors would regard as being suitable for the wife of a priest to be wearing. I train fully dressed as well.

Tarasios of Ardlark arrived bringing not only Theodoret Mauropous, or Blackfoot, the Metropolitan of the Plains, the only Insakharl to have reached that rank for some time, but also Abbot Michael Bardanes, of the Abbey of Saint Petrox in Ardlark and Imam Iyād ibn Walīd, of the mosque in Ardlark who, it seems is well known to several of the Mice.

It was for the first time in the known history of Mousehole that a male voice could be heard calling the Faithful to prayer. I suppose that he is here to make sure we Orthodox are not conspiring against his people.

Theodora

*S*ajāh tells me that the beds in the village are filling up fast. The senior clerics are set up in the hall of Mice. Their secretaries, and their other staff, are all given houses, as are the Abbots and the Consiliarius. The numerous grooms, servants, and guards are sleeping in one or another of the barracks. The single men and women and girls of the village are all staying with families all around the village.

Astrid tells me of general disappointment among the non-clerical visitors that most of those that serve them are married, and that they have little contact with our single girls, except as an occasional glimpse as one scurries past on the way to her work. I think that is a good idea.

Ruth is happy that, with a priority having been given to their needs, the children from the school have all been moved into their own dormitories. The school is laid out by now and even has some parts fully complete.

Besides now having the first dormitories ready, even though they are crowded with two in each bed, the school also has two classrooms, a hall, and its own kitchen for Ruth to proudly show off to visitors. The children can display their use of languages, and as children always seem to be at such times, put on display for the visitors.

Ayesha

*O*ur visiting Imam has quickly found himself eagerly sought out by the men and women who follow Allāh wadhu in the village, and fully engaged in answering their questions. To the relief of some of the women, and indeed some of the men, he confirmed the validity of their marriages, even if they had been done by a kāfirūn priest. I told them so, but it is good to be sure I suppose.

He and Christopher are still undecided as to whether our village needs its own Mullah. Iyād thinks that we are still too small, while Christopher is the one who is arguing the need on behalf of us. May Allah the Merciful forgive my amusement when his vigorous advocacy caused Iyād to humorously point out that a Mullah is clearly not needed, as the Christian priest is more than sufficiently zealous on their behalf.

Sajāh

*I*t was just as well that I made prior arrangements for Guk to bring down extra grain and other supplies on the last few visits, and more will arrive. As it is, Verina has been working in the mill for many long hours, with Lamentations and Pass (who always seem to work together) to help her. Not only is the flour being used up, but so are a lot of our other stores. We need two ovens working to feed them just the basics of bread and pastry.

It is also lucky that the prelates have generally all provided a few horse loads of provisions. None of our visitors had expected that the small village would be able to fully provide for nearly double its number of people on its own resources. Thankfully, they are only here for a short time. I am sure that it is good for us to have them all here, but I will be well pleased when they are not.

Rani (36th Duodecimus)

A part from greetings, I get to see little of them. The last to arrive, just this afternoon, is Metropolitan Petros of Northern Darkreach, who has come all the way from Antdrudge. I am soon glad that he made it on time, as six of the long train of packhorses that he has with him prove to have a special cargo on their backs. This time I am the Princess who is talked to.

His Alat-kharl animal handlers quickly unloaded and began to set up outside the village wall in a fallow field. *For once there is someone to help me celebrate New Year in the right way. I nearly forgot my own traditions again. There are others who need to know. Where has Astrid gotten to this time?*

Rani (that night)

W hen it finally grew dark, the entire valley was treated to a display of fireworks.

His hometown not only makes hugron pir, the liquid fire used in the molotails, and the war rockets for Darkreach, but also more trivial explosives. These are more in demand in Darkreach than the deadlier products. In Darkreach, the more dangerous items are only needed for practice and to replace those that grow old and unstable, and their makers make their money mostly by selling the fireworks.

They sell a lot of fireworks. While common east of the mountains, such items are rare in the west, rarer even than the goods that are used for warfare, and against some dangerous beasts. I wonder if Shilpa has realised that she could buy and trade them. I suppose that she will realise it after tonight. Even Haven would like supplies of these.

I am so pleased to get to add to the event by showing off my best New Year's spell in a huge final blast that lights up the sky. I have not only boosted it from what it had been when I left home, but I have added to it the full extent of my stored mana. My wife mentioned to me that the priests present observed the range and size of the resultant blast, and seem to have taken in its implications for me casting a harmful enchantment very well.

Hulagu

It was just as well that, apart from Ayesha, the Mori watch the display from on top of the falls with the majority of the flocks being pastured behind us quietly in the Övs of the Upper Meadow. Even here the explosions are very noticeable. The herd beasts that had been left below would not have been impressed with the noise or the light.

Parminder

How do I explain to them what is happening? I am deluged with complaints from both the cats and the horses. I had already warned the eagles to stay away, and told the cats to stay inside. Of course, the cats ignored me. Maybe it will make them listen to me more next time.

The only animal in the whole valley that seems to have enjoyed the fireworks at all is Azrael, whom I noted, while watching the display from the roof, turned around to watch them before resuming her normal position.

Sajāh
Iˢᵗ Primus, the Year of the Water Goat, New Year's Day

It has been decided that the actual Synod will take place in the smaller Hall of Mice as only the hosts, the senior clerics, and a couple of attendants for each prelate will be attending, but the communal hall will be used several times a day for the services, reassembled for meals, and then converted back again to being a Church.

My staff and I are going to be very busy, particularly with so many idlers underfoot. We need to get rid of them. Eventually, in frustration, she arranged for Stefan to set up some competitions for the many guards and animal handlers out in the training area. *I can also have lunch served for them out there. That decision makes life a lot easier, and cuts down on the amount of ale being consumed.*

Theodora

*T*he opening service of the Synod, ushering in the New Year, has the hall packed. It sees the Investiture of Father Christopher as Bishop of the Mountains by the two western Metropolitans and Tarasius, three apparently being the proper number for such a task, and something that the west has not been able to do for some time. The Abbot or the Consiliarus has always been the person who has been filling the other place.

Christopher's first official act is to ordain Father Aziz as a new priest. However, Aziz was not the first Hob to be ordained. The Bishop is assisted in the service by Father Cyril, the former Dindarqoyun, who is on his way back to his flock in Dhargev after the Synod is finished. Father Cyril is a far happier and more confident man than he had been when we first met him.

The priests at Dhargev will still need more priests to provide services for the nearly two thousand Hobs that live in the valley, but Father Michael will be glad of adding even one more to his team. The new Bishop has only the two congregations for the moment, but then Metropolitan Cosmas has very few more, even if he does have the theoretical responsibility for the pastoral care of the Swamp and Haven.

Theodora (later in the day)

*T*he rest of the day is full of formal introductions and gifts for the new Bishopric as it is presented with marvellously embroidered altar cloths and vestments, with sacerdotal plate and with chalices. Furthermore, Tarasius has brought with him a tradesman, Leo, his wages paid and with his supplies following. Leo will be staying in Mousehole at least until Saint George's is complete. He is here to do the plastering and tiling and mosaics. Hopefully, he can teach Denny these things.

Metropolitan Basil has brought as his gift, supplies of coloured sheet glass and lead for the stained-glass windows of the Basilica. It will be up to us to experiment in how to put them together, but it is not work that must be done in a single day. I am sure that Bilqīs can work on it.

None had expected the Basilica to be as complete as it is, and all watched the work in progress with wonder at the speed with which so few workers manage to perform their tasks. Before their eyes a section of the first side dome of the nave began to take shape as workers walked in the air and the unskilled people helped by moving the carved stones around. We have them *made by Tãriq or Adrian to a set of drawings and marked according to the plans they have been given by Ruth.*

When they are eventually handed to Goditha, she consults her own set of plans, and lays and sets them in the correct place. Christopher, as a return gift, presented each of the Metropolitans with one of the marvellous stone-working chisels that he and his priests have prayed over and enhanced. The recipients are all sure that these will find a use in their areas.

Chapter XXXIV

Theodora
2ⁿᵈ Primus, the Feast Day of Saint Joseph

*T*he second session of the Synod, on the feast day of Saint Joseph, and the first real working day, consists of a mutual examination of beliefs to ensure that the eastern and western halves of the Faith were still Communicate. The Mice who are tempted to listen in to the conversations of the senior priests are driven out of the room by the esoteric and generally dry conversation.

On the other hand, I, as the hosting Orthodox Princess, am compelled to sit through the whole session and will be present for the rest. I nearly fell asleep several times during the first few hours, and rely on my servants to keep me awake. I was hoping to be brought out to feed or attend Aikaterine, but to my regret, others have attended to that task for me, except during breaks.

The sessions are made duller due to the assembled clerics being unable to find any significant differences that had developed between them, and indeed, even very few trivial ones. To my mind, where a comma fits in a document is scarce cause for excitement. Mind you, given how protracted and bitter all the records say that the Great Schism was, this lack of conflict is a relief to us all.

Theodora (late that night)

*N*ow that is decided, they then debate whether to enforce uniformity on the minor points, whether to stay with the practices that have become established within each church, or whether to simply allow people to make

229

their own choice. In the end, they have largely decided to allow local custom to prevail, and informing the people that other areas have other customs.

Christopher is probably the most relieved at that decision, given that the two churches under his care both have a record of permitting multiple marriage partners, among our other peculiarities, including my marriage. Despite the dullness of the day, by its very nature it ends in a very late finish to the last session, and Apodeipnon rolls straight into the midnight service.

Theodora (3rd Primus)

*T*he third session is devoted to the issue of whether to install a Patriarch or not. In the end it is decided that we are all too spread out, and many of our problems are often too local in nature for a matter to be referred to a Patriarch for a ruling, and then to have to wait to have an answer come back again.

It would be as if the only reason to have one would be to set up someone as mimic, or a counter to the Freehold Pope, and that is not a good enough reason for any of us. As it is, Tarasios is already serving as Ethnarch to the Emperor, representing the entire ecumen to him, as the Grand Ayatollah does for the Muslims, and that would have been the main function of the role.

In the west, Metropolitan Basil seems to have fallen into the same role of representing the Faith, this time to the Kara-Khitan of the north, although Metropolitan Demetrios is also in contact with a couple of Clans. Instead of having a Patriarch, we agree that meeting on a regular basis in a spirit of collegiality will be more appropriate.

Five years is thought to be a sufficient interval between Conclaves, although they also agree that they will gather more frequently if it is needed. At least it will give us time to get more building finished for the next session. It was also agreed that, as soon as things can be put on a more regular basis there, when its priests and life had settled down, a Bishop will need to be appointed for Amity, and also for the mountains.

Theodora (4th Primus)

*T*he discussion today hinges on a vexed question, and this time I have no trouble staying awake. The freeing of the Brotherhood, which we have already agreed will soon lead to the future creation of a Bishopric of Amity, has direly exposed the need for more true vocations. Several theologians have *already questioned the use of the words about women not being heard in church.*

Theodoret, the part-Kharl Metropolitan, likens the exclusion of women to the exclusion of non-Humans that had been normal until only a few centuries ago. I think I like the way he thinks. Some old writings have alleged that this passage in the Bible refers to chattering in the rear of a large church where the women were segregated rather than to preaching.

Kyrillus pointed out that, as time goes by, it is more and more the case in almost all walks of life, women are found in the same roles as men. Christopher points out that he is sure his wife would be a superb priest, as she has faith in abundance. He is right. He also notes that even the schismatics allow some role to the women of the Ursuline Order and those of Saint Agatha.

Iyãd pointed out that, although it was not generally known, an especially holy woman could be named as Mujtahideh. It is in the same fashion as a man could be made an Ayatollah.

Making sure that the door was closed and that the servants were excluded for the moment, he confided that his Grand Ayatollah, Alī ibn Yūsuf al Mãr, who had met her in Ardlark, had tasked him to begin to examine Ayesha for a possible elevation to such a role in the years ahead.

It seems that we, and I suppose that just means Christopher and I, are not to let her know of this, and it is one of the reasons he is reluctant to send a Mullah, unless it is deemed to be essential. This whole idea is bit of a surprise.

Theodora was asked her opinion on the whole question. *I have been included in most discussions. Is this why?* "I am gratified with what has been said so far. Can I point out that a woman can be just as pious as a man? Bianca and Ayesha both show that, and as my husband and I prove, can be just as capable."

She shared the revelation that her husband had regarding the Havenite position on who was suitable for education as a mage, and pointed out the number of women, with a chance of being strong mages, who would have been excluded from that option in that regard, and drew the parallel to the church leaving aside half of its congregation from consideration in the same way.

They are nodding in agreement. It is nice to have such people tell me that I make a most cogent point. It is finally agreed not to rush into a decision on such an important matter, and that all of them will think and pray on the subject, seeking opinion and opening debate among their own clergy and laity, and that this will be set as the major topic for discussion at the next Synod.

That is something they can all look forward to. I do have to agree that, on such a major question, a delay of only five years is not too long to take to think about and debate the issue. It is one that will surely raise some very strong feelings on all sides.

It looked like the next day would be the last day of the Synod. They were all pleased with the way that they had quickly worked through matters that could have kept them tied up for a very long time. While they were all enjoying the experience of the Synod, in this uncertain world their flocks may have need of them at any time, and they all realised that they could not stay secluded for any length of time.

Theodora (5th Primus)

*T*he next question to be raised is the relations of the Ecumen with the schismatics, and other faiths around The Land. The generally relaxed attitude to other faiths that is seen in Darkreach, and practiced in the areas of the West that are dominated by the Church is not duplicated elsewhere.

Iyād had to admit that in the Caliphate, while there is not active persecution, there is a strong discouragement of other faiths through adverse taxation and other means. He has proposed a joint visit from himself, with an escort drawn from the Muslim troops of the Empire, and myself, my escort being a group of fliers in a mix of faiths.

I do have the excuse of visiting my cousin, which I want to do anyway, and he will have the excuse that, while there have been diplomatic and trade visits from Darkreach, there has been no equivalent visit such as this Synod represents. He said that he will have to consult with the Grand Ayatollah and he, in turn, will have to consult with the Emperor, but he feels that it will not be a problem gaining their approval for this. All agree that this will be a good move.

The next issue to be raised is where we stand regarding the Swamp. In the recent turmoil, we know that people of both Orthodox and Muslim persuasion have suffered persecution there. Father Kessog is the only known priest in residence there and no surviving Mullahs are known about at all. It is decided that we Mice shall take the lead there, given that the blame for the attack that we made seems to have been laid on raiders from the Caliphate.

Subject to my husband's agreement, I propose a visit in our full might to each of the villages to look at the actual conditions that prevail, and where possible, consider rebuilding any destroyed Churches or Mosques. If we go on our saddles, it should enable us to stay away from any trouble if needed. The saddles are no longer a secret from the Adversaries now anyway.

A courier, or a message sent via Carausius, can bring news from Mousehole to Ardlark as to what congregations the Muslims still have functioning and what will be needed in the way of Mullahs or other support for them. Word about this can be sent to the Imams throughout the land so they can consider who to send.

Suddenly, we have discovered that this issue, which had been thought to be able to be easily dispatched, has taken up nearly a whole day on its own and we are still not finished with it. They will all be here at least another day.

Theodora (6ᵗʰ Primus)

*K*rondag *is the sixth day of deliberations, and it took some time for them to start due to the inevitable delays of the extended services that are needed on this day. Once started, they begin to discuss Haven. To the best of everyone's knowledge, apart from Saltverge, there are no Churches or Mosques anywhere in that land. However, there must be at least a travelling population who would need them.*

After the previous day, Theodora had thought that this question might come up, so after they had finished, she had asked her husband and others of the Mice who came from there, and none had ever heard of any facilities at all. *It is decided that a missionary Church will be the first step.* Theodora protested that the Mice needed all their priests, and Demetrios pointed out that he was already short of them due to the actions of Freehold.

Cosmas thought that he could free some up, for either the Swamp or Haven. Theodoret believed that he could perhaps send a couple, and Tarasios opined that, although they should have the expected visible guards, perhaps one or two of the Antikataskopeía, probably posing as servants, might be loaned for their ability to find out more information. He asked Iyād to explore the idea of obtaining any…ghazi…from the Caliphate for his missionaries when they came.

They wondered if it were possible to purchase sufficient land on Anta Dvīpa, End Island, which would be close to the docks, and still large enough to build a compound for both missions. It seems that the Church lacks funds for that but perhaps…how subtle of them. They are all suddenly looking in my direction. Theodora sighed. "We may be able to look at using some of our wealth to buy land. I will have to talk with my husband."

At least, it could also serve as a base for trade ventures. After the mid-morning break, Theodora passed on, from her husband, the opinion that if it were done properly, they could be set up in place before the authorities in Haven realised what was happening, or at any rate before they realised the scale of what they were going to do.

"She said that the rulers of Haven paid no attention to that island, and with the right staff in place, the area might even be given a clean-up of its criminals, which would have most of the residents of the island happy and others, the criminals who lived and worked there, very unhappy. The gods of Haven are not noted for being jealous of other religions, and they should have no problems with our setting up a church in such a place."

After an early lunch, they talked about the thornier question of Freehold. *It is a touchy one for Demetrios in particular. Over the last few years priests from Saltbeach, Glengate, and Deeryas have disappeared from their parishes only to appear later before a Dominican tribunal accused of heresy.* Iyãd was asked about any people that his faith might have in Freehold.

He laughed. "Whilst they are not forcibly converted, from what little I have been able to find out from traders, if there are any of my people there, they dress and act as their neighbours do and make no public worship. With the strength of the Inquisition, it is unsafe to do otherwise."

They have agreed that, until the situation in Amity settles down and they became more self-sufficient, and the losses of the war are made up, generally no-one is strong enough to do anything about Freehold directly, but what else can they do?

A full solution looks to be several cycles of years away at least. Metropolitan Tarasios pointed out that, if we at least prevent any more losses, or to put it another way, stopped any more gains on the part of the schismatics, then a solution might present itself in the fullness of time.

Basil Phocas, Consiliarius of the Basilica Anthropoi, is one who has more experience in dealing with the plains and the far west than the rest. He was asked his opinion. He thanked the Metropolitans of the East, as he referred to them, for their sending more members to join his Order, and proposed that he talk to the Exarkhos ton Basilikon. Now, for the first time, and with no more threat from the Brotherhood, and with the Compact in place, they had the forces to move into a more forward and active position.

While they would have to talk to the Kara-Khitan, he seems to think that, carefully explained, being more active should not be a problem with the tribes. They should keep their base and headquarters at Greensin with one file at least based there all the time, but he would suggest to the Exarkh that they move two files to Warkworth, two to Glengate, and two to Saltbeach.

At each location they will build themselves a Chapter house and its facilities. It will both make the people of each village feel safer, and will also make them better able to protect their priests. The other two files will be used to allow a rotation through the four locations for rest and for training.

It is now my turn to upset things. Theodora then pointed out what they had all forgotten; the existence of the New Found Land that Father Simeon had come from. *I had to point out that, with the resources of that land behind them, Freehold might be able to secretly grow in numbers and strength and again launch an attack on the rest, as it did at the end of the last Age. They all sat in silent contemplation of that idea for a while.*

Someone has to say something. "I will consult with my husband. When we go out again, once we know our way west, we already know that we must look at other lands. We will see what we can find out about that area, and perhaps we might even be able to disrupt their trade a little, as we know was done by some of their people to ours through the bandits. Our ship, on its own, may not be enough for this and we may need to seek help from elsewhere."

She looked at Tarasios. *He nods in thought. He takes my point. At least they agree that this, combined with the movement of the Basilica Anthropoi, will be the first stage of their approach, while Tarasios consults at home.* "More importantly, whilst we know that Archibald, the Baron of Toppuddle, was a servant of the Masters, we do not know who else in their land is, and we are sure that he was not alone. We may need to do far more there."

"It could mean war," said Metropolitan Petros in alarm.

"But, if we do not do something, war may still occur as they grow in strength...and it will not be on our terms," said the more politically aware Consiliarius. *He backs my position. The others eventually reluctantly nod in agreement. This policy will need to be reviewed when next we meet and may not last even until then.*

They adjourned for a celebratory feast that night before they again spread out back to their homes. *At least temporarily, the die is cast.* Theodora left the meeting more than a trifle giddy. *I left my sheltered home only a few years ago almost on a whim and simply out of boredom.*

Now, after having taken part in the Jirgah with the Kara-Khitan at One Tree Hill, and the Conclave of the North, although I am still not sure exactly what happened there, I have just sat through another important meeting... one that possibly, despite the lack of much direct military force among the attendees, is in the long run possibly the most important of the three by far.

Between the three assemblies, the political landscape of The Land is being redefined, perhaps for many years to come. The more that I think about it, what we just discussed in the Hall of the Mice might one day be regarded by scholars as marking the start of a new Age for the world. If it does, it would all date from the New Year that we just celebrated in my village.

Theodora (7th Primus)

The next day the village began to return to normal as their visitors started to leave. *The roads will be full of people for a few days at least. The logbook at Forest Watch will have more notes in it than it has had for a very long time.*

With the beginning of summer in only a few weeks we will be venturing into the Swamp, and when that is done, down the Rhastaputra again. Whilst we are already committed, some will wonder whether it is time to consult our seers again about whether we have agreed to the right course, and whether the quiet time of withdrawal is drawing to an end.

Chapter XXXV

Rani (7th Primus)

I feel quite unsure within myself. I must admit that it is a feeling that I am not used to. This religious gathering has agreed on a path for us to take, but although my wife played a part in it, and we did discuss some of the options between us on the nights before and after the decisions, I was not a part of it myself, and I never can be unless I change my religion.

What makes me uneasy is that prophesy has been an important part of our decision-making process from before we joined together right through to this time. Indeed, it has been at the core of our actions. Just because we have people from other places here, why have we abandoned what has worked so well for us in the past? Rationality and logic have their more limited places in making decisions, but I know that, in the long run they are no substitute for the proven strength of prophesy.

The last of our visitors, Metropolitan Cosmas, has just left and I can see our new Bishop returning to his house after seeing him off from the valley gate.

Without having decided, she found herself going outside to see him. He seemed surprised, particularly since she did not seem to be able to come to the point, and he moved her across to the seats on the veranda of the Hall of Mice as girls walked past them with linen and other items. Around them, as they sat in the sun, the village was starting to restore itself to some semblance of normality.

"Princess," he said. "There is something on your mind. You do not have to be in a confessional to talk to me. You know that. I am always available to listen to you." He fell silent, and they sat for a little while looking at people moving around, some already back in their normal working clothes.

I can see that up the valley, some of the flock are returning down the cliff path to the closer fields, and back to the stables. With the children now in their school outside the wall they can no longer be heard, but the normal sounds and smells of village life can be. We are returning to our time of quiet.

"A decision was made …" Christopher, by nodding, encouraged her to continue. "It was made by men…I mean by people… And every time we have made a decision in the past, we have done it differently: Hulagu gets drunk…I read cards…you look in your Holy book and now Dobun has started to go to…wherever he goes… We didn't do that this time, and I feel as if we have done it all wrong somehow. What if I am right?"

Again, Christopher nodded and after a little while he spoke. "You are right. I was wondering why I was feeling uneasy. We need—not everyone, but you and I, and our spouses at least—maybe Astrid and Basil, and Hulagu and Ayesha, and I suppose Dobun… At least we know that the Khitan will not talk to others without need. We need to do it the right way, as well."

He fell silent again, then smiled, and continued in a mildly amused tone. "We have become creatures of habit, have we not? We need to do things the way we are accustomed to, or we are uncomfortable…regardless of how sensible what we have decided seems to be.

"Perhaps it would be best if you were to tell your servants to take the night off and enjoy themselves with the others after all their hard work for the last week. Tonight, we will all eat in commons, and then meet after Hesperinos in your reception room. I will get my wife to organise for the others to be there."

I thank Ganesh that it is not just me who feels that way.

Basil

I like the peace and quiet of our village. It is so different to Ardlark and the crowds. I know everyone here, and what they are likely to do. Basil returned home after making sure that everything in the valley was secure. *Whilst they were vouched for by their Metropolitans, it is in my nature that I do not necessarily trust that many outsiders in my valley to be on their best behaviour for the whole time.*

I do have to admit, however, that except for a few drunken episodes that were cured by some time in the cells, I have largely been pleasantly surprised. I have, nevertheless, been hard at work for the last week, along with Lakshmi, Ayesha, Shilpa, and Zeenat, talking to the guards and servants…well, not just talking to them, but keeping an eye on them, and making sure that none of them stray, or go near treasure, or go where the major magic of the valley is stored. The Princesses think that where they keep the Mouse and the Horse is a secret, but it is up to me to make sure that it really is and that it stays that way.

Some know where the unused, lesser magic is stored...in a cell at the other end of the row to where they were kept as guests. We also now know a lot more of the gossip and rumours from their homes. It is well to hear how the common folk take the actions of their rulers. The new Compact of the North, for instance, is very well received it seems.

As he came up to his door, it was opened by one of the Brotherhood girls... *one of the two that have been staying with us during the Synod, and helping with the children since we no longer have Kaliope. What is her name? Oh, yes, I remember now. It is the worst of their names that I have heard so far, and several of them can only be regarded as being very unfortunate.* "Hello Sin," he said to the girl. *Fancy being named They Shall Confess Their Sin.* "Not moved back to the barracks yet?"

The girl started to say something, but Astrid, from behind her, interrupted the reply. "No, and she is not going to. We are going to keep her with us." Basil looked blankly at his wife as she continued. "You are a soldier, dear... whether you think that you are or not...and you are often a very busy one.

"It seems that now I, too, am a soldier... We have four children...two are underfoot, and two are at breast, and I am getting exhausted looking after you all. For the last week, despite having the visitors in the valley, it has been so much easier for me. Up to now, Sin has been sawing logs, and she cannot stand that work, and she tells me that she is not good at it at all."

"However, she is good at looking after children, and cooking, and washing, and looking after a house...much better than I am, in fact. I knew many years ago I was not meant to be a housekeeper. I am a hunter and a killer. Sin has consented to stay with us and help us, so she will be moving in with us, and we will be paying her a wage from our money. Is that all right?"

She is looking at me with that look on her face that all husbands know with dread. It converts what is openly a question inviting participation into a definite statement that is challenged by the husband only with extreme peril. This is one of the many times when the old saying of 'happy wife, happy life' makes such perfect sense.

"Of course, Puss. Welcome to our house, Sin. I will go and see Kaliope tomorrow, and make sure that she knows all about it for her bookkeeping. Have you let Atã know?" *The girl nods, so that is one thing done.* He turned to his wife. "Well, now that the young ones are looked after for the night, we have been asked to come and see the Princesses after Hesperinos this evening for kaf and a short talk about how things went."

Astrid

*H*e is speaking far too innocently and lightly. Astrid looked sharply at her husband. *He is even looking far too innocuous, but still staring at me for my reaction. I am sure that means that something is happening. I wonder what this is about. I thought that everything that could be decided has been sorted out by the Synod. Obviously, that is not the case.*

Theodora

*W*ell, despite us agreeing to these actions at the Synod, I expected this meeting. I am surprised that my husband thinks that we would proceed *otherwise. Of course, I expect what we find out tonight will fully back up what was decided on as being the best course. That is the way things are, or at least that is the way that they should be.*

That night they gathered quietly, sitting around while babies were fed. Basil checked that they were alone in the house, and that none were outside, while Rani explained the situation.

"Fear is still staying at the school tonight…luckily, she had already asked if she could. I just do not feel that we can go out of the valley without checking on things. Even though our course of action was agreed on by everyone as being the wisest path to take, I do not feel confident about making any moves, if we do not consult the omens that we have relied on up to now.

"I suggest that we see what we find out tonight, and then work out whether or not to tell the other people." She looked around. *No-one is dissenting from what she says, and several are nodding.* "Remember," said Rani, "what we agreed to do at the Synod sounded so right at the time. That is what we must think about during the readings." With relief she handed the cards to Bianca, who shuffled and cut them before handing them back to Rani. Rani began to lay them out on the small table in front of her.

One by one, she turned them over. *We all know the layout by now and are all looking eagerly at what is revealed. The first card is nearly as familiar as the layout itself.* "The Empress," she turned over the second card. *We have seen that before, too.* "The Four of Staves." *The third card, the way ahead, is unfamiliar, and it is upside down.*

On it four swords are interlaced with their points to the top of the card. In a nest made of their interlaced points, a man in pyjama pants is sitting cross-legged playing a sitar. In each corner, there are words in Old Speech, the same language that we have seen before on the cards. "The Four of Swords".

She paused before turning the last. *It is almost as if she is unsure if she should turn it. It is also an unfamiliar card, and it is also reversed. The card has two coins on each side of it, with a fifth sitting at its base.*

In between them, there is a depiction of a four-armed woman dressed in a sari and wearing a crown. She is standing under a leafless tree with its roots shown as being exposed, as if it has been ripped from the ground. In the top corners are two different words, but the bottom of the card seems to have only the same word repeated in each corner. "The Five of Talents."

Once again, Rani held her hands over the cards and closed her eyes before pausing for some time and then starting to speak. "The first card stands for the enquirers...for us, and once again we see the card of the Empress standing for women and our time of quiet, of childbearing, and of recovery."

"Our second card is the same card that told us to take time out of our endeavours. Now, that is in the past as it stands in the position of our history. These two cards, in this place, leave us in no doubt that our time for rest is over, and we are once again about to have to go out of our valley, and engage with the world." She stopped talking. *It is as if she is contemplating the path that lies ahead of us for a moment longer.*

She continued: "Our way ahead is shown by the Four of Swords. Normally, this card means a retreat from the battlefields of life, and especially from strife with colleagues and friends. It can also imply calm in the storm, and often a self-imposed exile. Reversed, however, it means a cautious re-engagement with the world after a period of rest.

"The words at the top say 'repose' and 'retreat,' while those at the bottom, which are the ones that apply now, say 'circumspection' and 'activity.' It is not a card for rash activity, or for rushing headlong into things, but a card of cautious engagement. I think that it very much applies to us, and the way we are going out again."

She turned to the last card, pointing at it. "On the five of talents, we see the goddess Lakshmi grieving and disconsolate. The words at the top read as 'worry' and 'loss.' When we see this card upright it means impoverishment and loss, and an overwhelming yearning for someone or something that is absent. The word on the bottom, which applies when it is reversed, means 'improvement'."

Her pretty brow furrows in thought. "Seeing the card is reversed, it talks of the reversal of a difficult situation, of gradual improvement and encouraging news. This is not a card of complete resolution; or of any resolution really, but I do not think that we expected any final outcome at this stage. These cards tell us that it is time to slowly emerge from the valley, and follow the path that we discussed at the Synod. They say that we need to be slow and cautious, and not make bold or dangerous attacking moves.

"If there are two paths and we have a choice, we should always take the most cautious option. The boldness may come later, but it is not yet. We will need to think again about what we are doing before we leave the more immediate area of Swamp, and Haven, and the mountains, and try to go further afield. If we slowly and cautiously follow this path, our chances…our prospects…will improve."

She stopped her reading as her voice trailed off, and then gathered her cards together before sitting back in her chair. Once that was done, she looked at Christopher. "Your Grace …" *Christopher is shuffling in his seat on being addressed that way…not only is he not used to it, but he is also still a trifle uncomfortable with it.* "I believe it is now your turn."

Christopher nodded, and led those of us of the Orthodox faith that are present in prayer. He takes his wife's Old Testament out, and with eyes shut, solemnly allows it to fall open. Slowly and deliberately, he places a finger carefully and delicately on a page. Only then does he open his eyes and look down at where his finger points.

"At least I only have one verse this time…let me see…it is the Book of Numbers, chapter thirteen, and verse seventeen, and it says: 'And Moses sent them to spy out the land of Canaan and said unto them. Get you up this way southward and go up into the mountain.' Well…" He stopped and blinked before looking around the room. "I think that once again we have our guidance. We are to go to the Swamp, to Haven, and into the Caliphate, as was already agreed at the Synod."

He grinned. "I am not trying to compete on this, but it is a much more precise direction than that which the Princess gave, although, as usual for us, they complement each other very well," he said happily. He then sat back in his chair, and reached for a sweet pastry as he looked at Dobun.

"Well, young man," Christopher began. *Dobun is a whole four years younger than our youthful Bishop, but he lacks the experiences that we Mice have crammed into those times, and without those experiences, he looks younger.* "I, for one, look forward to what you can add to what we have just seen here. When you have left here, go and see Lakshmi. Just knock on her workshop door. I have made sure that she knows that you will be along to see her tonight."

Dobun just nodded, stood, and left the room silently, as the others stayed behind to sit for a while and talk. *He already has a very serious look on his face, more than the usual Khitan lack of expression. He is starting to grow into his role.*

Astrid

"What is this I hear about you taking a servant?" Bianca asked Astrid as they dispersed. "Have you suddenly become a Princess, too?"

Astrid smiled. "No, I have just decided that we are too busy. I don't know how you are coping at present…and you won't be able to cope for long, now that your husband has a lot more responsibilities. We hardly see you as it is. I think that you need at least two servants. I have only taken one of the girls. You need two: one for the house and children, and one for Christopher as his secretary. Remember, I know what he is like. He can never find things that are not important to either healing or praying. It should not be your job to remind him that something needs to be done, or a letter needs to be written. He needs his own Andronicus."

"One of the girls came up to me, and wanted to do that sort of thing while the visitors were here," said Bianca dismissively, "and I turned her down. I am not a grand lady. I shouldn't have servants. After all, it is only such a short time ago that I was a servant. It is just wrong for me to put on airs and graces.

"No, it isn't. You are a grand lady, Your Grace…whether you want to be one or not. You are the wife of a Bishop, and so you should not be doing the washing for him. You proved at Greensin that there are other things for you to do that are more worthy for you. After the Princesses, you are the most important woman in Mousehole…whether you like it that way or not.

"The only one of us who is close to you in rank is Ayesha, and that is because she is the senior wife of a Tar-khan, but that is only a secular role, and you are religious, so you are far more important. I think you should go back and see that girl, and see if she still wants the job…and then see if she knows another girl who would like to look after your house." *To me the argument is irrefutable.*

Bianca

*A*strid *is right in what she says, particularly about Christopher, but also with my house.* Bianca kept walking beside her husband the short distance to her home. *I don't need to consult Christopher as he will think the same as I did, and will also be harder to convince otherwise. I will just set things up, and he will look bewildered, and agree with what I have done…that is, if he notices at all.*

There is even one of the girls waiting inside our house who has volunteered to look after the children for the evening. Perhaps she will be interested in helping me full-time. I will ask, and then, in the morning I will go and talk to Glad about helping Christopher. If they agree to this, then I will see Kaliope about us paying them.

Hulagu (8th Primus)

The next morning Hulagu and Ayesha gathered the others together in the Princesses' house. *Dobun sits waiting nervously. He is still not used to being Zönch, in addition to Böö. Even more he is not used to being the centre of attention. Most importantly, he is not used to the Khün khanatai knowing as much about the business of the Emeel amidarch baigaa khümüüs as happens here.*

That will change, and it needs to. At least here, in a time of change, and where we share övs with others as a part of daily life, and they share their secrets with us, we need to think about what changes we need to make to our customs to fit in. He may not be comfortable with this, but he will do as his Tar-khan asks.

When they were all seated, he started: "My spirit flew south over the land, and up over the mountains. To the south it felt confusion, and the ordinary troubles and hatreds of the town-dwellers. I felt hatred rising up to the sky between the two areas that tells me not to take people from one area to the other, or at least to hide them if we do." *He pauses for a while and looks at zürkh setgelee gartaa barisan khün to ask permission. She nods to him.*

"Go on," Ayesha said.

"I am worried about what is happening in the Caliphate. I do not think that there is a Pattern there, but there may be. I do not know what one feels like, but I looked for wrongness. There are certainly evil people who follow the way of the Masters all over. However, as I flew over the Caliphate someone, or something there, tried to fight my spirit.

"They tried hard, but they were on their own, and they lacked...something... something they wanted and needed to give them the power to completely stop me, and perhaps even to trap my spirit there...although they tried to hold me, they were not strong enough. Perhaps the Tenger Sünsnüüd, the Spirits of the Sky, aided me against them. However, this fight is one of the reasons that I am not sure if there is a Pattern there, as I could not look as hard as I wanted to.

"I did feel a great wrongness there, but it could have been that which fought me, an Aguu 251uns muukhai, a great evil spirit, perhaps." He stopped and this time looked hard at Hulagu before continuing. *He does not like saying this out loud before the others. He is used to keeping everything within the tribe.*

"I have told of this to those others of the tribes who were in the spirit realm last night, and they agree that it is we Mori, as the Clan who claim the mountains as our övs, our range, who must do something about it...I agree with that even though I lack the power to enter and leave the true world on my own if our opponents are prepared.

"From what I was told, I believe that we must look at the other areas before we enter the mountains, and I have no idea where to go when we do eventually go there. Seeing that they are the last that we go to, perhaps it will become apparent. I have a strong feeling that this may be the case.

"I also have a feeling that we will definitely need help there from the holy man that the Tar-khan's wife tells me will return to us." He stopped, shrugged, and looked around at the faces that were watching him. "That is all."

Theodora

*H**e really does not like sharing the secrets of the Khitan with us, does he?* "I thank you for sharing that with us, and we are all very grateful." *See...he looks better already.* "With what the three of you have found out and said, last night and now, I believe that we have a fairly complete picture of what is happening, and a more definite plan of action than that decided at the Synod...now we must decide on another thing...do we tell everyone what we have found out?"

She looked around. *I can see people nodding.* Bianca spoke first. "You must," she said. "People, even our new ones, do what you ask of them, because they trust you to do the right thing for them. If you do not tell them such an important thing, then you break that trust. In the end, despite your power and that of my husband, and of Ayesha's, as a ruler you only have the power you have because they believe in you and in your concern for them."

Bianca nodded towards Basil. "You don't even have to make an official announcement about anything. You just need to let Basil spread it around in casual conversation. It lets everyone know without raising concerns." *Yes, I suppose that does make sense, that way it just becomes understood by all, instead of people asking why it was not done publicly.*

Chapter XXXVI

Theodora (9th Primus)

*M*y *husband and I need to prepare many more devices before we go south into danger.* Theodora had sat down and thought about it. *I have drawn up a long list of what is needed. We can make do with the number of saddles that we have until next winter. However, we not only need more wands, but even far more protection for our people when we go into the Swamp.*

The shield tokens have proven their worth against the Brotherhood when it comes to open battle. When we go out, this time it is quite likely that we will find a hostile reception from at least some people. Once our mission becomes known, and the saddles seen, someone is sure to add three and three and reach a fist, and then finally the blame for the death of Glyn and others will descend upon us. We may need to fight our way clear.

Later, when we go on to Haven, it is quite possible that our activity could prompt a mage to cast an enchantment that will reveal what we have already done there. Our opponents might even have warned their minions what to look for…they should have, if they have any sense. We Mice need to be prepared for anything that is likely to happen.

Theodora (10th Primus)

*T*he *first, and worst, thing about demanding preparedness is that I cannot just get others to be ready. I too must be ready, and I cannot pretend to sit in my study and avoid it. Still, why did I allow that horrible woman to intimidate me into this torture? I have always been perfectly happy…all my life…to avoid all exercise when I don't need it, and I very rarely find that I need it.*

I have always put some time into practicing my weapons, but particularly since she returned from Ardlark, Astrid has become a demon on the subject. It is small consolation, but at least I am not the only one that Astrid has worked on. She has intimidated all the women into joining in at least one of her sessions, and she is making us all work hard.

Now that she has someone looking after her house and the older children, Astrid is free to decide to run three sessions, two of them during the day, and one held at night, so that no-one can plead that they are busy at the time. She does it every day, except for Krondag, and then Stefan works us on weapons. Even the Brotherhood girls are doing the lessons, despite what Astrid makes them wear.

Where has she gotten these ideas from? The men might like to see the women running around, and lifting things, and bending, and stretching in ways the body was not meant to while they just wear their kilts, but the women don't have to like it. Mind you, I have had to admit, even if only privately, and when I am being very honest, that my body is behaving better now than it had been.

To be honest, it looked like I was going to have a permanent soft and rounded belly showing after having Aikaterine. I know that several of my relations have done the same, but that fate now seems to be a distant memory. I am also more limber in bed, and Rani has used it all as an excuse to return to doing her exercises that make her hold strange shapes, and bend herself in ways the body is not meant to bend. At least that limberness sometimes leads to other fun things.

Now my husband has gotten Shilpa to start teaching that bendy art to others. I must admit that at least the steam bath thing is relaxing afterwards… but it is all hard work, and I am not used to being shouted at like that by an Insakharl. In the Palace, my instructors were much more deferential, and they called me 'Highness' and did not yell my name like a…I don't know what. She is even just calling me 'Dora.' Not even my mother did that.

To make it worse, Astrid might allow the others a light staff to work with, instead of a real weapon, but she takes off all her magic, and still waves that horrible great practice weapon of hers around as if it were a little wand. Doesn't she know that she is already the strongest person in the valley…even without all of that discarded magic?

The Hobs are in awe of her, and when they are up from the River Dragon, the former guards Jennifer and Vishal are hardly ever away from her side, and what she does and I am coming to hate is that Ariadne, when she is not making tiles and bricks, seems to always be at a class, and she even has her baby asleep in a basket, alongside a similarly ensconced Anna and Thorstein, as their mothers do their exercises.

What had happened in Ardlark on those days when Astrid had not been seen anywhere? Surely it was too short a time for all the new things the girl knows to have been picked up. The Granther must have made available some of the books similar to those Ruth had...but that still does not explain it all. Astrid now has muscles like some of the Palace Guard. Realisation might be slow, but finally it dawned on her.

I knew that I had seen those exercises being done somewhere before. I never paid them much attention, but it was sometimes hard not to...and besides some of the people doing them were good to look at...all muscles and glistening skin. Moreover, they, men and women, wore as little to practice in as Astrid does. All is now clear, except how she gained the knowledge so quickly, and why the Granther gave it to her.

I may resent it, but I cannot even claim that the men are exempt from it. After seeing the women labouring at it some of the men went to Astrid and asked for their own lessons. She has her husband run those, but she must be teaching him privately, as he only seems to be a tiny bit ahead of his students.

I suppose to be honest, most of the men, particularly those who are originally from outside, would not have been able to handle being ordered around so freely by a woman. I have new bruises and sore muscles after almost every session, and the Muslim men never would have joined in doing things like that with near-naked women.

Most of the classes are done in the closed hall, wearing only a kilt or a loincloth, although Verily, Goditha, Adara, and Bryony, and the Khitan women sometimes dispense even with those, and only the mothers who are nursing, or the more generously endowed, bind their breasts during it, or when we go out for a run a little way up the path to the falls and back.

Rani (11th Primus)

I eventually have a list of people who I think should be going to the Swamp that I am happy with. We might be trying to be cautious in doing this, but it will not be a quiet and inconspicuous trip. Mousehole will be showing itself in force, and there will be near thirty combatants going, and most of the saddles will be used. Some will need to be left behind in case of an emergency.

Reluctantly, I have followed Dobun's advice, and none of the people going are originally from Haven. Long ago, with my grandmother living in the same house, I learnt to follow the advice of a seer once you have sought it. I will never forget the embarrassment that happened to me at school one day when I thought to ignore the hint that my grandmother gave me.

My wife will have three lesser mages to back her up: Verily, Goditha, and Maria. Christopher will have two priests, Simeon and Aziz, in addition to Dobun as a shaman, and Astrid and Stefan have an impressive array of armsmen and women along. Those Khitan who are going will all hold in the air under Hulagu, with the Muslim men, Atã and Tāriq, and the three kataphractoi along as backup.

All of those in the air can use horse bows well, and Hulagu can also act as their own mage in the sky. Even if he has only a few lightly powered spells of his own, he at least already knows when to use a wand, and when not to waste it. That will leave eleven on the ground, and Astrid alone will be worth several more than that. She and Stefan have their own little groups, and have been working them hard to learn to co-operate in a fight.

Astrid has her husband with her, as well as Thord, Jennifer, and Thomas. Stefan has his wives, along with Ayesha, Tabitha, and Harnermêŝ. Astrid's group are better suited for close combat and Stefan's are superior for archery. Moreover, Verily, Maria, and Dobun all use fire-based cantrips, so they are naturally suited to using battle magic, and I have been teaching it to them.

It was a good thing that I made those protection devices. Only around half of our ground force has shields, although the number of spears is impressive, and Astrid has really been working on that aspect, and the mock fights that are happening every day between the two groups usually lead to one of the priests being called for. It is getting to be as bad on our training field as that arena exercise that we saw in Ardlark.

Harnermêŝ has also demonstrated his combat skill. It is not really wrestling, but it can disarm most people, and he can even knock them out and perhaps even kill them using just his hands or feet. He is happy to fight a person armed with a spear when he has no weapons at all, and that makes him a surprise package indeed.

Astrid is already taking lessons with him, and is very intent on adding his skills to her own. With Basil and Ayesha with them, they will definitely not have problems in the close environs of a town if we face just normal problems.

I have to acknowledge that we still have a long way to go. I remember what my wife said about the rule for the Darkreach armies. A simple foot soldier requires at least two years training to be effective, and a specialist requires up to four. We don't have that luxury. We are lucky with what we have, and we will have to act with that.

After seeing various people in action, except for a few of the cadre in the independent villages, few in the west have that Darkreach level of dedication to training. The cavalry may be well-trained, but the levy in Haven is just as bad as the soldiers anywhere else.

I will never forget what I was told of the stupidity of the pursuers the last time that we Mice were in the Swamp. Each of those who will be staying in *the air are working furiously to co-ordinate their activities, and to learn to obey the different orders they are given. For a start, some need to get used to a different voice to Astrid's calling orders.*

In addition to their arrows and spells, they each now have two of the molotails in strong leather containers, and Maria, Verily, and Goditha have even more of them. A pursuit on our foot would be very expensive to undertake, and the Mice going with them can easily destroy an entire town if they need to. Between them, they can imitate the blast of at least a small dragon.

Now I must work out when they should leave. She looked at her lists. *The woman on it with the most recent birth is Bryony, and Trystan is over three months old already. Lakshmi gave a note to Fear to bring home that told of the women who should not go due to pregnancy, and none of them are on my list anyway.*

I suppose that the best time for them to leave will be as soon as is possible. Sighing, she rose and went to fetch her wife and the others who would lead each group. *They need to organise their final practices, and to get ready the various items that they will be taking with them to help justify the trip to an innocent questioner. We do have to, at need; act as if we are innocently looking for markets and trade opportunities. It is a flimsy excuse, but it is better than none.*

Theodora (13ᵗʰ Primus)

*B**efore anything else can happen, it appears that, un-noticed by the rest of us, the Darkreach kataphractoi have made their decisions on who was going to have which girl as their partner and have got the other persons concerned to agree with them. Perhaps it was even the other way around. It is hard to tell here.*

Whichever it is, during the turmoil of the last few weeks, apparently some serious courting has been taking place. One after the other couples are going to see the priests, and the impending marriages of Menas and Maria, Neon and Tabitha, and Asticus and Zoë have been announced to the village.

Soon after those announcements, Anastasia added to the crew of the River Dragon by giving birth to Leukothea. *That reminds me of something I have meant to discuss with my husband when we get back from seeing the new mother.*

"Astrid is always complaining about children getting in the way of her fighting. Some of the tagma in Darkreach have many women serving in them, and they have found a solution. Once the children are off the breast, and sometimes even before, they take all the children who are too young to go to school, and they put them in one place, and have people to look after them.

"These carers are usually poor women who must work, and yet who have children of their own and so cannot do something else. We don't have any poor women here, but the idea is still a good one for us to think about.

"I know that Astrid, and Bianca, and we have girls in the house now, but others do not, and also might not want their children underfoot all of the time when they are small. I mean…our miller may not be married now, but she will need to keep working when she has small children, and the mill is not a safe place for little ones.

"In a normal village or tribe, there will be grandmothers and maiden aunts and other relations all over the place to do this work. It will be very many years before we have families that are large, and old enough to have them. We need to think of other ways of doing it." *At least Rani has agreed to think about the idea.*

Theodora

19th Primus, the Feast Day of Saint Winifred

The point of having people working as devoted carers for the young children was driven home to them when Alaine gave birth to her daughter, Surtak, and then on the first day of summer, Aigiarne gave birth to her daughter, Enq.

On the plains, when their parents were busy, or away for war or the hunt, the old women take care of the youngest children and the hearth, while the old men care for the slightly older ones and the flocks. The Mori have no older people to undertake this task…and they will not have them until well after the generation being born now have grown up and have children of their own.

Chapter XXXVII

Theodora (22ⁿᵈ Primus)

*W*ell now we have let Birchdingle know what happened in the North, and at Mousehole, and what is going to be happening over the next few months. The people there will want to move to a more wary stance, in case the residents of the Swamp grow…restless. In some ways, it is reassuring to be told, as Magister Cathal said to me:* "We are ready when you need us. If the time is not yet, we will wait." *In other ways it is not.*

We still have no idea what the prophesies of the Bear-folk involve exactly, and they are as forthcoming about them as the Khitan generally are about their affairs. They seem to think that we will work it all out on our own, and will let them know when they are going to be needed. They are not going to share the details, even with me, but they seem to feel that they have a destiny to assist at some time, when we decide, and that has to be enough for us.

Theodora (late afternoon)

*T*he village of Bathmawr has come into sight. We avoided it the last time we came this way. It lies beside the Murga River, a tributary of the Tulky Wash and the village itself sits, for some reason, a good hand of filled hands away from the river. The landings on it are within a good bowshot of the walls, but the residents would still have to carry things backwards and forwards between the two.*

Theodora, after stopping everyone well away and using a telescope to spy out the land, called Bryony up and asked why. "There are only a few places near here that the giant lizards can easily come to the water and drink," she said. "This is one. It easier to walk to the water than to rebuild the village after a herd of large animals has been down for a drink. Even though the walls will keep out stray animals, a big and impatient herd can easily flatten them."

She pointed. "See, their fields are hidden within close planted banks of trees for the same reason. Here a hedge needs to be a couple of filled hands high to be of any use. That is also why the village wall is made up of whole trees, some still living, and is so high. You will see that all the villages of the Free either lie on islands or have similar walls."

The village lay within two rows of standing stones which ended in a stone circle on a mound. Bryony pointed at the stones: "Even the temple stones are sometimes trampled. That circle is almost the tallest spot in the whole Swamp. If you stand on it, you can even see over the top of all the houses in the village and over the walls," she added.

Theodora shook her head, and called Astrid over to give her control of the approach. *I suppose that this all makes sense.*

Astrid

I send Stefan's group forward with Bryony out the front. One or the other of the cousins will be the ones contacting each village as we go. The Princesses hope that a familiar accent may help allay suspicion. I place more faith in them using their boobs to distract people. I spread the rest of our people out and we slowly move up behind her.

I want the rest of Stefan's group just behind Bryony, and the others just within archery range ready to react, if needed. Despite the cautious approach coming down to ground level, and advancing slowly at a horse height, a bell has begun to ring from somewhere in the village, and people are moving around in an agitated fashion. They must be expecting attack. She looked around.

There is a ferry scurrying to the edge of the river. People are moving into the trees that surround the fields, slipping between the trunks, and beyond the village, it looks like we are disrupting a market. Directing Menas, who had good eyes, to stay high; she brought the others slowly down to near ground level and then slowed them down still further.

From what I can see, that seems to have a good effect on them, and although they still move away from us, most of the people have at least stopped running, except that one who is gathering up chooks. It is now up to Bryony to gain us entry. Hopefully, whoever oversees the gate is a man, or at least likes women.

Bryony

*S*lowly, *I approach the gate. It is still open, even if another two people have appeared outside of it, and several are quickly squeezing past to duck behind them and get inside.* She looked up at the wall above her. *I can see a couple of other people peering down. I haven't been here for some time, and I wonder if what I knew then is still current.*

Behind me, there are many people ready to back me up at need, so I should try to look harmless. I will keep my bow in its case, and my spear tucked into its carrier straps. My bodice is laced loosely and low. That always seems to distract at least some. At least I don't have a baby at my breast to slow me down this time.

She came to a stop twenty or so paces away from the gate, beyond even the dry moat that surrounded the village. *Theodora has said many times that it is always best to keep outside the short range of a potential caster, and I approve of that idea, as I feel naked enough out the front of everyone as it is.*

The guards look like normal armsmen for the swamp in their motley appearance. One wears mail. From its appearance, it started its life in Haven. He has a round shield that also looks to be of Haven origin and a sword. Despite his armour and shield, his sword is a leaf-bladed local weapon. He holds that in his right hand, and he peers over the shield.

The next one is a woman, and she has bronze lamellar on her torso, with a skirt of studded leather strips worn over a cotton skirt. She has knee high boots with long bronze splints on the front. She carries a long spear with a large oval shield.

The last guard is another woman who wears leather, much the same as I do, but without the advantage of having as good a cleavage to fit within it. She carries a bow with an arrow knocked, but the arrow is uselessly pointing at the ground.

Here goes nothing. I need to make my local accent as obvious as possible. "Greetings, what is all the fuss about? Cannot some travellers visit without causing disruption? I wanted to let my friends try some of Domnhall's food, and then let our leader have a word with the Reeve Dympna." She paused and looked around.

More curious heads are appearing both through the gate and on top of the wall. "We have no intention of trading, even if we have some sample goods to talk to merchants about. I had forgotten that it was a market today. Are there any vacancies at the Virgin Bride, or will we have to stay at the Bull and

Bear?" She paused again. "Have you all been struck dumb? Is no-one going to answer me, or at least say hello?" She looked at the three in front of her.

The woman archer obviously has noticed nothing except my breasts. I doubt that she has even noticed that I have a face. Perhaps I have it unlaced too far. She is almost licking her lips. I am more used to that from men but will take the distraction either way. The other woman is looking at the saddle. The one in mail is possibly the one in charge, and he is also distracted, as his eyes flick from behind me, to my breasts, and then to the saddle.

"Who are you and why are you here?" he eventually asked.

Now I need to sound offended. "I am sorry, but why do we need to answer that? You are prying dreadfully. What gives you the right to do that when we have broken no laws?" She grinned inside herself. *What I have just said is what a good half of the local inhabitants would say, regardless of whether they were guilty of anything or not, and most would probably have said it a lot less politely.*

"You could be an invasion," the man said defensively. "How am I to know? I am a guard, and I ask questions of suspicious people, and keep a watch for invaders from Haven."

"You are right...we could be an invasion...but I see no Haven faces behind me, and if we are an invasion wouldn't we have invaded straight away, and killed people by surprise, instead of coming down to your level and moving towards the gate slowly? I have even put all my weapons away and have approached you with empty hands." She held them palm forward and wiggled her fingers at him to demonstrate the truth of what she had said. *See the dancing fingers.*

"She is right," said an older woman who was just emerging from the village. *She wears a bliaut made of green silk and is obviously prosperous.* "Don't be an idiot, Corc." She turned to Bryony. "I, however, can ask you anything I want, as I am the Reeve here, and you have just used my name, and I don't know you."

"My name is Bryony verch Dafydd..." *I need to be as confident as Astrid always is at such times.* "I was originally from Leidauesgynedig. I was here a couple of years ago, but you would not have noticed me. Since then, my family has been killed, and I was taken by slavers, and now I live elsewhere, but am back among the Free on a visit."

"Slavers from Haven?" the woman asked, obviously expecting an affirmative answer.

"No, they were from around here. The mage Glyn ap Tristan, the mage Conrad, and a man called Cuthbert, and another called Gwillam, among many others...they are all dead now. I had the pleasure of killing Cuthbert myself. They kidnapped a girl from here...several years ago now...her name is Dulcie...she was sixteen then...she is still back in our village, and several years before her, it was another girl called Aine."

She looks disappointed at who I accuse of the kidnapping, but at least there is a flicker on her face at the names I recite.

"We have had our revenge on them, but I still seek others who had a part in the kidnappings to wreak my justice on them." Bryony stopped and looked at all the faces on the wall and peering out of the gate. *The presence of something as unusual as the saddles is obviously overcoming the normal reticence of Swamp people to pry into other people's business.*

"Can we enter...and is there somewhere more private to talk? I am not used to discussing my business so publicly. We were hoping to spend the night here rather than in the bush. Once we are all inside and settled, then everyone else can all get back to having a market day."

The woman chuckled. "I am sure that flying ..."

"Saddles ..."

"...That flying saddles are far more interesting to them than a weekly market...but you are right. We need not talk in the open. You may let your friends approach and follow us inside." Bryony turned and nodded to her husband. He in turn turned and waved to Astrid before moving forward, followed by the rest of his group. Astrid started the others moving, leaving Menas in the sky until she was about to enter the village.

"Corc was right about one thing," said Dympna looking back, "you are set up more like an invasion than a group of travellers."

"Travellers we are, for the moment at least, and that we will stay, unless someone does something stupid and we need to change our purpose." Bryony smiled in an attempt to take the sting from what she had just implied.

"We come from a once secret valley in the mountains, and I will let one of our bards tell you the story, once we have all had some of Domnhall's food...I didn't lie...I haven't had it for ages. While we are used to good cooks in our village, and in some of the places where we go, his cold pork pies are the stuff of legends. Besides, we had an early lunch, and I am quite hungry again."

We are off to a tavern of three stories, much like those in Evilhalt, but built all of timber. The saddles were put away in the stables, and Stefan made sure the stable boy tried to fly one, and then was graphically told the consequences of letting other people touch them, and shown the rewards of keeping them safe.

Bryony

After putting things in their rooms, Bryony led them out into a square where a man was set up with food in a square building with three sides raised up to provide shade and to allow a breeze to blow through. *Everyone with us has at least some Hindi, so I will use it. Lots do, despite it being the tongue of the enemy.*

"Everyone, this is Domnhall. Try his food. Atã, Tãriq, if you want, don't touch the small, tall round pies" she pointed "They are filled with pork. The rest is just delicious." She and Adara started buying things, and alternatively stuffing their own mouths and Stefan's.

Theodora

Now we have all eaten enough, we repair to the tavern where Dympna is introduced to me, and I give a shortened version of our story in Arabic. I speak no Faen, and it seems that we both speak the mountain language better than we do Hindi. While this is going on, Christopher and the other two priests take themselves upstairs, and cast to see if a Pattern is concealed somewhere in the village.

The priests returned just as Theodora was finishing up. She raised an eyebrow in Christopher's direction, and he shook his head.

"So, while we are still looking for these people and their friends, on this trip we largely seek trade opportunities, to find out if there are any of our religion here, and to tell people about our school and what has been happening in the world. Tonight, we will tell the full story to your people, and they will hear what the real story was behind the push to have a war with Haven and many other things. Do you have a bard in town?"

"Yes, Adhamhnán," the Reeve replied.

"Well, make sure that he is along to hear us tonight. We have many tales of legend to tell."

"I would say that is inevitable. He is just there," she said dryly, as she pointed at a man clad in a bliaut and hose of blue and gold only a few paces away. "And by the look of him, is already hanging off your every word." The man bowed with a flourish and a smile. *I suppose that I should have guessed that we would have attracted his attention.*

Chapter XXXVIII

Theodora (the night of 22nd Primus)

That night, as many of the villagers as can fit, cram into the Virgin Bride. They hear Ayesha tell the tale of the village of Mousehole in their own tongue. It is not a short tale and goes late into the night. To an accompaniment of astonished gasps and applause they heard of the bandits and the freeing of the village, of the discovery of Dwarvenholme, the death of the Masters, the death of the Dragon, the raids around The Land, the destruction of the Brotherhood, and the freeing of Skrice.

Ayesha has been told how to slant her tale, and she stresses that the people who died had been tools of outsiders, and some had secretly worked in the interests of those outsiders for years, keeping it hidden from their neighbours. The raid on Sacred Gate has general approval, and it seems that the raid on Rising Mud is easily forgiven...after all, it wasn't done to their village, none of them suffered, and Bryony and Adara clearly had the right of revenge on their side anyway.

I had not really believed it when the cousins told me that this is what would happen. We are telling no-one of my lineage, or my origin, however. If any know the meaning of my eyes, that is for them to talk about. Dawn was lightening the sky when some of them made it into bed.

Basil

I am keeping an eye out in case there is someone present who has cause to hate us, and wants their own revenge, but I see no-one who is dubious. On the other hand, the priests tell me they see and feel plenty who are suspicious.

They are sure that many of those around us make their living by theft, possibly only from Haven admittedly, but theft it is none the less.

They are making no attempt to hide the fact that they are Christian priests, and during the night, a couple of people have come up to them and asked if they will be doing a service. Christopher has sent them away, and told them to gather any others, and come to Orthros. He has made sure that he asks about any Muslims, although none know of any.

At one stage during a break, Basil found himself talking to a fat and happy man who introduced himself as Saenu ap Owen ap Alwyn.

He happily announces that he is the local slaver. He buys most of his slaves from local entrepreneurs…so the suspicious ones could be kidnappers, and not just thieves. It seems that most of his slaves are redeemed by relatives from Haven when a message is sent about their fate back into that nation. If they aren't bought by relatives, then they enter the local markets, usually ending up down Iba Bay picking cotton, or even sometimes go on to the Caliphate.

He rarely must do that, and he has frequent visits from a trusted intermediary from Garthang Keep, which lies downstream. He expressed disgust at the selling of children for sex. "I have had children brought to me as slaves, but not for that sort of thing, and they are the ones most likely to be redeemed. Otherwise, they usually go on to make carpets.

"Children are much in demand in the Caliphate for that. Such taking and selling for sex gives our trade a bad name," he said. "I will keep an eye out for any of that. If I hear of it happening, how do I get a message on to you? Will it do to send it to the Bear People? I sometimes sell that way, or should I send it through Garthang?"

Somewhat in surprise, as the man seemed to be very much in earnest in his dislike, Basil agreed that either was as good a method as any.

Having established that, Saenu went on: "Now…not that I am likely to be able to have enough stock at any one time…but should it happen that there are several who are unredeemed at the same time, in other words enough to make it worthwhile, what is the market like for slaves going into Darkreach?" *He is well pleased with the answer.*

Christopher (23rd Primus)

*N*ext *morning, three families from the village are here for Orthros, and it is obvious that the smaller members of the families have never seen an Orthodox priest before, and it is a long while between visits for the others. In addition to the expected Confessions, there are nine baptisms, and a wedding* *of a very pregnant bride to be done, and it being her second child.*

I need to explain to them all about what was said at the Synod and promise them that I will see what I can do about getting them a Priest of their own. I have even been told that, as well as those in the village, apparently there are a few more families who live outside the village and they will not know that I am here.

With that, he went up to Theodora and announced that he couldn't leave the area without at least seeing them. *We are supposed to be travelling slowly anyway, and this makes us look even more harmless.* With lighter locals riding as passengers on the saddles to act as guides, the priests headed off. *Astrid has detailed the kataphractoi and Goditha to go with us as an escort.*

Bryony

"I have noticed," Rhod ap Cronin, who had introduced himself as the chief druid, said to Bryony and Adara, when he had been able to get them alone, "that you have priests of the Christians with you, but no druids, and the Hobgoblin, who should be the same faith as you, is a Christian priest." *He has a look on his face that manages to be both stern and quizzical.*

The girls looked at each other. *Shit. I was hoping to avoid this question.* It was Adara who replied. "We are now Christian, as well. The women who were in our village and came from down here felt abandoned. They only had contact with one of the Wicca, and it was one who had chosen the evil path and not the good. The Christians have been very good to us, our chief priest is a very holy man whom God smiles on, and our husband is a Christian, so we took his faith."

"Your husband? You share a husband between the two of you? The Christians let you do this?" *The man sounds astonished, almost shocked.*

Again, the girls looked at each other. Bryony sighed. *My cousin obviously thinks that she has said enough. I guess that it is my turn to speak and now I get to fill in the gaps in the story.* "There are a few things about our little village that Ayesha left out of the story when she spoke last night. These make us perhaps a little more unusual than most..."

Theodora

I *am quite disappointed. Although the village is a prosperous one, and the people seem hospitable, there is really nothing tradable here except for the local fruit, nuts, herbs, and spices. Unless they do a lot more with what they have, they really do need to raid Haven in order to bring any real wealth into the village. Such theft is vital for their prosperity.*

I can see Lakshmi and Lãdi coming here for the local specialties among the herbs and plants, once the locals accept their origin, but that is all. On the other hand, from what I have tasted, Aine has a good market here in her home village for any of her drinks. Most of the beers drunk in the Swamp, I have been told, are made of rice and even I realise that it is very poor, weak stuff.

Most of these people teach their own children in their homes, and it is obvious that few can properly read and write, let alone know much else about the world. It seems that only the rich employ professional teachers. No wonder they were so easily gulled by Glyn and his friends. No child in Darkreach would be as ignorant about their letters, and indeed about the world, as these people seem to be in their pride.

If we have any of their children come to the valley school, it would only be some who are thought to be potential mages. They will be the ones who want more than just an apprenticeship, and yet the parents do not want them to go to Sacred Gate to be taught by my husband's peers. Those that come will possibly have as much catching up to do as a Hob child...and the Hobs are working on fixing that situation as fast as they can.

It will not be until well into tomorrow that we will be able to go on to Dolbaden, and that lets our story, and the news that we bear about the events in the world, travel further and get around the area even more. It also leads to there being another packed house on the second night to hear the story being told again. At least the tavern keeper here will welcome us back.

Chapter XXXIX

Astrid (24th Primus)

*A**t least we get to sleep late. It is only a short flight due south to reach our next destination, but I am taking us on a high path. I want to see if our maps are right.*

She rose high enough that they could see the broadening stream of the Tulky Wash flowing down to Garthang Keep and its junction with the Rhastaputra. *To the left, the Bellingen River lies, only sometimes visible through the expanse of green, and disappearing at other times, into low swamps to re-emerge again as a river.*

Ahead lies the Buccleah, or, as Ayesha calls it, the Ziyanda Rūdh, and near the junction of the two are the vast earthworks of Dolbaden. At some time in the past, an area big enough for a village, with some room left over for fields and even grazing, has been enclosed by a vast earthwork or levee. All around the earthwork, an even larger and wider moat had been dug and a deep down-stream channel created.

There is a pair of long stone opening bridges. Unlike at Rising Mud, these are real bridges. I would guess that after they were built to cross its new course, the Bellingen was diverted, and the moat filled up with water to make the moat a new river channel. The old course has then been filled in, where needed, so that a besieger could not easily use it to divert the river from its new course.

Some has been left as spreading marsh to make it even harder to again change the river. I think that from the sky I can still see where the old path of the river is. From the ground I am sure that it would be unseen. Now the river has a permanent new path, and a big new island in it, one with stone leading down into the water. It is impressive.

On that island, a motte and bailey keep had been built, and then over

*time, destroyed. After many years of despoliation and neglect, it is all being
replaced. The wooden palisade of the round keep that had been first put in
place is now gradually being replaced by stone, even if the bailey and the
outer wall on top of the river levee are still made of timber.*

*The river on the downstream side is very deep, so although the river looks
not to be navigable for any distance above the village, river-going boats can
come upstream a short distance and dock. Several are tied up at the fenced
off harbour and what is there is not just simple wharves, but there are proper
piers, also.*

*According to the cousins, this makes it the main contact point between
the cultures of Haven and the Swamp, and all of the Swamp contributes to
its defence by paying a yearly levy to support ten times a pair of hands of
soldiers. They patrol the border and keep order there, although from what
Rani has told Theodora and I before we left, Haven often accuses the so-
called peacekeepers of providing most of the raiders.*

Once the village was clearly visible to them, Astrid again brought them
down closer to the level of the ground, and they came into the village over
the rice fields and the circle of dolmen, each set of rocks in the circle the
same as those that were found on the little island outside Mousehole, with two
standing stones and a third laid on top of them like a table.

*This time it is Adara's turn to go forward, and this time there is less fuss
about our entry. The distance between the first wooden bridge over the river-
moat and the keep, and indeed the height of the keep itself, must allowed
whoever is in charge of the defences to be able to assess what is happening
from a distance.*

Theodora

*Except that there is a more open appraisal of the military implications of
our mounts by those who meet us, the visit goes much the same as it did
in Bathmawr. In some respects, however, it is different. The Reeve, Conandil
ap Doreen, shows by his appearance that he has at least some Havenite in
his ancestry, and there are a pair of mages openly listening, a man and his
apprentice girl, who look to be almost straight from Haven except for their
clothes.*

*It seems that the garrison itself is quite divided over the prospect of war.
Some are all for it, some want peace, and some want their current maintenance
of a state short of hostilities to continue due to its more profitable nature.
Again though, I am surprised to discover that here, in what is basically a*

military village, the actions that we Mice have taken to exact revenge are taken by everyone as being completely in the right.

There is no doubt that having proved that the deaths of their families were the fault of Glyn and his friends, Bryony, Dulcie, and Aine were entirely justified in undertaking to kill them, or enlisting aid to help them do so.

It seems that some of those present lost friends in the pursuit, but their loss is generally regarded as being their own fault. They brought it on themselves, both by being persuaded to take part in it by people who, they now know, were in the wrong in the first place, and more importantly, by being so stupid about the way it was done.

Astrid's inventive use of the molotail to kill one of the mages had come down to them by gossip and is regarded as a great joke by all the soldiers. The Pattern was discovered after the survivors returned, and despite some attempts to keep its discovery secret, it is generally known about among many of the people...at least here.

What the reaction will be to us in Rising Mud and in Eastguard Tower, where most of the pursuers apparently came from, is a more interesting question. Astrid has told me that by the end of the night, bets are actually being taken on the subject among the soldiers, and several of the wagerers are openly sounding her out about the intent of the Mice in order to gain a better price.

There seem to be no Christians or Muslims that any know of in the district, but the region will certainly bear another visit. The village makes most of its income, that which does not come from trade or raiding, by growing and processing the herbs, nuts, and spices of the Swamp, and rows of potions of Cure-all and Tugyore, both used to repair the damage of battle, and rows of bottles and flasks of other drinks and pills sat on shelves in one apothecary's establishment.

Another shop specialises in Dadanth, and other medicinal potions, and we are able to make sure that everyone has plenty of the insect repellent, as well as buying an assortment of other items. The mages I saw earlier were there too, and I am sure they are really from Haven. They may be dressed like the locals are, but the man and his girl are foreign. With her knives, the apprentice looks more like Lakshmi when she is getting ready for a fight.

Given that there were few sources for jewels in the Swamp, the jeweller in the village probably spends a lot of his time working on gems that arrive to him in very different settings, or indeed without settings. Having said that, his work is superb, and he eagerly bought some of the items that I brought with me as samples, and grew truly excited when Astrid, who was acting as my guard, condescended to show her necklace.

Apparently, the stories that Giles had told about it are well known, at least in some circles, and he recognised what it had to be at once. We have to say no more to have him regarding us as having walked out of the legends. He ends up doing very well out of the visit. Several of us have bought items for partners who have been left at home.

At least Goditha and I bought from him, at any rate. "They might regularly steal from Haven, but they certainly cater to their tastes, too, and a trader going there could make a good profit." *Both of us bought nose jewels, and fine chains for our partners, and Goditha has also bought some for her adopted daughter.*

Basil

*B*eing a garrison town, of sorts, the largest tavern, although not the best in the village, was able, with cramming, to take far more people than that in Bathmawr. So many of the garrison are here that the brothel even closed for the night, and the girls that work in it sit and listen to the stories from the front row. Astrid looked at the expressions on their faces as they listened, and wondered to me how many of them will find their way north over time. She could well be right.*

Christopher has checked for a Pattern—quite openly—before we leave, and has even explained to those watching what he is doing and why. I am watching the bystanders. All seem to show a normal degree of curiosity, except for a senior druid and two of the Wiccans, a man and a woman, who are taking notes on everything, and seem to be professionally enthralled by what Christopher is doing, and are continually asking questions. Their students stand nearby talking to Aziz.

Bryony has discovered that Rhoddi ap Owen was no longer the Reeve of Rising Mud. He was one of those who had been killed in the pursuit. Urfai ap Carel is now the Reeve. Apparently, he is an elderly water mage, and had been one of the few mages left alive who still actively opposed the war. That may give us hope of avoiding conflict.

According to current rumour, and people were eager to tell her, he might have been popularly elected to the job in the turmoil after the attack, but apparently there are already people who are trying to tear him down again. The people she talked to are in two minds as to whether it is because those working against him want to try and return to the path of war...or if it is just to take his job. Who is mad enough to want to be a ruler?

Theodora

*H*aving talked to the people here in Dolbaden, I have decided that it is best *to go straight from here to Rising Mud. I know we are supposed to be cautious, but I have realised there is no point in delaying the visit. We could easily have gone to the villages close to the sea and then come back, but that is just delaying the inevitable.*

Rising Mud is always going to be the most likely spot for us to have any trouble, and leaving it behind us as a source of strife is not a good idea. We are best going there before the word of our visit to the Swamp reaches anyone there who might wish us harm. That way we Mice will at least have an element of surprise in our visit, and that could be more than handy for us.

Chapter XL

Astrid
25th Primus, the Feast Day of Saint Dwynwen

We are flying straight up the river, over the water, with the birds and the flying lizards thick below us. I am staying outside the range of a bow. We sweep over the occasional river trader, and some canoes, to the consternation of the occupants.

On both sides of the river, assarts can sometimes be seen. Once, on the right, the ruins of a long-lost town lay deep beyond the dense jungle margins of the river. The ruins are all covered in trees, and can only be made out as occasional walls. Some pyramids have their tops poking out of the vegetation and serve as small hills.

Simon of Richfield talked about the towns here in his book. I wonder if that was their capital of Maarleen. It should be somewhere here in the Swamp, along with another place called Thaaness. They had both been on rivers, but the names of the rivers that were used then are nothing like the two this river has now, or indeed of any other in the Swamp that I knew about.

As they flew, Astrid could see that the land rose slightly and gently to the south of the river, and that there is what might be a low ridge running parallel to the river in the far distance. *On this side of the ridge the water runs into the Buccleah and north, and then into the Tulky Wash before turning south into the Rhastaputra to flow down into the sea. On the other side of the ridge, it must flow more directly south.*

Taking herself higher, she could see an unbroken sea of green lay in that direction. *The ocean lies too far away to even give a hint of its existence, but at least the faint ridge is clearer. Ahead of me lies the vastness of our mountains, and somewhere there directly ahead, the Caliphate.* She brought herself back down to the others, and they flew on.

It was nearly time for lunch before Rising Mud was sighted. Once it was seen, Astrid moved them to the left of the wide stream so that they were now flying up the path alongside the river.

This time, as we approach the bridge, Stefan needs to make sure that his face is obscured. Of all of us, his is the most likely face to be recognised. Theodora has asked that we try to set up in town before anything is said that might bring too great a reaction. I think that she is being an optimist. I am sure that trouble is going to happen, and fairly quickly.

We can easily destroy this town if hostilities start, and we need to, but that is not the idea of the visit. We should at least try and seem just like innocent travellers until we tell our story. Caution, we must think of caution first. At least I don't have to trust my life to that rickety excuse for a bridge. That is more than caution enough for me.

Bryony

*B*ehind me, I bet that they are all holding their breath. Here is our first real chance to have a fight start. Our arrival was clearly seen. The crews working on the bridges and the structure of the village have even stopped what they are doing, and are watching as I approach the guard on duty.* "Hello Cothric." *The woman looks like she has seen a ghost and has nearly dropped her spear.*

"But…but…you were taken by Haven slavers…the night that they killed your family and your husband, Conan, died," the woman said.

"No. Like my cousin, Adara, behind me…wave to Adara…you haven't seen her for a while, either…I was made a slave by Glyn, and by your cousin Cuthbert, and by some other friends of theirs when they killed my family, among others, to help promote the war. That is why I came back with some friends, and we killed Glyn. You might not have known who did it, but it was us.

"I had already executed Cuthbert myself after he confessed what he had done." *I hope that you can hear the acid in my voice, you bitch. You made my childhood hell with your spiteful ways, and your pack of nasty friends. I think that she has. Her face has changed from surprise to anger. The woman looks ready to strike me.*

"I wouldn't even think of doing that if I were you. There is only one of you, and if you look at my friends, you will see several very strong mages. However, I don't need them. Unless you have gotten very much better than I remember, even I could easily take you on my own now, with or without weapons.

"We are here to see Urfai ap Carel, and tell him exactly what happened and why. We have all the records of the questioning, and are willing to swear under an enchantment as to the truth of them. I am fully justified in what I did by our laws and customs.

"It was your cousin Cuthbert who suggested that I be taken as a slave by his friends, while my husband and my family were killed. It is his fault that I was repeatedly raped. I am happy to say that he didn't die in a becoming fashion at all. He went to his death just like the coward that he always was."

She smiled. *I wish for once that I had Astrid's teeth to do justice to the smile that I am bestowing on her.* "Now we are all going to fly over to the village, and we are going to see Urfai. At least we hear that he had sense, and was not taken in by Glyn, and Rhoddi, and their lies. Remember what was found in Glyn's house? He was a tool of demons, and so was your late cousin. Were you?"

The woman is blanching again. Turning away and now ignoring her, Bryony flew across the water. I am not going to pay a bridge toll for a bridge that I am not going to use. Astrid was listening and had closed the others up behind her, and the Mice now flew in, two by two. As Bryony had guessed, Cothric made no alarm.

Bryony

*P*eople *are looking at us as we fly low over the island to the Horse and Imp. We will stay there again. I am enjoying coming home openly. The occasional person whom I know is seeing me, and like Cothric, they react as if I am returned from the dead. I might as well be. I am not answering anyone, but, from behind me I can hear Adara happily hail someone.*

Bryony brought her saddle to a rest in front of the inn and went to go inside. *I can feel my pulse racing. My husband, Ayesha, and Harnermês are landing. They will follow close behind me into the inn, while Adara prepares to talk to anyone who says anything outside. Astrid has quickly landed beside her while the rest stay low in the air. She will keep Adara safe.*

It took a while to arrange rooms. *It is Dithlau and the market is happening, but we are willing to share beds, so it is possible to get rooms. I am even able to negotiate for a shed of their own for the saddles. Not that anyone can fly them away, but they can always be disenchanted or otherwise harmed. Someone of our group will be sleeping with them anyway, probably the Khitan.*

She returned outside to see Adara already talking to Urfai as a crowd grew around them. *Astrid stands casually, leaning on her weapon as if it was a spear.* Bryony recognised one of the people pushing his way through the crowd, unnoticed by her cousin.

Oh shit. It is Ith. He is Glyn's brother, a huge man, an armsman, and a loathsome bully. I remember his leers and his wandering hands far too well. I admit that I was surprised that I did not see him last time that we were here.

He has made his living by raiding Haven, but then he always seemed to be more than a little wealthier than others who did exactly the same. It is obvious that my sister-wife has not seen him approach. Before Bryony could push out and say anything to warn Adara, Ith spoke in Hindi. *A space automatically, and rapidly, starts to clear around them as his words came out.*

"I am Ith, and you are the ones who came from Haven to treacherously kill my brother, and the other patriots, and to steal the money that had been set aside for expenses. I challenge you to combat one-on-one to prove what I say," he said to Adara.

Astrid

*B*efore any others among the Mice can react, my husband and I have made *our moves...my husband stands to the side, his hands resting on his blades, to make sure that none interfere in what is about to go down. I need some exercise. He uses Hindi, so I can as well.*

Astrid slid herself sidewise and planted herself right in front of Ith. Astrid's face was only a hand from Ith's chest, and she looked up at him. *He stands two hands taller even than me, and he is a lot wider across the shoulders. There is only a hand between my tits and his stomach. His breath smells. Does he never clean his teeth?*

Still, he is a lot smaller than an Insak-div. She spoke up as loudly as she could. "On behalf of Adara, and of Bryony, and of all of the other women and children that you and your brother, and the other one called Cuthbert kidnapped and sent into slavery from the Swamp to be raped, and often to die, and in the name of Saint Kessog, my patron, I will accept your challenge.

"I think that I am also supposed make mention of the families of your victims that you murdered, and then laid the blame on the people of Haven to try and start a war." She paused briefly and looked around. *It has not taken long for there to be a crowd surrounding us, but they stay well back out of the way.*

She smiled broadly up at the man. *He is looking stupidly at me and my teeth.* "Will it just be you that I am about to kill, or do you want to call for a friend to die with you?" She again paused briefly as Ith stood there with his mouth open. *He has no idea what has just happened, and I am not going to give him a chance to gain any advantage.*

"Now, if I have it right, seeing that you issued the challenge, I think it works that I get to set the rules...I am going to make them very simple rules in the hope that you can understand them. There will be no missile weapons used; no wands, no spells, no healing, and it will be to the death." She smiled up at him.

My confidence, and probably my teeth, set him back on his heels. He recoils back. He is not used to having his bluff called. "Now, don't you try and run away, and I hope you don't piss yourself like Cuthbert did before we even started to question him. It was so undignified.

"Just try and be a real man for the first and last time in your life. You will not get another chance." For the first time, Astrid now looked at the crowd. *They are already quickly moving back, clearing an area. Some have a horrified expression on their faces, while others look a lot more calculating. I think that I just saw two shake hands. The bets are going to start being laid.*

"Clear a space around us and be wary. There is more than enough room in this square for us to fight, but we have found that his friends are cowards, so he may well try and run away." She turned back to Ith. "If you want, you can say a prayer to the so-called Masters that you worship before you die in their service." *From the look on his face, I know that I have struck home.*

I can hear the mage beside Adara starting to splutter. "I am sure that she will be quick," *Adara is talking apologetically to him.* "We need only wait a few minutes until Ith is dead, and then I can introduce you to the rest of our people."

Ith turned and talked to a few people. *I am taking note of them, and I can see that Basil is moving around in that direction, to try to keep an eye as to where they go. Ith has taken off his cloak, put it on the ground, and got himself ready, flexing his massive arms and obviously making an attempt to intimidate me. I will go the other way, and so lean on my bardiche trying to look bored. What did Bryony say?*

"Stop wasting time. I formally accuse you of being one of the ones who killed Conan, the husband of Bryony verch Dafydd, and one of those who also killed her family. I also accuse you of raping her and selling her into slavery. Since I am acting on her behalf as her champion, according to the customs of this area, let any who has not come forward now to aid you interfere at their peril, and forfeit of protection. I call on the whole village of Rising Mud to witness this, and so enforce it." *Even some of Ith's friends are drawing away from him at that and Ith is turning on me with a snarl.*

"I am going to kill you for that, bitch." Without any more ado, he leapt at her with a sword that had suddenly appeared in each hand. *For a large man, he moves very quickly and lightly.* He swung one blade high at her head in an obvious threat, while the other thrust low towards the stomach. Astrid moved quicker.

Suddenly, although she had been leaning on it, the heavy bladed bardiche spun around almost as rapidly as a quarterstaff, and the bottom blade was deflected while the top one flew spinning out of Ith's hand through the air to land at the feet of some of the crowd.

A suddenly flying blade landing near on their toes sends them falling backwards in panic. Astrid continued the move and put the point at his throat. *His empty hand is opening and closing as if he is trying to get feeling back in it.*

"You are a very stupid man, as well as being slow, and you probably have a very, very tiny dick." *I can hear a few female giggles in the audience.* "I am going to be generous though, and I will let you have another try." She lightly pricked his throat, giving him a gentle push back. *Fear has gradually started to appear on his face. It took a while.* Ith stepped back, and drew a dagger in his free hand, and went to close again.

He is too late. As he stepped in, Astrid pivoted the blade into his torso, brushing aside the dagger. He shrieked in pain and surprise, as he was nearly cut in half by the blow, and his opened guts spilt on to the ground. He dropped his weapons and fell screaming, trying futilely to grasp and hold closed the huge open wound. Astrid looked down at him. "Goodbye."

She paused, and looked around at the faces of the spectators. "At this stage are there any more who wish to take up his cause, or speak for the filth that he is?" She smiled broadly at them. *They are shitting themselves.*

The circle around them both drew even further back. *Blood is pooling around this nithling…enough suffering.* Quickly, and out of mercy, she brought her bardiche down on the writhing and screaming man who lay on the ground trying desperately to stuff his guts back together even as he was dying. His head sprang off his neck in mid scream and his body spasmed.

"I meant what I said." Astrid looked around. *I may as well speak and drive the point home while I have their attention.* "This animal…" she kicked the body in front of her, "his brother, and their friends are responsible for all of the losses that were put down to raiders from Haven. They were not even patriots. Most were fools and the rest well…some knew who they worked for, but most did not. They worked for some evil creatures called the Masters.

"Remember the Pattern that was found at Glyn's house? It took at least one human sacrifice to make that. We have been destroying ones just like it all over The Land. If you come along tonight, you will be able to hear the story of how Ith and Glyn were traitors to you, and your people, and led you to your destruction. Hear how Bryony here," she waved one hand behind her, "and Adara, were taken...one as a slave for sex, and the other as a sacrifice to their dark gods, for a Pattern like the one here.

"We have records of the questioning, and are willing to be put under a truth spell to vouch for them. Ask Ith's friends if they are willing to do the same." She shook her hand.

Blood is dripping down the blade onto it and drops fly as I move. I am tempted to lick the blade, to watch the reaction, but I won't. Think caution...if I did that, from looking around, I think that half of the onlookers would faint. It looks like my quick demolition of the man, added to what I have said, has made the right impression on the watchers. I hope that we will not have much more trouble after this.

She turned towards the inn, only to feel a bolt of air pass her close by, and hear a scream erupt. She turned again, and saw a man being held to the ground by Basil. *My husband has both of his shortswords out and one is deep in the man's body pinning him to the ground, while the other is held at his throat.*

I can also see several knives are buried in the man. Both Ayesha and Bianca must have seen him start to move. Around him, the crowd is melting away and a clear space has already appeared. He might have been hoping someone else would help him. He might have moved, but it is clear that he has no support now.

"Do I keep him alive to question?" asked Basil.

Astrid turned to look at the mage beside Adara. "I believe that under the rules of this place, he already owes me his life, and so I will kill him later. It is though, I believe, your town. Do you want to know the truth from him? That way all here will hear exactly what happened, and what he was involved in, from his own lips."

The mage nodded and looked at the man on the ground. "Athgal ..." he said in a shocked and slightly quivering voice, "How could you?"

My turn to watch out at the crowd, as Basil rolls the man over and quickly shackles him, ignoring his screams as the knives dig further into him. He then rolls the man, Athgal, back over, removes the blades and pours a draft down his throat to stop him dying yet, as Bianca and Ayesha take their blades back.

"Cast no spells. Make no moves I haven't told you to make." He began to pat the man down, throwing aside a sword, daggers, wands, rings, an armlet, and any jewellery he wore. *The man tries to resist, but he is helpless before a practised professional. I keep watching the crowd, but no-one is moving to help him. They are not totally stupid then.*

Basil kept him off balance and slapped him often to keep him dazed and confused. *The crowd around us look like a whole school of fish that are stunned by Hop Bush leaves and floating on the surface. Their mouths even open and close as if gasping for air. I will bet that this nekulturny fool was someone of importance.* Astrid looked around past the crowd.

*I am sure that I saw what I want on the last visit here...there it is...this village has everything you need...*Once Basil had cleared the man, she went over and grabbed him...*Athgal*...by his belt and lifted him with one hand while the other held her bardiche, still dripping blood. *He is only newly healed, and the skin is not yet strong. He cries aloud from the pain as blood begins to leak onto the ground from his stomach as the new healing tears open.*

He is not a little man and there is an intake of breath through the crowd. Seemingly effortlessly, she lifted him and shook him as if he were a small kitten in a one-handed lift. She took him over to where there were some stocks. Basil followed and undid the shackles, and their captive was quickly secured in the stocks. Basil took up a position behind him as Astrid leant close and looked at him tenderly.

"Don't even think about trying to cast a spell, or even resisting what we are about to do. My husband takes very poorly to treacherous little worms like you, and he has his weapons hovering around your balls and your kidneys. We can keep cutting you and healing you as much as we want to...no-one will be able to object to it in the slightest, as you are the one who broke the rules."

Despite his pain, it is possible to see the man deflate like a pig's bladder that has been blown up and then kicked too hard, so that it bursts open. He must have acted on impulse. He will not live long to regret it. I think that his bowels may have opened, one way or another.

Theodora

*W*hat has been done to the girl? I must have been right about her training. She moves like the Guard, and with her charms on, she is as strong as any Insak-div, if not stronger. That giant of a man...on his own he had just as much chance against her as a baby would have done.* She put that thought aside for the moment. *Now, how did that spell miss Astrid at that range? That is the main question I must ask myself.*

*Admittedly, the spell came from a wand, but if you look at the damage that has been done to the tavern...*she turned and looked again .... *and if he had made the wand himself, then he must be fairly competent. I guess Astrid was just lucky...of course...lucky...oh, thank you, Granther. The charm of the Horse is already working for us.* She moved towards where the man hung waiting to die.

His face tells me that he already knows what his fate is going to be. It is time for me to get some answers, but what is that smell?

Theodora

*I*n the end, it was another local mage who cast the enchantment to make him speak, and that is better. These backward villagers will more trust one of their own.

Once he starts talking, after he has been forced to exhaust his mana, it turns out that he is a mine of information, and Basil is writing fast in that little notebook of his. For a start, it seems that Glyn was not the leader of the group here. It had actually been Athgal, staying in the background, who was the real prime mover of the so-called patriot movement.

The last time that we Mice were here, he and Ith had been down river, at Dolbaden, trying to whip up support there for their attack on Haven. They had been waiting there for the boats to bring their people and money down before they started off. They came back to discover that we had struck and destroyed their chance of an attack.

He speaks scathingly of the fools who had been willing to believe the lies they told, and how easy it had been to manipulate them. He may have just swayed the last villagers against him with that. They were going to avoid Garthang, and strike through the jungle at the farms around Peelfall. After the Pattern had been destroyed, the Masters had been sending them messages, but they suddenly stopped, after we struck at Skrice, no doubt.

That is how Ith had known who we are. He had been warned about the saddles. Since Urfai had become Reeve, they had been fomenting trouble in the background, and it was they who had been about to strike out at Urfai to remove him from his post and take his life. Once they did that, they were going to make themselves a new Pattern, and try and get back in touch with the Masters.

There is shock among the locals as he reveals that they had already chosen their dedication sacrifice. He names a girl, Ia verch Brica. From the reaction, she is watching. There she is. She is a young and beautiful woman, apparently one of the local Wiccan practitioners on the good side. Despite his position, Athgal is still licking his lips as he looks through his pain at the terrified-looking young girl clad in leather.

Athgal has gone on to say that Ith had been very upset over the death of his brother, and had been certain of winning, killing Adara, and then Astrid. He had never lost a fight before in his whole life, and that was one of the ways that they succeeded in getting their way. By winning, they would have been able to regain their ground, but with Ith's death, Athgal had seen all his plans in irreparable tatters.

It was frustration at seeing his efforts destroyed a second and probably final time that made him lose his temper and snap. It turns out that Athgal is even more slimy and repugnant than most of the Master's men we have questioned have been. Some of the local losses have not been people who have moved elsewhere, or even just been killed or sold. Rape and torture figure prominently in his listing of his own activities.

Basil

*T*he crowd are listening intently. I think that Rising Mud is going to be *a very law-abiding community—for the Swamp that is—for quite some time after this set of revelations. Everyone is already watching each other, and this scrutiny will probably ensure no such things ever occur again. The persecution of the Christians has been a part of the whole plan, also.*

Not only is word of that persecution supposed to get out and lead to more strife, but also, although the Druids can do it too, the Christian priests are far better at telling good from evil, and the conspirators wanted to be rid of that risk. It was a bonus for them that the priests are easily made out to be a foreign enemy, and seen as tools of the outside world.

By the time we have finished speaking, another man has been stopped from fleeing by his neighbours, and four who were here earlier, but who left before the questioning started and they were named, are being sought by posse. Parties have been sent to various houses, and some items recovered. The elderly Urfai is in a state of shock over what has happened to his township, and he is not the only one in the village.

It is obvious that their supposed self-reliance has only meant an isolation from each other as they each assiduously ignored what was happening around them. The smug independence of Rising Mud will never be the same again, as it is revealed how completely they had been played as fools by the minions of the Masters.

During the questioning, Father Kessog has emerged from the crowd and joined the Mice on the side. It seems that he had, only the day before, returned to the village in disguise, and had been keeping a low profile while he worked out what to do next. It must seem to him that he will not have to stay hidden any longer.

Astrid let Athgal out of the stocks and gave him his sword and dagger back before killing him. *He was either not a very good swordsman, or else his heart had left him well before the point of her bardiche went through it. She didn't even pause in her stroke, pulling the blade back out as he swayed and swinging it around to kill him a second time after his cure cut in, by casually removing his head. I think that she has been holding back in practice.*

Astrid again demonstrated her strength by casually throwing him and Ith into the river, keeping everything that was useful or valuable that was on their bodies, or in Ith's case on the ground, as her rightful spoil before the Mice headed off to their houses to claim what was there.

Afterwards, the Christians among the Mice trooped off to the burnt remains of the Church of Saint Mark. *The Bishop has openly held a service in the ruins. By this deed, I think that he is actively challenging any of the many passers-by to say anything about it.*

It does not seem likely that this will happen, as several of those standing and watching, and I would say standing guard over us, are Wiccan celebrants. After the service, Father Kessog was then told how his children, Angharad and Cadfael, were doing at the school, as each side brought the other up to date. *I get to start circulating again, although it is hard to be invisible with so many watching the questioning and my part in it.*

Theodora

*A*fter that, and with the bloodstains left on the ground in front of the tavern as a reminder, the rest of the day is fairly uneventful. The story that Ayesha tells this night, in a packed tavern, is told to a very respectful silence. After having seen what they have seen, and heard the truth direct from Athgal's lips, the people of the village, and in particular Urfai, are very willing to believe the rest of the tale.*

The young witch Ia, who is not even as old as most of the Brotherhood girls back in the valley, sits in the front row. Her large violet eyes are gradually becoming as round as saucers as she realises how close she has come to a terrible fate when the knives and what they do are described. She is looking on Astrid as a man lost in the Dry Plains would look at a water bottle that has suddenly appeared in his hands.

One more of the blades has been found in Athgal's house, and has been displayed for all to see. Also sitting in the front row near Ia are several other young women, all of whom have been subject to the attention of one of the dead men, intently listening to how the Mice might have changed their fate, and indeed, might still be changing it.

Theodora (much later that night)

W*e are nearly finished, and I am sure that it is nearly dawn, but not one person has left to go and sleep.* She looked around at the people watching entranced.

I am sure that Astrid…or maybe it is Bianca, or Ayesha…at any rate one of them…seeks out brothels deliberately. That row of young women must be from one of the local brothels from the way that they are dressed, with even less left to the imagination than Bryony and Adara leaves in the matter of cleavage, and length of skirt, and from the way the local men look at them.

Some of the people around them might have looked excited by everything that is happening but most of the girls look…stunned…that is the only word that can be used. I wonder if they are thinking about some of the men that they have had, and what might have become of them, or perhaps even how they might bring change to their lives.

So much for us coming here and being quiet. We tried, but even when we try, some things just seem to happen. My husband cannot blame Astrid for having set off what happened. She just reacted to the local men. As it turns out, it was probably for the best. What has happened here today will spread through the Swamp faster than a rumour through the Palace, and this will lend credence to our story.

Even if we were to pack up and go straight home tomorrow, we would probably have achieved most of our aims. Astrid's swift, humiliating, and ruthless dispatch of Ith, along with the testimony of Athgal, will in the long run probably make as much impression throughout the Swamp as our victory over the Brotherhood has done in the North.

Glossary

Adversaries: the major protagonists behind the evil that is infesting Vhast.

Agatha, Saint: a Christian Saint, Feast Day 3rd Secundus, she is the patron of victims of rape and torture, and is invoked against fire and earthquakes. Her Order run shelters for abused women throughout Freehold.

Aguu süns muukhai: a Khitan phrase for an Adversary (lit. great evil spirit).

Alat-kharl: one of the Kharl tribes of Darkreach, they are most usually found working in the trades or mining.

Aldhelm, Saint: a Christian Saint, Feast Day is 25th Quinque, he is the patron of scholars.

Alkahest: from Arabic, an acid.

Allāh wadhu: an Arabic phrase, literally 'the one God.'

Amitan: the Khitan Clan of the Bison, who are based along the western coast of The Land, between Freehold and the Brotherhood (or Amity).

Amity, the Forest of: this is a small forested area that is only a trifle smaller than the Brotherhood that it protects from the Khitan. It later is the name taken by the villages of that area once the Brotherhood falls.

Anastasi, Feast of: an Orthodox Christian Feast on the 17th Quinque, the main day of Easter celebrating the Resurrection.

Anta Dvīpa: an island in Pavitra Phāṭaka, mainly inhabited by the lowest castes and foreigners. Its name means End Island.

Antdrudge: a northern Darkreach town, a place of industry, and one of the few places with a large supply of petrochemicals.

Antikataskopeía: the Darkreach 'secret police,' an arm of the military who are concerned both with criminal investigation and treason.

Apodeipnon: literally 'after-supper,' this is an Orthodox service performed after the evening meal prior to bedtime.

Arden Creek: a long, but never strong, stream draining the southern plains. It enters the sea at Saltbeach.

Ardlark: a major city and capital of Darkreach.

Arnflorst: see Shunned Isle.

Asvayujau: the Hindu Goddess of good luck, joy, and happiness.

Az: the Khitan word meaning 'luck.'

Azrael: a gargoyle brought to Mousehole by Father Christopher. Despite the name, she is female. Gargoyles eat evil spirit creatures.

Bagts Anchin: an animal and a Khitan clan, that of the Pack-hunters.

Baloo: a village of the former Brotherhood.

Bardiche: a pole weapon with a very long blade that is joined, at one end, to the shaft and at the other forms a spear-like point.

Bartholomew, Saint: a Christian Saint, Feast Day 13th Sixtus, his patronage is to tanners and leatherworkers.

Basilica Anthropoi: a Holy Order of warrior monks of the Orthodox Church west of the mountains. They are heavily armed, and ride as kataphractoi, or kynigoi depending on their role. They bear the Chi-Rho on their shields, and the leader of a group will have a painted icon there.

Bathmawr: the most northerly of the settlements of The Swamp on the Murga River.

Bear-folk: a group of humanoids who have a high number of bear-based shape-shifters among their population. They live just north of the Swamp.

Bellingen River: a tributary of the Buccleah River in The Swamp.

Beneen: a large plain in the south of Darkreach scattered with towns and villages of herdsmen.

Big One: what the Neronese call the Insak-Div.

Birchdingle: a Bear-folk settlement.

Bliaut: on women, this is a long flowing gown with larger open sleeves. For a male, it is tights and a short tight and belted tunic, also with large open sleeves.

Blood-Letter: the drakkar (what many would call a Viking ship) sunk by the River Dragon on the way north.

Böö: a Khitan word for a shaman or shamanka.

Boyuk-kharl: the largest and most intelligent of the Kharl races. They are often found in independent units and at sea.

Brotherhood, The: the Brotherhood of All Believers were militant semi-Christians of an extreme Puritan type, with a focus on literal truth and rigid obedience, as well as hidden human sacrifice. They have been wiped out.

Bridget, Saint: a Christian Saint, Feast Day 10th Sixtus, her patronage is to dairymaids, blacksmiths, poetry, and compassion to the poor.

Buccleah River: a large tributary of the Tulky Wash in the Swamp. In Arabic, in the Caliphate, it is known as the Zuyanda Rŭdh.

Bucinators: name for players of a trumpet who are used to command attention and make signals in Darkreach.

Bulga: an independent village on the north coast of The Land.

Bull and Bear, The: a tavern in Bathmawr.

Burning, The: a dread disease that causes people to go mad and destroy things. Less than one person in twenty survived the years that it raged.

Caliphate: a Muslim Kingdom nestled high in the south of the Great Range.

Catherine, Saint: a Christian Saint, Feast Day 24th Duodecimus, patron of any trade involving a wheel and chaste women.

Cenubarkincilari: a small Hobgoblin tribe in the southern mountains. The name roughly means 'Southern Raiders.'

Christopher, Saint: a Christian Saint, Feast Day 25th September, his patronage is to travellers, and in regard to water and sudden death.

Chulün Arlüd: a Khitan phrase that literally means 'Stone Islands.' See Pavitra Phāṭaka.

Clare, Saint: a Christian Saint, Feast Day 6th October. She is the patron of needle-workers, clairvoyants, and goldsmiths. She is invoked against eye disease.

Columba, Saint: an Orthodox Saint, Feast Day 9th Sixtus, his patronage is to Abbots, and other religious leaders.

Cold Keep: the most northerly town in Darkreach.

Consiliarius: the chief priest of the Basilica Anthropoi.

Confederation of the Free: a very loose alliance of villages and towns spread through the jungles and bogs between Haven and the mountains. It is known as a lawless place to most.

Constantine, Saint: a Christian Saint, Feast Day 24th December, his patronage is towards rulers.

Cosmas and Damien, Saints: brothers and Orthodox Saints, Feast Day 7th Duodecimus, their patronage is to medicine, and in particular, surgery. They are always depicted together and are always in Caliphate dress.

Cure-all: a plant of the Swamp that makes a powerful curative potion for most diseases.

Cyricus, Saint: a Christian Saint, Feast Day 16th October, his patronage is to orphans.

Dadanth: a jungle shelf fungus that can be made into an unguent that repels insects.

Darkreach: this is a multi-racial Empire that takes up the eastern third of The Land east of the Great Range. It is ruled (and has been since known time began) by Hrothnog.

Dating: Years run over a 48-year cycle; with the twelve zodiacal signs that are used on Vhast along with the elements of Earth, Air, Fire and Water. There are twelve months of equal length, each having six weeks of six days. The first parts of this story take part on the Year of the Water Dog. A year thus has 432 days so a year on Vhast is nearly a fifth longer than a Terran year. A person who is fifteen on Vhast will be eighteen on Terra.

Deathguard Tower: a strongly fortified village with a large garrison that watches over the burial mounds that cover the Funereal Hills.

Deepavali or Diwali (5 to 10th Undecim): or 'row of lamps,' a very important Festival celebrating the killing of the demon Narkasura.

Deeryas: A village on the southern fringe of the plains.

Devi: a major Hindu goddess, the mother principle.

Dhargev: a Hobgoblin village in the Southern Mountains. The main settlement of the Cenubarkincilari tribe, the name means 'Our Home.'

Dochra: a village on the main road of Darkreach. It is a fertile oasis.

Dolbaden: a town and fortification on the Bellingen River in The Swamp.

Domenic, Saint: a Christian Saint, Feast Day 6th Sixtus, he is the patron of teachers. The Order of Saint Domenic, once teachers are, since the Great Schism, now mainly seen as the Inquisition.

Drakkar: a low build, clinker hulled craft of the northern seas. They are fast and very seaworthy, but with no shelter on board and little in the way of cargo space.

Dromond: the large warships of Darkreach that use a combination of sail and oar, or rarely, are propelled by their own magic. They are the most powerful warcraft around The Land and many are armed with rockets and fire weapons.

Dry Plains: a large semi-arid area of Darkreach between the mountains and Ardlark.

Dwarf (Dwarves/Dwarven): a race of short humanoids that tend to live below ground. Most people cannot tell if there are female dwarves as all of them are bearded and similar in appearance. They are skilled miners and artisans.

Dwynwen, Saint: an Orthodox Saint, Feast Day 25th Primus, patron of both lovers and sick animals.

Easter: a Christian festival celebrating the death and Resurrection of Christ.

East Zarah: the tallest of the mountains on Neron Island. It is also the most southerly and eastern of the several peaks there.

Eid ul-Fitr: the Muslim Feast at the end of Ramadan, the Feast at the Breaking of the Fast. 1st December. It is a very joyous event.

Eldest Gods: a winged race of Creators in the legends of the Hobs.

Eloi, Saint: a Christian Saint, Feast Day 1st December, his patronage is to goldsmiths, jewellers, and farriers.

Emeel amidarch baigaa khümüüs: a Khitan phrase describing themselves. It literally means 'people who live in a saddle.'

Erave, Lake: this is almost a small sea and lies on the Rhastaputra River to the west of the mountains.

Erave Town: a town on the southern shore of Lake Erave.

Ethnarch: in Darkreach Greek, it is a person who represents an ethnic group or religion when speaking to the Emperor.

Evilhalt: a town at the very northern tip of Lake Erave.

Exarkhos ton Basilikon: the title of the Commander of the Basilica Anthropoi.

Faen: the language of the Swamp.

Fagus trees: a deciduous tree of the mountain slopes, or their semi-deciduous cousins. On Terra, they are *Nothofagus* (sin *Fuscospora*) *gunii* or *N cunninghamii*.

Forest Watch: a Darkreach outpost on a large hill in the Great Forest. On a clear day, it has a view of most of the central mountains area, and in particular, the approach of an army to the Darkreach Gap.

Francis, Saint: a Christian Saint, Feast Day 4th October, his patronage is to animals.

Freehold: a kingdom that takes up much of the west of The Land, 'sharing' some of the land uneasily with the Khitan. Its Queen is Daphne IV Acer, Baroness Goldentide. She is unmarried, and has sat on the throne for ten years.

Ganesh: an elephant-headed Hindu God of divination, knowledge, and prophesy. He is often called 'the remover of obstacles' and he rides a mouse.

Garthcurr: a large town in the south of Darkreach.

Gasparin: a very hot spice.

George, Saint: a Christian Saint, Feast Day 23rd Quattro, his patronage is to cavalry and to those who fight dragons and demons.

Ghāt: a general Hindi term for a wharf, a landing, or a set of steps leading to the water.

Gil-Gand-Rask: a large island in the Southern Seas. Gil-Gand is the city on it.

Glengate: a town to the west of Lake Erave on the path to Freehold.

Granther: a term used in the Darkreach Imperial family to describe an older relative. 'The Granther' is always Hrothnog.

Great Schism: around 470 years before the start of the books, under King Roger III, the Christian Church in Freehold 'reformed' and installed a Pope who claimed authority over the whole Church. The resultant schismatic group became the Catholic Church.

Greatkin: the capital of the Brotherhood on the north-west tip of The Land in clearing of the Amity Forest. It was once known as 'Graemsle.'

Greensin: a town north-west of Evilhalt. It is the home of the senior of the western Metropolitans of the Orthodox Church.

Greenskin: a slang term sometimes used in a derogatory way, for anyone of the Kharl races (even the Hobgoblins, who are grey-skinned).

Gupta ke Dvīpa: Hindi for 'Gupta's Isle'; a home for the rich, it is park-like and green.

Hand: as a basic unit of measure, it is made up of six fingers (1.7cm each) and so is 10.2cm long. Six make a cubit. A hand of hands (or a filled hand) is thirty-six.

Harijan: the lowest caste of Haven society. It includes all the less prestigious occupations.

Haven: a nation at the mouth of the Rhastaputra River.

Herjolfssness: a cape and the most southerly point of Neron Island.

Hesperinos: performed at sundown, this is the beginning of the liturgical day for the Orthodox.

Hob or Hobgoblin: one of the larger humanoid races of Vhast. They have hard grey skin and are very strong and are, to Humans, quite ugly.

Holy Trinity, Feast of the: a Christian Feast that celebrates the triune nature of God, it is held on 24th Sixtus.

Homobonus, Saint: a Christian Saint, Feast Day 13th November, his patronage is to cloth workers.

Hop Bush: a tall shrub of the mountains. Among other things, it can be used to cause fish to float to the surface or for medical purposes.

Hugron pir: a chemical mix that we would call Greek Fire or perhaps napalm.

Humans: the most common intelligent race on Vhast. They have a wide variety of original origins, but despite when they come from, all of them seem to have been on Vhast for about the same amount of time.

Iba Bay: a broad and deep bay formed to the east of the vast delta of the Swamp rivers.

Insak-div: the largest of the Darkreach races, and often referred to in the West as Dark Trolls (although they are largely dark green in colour). They are over twice as tall as a Human and a lot broader.

Insakharl: this is not a distinct race, but a name given to those who have part-Human and part-Kharl ancestry.

Inshallah: an Arabic word that best translates as 'if God wills it.'

Isci-kharl: one of the Kharl tribes of Darkreach. They are large, strong, and not overly bright.

Jade Mountain: a high series of mountains south of the road to Ardlark in the Dry Plains. They are high enough to have their own weather and the slopes and tops are green and verdant in an arid area. It is a popular holiday spot for nobles and rich. Jade is found here.

Jirgah: a Khitan word that best translate as 'conference' but could also be used to mean 'meeting' or even just 'decision making body.'

John Crysostum, Saint: an Orthodox Christian Saint, Feast Day 13th November, his patronage is to priests, peacemakers and those who seek a simple life.

John the Baptist: a Christian Saint, Feast Day 29th Sixtus, he is patron of pilgrims and those who travel for the faith.

Joseph, Saint: a Christian Saint, Feast Day is 2nd Primus, his patronage is towards fathers.

Joseph of Aramathea, Saint: a Christian Saint, Feast Day 31st September. He is the patron of quests and of those who arrange funerals.

Jude, Saint: a Christian Saint, Feast Day 16th Undecim, he is patron of those with forlorn hopes.

Kãfirũn: an Arabic word, it means an 'Unbeliever.'

Kara-Khitan or Khitan: a group of mounted tribes who claim and occupy most of the plains.

Kartikeya: the Hindu God of War.

Kataphract or Kataphractoi: a very heavy cavalryman (or woman) usually from Darkreach. They ride an armoured horse and are themselves armoured. They employ a variety of weapons depending on range and target. They charge with their knees touching.

Kentarkhion: a Darkreach military unit larger than a company and smaller than a bandae. Depending on role, it will have several hundred people in it.

Kessog, Saint: a Christian Saint, Feast Day 10th Tertius, patron of those who fight monsters on land. He is taken as a Patron Saint by Astrid.

Kharl: one of the races of Vhast. They are the most common form of humanoid after Humans. They vary greatly in appearance, but often have some animalistic features. There are several distinct tribes among them.

Kharlsbane: a Dwarven settlement in the Northern Mountains of The Land. Thord comes from there.

Khün khanatai: a Khitan phrase used for all non-Khitan, literally 'walled in people'.

Kichic-kharl: the smallest of the Darkreach races. They are around the same size as a Goblin. In Darkreach, they are the scouts, and often, the sailors.

Knorr: a clinker-built ship of the northern seas. They have a very low aspect ratio, and so are slow and capacious. They are also very sea-worthy.

Köle: Khitan term that means something similar to both captive and slave. It is for a term that is usually five years.

Krondag: the Sixth day of the week and the Holy Day for many religions, including the Christians.

Kshatya: an upper Havenite caste. It consists of warriors and rulers.

Kynigoi: riders with any level of armour riding unarmoured horses. Their primary role is skirmishing and harassing as well as scouting. They mainly use bows in combat.

Kyriaki tou Pascha: the Greek for 'Easter Krondag.'

Laylatul-Bara'ah: a Muslim Holy Festival, the Night of Record, when Allah records your deeds for the year ahead. It is held on the 15th of October.

Leidauesgynedig: see Rising Mud.

Luke, Saint: a Christian Saint, Feast Day 18th October, patron of physicians.

Maarleen: A city in The Swamp from before The Burning, and its capital. It is now in ruins and mostly forgotten.

Magnus, Saint: an Orthodox Saint, Feast Day 36th Sixtus, he is patron of the North and icy wastes.

Mark, Saint: a Christian Saint, Feast Day 23rd September, his patronage is to ferrymen, as well as thieves and robbers.

Masters, the: a group of undead mages who once had control over Dwarvenholme.

Matthew, Saint: a Christian Saint, Feast Day 16th November, his patronage is towards all professions that deal with money (bankers, tax collectors, etc).

Maurice, Saint: a Christian Saint, Feast Day 9th September, his patronage is to infantry, and dyers, and he is always depicted with dark skin. In Darkreach, it is dark green.

Menna, Saint: a Christian Saint, Feast Day 15th November, his patronage is to traders and merchants.

Metal Hill: a large hill on the north of the road to Ardlark. It has an iron mine.

Methul River: the river that comes out of the Darkreach Gap and then heads north to reach the sea at Wolfneck.

Metropolitan: the title of an Orthodox 'arch-bishop'. Unless a Patriarch is created, it is the highest rank in the Orthodox faith and a Metropolitan, although still subject to a Synod, is theologically supreme in their area.

Mistledross: a village in the south of Darkreach. It is in one of the few parts of The Land that regularly experiences earthquakes.

Molotail: these are glass containers of hugron pir, a hypergolic liquid. We could call it Greek Fire, or perhaps napalm.

Months: although there is some local variation, generally in The Land the twelve months, in order, are: Primus, Secundus, Tertius, Quattro, Quinque, Sixtus, September, October, November, December, Undecim, and Duodecimus.

Mori: a Khitan word for the animal and clan of the Horse. Moriid is the plural form.

Mousehole: a free village in the Mountains ruled by the Princesses Rani and Theodora.

Mouthguard: a Darkreach fortification that sits on an island in the Methul River in Darkreach Gap guarding a bridge. It is starting to have a small village form on its southern side.

Mujtahideh: the title of a high female religious figure in the Islamic faith.

Murga River: a tributary of the Tulky Wash, the Swamp village of Bathmawr is on it.

Nameless Keep: a major fortification and army base in Darkreach on the eastern end of the Darkreach Gap.

Nekulturny: an insulting word in the Wolfneck dialect of Darkspeech that literally means that a person is uncultured.

Neron Island: an island to the north of The Land, the last inhabited island. The village of Skrice is there.

Nicholas, Saint: a Christian Saint, Feast Day 3rd Tertius, his patronage is to both perfumers and to children. A Church and orphanage at Greensin are dedicated to him.

Nicodemus, Saint: a Christian Saint, Feast Day 2nd October. He is the patron of both the curious and those who defend the innocent.

Nithling: an insulting word in the Wolfneck dialect of Darkspeech that means, roughly, that a person is nothing and is beneath notice or contempt.

Northern Hills: a group of small mountains in the northern forest which is an area of Dwarven settlement.

Nu-I Lake: a very salty lake in the Dry Plains near Dochra. It is fed by the spring that feeds the oasis.

Old Gods: a name for the Adversaries that is used in the north, and by the Hobs.

Old Lobster, The: a tavern in the Darkreach village of Dochra.

Onam: a Hindu Festival held on 23rd Sixtus. It is a harvest festival.

One-Tree Hill: the battle ground beside Teni Creek, where the armies of the Brotherhood were broken. A Concord was struck there between the Kara-Khitan and the North.

Ooshz: an independent village on the southern edge of the plains.

Orthros: the first Orthodox service of the morning. It usually starts before sunrise.

Our Lady: Mary, Mother of God, Feast Day 12th November, patron of motherhood.

Our Lady of the Sorrows: the Orthodox Basilica in Greensin.

Outville: an independent village of the north. The people there are Human and mainly Orthodox.

Övs: the Khitan word for 'grass,' it can also be used to describe the territory of a group.

Pandonia, Saint: a Christian Saint, Feast day 26th Sixtus, she is the patron of goose girls and other female herders.

Pavitra Phāṭaka: also known as Sacred Gate and Chulün Arlüd. It is the capital of Haven.

Peelfall: a town in the north of Haven.

Peter or Petrox, Saint: a Christian Saint. His Feast Day is 18th Secundus and his patronage is to evangelists. 'Petrox' or 'Petros' is the preferred form in Greek.

Phocas, Saint: a Christian Saint, Feast Day 14th Sixtus, his patronage is to farmers and gardeners.

Pious Smith, The: a large tavern in Greensin on the main square.

Platys Dromos: a Darkreach term for the Imperial Freight Service that haul strategic cargo around the Empire. They are expected to travel 32km (a Stathmos) a day on good roads.

Ploi_gós: a term used in Darkreach as the job title for a harbour pilot.

Presbytera: the title given to the wife of an Orthodox priest or Metropolitan.

Ramadan: the Muslim Holy Month of November when no food is eaten by most people during the hours between sunrise and sunset.

Rangers: what passes for a military in the village of Wolfneck. They are scouts and hunters more than anything else, and fight from cover with bows if forced to fight.

Rhastaputra River: the main river draining the mountains and area just to the west of them in the south.

Rising Mud (Leidauesgynedig): a village in the Swamp built on islands of mud behind wooden walls.

River Dragon: a brigantine owned by the Mice. It has Olympias as a Captain. It is gradually being equipped with formidable magic.

River's Head Inn: a new tavern in the Darkreach Gap near the head of the Methul River.

Sacred Gate: see Pavitra Phāṭaka.

Saltbeach: an independent village on the southern edge of the plains.

Sasar: a strategic crossroads town in the Dry Plains of Darkreach that also has one of its two iron mines. It is a town of red dust.

Sebastian, Saint: a Christian Saint, Feast Day 18th December, patron of archers.

Shayk: an Arabic word that means, roughly, a wise man.

Shunned Isle: also called Durham Rock, or Arnflorst (its original name as a city), it is the furthest north of the chain running up from the Northern Mountains.

Skrice: the only large village on Neron Island.

Sleepwell: a forest tree that can be made into a potion that acts as if the drinker has had a night's sleep.

South-West Mountains: the only real hills in the west of The Land and home to several Dwarven villages.

Southpoint: the southernmost town in Darkreach.

Sowonja: this is the language of the Brotherhood. It is derived from Latin, and the 'j' is pronounced as 'h.'

Strategos: a Darkreach military rank. It roughly equates to a General or Admiral.

Sünsjims: the Khitan name, literally 'spirit berry' for Spearleaf, a trance-inducing hallucinogen.

Swamp, The: the common name for the Confederation of the Free.

Swithun, Saint: a Christian Saint, Feast Day 15th Undecim, his patronage is regarding the weather.

Tagma: a Darkreach Army unit. It is roughly equivalent to a division.

Tar-khan: the head of a Khitan Clan.

Teni Creek: a small watercourse leading down from the plains near Bulga. It plays a major role in the battle of One-Tree Hill.

Thaaness: a large city in The Swamp from before The Burning. It is now in ruins and almost forgotten.

Thomaïs Saint: a Darkreach Orthodox Saint, Feast Day 25th December, her patronage is to all of Darkreach, and is credited with bringing the faith there.

Toppuddle: a major town in Freehold near the South-West Mountains. Its Count, Archibald, was killed by the Mice. It was once known as Topudle.

Tugyore: a lichen from Swamp that makes one of the most powerful curative potions known.

Tulky Wash: a river that goes from the mountains, through the area of Mousehole to the Bear-Folk, and the Swamp before entering the Rhastaputra at Garthang Keep.

Ünee Gürvel: a Khitan clan, that of the Cow-lizard.

Ursula, Saint: a Christian Saint and patron of virgins, Feast Day is the 6th of September. Bianca takes her as her patron saint.

Üstei akh düü: a Khitan term for their totem animals, literally 'fur siblings.'

Vasant Navrati: a quarterly Hindu festival held on 12th of the months of Secundus, Quattro, September, and December. It celebrates the power of the genetrix.

Vindur-skefi: a Darkspeech phrase in the Wolfneck dialect, 'Wind-strider' and it is the name of the Drakkar taken from Astrid's old betrothed Svein.

Virgin Bride, The: a tavern in Bathmawr.

Vyāpārī Dvīpa: the Merchant's Island in Pavitra Phāṭaka.

Walstan, Saint: a Christian Saint, Feast Day 30th Quinque, patron of agricultural workers.

Warkworth: a free village in the west of The Land on the edge of the Plains. It lies on a sea-cliff between The Brotherhood and Freehold. It is on Pulletop Creek.

Weeks and days: each week on Vhast has six days. Generally, across The Land, these are given the names: Firstday, Deutera, Pali, Tetarti, Dithlau and Krondag. Kron is the name given to the sun. The definitions and roots of some of these names are unknown.

Winifred, Saint: a Christian Saint, Feast Day 19th Primus, one of the patrons of healing.

Wolfneck: a village of people who are mostly Human, but who have a lineage that is part-Kharl. It is in the north of The Land. It is the original home to Astrid.

Wolf's Warning, The: a large tavern in Greensin.

Yamyam: or more fully 'Devartetilcu Yamyam,' a Hobgoblin phrase, literally 'wall-striking monsters,' a name that Ariadne's artillery group call themselves.

Yama: the Hindu God of death and justice.

Zim Island: an island in the south that is completely covered in an un-named ruined city. It has dense jungle between its buildings and Kraken Weed around it.

Zönch: a Khitan word for a prophet or seer.

Zürkh setgelee gartaa barisan khün: a Khitan phrase, (literally 'One who holds my heart in her hands') that is used for a deep love.

Cast

Aaron Skynner: in his 30s, a tanner and widower from Glengate, comes to Mousehole seeking a wife. He marries Aine.

Abel Skynner: the son of Aaron and Aine.

Abhaidev: (Free of Fear) the son of Shilpa and Vishal.

Achmed ibn Atã: the son of Atã and Umm.

Adara ferch Glynis: a cousin of Bryony from Rising Mud and in love with her. She was rescued from the Master's servants in Pavitra Phāṭaka. She marries Stefan in an arrangement that allows her to share her co-wife with him. Her identical twin daughters are Finnabhair and Sinech.

Adhamhnán ap Ith: a bard in Bathmawr in the Swamp.

Adrian Digge: a young miner from Saltbeach who travels to Mousehole and marries Verina.

Aelfgifu: the 11-year-old adopted daughter of Eleanor and Robin. She was a slave to the bandits.

Aigiarn (Nokay Aigiarn Buriad): late of the Lion Clan, she marries Hulagu, and their daughter is Enq.

Aikaterine Rai: the daughter of Theodora and Rani (courtesy of Rani's unknowing brother).

Aimee Tate: the Mayor of Glengate and retired trader.

Aine ferch Liban: a former slave from Bloomact in The Swamp, she is now the brewer and distiller for Mousehole. She marries Aaron. Their son is Abel.

Alaine (Boladtani Alaine Buriad): late of the Eagle clan, she marries Hulagu, and their daughter is Surtak.

Alia bint Asad: the daughter of Asad and Hagar.

Alice: the daughter of Fortunata and Norbert, twin sister of Bryan, sister of Valentine and half-sister of Bishal.

Alĩ ibn Yũsuf al Mãr: the Ayatollah Uzma or Grand Ayatollah of Darkreach and head of the Muslim faith there.

Amos Ostrogski: the younger brother to Stefan, he is a leatherworker in Evilhalt.

Anahita (Vachir Anahita Ursud): a Khitan girl and former slave from Mousehole. As Hulagu's köle, she is the mother of Būrãn and Baul. She becomes one of the Clan of the Horse, and marries Dobun along with Kāhina.

Anastasia Tarchaniota: an Insakharl sailor sent from Darkreach to help crew the River Dragon. She is married to Cyrus and their daughter is Leukothea.

Andronicus Fotiou: the secretary to the Orthodox Metropolitan of the North at Greensin.

Aneurin ap Stefan: a son of Bryony and Stefan, brother of Trystan.

Angelina Cheila: a daughter of Nikephorus and Valeria, twin sister of Eugenia.

Angharad verch Kessog: the 10 years old daughter of the Orthodox priest of Rising Mud and sister of Cadfael. She is a student at the school.

Anna Astridsdottir: the second daughter of Astrid and Basil, sister of Thorstein.

Archibald Neville: the Count of Toppuddle and servant of the Masters. He is killed.

Ariadne Nepina: an Insakharl (part Alat-kharl) from Antdrudge. She is partly trained as an engineer, but wanted a quieter life as a brick and tile maker and layer after her parents are killed in an accident. She moves to Mousehole and marries the Hob Krukurb. Their daughter is Nikê.

Arnor Thrainsson: the son and apprentice of Thrain Vigfisson from Neron Island, he is also an Air mage. His mother is Ingrid Holmsdottir, and his sister is Groa Thrainsdottir.

Arthur Garden: a farmer and youngest son (of four) from Evilhalt. He comes to Mousehole seeking land and a wife. He was talked into coming by Ulric. He ends up courting and marrying Make.

Asad ibn Sayf: a widower from Doro. He is a farmer and becomes the husband of Hagar and Rabi'ah. His daughter with Hagar is Alia, and his son with Rabi'ah is Rãfi.

Asticus Tzimisces: one of three kataphractoi (heavy cavalry) from Darkreach who comes to join Mousehole and is sent straight into the fray against the Brothers.

Atã ibn Rãfi: a widower from Mistledross. He is a timber-feller. He becomes the husband of Umm and Zafirah. His son with Umm is Achmed, and with Zafirah is Sughdī.

Athgal Dewin: Air mage of Rising Mud, and friend of Glyn and It hap Tristan. He attempts to kill Astrid, and is executed after confessing under a compulsion spell. He was the real leader of the push to war with Haven.

Atli Runeson: a Water mage from Wolfneck.

Astrid Tostisdottir (the Cat): an Insakharl girl from Wolfneck, in the far north of The Land. She is married to Basil. Her first children are Freya Astridsdottir, 'the Kitten,' and Georgiou Akritas, and the second set are Anna and Thorstein. Her youngest brother is Thorstein, now a priest.

Ayesha bint Hãritha: an assassin of the Caliphate assigned by a Princess to guard Theodora. She is a minor daughter of the Sheik of Yãqūsa. She eventually marries Hulagu as his senior wife, and has Hãritha, his fifth child, and her first.

Aziz (Azizsevgili or Brave Lover): a Hobgoblin captured during the attack on Mousehole. He falls in love with Verily, converts to the Orthodox faith, and marries her. Their sons are Saglamruh (Strong Spirit) and Sunmak (Gift). Daughters Qvavili (Flower) and Fear. His former name is Saygaanzaamrat (Plundered Emerald).

Æirik Lærði: a sage and teacher and survivor from Neron Island. He is married to Kadlin Vitur, another sage and teacher.

Basil Akritas or Kutsulbalik (nickname from great-grandfather): a mostly human (one sixteenth Kharl) Insakharl, and an experienced officer of the Antikataskopeía. He is married to Astrid and living in Mousehole assigned to guard Theodora by Hrothnog. Their first children are Freya Astridsdottir, 'the Kitten,' and Georgiou Akritas, and the second set are Anna and Thorstein.

Basil Phocas: the Consiliarius or chief priest of the Basilica Anthropoi.

Basil Tornikes: the Orthodox Metropolitan of the North at Greensin.

Baul (Hulagu Baul Buriad): a son of Anahita and Hulagu, full brother of Būrān.

Beth Farmer: a daughter of Giles and Naeve, sister of Peggy.

Bianca Palama: a foundling from Trekvarna now living in Mousehole and married to Father Christopher. Their first children are Rosa and Francesco. Their second are Diogenes and Rhodē.

Bilqîs al-Yarmūk: a tiny girl, from a trade background in the Caliphate, she now lives in Mousehole as an apprentice mage. She has some ability as a glassblower. She marries Tāriq as his senior wife. Their daughter is Zainab.

Bjarni Drallingson, Father: a junior Orthodox priest in Wolfneck and later at Skrice.

Bryan Black: the son of Fortunata and Norbert, twin brother of Alice, brother of Valentine and half-brother of Bishal.

Bryony ferch Dafydd: a freckled red-head from Rising Mud in the Swamp. Her husband (Conan ap Reardon) and father (Dafydd ap Comyn) were killed at her wedding, and she was brought to Mousehole as a slave. She is now married to Stefan, and her sons are Aneurin ap Stefan and Trystan. She is cousin, lover, and sister-wife to Adara.

Būrān (Hulagu Būrān Buriad): the daughter of Anahita of the Axe-beaks and Hulagu.

Cadfael ap Kessog: the 12-year-old son of the Orthodox priest of Rising Mud, and brother of Angharad ferch Kessog. He is a student at the school.

Candidas Psellus: supposedly an animal handler for Carausius from his second trip, he is actually a member of the Antikataskopeía.

Carausius Holobolus: He is a Darkreach trader in fabric, spices, or anything else, and is the first to stumble upon Mousehole. He makes a lot of money there. His guards are Karas and Festus, his animal handler is Candidas, his wife is Theodora, and his daughter is Theodora Lígo.

Cathal Ageddillixson: the Magister (leader) of the Bear-folk village of Birchdingle. He is a shaman and a shape-shifter.

Christopher Palamas, Father: the chief Orthodox priest for Mousehole and husband of Bianca. Their first children are Rosa and Francesco. Their second are Diogenes and Rhodē. He is a very holy, but diplomatic man, and a dedicated healer. He becomes suffragan Bishop of the Mountains.

Cnut Stonecleaver: the Dwarven Baron of North Hole in the Northern Mountains.

Conan ap Reardon: the first husband of Bryony who was killed on their marriage night.

Conandil ap Doreen: the Reeve (the head of the village) of Dolbaden in the Swamp.

Conrad ap Guto y Swynwr: a mage from The Swamp, sent to Mousehole after the Hobs have supposedly cleared it. He is executed for his part in the death of Bryony's family.

Corc ap Gwern: a guard at Bathmawr in the Swamp.

Cosmas Camaterus: the Metropolitan of the Orthodox Church for the south-east of The Land (from Evilhalt and including Haven and the Swamp). He is based in Erave Town.

Cothric verch Manod: a female guard at Rising Mud, she is a cousin of Cuthbert.

Cuthbert y Warchod: a bandit armsman from The Swamp sent to Mousehole after the Hobs have supposedly cleared it. He is executed for his part in the deaths of Bryony's family.

Cyril, Father: see Dindarqoyun.

Cyrus Tarchaniotes: an Insakharl sailor sent from Darkreach to help crew the River Dragon. He is married to Anastacia and their daughter is Leukothea.

Danelis Alvarez (nee Romaia): a former slave originally from Warkworth, she now lives in Mousehole. She marries Father Simeon. Their children are Epanxer or Brave, and a daughter, Mehre, or Silver.

Daniel Mason: the second child of Goditha and Parminder.

David Granger: a wealthy farmer, kataphractoi, and Mayor of Outville.

Demetrios Choumnos: Orthodox Metropolitan responsible for the southern independent villages, he is based at Bridgcap.

Denizkartal (sea eagle): a Boyuk-kharl, Olympias' bosun on the River Dragon, and her eventual husband. Their daughter is Thalassa.

Denny Pollard: a young shearer from Ooshz who travels to Mousehole. He marries both Lamentations and Pass.

Dindarqoyun: the last druid apprentice of the Cenubarkincilari. He had not yet chosen his adult name and his child name means 'Pious Sheep.' He has been studying in Greensin to become an Orthodox priest and returns to Dhargev as Father Cyril.

Diogenes Palamas: the second son of Bianca and Christopher, twin of Rhodē, and brother of Rosa and Francesco.

Dobun (Tömörbaatar Dobun Buriad): late of the Axe-beaks, he becomes shaman of the Horse, and marries Anahita and Kãhina.

Domnhall y Dalaff (the Tall): a superb cook, and server of prepared food in Bathmawr in the Swamp.

Dulcie: a former slave from Bathmawr in The Swamp. She is now the Mousehole carpenter and marries Jordan. Their daughter is Rebecca.

Dympna verch Mugain: the Reeve (village leader) of Bathmawr in the Swamp, she is a notary.

Egil Thorgrimmson: the Jarl (Earl) of Neron Island and its ruler. He is an enthusiastic supporter of the Old Gods and dies in battle defending his island against the Mice.

Eleanor Fournier: caravan guard from Topwin in Freehold. Once a slave, she now lives in Mousehole and works as a jeweller. She is married to Robin Fletcher, and is one of the first in the village to fall pregnant. They have adopted Aelfgifu, Gemma, and Repent, and have a daughter, Bianca, and twins Michael and Sara.

Elizabeth Hurrell: an orphan from Trekvarna in Freehold and former slave who now lives in Mousehole. She is a skilled musician and assistant brewer. She is married to Thomas and mother of Virginia.

Enq (Hulagu Enq Buriad): the daughter of Aigairne and Hulagu.

Epanxer Alvarez: (or Brave) the son of Father Simeon and Danelis and twin brother of Mehre.

Erika Whittaker: a girl from Warkworth. She marries Nadia, and becomes an assistant to Kaliope.

Eugenia Cheila: daughter of Nikephorus and Valeria, twin sister of Angelina.

Fãtima: comes from an unknown background in the Caliphate, she was a slave in Mousehole. As Fãtima bint al-Fa'r (Fatima, daughter of the Mouse) she is now married to Hrothnog as the Empress of Darkreach and Ambassador of the Mice. They have a son.

Fear: the daughter of Aziz and Verily. Her identical, but larger, twin is Qvavili.

Fear the Lord Your God Thatcher: 10 years old, she is the adopted daughter of Rani and Theodora.

Fergus Leonhardson, Father: the second most senior Orthodox priest in Wolfneck.

Festus Skudnŷ: an Insakharl guard for Carausius Holobolus.

Finnabhair Ostrogski: the daughter of Stefan and Adara, and identical twin sister of Sinech.

Fire: see Kaliope.

Forth: more fully, I am Now Come Forth. She is a former slave who ended the resistance at Baloo by hitting the last priest leading fighting over the head with a frying pan. She becomes Mayor and the functional leader of Amity.

Fortunata Esposito: a former slave in Mousehole and a dressmaker. She becomes an apprentice mage and co-wife to Norbert with Sajãh.

Francesco Palamas: the son of Bianca and Christopher, twin brother to Rosa.

Freya Astridsdottir: the twin sister of Georgios Akritas, daughter of Astrid and Basil. They were the first children born in Mousehole to live. She loves cats and is accepted by Dire Wolves.

Gennadios Boutoumites, Father: the senior priest of Saint Menna's in Ardlark.

George Pitt: the oldest son of Lakshmi and Harald.

Georgios Akritas: the twin brother of Freya Astridsdottir, daughter of Astrid and Basil. He is named after Basil's father. They were the first children born in Mousehole to live. He is accepted by dire wolves.

Gildas Vhorternson, Father: the only surviving Orthodox priest on Neron Island. He is married to Vigdis Æsirsdottir.

Giles Ploughman: a former slave and farmer at Mousehole. He is married to Naeve. His first daughter is Peggy Farmer and his second is Beth. He also makes cheese.

Glad: the name by which We Declare Unto You Glad Tidings is known. She is a former Brotherhood slave girl who becomes Bishop Christopher's clerk.

Glyn ap Tristan: a mage in Rising Mud and servant of the Masters. He has one of their patterns in one of his outbuildings. He was killed.

Goditha Atalante: the daughter of Harnermêŝ and Jennifer Wagg. Known as Goditha Littlemouse, and soon as Goditha the Fleet.

Goditha Mason: a former slave from Jewvanda. She is sister to Robin Fletcher, and married to Parminder. She is the mason of Mousehole and an earth mage. She is regarded as the father of Melissa and Daniel Mason.

Gorthang Taverner: an Insakharl who is building an inn, the River's Head, near the start of the Methul River in the Darkreach Gap.

Groa Thrainsdottir: the daughter of Thrain Vigfisson, the senior refugee mage of Neron Island, and Ingrid Holmsdottir, and sister to Arnor Thrainsson. She goes to Mousehole as a student.

Guk or Gukludaashiyicisi (strong carrier): a mature hobgoblin of the Cenubarkincilari and a carter around their tribe. He becomes their first trader to the Dwarves. He decides to call himself Guk outside Dhargev.

Gundardasc Narches: a Kichic-kharl cook and sailor added to the River Dragon in Southpoint. His wife is Galla.

Gurinder Sen: the 14-year-old sister of Parminder.

Gwillam ap Aled: a bandit armsman from The Swamp who is sent to Mousehole after the Hobs have supposedly cleared it. He is executed for his part in the deaths of Bryony's family.

Habib Asen: the merchant who unwittingly helped Theodora and Basil first leave Darkreach.

Hagar al-Jamila: a former slave from a farming family outside Dimashq in the Caliphate, she lives in Mousehole as the village butcher. She becomes senior wife to Asad along with Rabi'ah. Her daughter is Alia.

Harald Pitt: a former slave and miner at Mousehole. He marries Lakshmi, and their sons are George and Henry.

Harnermêŝ: (Har-ner-meess): a young man from Gil-Gand-Rask, who becomes Jennifer's lover and joins the River Dragon, their daughter is named Goditha.

Haytor: (Pretty Bull) a Hob who joins the Mice for the campaign in the North. He goes on to work for Guk.

Hãritha bin Hulagu: the son of Ayesha and Hulagu.

Henry Pitt: the second son of Lakshmi and Harald.

Hrolfr Strongarm: the Dwarven Baron of Oldike in the South-West Mountains. Father of Ragnilde.

Hrothnog: the immortal God-King of Darkreach, and great-great-grandfather of Theodora. He is now married to Fātima. At the start of the books, his race is unknown, but not human. In this book, he is named as Hrąthnąrg (pronounced as 'Raathnaargh' by the Hobgoblins). He is one of the Daveen.

Hulagu: a young Khitan tribesman with ten toes. His tribe and totem is the Dire Wolf. He becomes a part of Mousehole. His children are Khātun & Yesugai (with Kāhina), Bŭrăn & Baul (with Anahita) and Hăritha (with Ayesha). He marries Ayesha, Aigiarn (daughter Enq), and Alaine (daughter Surtak) and becomes Tar-Khan of the re-born Clan of the Horse.

Huma: the daughter of Norbert and Sajāh, younger sister to Bishal.

I am Now Come Forth: see Forth

Ia verch Brica: a young and very beautiful Wiccan priestess chosen as a sacrifice by Athgal in Rising Mud. She has a raccoon familiar called Maeve.

In Flaming Fire Take Vengeance on Them That Know Not God (Fire): see Kaliope.

Ingrid Holmsdottir: the wife of the senior refugee mage of Neron Island, Thrain Vigfisson. She is the mother of Arnor Thrainsson and Groa Thrainsdottir.

Issac Philes: the third child of Ruth and Theodule.

It Shall Come to Pass: see Pass.

Ith ap Tristan: brother of Glyn in Rising Mud. He was out of the village on the first raid there, and is killed by Astrid on the second visit.

Iyād ibn Walīd: the Mullah of the main mosque in Ardlark.

Janibeg: the Tar-khan of the Ünee Gürvel, the Clan of the Cow-lizard.

Jennifer Wagg: a young woman, guard, and sailor, from Deeryas. She was rescued from the Master's servants in Pavitra Phāṭaka, where she was brought as a sacrifice. She ends up as partner to Harnermêŝ. They marry before the birth of their daughter, Goditha Atalante.

Joachim Caster: a mage, and the Mayor of Warkworth.

John Hyde: a wealthy farmer and currently Mayor of Bulga.

Jordan Croker: a journeyman potter from Greensin. No more potters are needed there, and he came seeking a place to settle and a wife. He marries Dulcie. Their daughter is Rebecca. He also makes salami.

Kadlin Vitur: a sage and teacher and survivor from Neron Island. She is married to Æirik Lærði, another sage and teacher. She later becomes Captain of Skrice.

Kaliope: (beautiful voice) the name taken by In Flaming Fire Take Vengeance on Them That Know Not God when she is baptised. She is the 16-year-old widow of a Brotherhood priest taken captive at Peace Tower and brought back to Mousehole. There she marries Thorstein. Their twin daughters are Bernike and Iris.

Karas dol Krum: he is an Insakharl guard for Carausius, a Darkreach trader in spices etc.

Kāhina (Bodonchar Kāhina Jugin): Hulagu's köle and mother of Khātun & Yesugai. She becomes one of the Clan of the Horse, and marries Dobun along with Anahita.

Kessog Aerobindus, Father: the Orthodox priest in Rising Mud. He went into hiding.

Ketill Söngvari: the son of Koll Hjortson and Signy Skáld, a family of bards and Orthodox survivors of Neron Island.

Koll Hjortson: married to Signy Skáld and father of Ketill Söngvari. They are a family of bards and Orthodox survivors of Neron Island.

Krukurb: (Strong Frog) one of the Hobs who join the Mice for the campaign in the North. He later marries Ariadne. Their daughter is Nikê.

Kyrillus Dabatenus: the Metropolitan for Beneen and the South of Darkreach, based in Garthcurr

Lakshmi: a former Havenite, she has converted and is now Orthodox, and married to Harald Pitt. Their eldest son is George, and their second is Henry. She is the apothecary and midwife for Mousehole.

Lamentations: a slave girl from the Brotherhood brought to Camel Island to be sacrificed to establish a master pattern. She is usually called Lamentations. Originally known as 'There Shall Be Lamentations,' Bianca thought that her name was 'There Shall Be Lemons.'

Lawrence Woolmonger: a rich farmer and Mayor of Bidvictor. He fought at a kataphractoi at One Tree Hill, and as Stefan's lieutenant at Peace Tower.

Lãdi al-Farãma: a former slave from the Caliphate, she is the chief cook at Mousehole and very skilled. She marries Nathanael.

Leif Galdrar: the second most important mage in Wolfneck. He is an earth mage.

Leo Makrembolitissas: a mosaic and tile worker sent to Mousehole during the Synod to work on St George's Basilica.

Leukothea Tarchaniota: the daughter of Anastasia and Cyrus.

Loukia Tzetzina: cooper and cabinet maker from Mistledross. She lost her family in an earthquake and has moved to Mousehole.

Make Me to Know My Transgressions: young woman from the Brotherhood brought as a slave to restock Mousehole. She is usually called Make. She marries Arthur.

Maria Beman: a kidnapped woman from Greensin, daughter of Johann Beman, brought to Mousehole by slavers after it was freed. She is now learning to be a fire mage.

Mark Durrant: a rich farmer and kataphractoi from Outville.

Masters, the: the animated skeletons of the old Dwarven Druids with the ability to use magic as air-mages. They may now longer exist, or there may be more somewhere.

Maurice Eudokias, Father: a junior Orthodox priest at Wolfneck.

Mehre Alvarez: (Silver) the daughter of Danelis and Simeon and twin sister to Epanxer.

Melissa Mason: daughter of Goditha and Parminder, elder sister to Daniel.

Mellitus Opsarus: an Insakharl customs officer at Mouthgard.

Menas Philokales: one of three kataphractoi (heavy cavalry) from Darkreach who comes to join Mousehole and is sent straight into the fray against the Brothers.

Michael Bardanes: the Abbot of the Abbey of Saint Petrox in Ardlark

Michael Fletcher: son of Robin and Eleanor, twin brother of Sara, and full brother of Bianca. Adopted sisters are Aelfgifu, Gemma, and Repent.

Michael Lagudes, Father: the chief missionary priest to the Cenubarkincilari. He is married to Sophronia.

Mongka: the Tar-khan of the Amitan or Bison. He is known as Mongka the Greedy.

Murgṛtt: an Insak-div killed by Astrid in the attack on East Zarah.

Mũsã ibn Nasr: Hrothnog's secretary and assistant.

Nacibdamįr (noble iron): a young Hobgoblin and chief of the village of Dhargev, and of the Cenubarkincilari, the southern Hobgoblins. The 'į' is a long & drawn out 'i.'

Nadia Everett: a girl from Warkworth, she marries Erika and becomes a mason.

Naeve Milker: a former Freehold dairymaid and former slave who now runs the herds of Mousehole.She becomes an apprentice mage and marries Giles. Her first daughter is Peggy Farmer and her second is Beth.

Nathanael Ktenas: an Orthodox pastrycook from Ardlark who comes to Mousehole for Lãdi.

Neon Chrysoloras: one of three kataphractoi (heavy cavalry) from Darkreach who comes to join Mousehole and is sent straight into the fray against the Brothers.

Nikephorus Cheilas: a senior Palace servant from Ardlark, he is now married to Valeria and father to her children, Angelina and Eugenia.

Nikê: the daughter of Ariadne and Krukurb.

Norbert Black: he is skilled as a blacksmith, weapons smith and armourer and kept as a slave in Mousehole. When he gets free, he marries both Fortunata and Sajãh. His sons are Valentine (with Fortunata) and Bishal (with Sajãh). He later has younger twins, Bryan and Alice, with Fortunata, and another son, Huma with Sajãh.

Olympias Akritina: Basil's sister, she is a junior officer in the navy in charge of a small fast scout and messenger boat. She becomes Captain of the River Dragon, and a Darkreach Epilarch (small-unit commander) in charge of all Darkreach vessels beyond the Great Range. She marries Denizkartal and their daughter is Thalassa.

Panterius Lydas: the Strategos or General of Darkreach Intelligence (the Antikataskopeía).

Parminder Sen: assistant cook and sometimes dressmaker at Mousehole, she marries Goditha and is sister to Gurinder. She becomes an apprentice mage and is a xenotelepath. Her daughter is Melissa Mason, and her son is Daniel Mason.

Pass: a slave girl from the Brotherhood brought to Camel Island to be sacrificed to establish a master pattern. In full 'It Shall Come to Pass.'

Pąrlakmugąni: a bard of the Cenubarkincilari Hobgoblins. The 'ą' is a long and drawn out sound.

Peggy Farmer: eldest daughter of Giles and Naeve.

Petros Lydas: the Metropolitan of the north of Darkreach. He is based at Antdrudge.

Procopia Ampelina: a Praetor of the Antikataskopeía in Ardlark and former commander of Basil.

Qvavili: (or Flower), daughter of Aziz and Verily. Her identical, but smaller, twin is Fear.

Rabi'ah: a poor spinner and weaver from Ardlark. Her drunken father sold her into slavery. She is sent by her Imam to Mousehole. She marries Asad.

Ragnilde Hrolfrson: despite her name following Dwarven practice, she is the eldest daughter of Baron Hrolfr Strongarm of Oldike and she is the betrothed of Thord.

Rahki Johar: a harijan servant from Haven. She was rescued from the Master's servants in Pavitra Phāṭaka.

Rani Rai: a former Havenite Battle Mage and now co-Princess of Mousehole. She has broken caste, is married to Theodora, has adopted Fear, and is regarded as the father of Aikaterine.

Rebecca Croker: the daughter of Jordan and Dulcie.

Repent of This Thy Wickedness: a 6-year-old slave brought from the Brotherhood to help restock Mousehole. She is adopted by Eleanor and Robin.

Rhaldraht: an Insak-div Starşiyrang (Sergeant) from the Imperial Guard who teaches Astrid how better to use her new weapon when she is in Ardlark for the wedding.

Rhod ap Cronin: the chief druid at Bathmawr.

Rhoddi ap Owen: he was Reeve of Rising Mud. He was killed in the raid of the Mice that killed Glyn.

Rhodē Palama: the second daughter of Bianca and Christopher, twin of Diogenes, and brother of Rosa and Francesco.

Robin Fletcher: a former slave, fletcher, and bowyer for Mousehole. He is married to Eleanor, and they have adopted Aelfgifu, Gemma, and Repent, and have a daughter, Bianca, and twins, Michael and Sara. He is the brother of Goditha.

Rosa Palama: a daughter of Bianca and Christopher, twin sister to Francesco.

Roxanna: the 12-year-old adopted daughter of Sajāh, Norbert, and Fortunata.

Ruhayma: the 13-year-old adopted daughter of Sajāh, Norbert and Fortunata.

Runa Gildasdottir: the eldest daughter of Father Gildas and Vigdis Æsirsdottir. She was the first sacrifice to the Old Gods on Neron.

Ruth Hawker: a former Freehold merchant and now teacher of the village children in Mousehole. She is married to Father Theodule, and their identical twin sons are Joshua and Jeremiah.

Saenu ap Owen ap Alwyn: a slaver from Bathmawr.

Sajāh bint Javed: from the Caliphate, she is the Seneschal of Mousehole under the Princesses. She is the second wife of Norbert Black. She is the adopted mother of Roxanna and Ruhayma, and mother of Bishal & Huma.

Sara Fletcher: a daughter of Robin and Eleanor, twin sister of Michael, and full sister of Bianca. Adopted sisters are Aelfgifu, Gemma, and Repent.

Shilpa Sodaagar: a former Havenite trader and slave in Mousehole. She takes Vishal as her partner. Their son is Abhaidev.

Siglunda the Wise: a mage and midwife, Captain (village leader) of Wolfneck.

Signy Skáld: married to Koll Hjortson and mother of Ketill Söngvari. They are a family of bards and Orthodox survivors of Neron Island.

Simeon, Father: a Catholic cleric and werewolf who is born in Xanthia in the Newfoundland. He flees from there, and ends up in Mousehole through the offices of the Bear people. He converts to being Orthodox and marries Danelis. Their children are Epanxer, or Brave, and a daughter, Mehre, or Silver.

Simon Rothson, Father: the Senior Orthodox priest in Wolfneck.

Simon of Richfield: a traveller and chronicler from before The Burning, and even from before the Schism of the Church. He wrote a book called 'My Travels Over the Land and Beyond'.

Sin: more fully, They Shall Confess Their Sin. She is a former Brotherhood slave girl and becomes the domestic and child minder for Astrid and Basil.

Sinech verch Stefan: the daughter of Stefan and Adara, and identical twin sister of Finnabhair.

Skap Hjalmarson: a Neronese follower of the Old Gods who is captured, and tells about the Masters, and the Old Gods.

Snæbjorn: a junior earth mage on Neron Island and follower of the Old Gods. He is killed by Ayesha during the attack on East Zarah.

Snorri Trueheart: a Dwarven Count, and the ruler of Copperlevy in the Northern Hills.

Sofronia Lagunda: wife of Father Michael in Dhargev.

Stefan Ostrogski: a young soldier from Evilhalt. He is now in charge of the militia of Mousehole, and is married to Bryony and her cousin Adara. His sons with Bryony are Aneurin ap Stefan and Tristan. His identical twin daughters with Adara are Finnabhair and Sinech. He is also a leatherworker and has an inherited magical sword called Smiter, and another, anti-dragon sword called Wrath.

Surtak (Hulagu Surtak Buriad): the daughter of Alaine and Hulagu.

Svein Steinarsson: a man of Wolfneck and 'suitor' to Astrid. He had a Kharlish appearance, was a violent drunkard, and around 40 years old. Owned a ship and was a rival of Astrid's father. He was the Northern agent for the Masters. Astrid kills him.

Tabitha Worral: born in a farming hamlet near Erave Town, she now lives in Mousehole as an assistant carpenter and cook. She has one green eye and one blue one. She marries Neon.

Tarasios Garidos: the Orthodox Metropolitan of Ardlark and the east of Darkreach.

Tãriq ibn Kasîla: a quarryman from Silentochre. He becomes husband of Bilqîs (daughter Zainab) and Yumn.

Thalassa do Denizkartal: the daughter of Denizkartal and Olympias.

Theodora Cephalou: wife of Carausius and mother of Theodora Lígo.

Theodora do Hrothnog: a great-great-granddaughter of Hrothnog. She is not entirely human, a mage, and at over 130 years, is far older than the late teens that she appears to have. She is now Princess of Mousehole, with her husband, Rani and their adopted daughter, Fear, and daughter, Aikaterine.

Theodora Lígo: daughter of Carausius and eventual wife of Candidas.

Theodoret Mauropous, or Blackfoot: the Metropolitan of the Plains, an Insakharl based at Axepol.

Theodule Philes, Father: a former monk, and now assistant to Father Christopher at Mousehole. He marries Ruth, and their identical twin sons are Joshua and Jeremiah.

Theophilus Kafatos, Abbot: in charge of the Orthodox monastery situated at Greensin, that of Saints Cyril and Methodius. He is also in charge of the training of new priests and monks.

There Shall Be Lamentations: see Lamentations.

They Shall Confess Their Sin: see Sin.

Thomas Akkers: a younger son and farmer from near Bulga. He comes to Mousehole seeking land and a wife. He marries Elizabeth and they have a daughter Virginia.

Thord: a shorter and broad humanoid of the species locally known as a Dwarf. He comes from Kharlsbane in the Northern Mountains, but is now Mousehole's Ambassador to the Dwarves. He rides a sheep called Hillstrider. He is known as the Crown-finder to the Dwarves, and is engaged to Ragnilde.

Thorfinn Deepdelver: a Dwarven Duke, and the ruler of the Northern Hills.

Thorkil Mauritson: an outlaw from Wolfneck among Dharmal's brigands. He was killed in the attack on the bandit village. He was a paedophile.

Thorstein Akritas: the second son of Basil and Astrid, twin brother of Anna.

Thorstein Tostisson, Father: a priest in Wolfneck and youngest brother of Astrid. He moves to Mousehole and marries Kaliope. Their twin daughters are Berenike and Iris.

Thrain Vigfisson: an air mage, and the senior refugee mage of Neron Island. He is married to Ingrid Holmsdottir and father to Arnor Thrainsson (who is also his apprentice) and Groa Thrainsdottir.

Trystan ap Stefan: the second son of Stefan and Bryony. He is named after her murdered little brother.

Umm bint Wā'il: a slave of the bandits from a poor farming family in the Caliphate, she is now a spinner and weaver in Mousehole and helps in the kitchen. She is now the senior wife of Atā ibn Rāfi. Her son is Achmed.

Urfai ap Carel: an elderly and powerful water mage, and now Reeve of Rising Mud. He opposed the war.

Valeria Cheila (nee Lobb): a girl from Deeryas on the south coast, she is now the servant of Rani and Theodora and has married Nikephorus. Mother of Angelina and Eugenia. Her brother, James, joins her in the valley.

Verily I Rejoice in the Lord Tiller (Verily): a former Brotherhood slave, and slave in Mousehole, now an assistant cook, and apprentice mage in Mousehole. She can 'smell' magic and has married Aziz. Their sons are Saglamruh (Strong Spirit), and Sunmak (Gift). Daughters, Qvavili (Flower) and Fear.

Verina Gabala: an Orthodox miller from Mistledross. She leaves Darkreach after she loses her family in an earthquake and ends up in Mousehole married to Adrian Digge.

Vigdis Æsirsdottir: a survivor of Neron Island. She is married to Father Gildas Vhorternson, the only surviving Orthodox priest from the island.

Virginia Akkers: the daughter of Thomas and Elizabeth.

Vishal Kapur: a young armsman from Haven. In the pay of the Master's servants, he is captured and then joins the Mice. He is taken as a partner by Shilpa. Their son is Abhaidev.

We Declare Unto You Glad Tidings: see Glad.

Yesugai (Hulagu Yesugai Buriad): the son of Hulagu and Kahina, the full brother of Khãtun.

Zafirah: a poor spinner and weaver from Ardlark who sells herself into slavery to pay the family debts. She is sent by her Mullah to Mousehole. She becomes junior wife to Atã and their son is Sughdï

Zamrat: (Zamratejedehar (Emerald Dragon): she is a Hobgoblin, and third daughter of Guk. She was the first outside student at the school.

Zeenat Koirala: a Harijan and former prostitute from Haven, rescued and brought to Mousehole.

Zoë Anicia: an Orthodox baker from Mistledross. She loses her family in an earthquake and ends up in Mousehole.

Details of Mousehole

Explanation: All shops and trades will have a quality associated with them denoting level of service, how good their items are etc. As an example Mousehole has Norbert Black. He has blacksmith Q5, weaponsmith Q5, and armourer Q5. He is a generalist and can do most work using iron. He is not particularly good, but he is competent in all his areas.

A craft or vocation followed by a number indicates the competencies that the person holds. Norbert is has six competencies in Trades. The vocations mentioned are Trades (any actual Craft), Vagus (an unspecialised general category), Professional (indicates some formal education), Illicit (made their living beyond the, usually as a thief and/or prostitute), Armsman (a soldier or guard), Scout (a person who seeks paths and usually is an archer), Cleric, and Mage. Clerics and Mages have their Piety or Psychic Ability listed and, for mages, their Element and Moon (where known). Characters often have skills listed after a colon. Anything of 3 or above is at a level where a person can make a living at it.

Sometimes more detail is given. For instance there is Rani Rai (Mage C9[19FD]). This means that she is currently a 9 competency mage (which is fairly powerful for a village enchanter), that she has a Psychic Ability of 19 (which is a high level) and that she is a Fire mage of the sign of the Dragon. This indicates her area of specialty in her spells (which is destruction and war).

Mousehole

This is a very small village of less than 65 inhabitants on the track from Mouthgard down to the Swamp. It was a bandit hideout, but is now free. The rulers are the most powerful mages in the area and there are minor mages. It produces dark rubies, antimony, Healbush, Sweet Ali and Lying Miriam. Potions are available. There are many more women there than men and the women come from all parts of The Lland and all are beautiful.

There are many children who are not mentioned. The Inn is the Mouse Hall and the villagers call themselves Mice. They use a compulsory militia to defend themselves. This militia includes a flying carpet and many saddles and rings of invisibility. The local cheese is a cheddar variety. It was known in Old Speech as Muzel. In the hills two days north of the village is a supply of gypsum that has not been mined since The Burning at least. There are no shops, as such, although items are available for purchase at workshops.

All of houses backing the surrounding cliff will extend into the cliff. Some go back a very long way and will be used, eventually, for maturing cheese and other activities that need a constant temperature. There is around 3m of elevation between levels. All of the buildings in the front and middle rows have two levels. Very few of the houses of the last row are of more than one level, but may be the same size due to going back into the cliff.

This mostly illustrates the village as it is by the end of *Engaging Evil*. Most of the people not mentioned here are still living in the Hall of Mice or in the old barracks as are most of the single people. Most of the houses are empty at this stage and only those listed are repaired enough to be lived in.

1. Watchtower on the wall
2. Wider section of wall around gate
3. Smithy: Norbert Black (Trades 6: Blacksmith Q5, Weaponsmith Q5, Armourer Q5), Sajāh bint Javed (Vagus 7: Housekeeper Q9, Administration Q3), Fortunata Belluci (Vagus 5: Dressmaker Q6, Embroiderer Q5, workshop at #23)
6. Stable (extends under next level)
7. Bandit Barracks
8. Mages building/ Hall of Mice: Orthodox priests (Father Christopher Palamas, Cleric 6^{23} and Presbytera Bianca, Vagus 4), (Father Theodule Philes, Cleric 7^{15} and Presbytera Ruth Hawker, Trade 6, Professional 1: Sage 6F36, Teacher 4)
11. Kitchens: under Lādi al-Yarmūk (Trade 2, Vagus 7: Cook 9, Sex Appeal 5, Dance 6)
12. Village hall
16. Pool of fresh water
19. Apothecary and healing chapel: used by the priests and Lakshmi
21. (by this book) Pastrycook: Nathanael Ktenas (Trade 8), an Orthodox pastrycook from Ardlark who comes to the village for Lādi
22. Leatherwork: Stefan Ostrogski (Armsman 5, Trade 4: Leatherworker 4) and Bryony verch Dafydd, (Scout 4, Vagus 1)
23. Dressmaking and tailoring (used by Fortunata and Astrid)
26. Miner & physician (residence): Harald Pitt (Trade 7: Miner 9, Value

Gems 4), Lakshmi Brar (Vagus 5, Illicit 2: Physician 4, Value Gems 2, Sage E400)

27. Farmer and Dairy: Giles Ploughman (Vagus 6: Farmer 4, Husbander 4, Cheesemaker 4, makes cheese at # 110) and Naeve Milker (Vagus 4: Husbander 5)

28. Bows: Robin Fletcher (Trade 5: Bowyer 5, Fletcher 6), and Eleanor Fournier (Armsman 5: Jeweller 7)

29. Brewery: Aine Bragwr (Trade 6, Vagus 2: Brewer 7, Distiller 3, Vintner 3)

30. (by now) Bakehouse: Zoë Anicia (T4: Baker 6, Pastrycook 3)

31. Barracks originally used as slave quarters

32. Guard room

53. Goditha Mason (Vagus 5, Mage $2^{17E?}$: Mason 3, Carpenter 1) and Parminder Sen (Vagus 3, Mage $C2^{16S}$), Goditha is unsure as to her exact birth date and is self-taught in her crafts. Parminder is a rare Spirit Mage.

55. Princess' House: Theodora do Hrothnog (Mage 11^{20AB}, Noble 5, Bard 4: Rhetoric 6, Gambling 10, Sex Appeal 6, Courtier 5, Music 10 – in various instruments) and Rani Rai (Mage $C9^{19FD}$: Astrologer 7, Teacher 7, Alchemist 4)

57. also Basil and Astrid

58. Basil and Astrid: Basil Akritas (Armsman 4, Vagus 8: Athlete 4, Courtier 4, Physician 4, Housekeeper 4, Cook 4, Tracker 4), Astrid the Cat (Scout 5: Sailor 3, Tailor 4, Bushwise 2, Wilderness Survival 2, Tracker 4, Hunter 3)

59. Father Thorstein Tostisson (Cleric 2) and Kaliope (Vagus 2: Linen-maker 5, Housekeeper 3, Cook 3, Play Organ 4)

62. Verily I Rejoice in the Lord (Vagus 4, Mage $C2^{21F?}$, Illicit 1: Juggler 4, Sex Appeal 3, Cook 3, Music 6) and Azizsevgili (Armsman 4: Mountaineer 4, Wilderness Survival 2, Tracker 2, Trapper 2, Bushwise 2). Verily is very unsure of her birth date.

90. Spring emerging from cliff

110. Cheesemaking and storage for Giles.